The Tangled Life of Tabitha Grey

The Tangled Life of Tabitha Grey

Amelia Wildwood

First published in the UK in 2026 by Bedford Square Publishers Ltd,
London, UK

bedfordsquarepublishers.co.uk

A CIP catalogue record for this book is available from the British Library.

ISBN
978-1-83501-420-2 (Paperback)
978-1-83501-421-9 (eBook)

2 4 6 8 10 9 7 5 3 1

Typeset in 11 on 13.4pt Adobe Caslon Pro
by Avocet Typeset, Bideford, Devon, EX39 2BP
Printed and bound in Great Britain by
CPI Group (UK) Ltd, Croydon CR0 4YY

The manufacturer's authorised representative in the EU for product safety is Easy Access System Europe, Mustamäe tee 50,
10621 Tallinn, Estonia
gpsr.requests@easproject.com

This book is dedicated to Pop-pop, Dandy, Man-Mountain and the Pipsqueak. You all brought me back to romance, one way or another.

Chapter 1

'A LITTLE TO THE left.'

Teetering on the ladder, I couldn't turn my head enough to look at her. 'Your left or my left?'

'… we're facing the same way,' Emma pointed out.

'I know. I meant more – is it actually left or what you think is left?' I clarified.

There was a long pause and I didn't have to turn around to know that Emma was holding up her hands, making an 'L' with both. She'd never been good with directions. Once, when we'd been set to meet at the sprawling Great Amwell car-boot sale, she'd told me she was 'over on the right, near the entrance'. I'd spent half an hour looking for her, confused because the entrance was on the left, and eventually realised she was at a different car-boot sale entirely, over in Baldock. So maybe it wasn't really 'directions' so much as 'practicalities' in general. But, then again, she was a creative genius, so that sort of went with the territory.

Still, she was my best (only) friend, well, the only one who wasn't one of Richard's mates' ever-changing girlfriends. At least she was here, helping me. Even if she was also my employee, so she sort of had to be.

My employee. God, that sounded so official and business-y. I was a businesswoman, officially! Twenty-seven years old and I was about to flip the 'Open' sign on my own shop. The sense of accomplishment was dizzying. Or perhaps that was just the effect of standing on a rickety ladder. I glanced down and caught an eyeful of the unforgiving cobbled street below. I'd always found it charming but, just then, I couldn't help wishing for a more stable foundation for my DIY efforts.

I waited, my arms starting to ache as I held the heavy drill in one hand and the sign with the other. I'd already affixed it at one point, and I was more than ready to be done with heights for the day.

'My left,' Emma finally said with confidence. 'As in the left that is actually the left.'

I raised the drill to the wooden trim and tried not to wince at the loud noise as it bored a hole. A few quick bits of hardware later and presto! Dad's advice hadn't led me wrong. Richard would be proud – though he'd probably also tell me I should have waited for him to do it. Even though he had to look up a YouTube tutorial on how to hang a picture.

I climbed down the ladder and looked up at the sign for the shop – my shop. It still gave me a tiny thrill to think it. Emma had painted it for me, drawing the name 'Ewe and Me', with each letter illustrated as a different craft supply we sold – ribbon, thread, yarn, a measuring tape, buttons, etc. It looked adorable.

And crooked.

'I think I meant your left, or like… right,' Emma said, wincing. 'Whoops!'

I looked up at it, debating the merits of taking it down right now or having a cup of tea first. We'd been setting things up all morning, trying to finish the last few tasks before the grand opening at the weekend. Only a day away now. With only the two of us, it had been a slog, but I was no longer five scrolls from the end of my phone to-do list and things were looking up. At least the nightly spiralling into 'what have I done?' territory was a thing of the past. Mostly.

'Is it really noticeable?' I asked, trying to gaslight myself into thinking it wasn't that bad. 'As in, if you were just casually walking by, would you be all "Look at that stupid wool shop with the crooked sign!" or would it be more like "Ooh! A wool shop! What a lovely sign!"?'

Emma seemed to consider for a moment. 'I think split the difference and say, "Oh, wow! A lovely wool shop – and what a quirky, crooked sign!"'

I sighed and chewed my lip. 'Eh, good enough for the next half-hour – let's have a tea and consolidate our strength. I'll summit the ladder again later.'

Together we entered the shop, sending the bell by the door jingling. I'd dreamed of owning a cute little wool shop in the high street in the winding Tudor streets of Leaford ever since I made my first proper jumper at thirteen. Not just any shop but specifically this one, with its red-brick exterior, cobbled side alley and half-timbered frontage. When I was growing up, it had been a sweet shop, but now the giant jars of sherbet pips and cherry lips were in a larger unit opposite the library. My own real shop, with a bell by the door and a clean sparkling bay window filled with bright balls of yarn and crochet projects I'd made to delight and draw in customers.

In my dreams, however, I'd had help putting up the sign from my boyfriend. Unfortunately, Richard was once again off somewhere 'networking'. I didn't begrudge him the time – he was trying to start his own business as a property developer, after all – but he had promised. He was also the one with the tools in his car – he'd taken mine to fix 'something at work'. Luckily, I'd helped myself to them before he drove off. What he needed to fix as an estate agent, I had no idea.

'Thinking about Richard?' Emma asked, ducking through a bead curtain she'd made of tiny recycled bobbins and clicking on the kettle.

'It's scary, how you do that,' I said, following her. The 'staffroom' behind the counter was only large enough for two breakfast-bar stools, a narrow counter with a kettle and microwave, and two lockers for our personal items. Emma leant against the counter and shrugged, sending her multiple strings of crystal beads swaying.

'One of my many magical powers… besides it's written all

over your face. You've been glum ever since you turned up this morning.'

I glanced at the kettle, a vintage chrome monstrosity I'd brought home from Aunt Lou's cottage after clearing it out a year ago. The tab inside said in all caps 'DO NOT FILL PAST HERE' and, as a child, I'd always been terrified that it would explode like a claymore if I added a teaspoon too much water. I used to sprint into the hallway as soon as I'd turned it on. The same with Lou's beloved pressure cooker. Now it was a pleasant reminder of my favourite aunt and the many cups of tea we'd shared as she taught me to crochet in her woodland cottage all those years ago.

'At least he called,' I said. 'He's got to take every opportunity going, I suppose. It's not like he has an inheritance to fall back on to get his business off the ground.' I winced, aware that I was parroting one of Richard's lines. He'd really wanted me to invest in his business, in our shared future. But this place had been a dream of mine for so long and it seemed only right that Aunt Lou's money went towards it.

A few days ago, he'd dropped into conversation that I could still recoup a lot of the inheritance money I'd laid out by selling off the stock wholesale and surrendering the shop lease. I think maybe he was trying to make me less anxious by reminding me I had options. Which wasn't really helpful and didn't make me feel better. Still, at least he'd tried. He'd been so excited when I found out how much I was inheriting, it had been so awkward to have to tell him I had plans for the money, but he'd been really understanding.

'Hmm,' Emma muttered. 'Well, as long as he pulls his weight at the grand opening.'

'He will. He's really excited.'

I was overselling it. He hadn't said he *wasn't* looking forward to it, though, which was basically the same thing.

Emma made me a regular Yorkshire Tea and herself one of her witchy blends. We'd met on jury service, of all places.

Both of us freshly eighteen and unsure why on earth we'd been handed this responsibility so early in our adulthood. I'd been drawn to her because she wore a lot of velvet and handmade jewellery. She'd also had a magazine she was willing to share and, as it turned out, jury service was really boring. We'd gone out to lunch that first day in the dreary Fenlowe high street and she'd read my tarot cards over a jacket potato. I'd crocheted her a card cosy the next day and we'd talked about our childhoods. Emma had grown up in Ireland but was about as different from her staunch Catholic parents as I was from mine. Both of us the black sheep of our families.

Emma's interest in the supernatural was already working its way into the shop. There were several crystals in my till and a special piece of paper hidden above the door with a mysterious symbol on it. I wasn't really a believer in anything like that but, as we were a new business and I'd given up my job as a library assistant to do this, I needed all the luck I could get. Aunt Lou's savings wouldn't keep us going forever.

Perched on stools, we sipped our respective teas and soaked up the feeling of all our work coming to fruition. At least, I was soaking it up. I couldn't vouch for Emma. But it had been an intense few months of effort. First all the paperwork – the deposits, ordering stock and setting up insurance and electricity, all the boring bits. Then we'd had to roll our sleeves up and banish the remnants of the nail salon this place had been before. From the bubble-gum-pink walls to the dust-encrusted crystal chandelier and the leopard-print vinyl flooring. Not one inch of the place had been well painted or properly finished and there had been pink paint spattered on the kitchen sink, the ceiling and the floor. As if Mr Blobby had been massacred there. Half the floor had been rotten from a leaky sink and we'd had to replace the boards and install new flooring.

Now the shop was back to its old-fashioned roots, painted a blessedly neutral cream colour, with all the brightness coming from the stock. The walls were covered in timber shelves holding different weights and types of yarn, from traditional wool to cotton to bamboo and alpaca. From the high-priced cashmere at a whopping fifteen quid for fifty grams, to the bumper acrylic yarns sold by the kilo – bright, fun and cheap. Primary and secondary colours, ombré, confetti, colour-changing and self-patterning yarns, all tucked neatly into pigeon holes and labelled in Emma's precise bubble writing.

On top of the shelves down the centre of the shop were paint dipped jam jars full of colour-coded crochet hooks and knitting needles. Then plastic tubes of buttons, wicker baskets of zips and elastic. Rolls of ribbon were mounted behind the till and over each section was a tapestry I'd crocheted, indicating what could be found there.

It had been a long road and yes, there were times when I was prying up floor vinyl at one in the morning that I wanted to cry (and did, though I kept working through it), but it was worth it. We were finally ready to open.

'Do you know your sign's crooked?'

With one notable exception.

It was Maeve, from the Scrummy Cup Bakery down the road. She'd heard all about the remodel every time I stopped in for fortification in the form of boiled fruitcake and tea – before the kitchen was serviceable. Delights like cake pops and pumpkin spice had yet to reach us in Leaford. Something which I was actually sort of happy about. I'd take a slab of tiffin over some biscotti any day.

'Is it?' Emma asked, smiling pleasantly as Maeve put her head through the bobbin curtain. Bless her for remaining cheery no matter what, she was made for customer service. 'Thanks for telling us.'

'No problem.' Maeve beamed and looked around the kitchen. Her candyfloss perm was tinted pink, and the crinkles around her eyes were iced with matching pink frosted shadow. She reminded me of my aunt – she was also a bit of a magpie with colour and sparkle, and she was always smiling. Today Maeve was wearing three rhinestone brooches on her café-issue tabard, and a pink mohair beret on her head.

'I meant to say last time you were in the café – I need some name tapes for my granddaughter's school uniform. Do you have any in?' she asked.

'Sure, let me get some.' I got up and headed for the 'sundries' section.

'Oh, love, don't worry about it. As long as you have them, I'll pop in on Saturday.'

I plucked up a packet and returned to her, passing it over. Behind me the bell jingled, and I couldn't hold back a smile. My shop was already attracting attention and we weren't even fully open yet.

'On the house,' I told Maeve. 'Consider it a thank-you for dropping those scones round the other day.'

'They were just leftovers,' Maeve protested, but she accepted the name tapes and smiled at me. 'I can have my Ian come round to help with the sign, if you like – he bought a fancy drill and he's never used it for anything except pretending it's a ray gun to scare the dog.'

I stifled a laugh. 'I think we're good but I'll keep him in mind.'

Maeve left and I turned to see who'd come in while we were talking. A familiar dark head of meticulously styled hair was bobbing down the pattern-book aisle.

'Richard!' I darted after him and he caught me in a hug, lifting me off the ground as if we were in a film. 'I didn't know you were going to be able to make it.'

'Finished golf early – but I got a firm offer to invest in Hollings Property Development,' he said proudly. He was glowing with a light tan from being out on the greens several times already this month and he smelled of cut grass and crisp G&Ts. I pressed my cheek against his polo shirt and breathed him in: my sophisticated, fancy boyfriend, who golfed.

'I'm glad. We've been setting up in here – finally got all the buttons out. Just got to fix the sign.'

'I saw, it's a nice sign.'

'It's crooked,' I snorted.

He grinned. 'It is, but that'll only take a minute to put right. You should have waited for me to do it but, by the time you've made me a tea, it'll be done.' He kissed my forehead and gave me a squeeze. 'And don't go giving your profits away before you've even made any. This is your business, not a charity.'

He said it gently but my cheeks burned nonetheless. It was just some name tapes, barely a three-pound order. But he had a point. It wouldn't take long for me to give away a fortune in 'little bits' here and there. I'd have to watch that, especially now all my inheritance, bar a few hundred in my savings account, was sunk into this place. I was glad he was there to remind me to be sensible. Emma was my rocket to the stars, but Richard kept me grounded. They were a good team. Even if they didn't like each other much. It was nothing personal, they were just very different. Emma was all recycling, meditation and animal rescue. Richard was more… next-day delivery, protein shakes and marketing podcasts. The only thing they had in common was me.

I went back to the kitchen to refill the kettle. In its reflection I saw my flushed face, slightly frizzed-out ginger pigtails and a paint-spattered T-shirt I'd won on Brighton Pier five years ago. I winced. Not exactly the look boyfriends dreamed of coming home to. Still, now the shop was basically ready, I could start dressing up again. After all, when Richard met me, I was working in the library, in smart skirts and tights with Mary Jane pumps. He'd been bemoaning the fact that I now lived in painty, wrinkled jeans and trainers. Or, heaven forfend – my Crocs.

'That Richard?' Emma asked, looking up from her phone, perfectly plucked inky brows drawn together.

'Yeah, he's fixing the sign.' I smiled. 'My hero.'

'Great,' she said, her smile not quite reaching her eyes. I chose to ignore it, as she'd never been the biggest fan of shiny-shoed businessmen or landlords and Richard was set on becoming both. 'Roll on opening day!'

I toasted her with my mug and fizzed with excitement. Just one more day and I'd officially be the owner of a fully functional craft shop. Aunt Lou would have been proud.

Chapter 2

SATURDAY MORNING ARRIVED BRIGHT and clear. My alarm woke me at six sharp and, while Richard groaned into his pillow, I slid out of bed and into the bathroom. It was my first day as a proper shopkeeper and I wanted to look my best.

I'd slept all night in heatless curlers – much to Richard's amusement – and carefully unfurled my ringlets under the sterile fluorescents of the bathroom. I was hoping that eventually turning them on wouldn't make me wince. To be honest, ever since we'd moved into the apartment, I'd thought the place gave off a slightly surgical vibe. The bright white lights, gleaming white tiles and all the glass partitions made me feel as if I was about to be quoted for a new filling and a tooth clean. The chrome and leather furniture Richard had picked out didn't really soften the place at all, but at least it always looked clean. Though there was a part of me that longed for overstuffed pillows, dusty bookshelves and dim lamps shedding golden light of an evening. Even my vintage record player was tidied away into a seamlessly integrated cupboard and most of the things from Aunt Lou's were in storage.

The apartment block stood out from the other buildings in Leaford too. Its siding and mirror-filmed windows a far cry from red bricks, leaded glass and whitewash. It was like living in a spaceship that had crash-landed by the canal.

I washed my face and started applying toner, serum and moisturiser. The little morning ritual helping to calm me. Today was my first day with actual customers and, even though I had plenty of experience with the public, that was at the library. This was for my own business, something I was passionate about and had put myself out there for. After all, if the shop failed, that was me and Emma out of a job and it'd all be my fault. My stomach was flip-flopping with nerves already.

As I finished up my BB Cream and started tapping on some cream blusher in a sweet, rosy pink, Richard came in behind me. He smiled at me via the mirror.

'Very cute,' he said, before jumping in the shower.

I took my make-up into the bedroom to finish up, so the steam wouldn't make my hair frizzy or get into my powders. After dabbing on some low-maintenance lip stain, I got dressed in the outfit I'd laid out for myself last night. Like a kid getting ready for their first day of school. Copper-coloured loafers, burgundy tights, a brown tweed skirt and a cream blouse dotted with tiny embroidered terriers. They looked just like Pete – Aunt Lou's faithful Jack Russell.

As a finishing touch, I found the bracelet Emma had gifted me for Christmas – a sterling-silver charm bracelet. She'd combed every antique shop and eBay storefront, looking for as many themed charms as possible, all of them reflecting things I loved – a cowboy boot for country music, a terrier, crochet yarn (obviously), a latte, an autumn leaf and dozens of others. It was my prized possession and today was the perfect day to wear it. For luck.

My phone jingled with a text from Emma herself, as if she knew I was thinking about her. It was a mess of emojis and kisses with 'opening day!!!!!' in the centre in pink. I sent back a few popping champagne bottles and anxious faces.

I made breakfast while Richard got ready, packing an insulated bag with extra for Emma, as she was going to have a busy day too. The kitchen was just as sparse as the bathroom – rectangular brushed-steel sink, white countertops that showed every stray piece of peppercorn, and mountains of chrome gadgetry for making coffee, which I was not meant to touch.

It was all very finicky and I was more of a tea person first thing anyway.

Richard emerged to find me plating up the last of breakfast – fortifying potato farls with crispy bacon, poached eggs and sweet caramelised tomatoes.

He pulled a face. 'Bit much just for breakfast, isn't it?'

I set my mug of tea down by my plate, heart sinking. 'It's going to be a long day. I thought you'd want something a bit more substantial than a smoothie.'

Richard shrugged. 'There's probably more protein in my smoothies, gram for gram. Less fat too,' he added, eyeing the bacon and its crispy brown edges.

'Well, I've made it now,' I said, trying to breeze past it. 'Special breakfast, just for today.'

Richard pulled out a chrome and white-leather stool and sat down. 'I suppose just once is fine. As long as it doesn't get to be a habit.'

'You'll burn it off at the gym anyway,' I teased, twisting the pepper mill over my breakfast. 'They see more of you than I do.'

Richard smirked and dug into his egg, letting the yolk stream over the crisp and fluffy farl. 'You know me – always trying to push myself.'

I cut into my egg, preparing the perfect bite for myself. 'I might have to take your measurements again – don't want to have you hulking out of your cardigans.'

Richard's lip curled at the edges in a cat-like smile, but he didn't comment. I would apparently have to drop less subtle hints if I wanted him to submit to the measuring tape again. I'd already made him several jumpers and cardigans in our three-year relationship. He'd even come to me with pictures for some of them – designs he'd seen from Ralph Lauren and Missoni, from which I'd improvised patterns for dupes.

My current project, however, had been in the works ever since I'd decided to set up the shop. It was a sort of peace offering for not having invested Aunt Lou's money with him to start buying and developing properties. I'd been keeping it at the shop and working on it in breaks from the renovations. If he'd grown extra arm muscle in that time, I'd be devastated.

'Right then,' I said, once breakfast was done and I'd put all the washing-up in the dishwasher. 'Shall we go?'

'I suppose.' Richard went to grab a cream cable-knit cardigan to throw on over his blue shirt and beige chinos. It wasn't one of mine. Some factory-made creation from Topman – nice, but I couldn't help wishing he'd chosen one of my pieces to wear to the shop opening. Not wanting to nag, I just smiled at him, grabbed my bag and my water-bottle holder, and we left the flat. I always found it a bit of a relief to get out into the hallway, where there was at least carpet and some of the walls were painted a cosy sage green. It somehow felt homier in the shared corridor than in our spaceship of a flat. Not that I hadn't tried to warm our place up a bit.

I'd spent over two hundred hours, all told on a Moroccan-tile-design throw and matching cushions for the angular white leather sofa. Fourteen balls of yarn later and I'd finished it up, and it had sort of helped. The design was meant to be bright and festive but I'd toned it down a little for the sake of Richard's preferred aesthetic. Most of it was in shades of grey, from dove to slate, in a lovely gradient, edged all over with robin's-egg blue. I'd used the same colour scheme for a bedspread in our room, covered in three-dimensional flowers and leaves made of popcorn and pompom stitches. Though Richard found it too warm and preferred the Kingsley quilt from The White Company that his parents bought us as a flat-warming gift.

We left the block of flats, or 'apartment complex', as it was apparently meant to be called, and walked over the curved brick bridge and into Leaford proper. The bridge over the river separated the newer part of town from the old. We lived amongst newer terraces built in the style of the original homes of Old Leaford. Over the other side it was the real deal – Tudor timbers and diamond-glass windows with leaded panes. Storybookperfect and also prohibitively expensive. The rent on the shop was high and, were it not for Aunt Lou's money, I'd never have been able to afford it. Her cottage had been rented, but she'd lived frugally and left me a lot of savings. Now I just had to get the shop off the ground before the first rent payment outside of what I'd already paid.

The river joined up to the canal which ran behind the library where I used to work, bordering Leaford. The river was narrower, more of a glorified stream, which wound its way through the town under various bridges, bisecting the old and new graveyards, and then up through the park, past the Victorian bandstand and all the way to our apartment block. Sometimes when I was a lot younger, I'd thought of Leaford as its own island, between the two waterways. It had been magical, being able to wade there all summer, building dams and rock islands and watching the swans, dragonflies and frogs. Sometimes I wished it was still socially acceptable to go paddling of an evening.

I enjoyed the walk, the morning air crisp and fresh, as only the start of autumn can be. Still golden with traces of summer but mellower and softer. Nearly sweater weather. I couldn't wait. I had hoped to have time to make myself a new hexagon cardigan before it got too chilly. I'd found a nice design in pastel pink, yellow and blue. But Richard's jumper was taking longer than I'd thought, and anyway, I could make a cardigan for myself any time.

We passed the newsagent's and then the everything shop, where Maeve's husband Ian sold exactly that – everything – from the nameless unit with its creaking spiral staircase up under the eaves. Birthday cards, disposable barbecues, hair accessories and spring bulbs, all neatly shelved and labelled like an old-timey general store in a cowboy film. He even wore an apron and kept a pencil behind his ear. 'Sally's Sweets' wasn't open yet and Sally herself was probably already at her first job as the school receptionist. Every day at three she rushed down to open the shop before the kids were released for the day. Her little red moped the herald of the chaos that was to come at ten past.

Maeve gave me a wave through the bakery window as we passed and I waved back. Richard was on his phone, looking at Twitter and occasionally glancing up to navigate the cobbles. Finally, I saw the sign for 'Ewe and Me'. This was really happening.

'Hiya!' Emma was already outside the shop front, wearing an ankle-length purple duster I'd crocheted for her in an ombré, from lilac to darkest aubergine. She twirled to show it off and then handed me a steaming bamboo travel cup with one of my handmade cosies on it.

'Made you a chai before I left home – should be perfectly drinkable by now.'

'Thank you!' I handed her the insulated bag I'd squirrelled away into my handbag. 'Bacon farl?'

'God, yes.' She dug the sandwich out and bit into it, humming her enjoyment. 'You're the best,' she said, through a mouthful of soft white dough and tomato sauce. If you didn't know Emma, you'd probably assume at a glance that she was veggie, or vegan. But her love for animals came from a distinct 'circle of life' approach to the universe. Something I'd tried to explain to Richard more than once when he made jokes about lentils and tofu. Which I was attempting to train him out of.

'Morning,' Richard said, eyes following the scattering of crumbs over her purple T-shirt. 'Shall we go in?'

I unlocked the door with ceremony and waved them through. As I snapped on the lights and breathed in the scent from my handmade wardrobe sachets hanging by the door, I smiled. Opening day! I felt like a little girl waiting for people to come to my birthday party. I wished I'd brought some cake in, to be honest. But I'd have had to buy it – baking was a skill I'd never mastered. Like most things.

Part of why I owed Aunt Lou so much was that she'd taught me to do the one thing I was any good at: crochet. I'd spent my childhood never really finding my own niche. I wasn't sporty or particularly clever. I liked to read but not enough for it to be my 'thing'. I was politely removed from recorder club after failing to master 'Three Blind Mice' after several months of wincing tutelage from Mrs Bennet (who retired shortly thereafter – which I took slightly personally). I sucked at drama, couldn't learn chess, got scared by video games, and my inability to do so much as a forward roll nixed me from gymnastics. Then Aunt Lou put a hook and yarn in my hands and finally, for the first time, I was good at something. It came so easily, so joyfully. I didn't just find my 'thing' – I found an outlet for all the stress and anxiety of growing up. All thanks to her. It was like she'd introduced me to the me I was meant to be.

'Oh, before I forget.' Emma set her farl down carefully on the strawberry-patterned napkin I'd wrapped it in. 'Here – first-day present.'

'Aww, you didn't have to,' I said, taking the small package from her nonetheless. It was something hard inside a striped paper bag, sealed closed with glittery tape.

'May it bring you luck,' she said.

I opened the bag and pulled out a keyring. Part of it Emma had obviously engraved herself, punching 'Tabitha's Keys' into it on one side and 'Ewe and Me' on the other. Alongside that, she'd used jump rings to attach a yellow crystal point and a string of beads made out of something orange-red and sparkly.

'Citrine and goldstone – for prosperity and wealth,' she explained. 'Also, they're pretty, so…'

'I love it.' I hugged her and then held it out to show Richard. 'Isn't it so nice?'

'Very… cute,' Richard said.

Emma smiled at him, but I saw her eyebrows twitch upwards. Any time witchy stuff came up, it was a reminder of how much they were polar opposites. Whilst that was good for me, because I benefited from their varied energy, they did tend to rub each other up the wrong way. Two cats warily circling each other, ready to start hissing and swiping at each other if I turned my back.

'So where do you want me?' Richard asked, looking around the shop. 'I suppose I can do a few hours on the till?'

He had actually offered to spend the day helping out, so I hoped it would be more than that. Maybe he just meant that he'd move on to something else after a while, so I could take a break from being on my feet.

'That would be great – then I can talk to customers, give them advice if necessary.' I turned to Emma. 'And if you could restock throughout the day and make some more of those crystal stitch markers out back, that would be amazing.'

Emma patted her capacious tote bag. 'Brought my wire and my beads – I'll be churning them out.'

'Perfect.' I shook my hands out, discharging some excitement into the air. 'All right then, I'll flip the sign to "Open" and… we'll see what happens.'

Chapter 3

Absolutely bloody nothing, as it turned out.

Not one single customer in nearly three hours. Unless you counted Maeve, who came by to wish us well on her tea break. After the first half-hour I was slightly embarrassed, watching Richard sit at the till, swinging from side to side on the stool. After another hour had passed, it was downright humiliating. By the three-hour mark, I could feel sweat prickling down my back in my desperation for someone, anyone, to please visit the shop.

Richard didn't say anything but I could see him thinking, 'This is what she did with all that money? We could have been renovating properties and making a fortune right now.' The worst part was that he was right. My inheritance could have got us a project terrace house at auction. With the time and effort I'd spent on the shop, we could have easily flipped it for a great profit. Property prices around Leaford were rising exponentially and even the modest terraces were selling for over three hundred grand. But I felt guilty taking a starter home from someone who might want to do it up themselves. The shop was meant to be the better option.

Well, that was blowing up in my face.

Standing in the empty aisles, I was starting to think I'd made a massive mistake. The cooked breakfast I'd eaten was congealing into a hard lump in my stomach and my heart was doing panicky little flutters every time I checked my watch. The golden sun moving around the dial seemed to mock me. Every tick of the second hand sounded like a pound coin hitting the floor.

At the three-and-a-half-hour mark, Richard sighed and slid off the stool.

'I think, if it's okay, I'll head back to the apartment – I've got some things I could be doing. You know how it is,' he said, stretching his back out. 'Calls to make, investors to lock in.'

'Sure, that's fine.' I didn't have it in me to ask him to stay. I mean, he'd promised to help me out for the whole day but there wasn't exactly anything to help with. Since he'd taken the day off from working for the estate agents, he could at least get some stuff done for his own business.

For a *real* business, I thought miserably. The one I could have invested in, for us and our future.

'See you later, okay?' He stopped for a kiss on his way out of the door. 'Don't stress, all right? You'll do fine.'

I gave him what I hoped was a convincing smile and waited until the bell had sadly chimed behind him before rushing to the back room.

'This is a disaster.' I collapsed onto a stool and looked at the array of gorgeous stitch markers Emma had made – which no one was coming in to buy.

'It's only been a few hours – it's still the morning. You just wait until everyone's had a chance to wake up and get into town. We'll be swamped.' Emma looked up and her smile was so confident and unwavering that I couldn't help but believe her.

Still, I wasn't above having a little whinge.

'I just thought it would be, you know… this big event. There's no other shop like this within a forty-minute drive.'

'I know, hon, and it is an event. I mean, we're open – we did it, you did it! We have built it and so they shall come.'

'Are you quoting the Bible? Can witches do that?'

'We can, but it's actually from *Field of Dreams*,' Emma laughed. 'Now sit your arse down and get to work on your jumper and I'll go out on the floor for a bit. Give you a break.'

'A break from nothing,' I muttered, and Emma swatted the back of my head as she passed by.

She had a point, though. Richard wasn't around and it was the perfect time to put some serious work into his jumper. I'd only half finished the body and still had a whole other sleeve and all the edges to do afterwards. I dug my project bag out of my locker and stroked the insanely expensive cashmere wool. It was kitten-soft and so very snuggly. I'd even picked out colours I knew Richard would be able to put with everything in his wardrobe – oatmeal, camel and coffee, with navy in the edges for contrast.

With my crochet hook in hand, I found my stitch marker and carefully removed it, re-inserting the hook into the last stitch. The pattern was quite complicated and was designed to mimic a more traditional cable-knit style. As much as I loved crochet, I'd never really been fond of knitting. I could do it, but it didn't relax me. It wasn't as effortless as crochet felt. With crochet I could just zone out and get into a good rhythm, knowing I was doing something I was good at. It was like meditation for me.

I stopped checking my watch and the time seemed to fly by, stitch by stitch. It wasn't until I heard Emma talking to someone that I realised there was a customer in the shop. I stopped working and listened. Customers, plural.

I quickly put the jumper away and slipped through the bobbin curtain. There were three customers in the shop, two young women browsing and one older lady chatting to Emma at the till. I flashed her a smile.

'I was about to call you,' Emma said, looking pleased with herself. 'Those two ladies over there are looking for recommendations on yarn for a baby blanket.'

'Perfect,' I beamed, and then turned my smile on the customer at the counter. 'Did you find everything okay?'

'Mostly,' she said, eyes crinkling as she smiled. 'I was looking for one of those light-up hooks too.'

I laughed. 'Can't have that. I don't think we have any in stock right now but I can definitely find one for you and order it in if you leave your details. Are you local?'

'Oh, yes. I'm here all the time – meeting my friend for coffee. Catching up on the gossip.' I slid her a form to put her details down on and she printed them carefully in clear, Biro capitals, her sugar-almond nails catching the light. 'She's been on the phone to me already today, telling me all about that squatter up by the viaduct.'

'Squatter?' Emma finished placing the woman's balls of angora into one of our brown paper bags and frowned. 'Are there even any buildings up that way? Aside from the houses in Riverside Park but, if anyone tried to squat in one of those, the police would be there within five minutes.'

I nodded in agreement. Riverside was the posh part of Leaford, even more so than the old high street. Famous people were said to live in the gated homes there, as well as Leaford's rich and powerful, like Carmel Gould, who headed every charity committee in town and had Harrods deliver to her home weekly.

The woman shrugged. 'Squatter, river person, drifter, whatever you call them. There's a boat up there – not as far as Riverside. An absolute wreck, she said. Saw it while she was out walking her dog in the small hours. It's not safe, is it, having God only knows who lurking around like that?'

My smile had gone a bit stiff. It wasn't that I had a particular kinship with people living on boats but I'd never liked the small-mindedness that came with living in a small town. I still remembered how people had whispered about Aunt Lou and her 'friend', Gail. I'd only been about seven the first time another kid told me my aunt was a 'lezzer' and asked if I was one too. Other people's lives were their own business, and what they didn't want to share was theirs to keep.

'That's all ordered for you,' I said, gently forestalling any further comments about the boat. 'I'll just go and help these ladies.'

I excused myself and went over to the other women, who were comparing colours of yarn. I directed them to the 'supersoft' baby range and the double-knit baby yarn in acrylic. Something that would stand up to a lot of washing without losing its vibrancy and softness. By the time they'd selected six skeins of pastel rainbow yarn and a pattern book, the woman from before was gone.

Emma rang up the sale and even managed to upsell one of the women one of the page spreaders we had at the front counter. A sort of weighted, arched piece of wood with a sliding number scale on top, so you could use it to count stitches while it held your pattern book open.

Once they were gone, Emma turned to me and raised one of her perfectly shaped dark brows. 'Told you we'd have customers – that's three! And an order!'

'That is good and, yes, obviously you were right, as always,' I joked. 'Even if she was a bit…' I pulled a face.

'NIMBY?' Emma filled in, then shrugged. 'You know it's always been like that round here. This place is just a bit old-fashioned. Not everyone – just, you know, some people. Remember when they wanted to build that wind farm and suddenly everyone and their dog was an expert on bird migration and ultrasonic waves that made your ears fall off, or whatever it was.'

I giggled, remembering the heated town-hall debates and the leaflets that had come through the door at the apartment block. The ones showing a landscape dominated by a wind turbine several times larger than any I'd ever seen, the pristine pasture below littered with photoshopped kestrels and hawks, mown down by the scything blades of the dreaded windmill.

Sadly, the campaign had worked. Though the new bypass announced later that year had cut right through that pasture anyway. It was a shame, aside from the woods by her cottage, it had been one of my aunt's favourite places to forage for wild dyes for the wool she'd bought from local farms. I could still remember the smell of the blackberry dye, and the way it had stained my nail beds. Mum had despaired of it ever coming out. I still had a scarf Aunt Lou had made for me with that yarn. I didn't dare wear it out in case it got lost. I kept it for when I was sick at home.

'Still, we don't get a lot of boats coming through,' Emma said, tidying up the little baskets on the counter. 'We're not exactly a tourist hotspot.'

'Maybe they're just living on it. People do now – there was a bit about it on *Gardeners' World*. Someone with a roof garden on their narrowboat.'

Emma chuckled. 'Since when do you watch *Gardeners' World*?'

'I was at Mum and Dad's for Sunday lunch a few weeks ago. Dad had it on in the shed – I think mostly for background noise, not because he suddenly has an interest in gardening. He paved ours over ten years ago and, as far as I know, he's never looked back.'

It was admittedly meant to be a sort of minimalist, modern garden at the time. Stone slabs, gravel, a fountain and a grand total of three spiky plants in a triangle around the garden. Only said plants had perished in their first frosty English winter, and had never been replaced. So now the garden was giving less 'zen' and more 'abandoned quarry'. Mum didn't seem to mind, as long as she had access to the whirligig washing line and a place to tan or have barbecues in summer.

'It's like this new trendy thing, right?' Emma said. 'Like those people that spend half a million quid on a van with a king-size bed and a bidet and then try and park it down tiny lanes.'

'I guess,' I said. 'Kind of cool, though. I mean, being able to travel around but always having your home with you.'

'Like a snail,' Emma said, pulling a face. 'I mean, I love travelling but I know you're more of a creature-comforts girl.'

'I just like my own stuff, you know? Nothing like a cup of tea made in your own mug at the end of the day.'

Emma laughed. 'Hint received, I'll go and stick the kettle on.'

I chuckled as she went. I hadn't been kidding, though. Not really. Leaford had been my home since birth. Mum and Dad lived just outside of it, in a 1950s prefab painted shell-pink and studded with plastic butterflies. I'd gone to school here and spent one or two school holidays a year living with Aunt Lou in her cottage on the outskirts. Mum liked to throw dinner parties and cocktail nights, and her sister was more than happy to babysit me on weekends too. Her house was my idea of heaven – full of books and craft projects and quiet evenings with just the radio on. Compared with the blaring TV at home, with Mum and Dad shouting questions to each other from different rooms and their friends and extended family stopping by to shout and laugh along with them, it was bliss.

If Aunt Lou had lived on a boat, I'd have asked her to trundle it off to Bristol, where I went to university. It would have been wonderful to be able to shut myself away in that haven of peace and quiet to escape from the city. Even if the idea of being a snail wasn't exactly flattering, I couldn't deny the idea had appeal. If home was where the heart was, why wouldn't you want to take it with you wherever you went?

Chapter 4

Later that afternoon, Mum and Dad popped by to 'see how we were getting on'. Even though the shop was quite busy by then – well, busy compared with that morning's humbling lull – I still heard them coming.

'... lived in this town my entire life and now they want me to pay for the privilege of spending money in the shops. Two pound ruddy fifty an hour! It's not on. I mean...'

'Mum, Dad!' I called, cutting off the next part of Dad's rant, which I knew from experience would involve the much-promised and never-delivered wheelie bins, the time Dad got a ticket for 'just stopping to say hello to Stanley from the pub' and the former dog warden who'd been 'having it off' with 'her on the council'.

'Hello sweetie,' Mum beamed, air-kissing me on each cheek. She had to get up on her tiptoes to do it, despite her habitually high wedge sandals – worn in all weathers bar actual snow. I've been taller than her since I was fifteen – 'that's your father's genes', she used to say. My mother, who shopped the petite range until she was nine months pregnant and whose feet still fitted into children's shoes, made me feel sometimes like a galumphing giant.

For years I had this little theory, brought on by too much Jacqueline Wilson and *EastEnders*, that I was actually Aunt Lou's daughter and that Mum was raising me for her because Lou wasn't married. Even though it was the late nineties and, honestly, who would have cared? Lou and I were both pale, turning pink instead of brown in the sun. We had the same reddish hair and she was tall and curvy like me. Mum was short, slim as a whippet and tanned to a crinkly mahogany. Her hair was chestnut brown and she'd worn the same shade of sticky cerise lipstick and nail polish my entire life. With her loud laugh and her clattering heels, Mum was tailor-made to be the 'fun aunt'. It seemed wrong that she was my mother and quiet, bookish Lou was my aunt. I loved them both dearly, but sometimes I still wondered if there had been some kind of mistake. Cosmically speaking. Sometimes I suspected Mum felt the same.

'All right, love? Looks very smart in here,' Dad said, peering around cluelessly. Bless him, he didn't know a crochet hook from a shoe horn but he always tried to show interest in me and my hobbies. He'd worn his sunhat too – one of the first things I'd ever made him, from a pattern that was quite floppy and atrocious really. A khaki creation in cotton yarn, but he'd had it for years and mostly wore it while sunbathing with Mum in the garden. Just the hat, a twenty-year-old pair of 'designer sunglasses' he'd bought in Crete and his alarmingly snug denim shorts, which now buttoned under his fish-white barrel of a stomach.

'It's been a day,' I said, and hugged him. 'But we've had quite a few people in.'

'Including us now. Wow, look at all the diddy little… things!' Mum said, using her inside voice, so probably only the next street heard her. I suppressed a smile as she looked over the unfamiliar collection of crafting items. She picked up a ball of fuchsia and violet marbled yarn. 'I'll take three of these.'

'Mum, you don't crochet. You don't have to buy stuff,' I laughed.

'It's for you – so you can make me another one of these fab tops.' She did a twirl to show off the bust-hugging vest I'd made her. 'Adriana from Pilates wants one too, so I'll get you some more wool for that.'

It was pointless trying to fight it. I didn't really mind making things for Mum's friends but it did get a little overwhelming at times. Like when she'd planned that girls' trip to Majorca and told fifteen of her friends that I'd make them all matching beach totes. I'd worked like a demon on those for weeks – Richard told me I was miming crochet while I slept. Then some of them hadn't picked theirs up in time and three more had ditched them at the airport because of the baggage limit. Mum lost hers off a pedalo and someone else traded theirs for a jug of sangria from a stranger after the bars closed.

Mum pottered about gathering up 'wool' – I'd tried to teach her that not all yarn was wool but it landed on deaf ears – and Dad nudged my elbow.

'Looks great, love. It really does. Richard did some bloody good work in here – I always said he was a good pick for you. Someone with a business head and hardworking hands. He'll always be able to take care of you. Just like I do for your mum.'

I forced a smile. Dad was just a tad old-fashioned, at least where men were concerned. Possibly because he adored Mum down to his bones and moved heaven and earth to give her anything she wanted – from decking to yearly holidays in the sun. He'd been a big supporter of me going to university, working and living in my own place. And he'd taught me to use Rawlplugs, a spirit level and a circular saw (hazards of being a contractor's daughter). He'd taught me car maintenance too. But he was still very much of the opinion that, even if I knew how to unclog a sink or tile a bathroom, I shouldn't have to do so. I hadn't the heart to tell him that Richard had corrected the sign placement and that was about it. Dad adored Richard and, anyway, what did it really matter who did what? The shop was up and running now and it looked great.

'Tabby.' Mum appeared at my elbow, carrying a large brown paper bag filled with skeins of yarn, which she handed off to me. 'I've just had your father bring the patio heater out of storage. We're having one last big bash before it gets too wet to use the garden bar. You must bring Richard over. It's been ages since we had you both there for a real knees-up.'

'We'd love to, I'll check when he's free,' I said, privately thinking that her 'luau' had only been three weeks ago and I was still a little wary of downing any more of her 'speciality drinks' after whatever had been in that pineapple thing. Paint stripper and neat acetone was my best guess. Mum mixed drinks like a fresher at uni – everything went in, with unpredictable consequences.

'I'll be doing invites for Bonfire Night and my big Christmas do soon,' Mum said, glossy pink nails tap-dancing on my arm in excitement. 'You never know, by then I could be introducing Richard to everyone as your fiancé,' Mum sing-songed.

'All right, ease up a bit,' Dad chuckled, using his sixth sense for when I was close to having had too much of Mum for the day. 'We'll leave you to it, love – all right? But we're very proud, aren't we, Pen?'

'Very,' Mum nodded. 'And Louise would be too.'

I smiled at that, a mixture of happiness and grief twining together inside me into a strong cord wrapped around my heart. 'I hope so.'

Mum gave me a hug. I knew she missed her sister as much as I did, probably even more so. After all, they'd grown up together – sisters, best friends, total opposites. I clung to her and breathed in Mum's scent – vanilla body spray and biscuity fake tan. In moments like this, she felt like my mum, rather than a glitzy aunt or sassy neighbour. Then she pulled back and started trying to 'make something' of my hair.

'I don't know where you get this frizz from, probably your dad's side,' she muttered, stepping back and smoothing her own sleek bob.

I felt sad all over again. Just once I wanted her to just be content with me – not to jump on the scale right after to compare us and come out the 'winner'.

Mum and Dad left to go and stock up on Malibu and amaretto (I winced, imagining the carnage unfolding around the cocktail bar in their garden already). I let out a long breath and fiddled with my charm bracelet, tapping my fingernail on a miniature porcelain teacup. It wasn't that I didn't love my parents to bits, but they were just sometimes a bit… much for me to cope with. We were very different people and sometimes I felt as if we were from different cultures, exchanging gifts and customs that the other side didn't really get but wanted to appreciate nonetheless.

Emma shot me a sympathetic look as I retreated to the counter. 'Cup of tea?'

'I must be made of it at this point,' I sighed. 'But if you're offering.'

She grinned, but then her face fell a bit. 'Did they ask where he was? Richard, I mean?'

'No… I suppose they just assumed he was off doing something…' the words 'more important' bubbled up in my throat like a pineapple-cocktail-flavoured burp. I suppressed them with a shudder, '… else,' I finished, instead.

'Yeah, probably that,' Emma said, and smiled again, but not as widely. I tried to send her a mental message to please not poke that particular sore spot too hard. I'd never wish I didn't have Emma in my life but sometimes – on rare occasions – she could be just a little bit *too* honest. A bit *too* perceptive. I was trying to get my business off the ground and deal with Lou not being around any more. I couldn't add dissecting my relationship on top of all that. It was like a car – if it was running fine and there were no warning lights blaring at me from the dashboard, why would I go poking around under the bonnet looking for problems? That would just be creating stress that didn't have to exist. As long as Emma didn't tell me an MOT was due, I could ignore it.

Not that there was anything to ignore. As long as I didn't go looking for trouble, I wouldn't have to ignore it. That was the genius of my system.

All in all, I had seven cups of tea that day. That was an average of one per two customers. If we carried on like that, I'd probably end up drinking our profits away, one Yorkshire Tea bag at a time. At least we'd had customers, though. That was something. Fourteen of them! Double digits. True, one of those was Mum and another was Maeve from the bakery, who'd bought a single spool of white cotton. But still, they counted.

After five I closed up and we straightened the shop shelves and hoovered the place pristine again. There wasn't much restocking to do. We'd sold quite a bit of yarn but Emma had already refilled the baskets from the wholesale cupboard beside the staffroom.

Outside, in the golden glow of the early autumn sunset, I finished locking up and Emma gave me a patchouli-scented hug. The church bell chimed for six in the distance, which meant it was five to. It'd be getting dark soon.

'The hardest part's over,' Emma promised me, her breath tickling my ear. 'First day all done with. From here on, it only gets easier.'

I squeezed her back and wanted to believe her, but I felt doubt closing in on me. As soon as she'd disappeared in the direction of the (extortionately priced) car park, I was alone with the little voice in my head that wanted to know exactly who I thought I was fooling.

I hated that voice. Mostly because it usually made really good points.

Fourteen customers, I thought, as I walked the sun-drenched road home, taking the long way via the park and over the bridge to see the ducks and their one adopted goose sibling. Were fourteen customers enough to sustain my business, given the high rents in the area? The spot had great foot traffic, sandwiched between the shoe shop and a little gift place, which was part of why I'd picked it, that and I loved the little shop front's quirks. But what were the odds of people passing by every day who needed yarn or buttons?

I hugged my arms around myself as a chilly breeze lapped over me, bringing the damp smell of rotting leaves and pond water. It felt like I was waking up from a feverish dream. All this time I'd been preoccupied with making the shop a reality, finally making good on the dreams I'd talked about with Aunt Lou, and now that it was real, I was left wondering if I'd made a big mistake.

Richard was coming out of the front door of the apartment complex as I arrived. I smiled at him, clocking the gym bag over his shoulder with a twinge of irritation. He was going out right now? I quickly checked myself. He'd been working all day, first at the shop and then back here on his business. He deserved a break.

'Tabs, how was it?' Richard asked, stopping to give me a quick kiss.

'Good… eventually. We had fourteen people in,' I said, trying to sound as enthusiastic as I'd felt when talking to Emma.

'Your parents stopped in then,' Richard smiled. 'I rang to remind them.'

That stung a bit. Had they needed reminding? 'They did, yeah. We're invited to Mum's final garden party of the season, by the way.'

He pulled a face. 'I probably won't have time but we'll see. Got to get to the gym but I'll be home later, okay?'

'Cool, see you then,' I said and he hurried off, putting his earphones in as he went.

It was fine. I didn't really want to give him the blow-by-blow of the opening day anyway. It would be nice to have some time to myself. Open a bottle of pink wine, put my feet up in front of the TV and work on Richard's jumper. I couldn't wait to surprise him with it.

Chapter 5

'DONE!' I FINISHED SEWING in the final end, tucked my large-eye needle away in its plastic tube and held the jumper up triumphantly. 'I mean, aside from the final wash and block, but… done with the actual construction. Finally.'

Emma, counting our float into the till, beamed at me. 'It looks gorgeous – sometimes even when I've watched you making things, I can't believe they're not from a shop, you know? It just looks so perfect.'

'Thank you.' I smiled to myself and stroked the supersoft cashmere. 'I think this might be the nicest thing I've ever made. I can't wait to show Richard. He's going to be so surprised.' I folded the jumper into a tote bag and stretched my back out. I'd been sitting behind the counter working on it for several hours now and my spine and wrists were paying the price. I rolled my wrists and winced as they clicked.

Emma pulled a face. 'You should take more breaks. That is not a good sound for your bones to be making… sounds like breadsticks under a car.'

I snorted. 'Maybe we should start selling wrist supports. I know I should take more breaks but I wanted to get the jumper finished before it gets really cold outside. It's not like we've been busy otherwise.'

Emma looked like she wanted to argue, but the facts were not on her side. Opening day had been sort of a high point, customer-wise. I had a little Post-it tally going on behind the counter and, since then, the most people we'd had in on one day was seven. Most days we only got one or two and the number of actual customers who bought things was even lower. The jumper was a distraction if anything. I didn't want to confront the horrible truth – that, after only a few weeks, my business was failing. And I didn't know what to do about it.

Richard had been so supportive over the past fortnight. He'd dropped by three times to bring Emma and me coffees from the Costa on the roundabout outside of town. He looked around the shop every time and said it wouldn't be quiet forever and that soon everything would work itself out. But him being nice only made me feel worse. I could tell that he was tallying up how much money I'd wasted on this silly little fantasy. Money that could have set his business up and ensured we were provided for in the years to come. I'd gambled our future away on a whim.

Emma was trying to keep me buoyed up as well. She'd brought in a bowl of herbs and special crystals that now lived underneath the till. Aside from smelling pleasantly of cinnamon and mint, it didn't seem to be doing much. She spent ages looking at the door as if trying to manifest someone walking through it and she'd added some ideas to my brainstorming pad, where I was trying to come up with ways to bring in some cash.

So far, I had 'crochet/knitting classes' and 'beginner kits' down in sparkly green gel pen, right above 'fire + insurance fraud?' and 'pray for the *Bake Off* team to start a knitting show'. Emma had added 'coffee morning' and 'stitch and witch', which I had assumed was a spelling mistake but it turned out she was being literal.

'So many of my friends want to learn to make, like, tarot-card pouches, wand cosies, hats…' she'd said, shrugging. 'I could get half the coven in on a Wednesday night, no problem – just so long as we've got wine and some Stevie Nicks to listen to.'

I'd actually dug out several Fleetwood Mac LPs from my collection and had them on standby, just in case I needed to set up an impromptu coven meeting. That was how desperate I was. But I couldn't see how any of our ideas so far could save us. Did anyone even want crochet classes? I'd floated it with Richard and he'd pointed out that YouTube was free. He had a point.

I had the first five months of rent covered by my inheritance, but by that time I needed to be in the black. Otherwise, my short-lived tenure as a shop owner would be over and I'd be unemployed and stuck with a mountain of unsold merchandise. I'd also have made my best friend jobless. Way to go, Tabitha.

'Why don't you take a long lunch and go and show Richard the jumper? Cheer yourself up a bit?' Emma said, stirring one of her special tea concoctions with a Biro. 'I don't mind manning the fort.'

Well, the fort was empty, wasn't it? It hardly needed manning at all. Still, the idea of surprising Richard, perhaps with something nice from the bakery as well, sounded like just the little lift I needed.

'As long as you don't mind…' I said, still sort of on the fence about it.

'I don't. In fact,' Emma crossed her arms over her chest, beads clattering. 'I am ordering you to take a long lunch. As your friend. As your employee, I am merely suggesting it.'

'Gotcha,' I said, laughing. 'Okay, well, then I will pop home for a bit. But I'll bring you back something from the bakery – as your boss. Because then it's tax-deductible.'

I gathered up my tote bag and handbag, then headed to the bakery. Their boiled fruitcake was my favourite – moist and packed with shiny red cherries. But Richard didn't have a single sweet tooth in his head, so I got his favourite rosemary and sundried tomato focaccia instead, plus a sparkly flower-shaped cookie for Emma for later.

Maeve was the one at the counter, serving. Today her tabard was studded with a collection of enamel animal brooches – terriers, horses, field mice and fauns gambolling freely across the hills and valleys of her chest. Her hair was freshly tinted pumpkin-orange and she had a laser-cut necklace of autumn leaves around her neck.

'Love that necklace,' I said, as she was bagging up my purchases. 'You're all ready for the season then.'

'I'm just happy summer's over – it gets so hot in here. Besides, Halloween is my favourite theme to bake for. Apples, cinnamon, pumpkin pie and cinder toffee.' Maeve looked wistfully at the display case, still full of summer goodies – flower cookies, lavender cake and ice-cream-shaped cupcakes. 'Roll on October, that's what I say.'

'Oh, don't! I'm meant to be contributing to the harvest display at the library,' I confessed, feeling a tinge of worry. I'd promised to do it while I still worked there and it felt mean to pull out after I'd left my job to start the shop. Every year all the local schools, shops and societies contributed something to the display in the giant bay window of the library. I had volunteered to do some crochet pumpkins and felt-leaf garlands. All the supplies were still sitting untouched in the flat. I'd been too busy to make a start.

'It'll be a good one this year. I'm doing a salt-dough cornucopia and my granddaughter's class are making local points of interest out of cardboard. She's already robbed me of three Pringles tubes. I wouldn't have minded but I wasn't done with them – there's just a massive bowl of crisps in the microwave now.'

I chuckled. 'Well, if she needs any extra supplies, you know where to send her. What's she making?'

'Manor Park Farm – with the silos and loads of plastic cows – and a dragon,' Maeve shrugged. 'She's very creative. Apparently there was a bit of a kerfuffle because one of the other girls wanted to make that boat that's turned up near the viaduct, but some of the mums are doing a campaign to have it moved on, so they took it as an act of protest, so she's put it on its end and turned it into the clock tower for the church.'

I snorted. 'Protest? Jesus… so it's still up there then? Thought it would have moved on after a few days once whoever owns it realised there was nothing around here to do, tourist-wise. I mean our only claim to fame was the brewery and that shut down years ago.'

Maeve shrugged. 'You still catch a whiff of yeast on damp days. But I've no idea what anyone would come here for, or whose boat it is. I asked around and no one's seen anyone on it. My Ian went for a walk up that way – not on purpose, he got lost coming home from The Kingfisher in the dark – but he said there were lights on and someone was watching him out of the window. Didn't even blink apparently, just stared after him.' She shuddered. 'Gave him the willies and had him home in double-quick time anyway. The shepherd's pie was barely browned.'

I could see why he'd been freaked out. The back of my neck was tingling just thinking about it. How creepy. I was still thinking about it afterwards, while I walked to the apartment complex (why couldn't we just say 'block of flats' like normal people?). As much as I loved Leaford, a thriving holiday destination it was not. Aside from the Travelodge out by the tiny two-platform railway station – used exclusively by travelling salesmen and family visiting for weddings and funerals – we had nothing around for anyone to visit. People did not come to Leaford for their holidays. They retired here to raise spaniels or grow courgettes that would only ever get second place in the yearly fair.

That got me thinking about the pumpkins for the display again. I'd have to start them soon. We were already well into September and time was running out. Maybe I could cheekily get Emma to cut out leaves for the felt garlands. After all, it wasn't as if we were snowed under at the shop these days. My wrists twinged and I shifted my bags around to try and take the strain off. Emma was right, I did need to start taking more breaks from the crochet. Or invest in some of those icepack wristlets.

I had to put my bags down to unlock the front door, elbowing it open as I bent to retrieve my things. 'Rich? I'm back for lunch, and I've got something to show… what the fuck?'

'Tabs! You're early!' Richard exclaimed, leaping to his feet and grabbing the Moroccan tile blanket to wrap hastily around his waist.

The naked woman on the sofa discreetly covered herself with the matching cushion, her face a mask of shock. She was very pretty, I couldn't help but notice. Tanned and toned and with a high blonde ponytail that was understandably a little crushed and messy from being smooshed into the sofa. There were two coffee cups on the table – my hand-painted ones from the weekend course I did with Aunt Lou – and it was that more than anything else, oddly, that brought tears to my eyes.

'I… I'm so sorry,' the woman said. 'I didn't know he… Ricky?' She turned to him for help and I could hear her bum squeaking on the leather sofa as she squirmed. The only noise in the horribly silent flat.

Richard just stood there, eyes darting about as if for inspiration. Finally he wetted his lips.

'Now, Tabs… don't overreact…'

Chapter 6

It was, in retrospect, a mistake to try and beat Richard to death with baked goods in a paper bag. I was going to be finding raisins and cherries all over the living room for weeks.

I also didn't have anything left to comfort-eat.

Richard and his unnamed tart (that's mean, she was probably lovely – definitely seemed surprised to meet 'Ricky's' *girlfriend*, and did offer to wash the cushion cover, which was very nice of her… the cow) left once I started shouting, and then it was just me, alone with the sound of the washing machine as it chugged away, stuffed full of every soft furnishing that was on the sofa. My special mugs were drying by the sink but, honestly, I didn't think I'd ever be able to look at them the same way again. I hated him for that. Of all the mugs he could have picked.

The mugs were still important memories I made with Aunt Lou but everything else… I didn't think I'd ever be able to so much as sit on that blanket again. It was tainted. All the hours I spent on that blanket and the cushions. Hours thinking about how they were going to make our apartment (flat, it was a fucking *flat*) a home, that one day I might pass them on to our children. God, I was such an idiot. I was struck by a wave of humiliation so strong that I nearly cringed myself into a little ball on the floor.

I took out my phone as a distraction, realising the time as I did so. I should have been back at the shop a while ago. Emma hadn't messaged me. She probably thought Richard was so happy with his present that we'd decided to spend the afternoon together.

I quickly tapped out a text to her. *The sweater curse is real. Taking rest of the day off.*

The curse was something I'd heard about on every online crochet group and in many wry post-break-up TikToks, but I'd never thought it was anything to be seriously worried about. How could it possibly be a real, observable phenomenon that making a partner something as big and time-consuming as a sweater was a one-way ticket to suddenly being single? In my years with Richard, I had let it slip my mind. I'd naïvely thought I was somehow immune, given how much of my work was hanging in his side of the wardrobe. But, apparently, I'd been on borrowed time, and the cashmere jumper had finally triggered the universe into delivering a kick to my stupid, trusting face.

A moment later a reply came through. *Oh, hon. Red or white?*

Vodka, I replied.

Unable to sit still a moment longer, I went into the surgically clean kitchen and tore several bin liners off the roll in the drawer. I walked into the bedroom as if in a trance and opened the wardrobe doors. There were all the jumpers, cardigans and vests I'd made for Richard since we'd got together. The time-consuming patterns I'd created to duplicate designer pieces, the birthday and Christmas presents. Scarves, hats and all the other accessories in a storage container at the bottom. The only things I was good at making, the one skill I was proud of, and it wasn't enough. None of it was enough.

I started taking the big items down off their hangers, one by one. This one I'd worked on at a lazy picnic in the park while Richard napped. This had been in my bag on our first weekend away. A pair of socks I'd made while he was on a lads' weekend and I'd missed him. A hat I'd bought the yarn for while we were on a mini-break in Cornwall. I did it slowly at first, then faster and faster, until I wasn't folding them any more, but stuffing them into the rubbish bags. I threw the bedspread on the floor. They'd probably been in here too. I felt ill just thinking about it. I stripped the sheets off the bed.

Twenty minutes later, when the door buzzer went, I had two black plastic sacks in the living room, stuffed with crochet. I'd probably be able to fit the stuff I was still washing into there. But what I'd do with it all then was anyone's guess. I'd intended to throw it all away when I started but now I was starting to weaken. It was so much work, so much time. Hundreds, well... probably more like thousands of pounds' worth of supplies and work-hours. How could I just throw that in the big Biffa bins outside, with the pizza boxes and leaking sacks of rubbish?

'Hello?' I said into the intercom.

'It's me – I closed early,' Emma answered. 'If you don't want company, I can just drop off the vodka and leave?'

'No... no, come up.' I buzzed her in and opened the door, rubbing at my face in a futile attempt to make it look as if I hadn't been crying, but I had been, eyes running and sobs choking me as I cleared out the wardrobe of every stitch I'd ever made for my now ex-boyfriend.

Emma arrived in the lift and immediately hugged me, her arms weighed down with two bags for life. I heard bottles clink and felt the cold brush of a carton of ice-cream against my arm. God bless Emma.

I let her into the flat and shut the door. She approached the sofa but I herded her towards an armchair instead.

'What happened?' Emma asked. 'Unless you don't want to talk about it right now?'

'He...' I had to stop and dig the vodka out of the bag, taking a shot out of the bottle, neat. I coughed – as I was nowhere near hard enough to drink straight booze like that. What was I thinking? 'He was here, with someone else. A woman.'

Emma's eyes widened. 'That son of a bitch. Oh my GOD, how DARE he?'

That was exactly the energy I needed and I welcomed it, letting her outrage wash over me. It was like being wrapped in another hug – protective and warm.

'And they were...' Emma pulls a face. 'Do you want me to strip the bed?'

'Done it... and they were on the sofa.'

Emma looked at the sofa like it was diseased. 'Jesus... and, shit, wasn't that blanket on there? That took you forever!'

'I know,' I said, and burst into tears again. It just all crashed down on me in another relentless wave. It wasn't about the time I'd wasted on the blanket. It was about the time I'd wasted on Richard. Three years of my life, gone.

Emma left her armchair and came over to hug me tightly. 'It's okay. I mean, it's not, but he's the one who's a dipshit. You did nothing wrong and he never deserved you anyway. I'm just sorry you had to see... that.' I felt her shudder theatrically and my sobs turned into a choked giggle.

'Let me get you a glass and some tissues.' Emma pulled back, looking at me intently, her witchy green eyes flashing. 'And also a courgette and some nails – an aubergine would also work. Or a baby carrot.'

'You are not hexing him,' I spluttered, welcoming the laughter as it broke apart the lump in my chest.

Emma pulled a thoughtful face. 'Hmm... okay. To be fair, I doubt you have any black candles or spicy peppers here. But I owe him at least one tiny hex, like, may he always fail to spot the speed camera, or... run out of toilet paper after the shops have shut.'

I giggled and she fetched some glasses with ice and poured us vodka and lemonades. Heavy on the vodka – in that the lemonade was in a separate, unopened can, which we both ignored. At least the ice made it easier to get down me.

'Is that his stuff, in the bags?' Emma asked, glancing at the bulging black sacks.

'It's stuff I made for him.' I downed the chilly vodka and refilled my glass. The ice had barely melted. 'I don't want to look at it any more. Especially not the blanket.'

'There's so much of it though...' Emma trailed off doubtfully.

'That's a lot of work. You sure you just want to bin it? I could always store it for you for a while until you've had time to process and then you can deal with it?'

It was tempting, but I shook my head. 'I'd know it was there. I just need it gone. Out of my life for good.' I sniffed and looked into the pink depths of my glass. 'I thought I was going to marry him, Emma. I thought he was it, you know?'

I felt cold inside, suddenly rootless and empty. The future I'd imagined with Richard was just… gone. There was nothing in its place. I kept accidentally thinking about him because he was in all parts of my life – memories and plans and every inch of the present. It all now had a Richard-shaped hole torn through it. My insides cramped in misery every time I spotted something that reminded me of him and just then, that was everything. From the fruit bowl we'd carted back from a Spanish holiday, to the way he arranged all the shoes upside down by the door, even the weird little white dab of gloss on the floor where we'd painted the room together. Richard was everywhere and yet his absence felt like it would crush me. Yet every time I thought of the dreams I'd had for our future, the image of our smiling faces at a wedding, a christening… it was all replaced by the visual of him with that woman on our sofa.

'I know… I'm sorry.' Emma perched on the side of my chair with a sigh and let me cuddle her, wrapping her arms over my back. 'I think I'm just… you put so much work into that stuff and it just breaks my heart to see you throwing it away like it's worthless. He's the worthless one. You're worth like… a million quid. A billion.'

Even as I felt gaping holes open up around me, I realised she had a point. At least about the crochet. It wasn't worthless and it would be a waste to throw it all away. I'd loved making every single piece and just because I didn't want to see them any more, that didn't mean they deserved to be mulched up with old tea bags and cold beans, then buried in a landfill. The idea of it made my chest hurt even more than the loss of

Richard on its own. At least this pain I could do something about.

'I'll take them to the charity shop,' I said decisively, a tiny bit of future planning reclaimed. 'In the morning. They deserve a fresh start.'

'Yeah…' Emma squeezed me tighter. 'Fresh starts all round, okay? And if you change your mind about that hex… just let me know and I'll pop to Tesco for a cocktail sausage.'

I snorted into her shoulder and Emma giggled. I felt lighter. Maybe it was the vodka or maybe it was the company, but suddenly it didn't feel like the end of the world any more. It just felt like what it was, the end of a very shitty day. Still not great, but not insurmountable either.

'You want to order pizza? My treat?' Emma asked, getting her phone out. 'That place that keeps shutting down and then reappearing at another address is back on the apps now.'

I sniffed. 'Good… I like their garlic bread.'

'It is great – and filthy, I'll get double.'

Emma tapped at her phone, wandering around the stark flat and humming. I knew that was her way of subtly breaking up the 'bad energy'. If she had her way, no doubt she'd be purging Richard's essence with herbal smoke and her massive old school bell. Out, foul demon! Out!

I dabbed at my face with a tissue and told myself that I was going to be fine. It was just a break-up, an ugly one but still. No one had died. This was nothing like losing Aunt Lou to the fucking evil bitch that was breast cancer. That had shaken my foundations, this was just a broken window. One I could board over and carry on, patching up the Richard-shaped holes with new plans and new people.

That thought brought me to the realisation that my actual home was probably not going to be mine for much longer. God, what were we going to do about this place? We split the rent and I'd never be able to afford it on my own. I'd have to move. Richard was going to want to come by for his stuff and I'd have to see him again. This wasn't over just because he'd fled the scene of the crime. All the messy loose ends were still dangling all over the place.

I felt a fresh wave of pain as I thought of what it would be like to tell my parents. Mum was expecting Richard to propose to me soon. She probably had a little schedule in her head already – engagement party, dress shopping, hen do, wedding, the inevitable baby shower. She'd probably already come up with signature cocktails for our first five anniversaries and had Dad draw up plans for a play area in their garden.

Now it would all crumble in front of her. I'd have to start over again, only with Mum's warnings about me 'getting on in years' coming more frequently and at a higher pitch. I wasn't following the timeline she'd lived by. I was falling behind her. At my age she'd already been married, had me. I was already twenty-seven, a hop, skip and a jump from the big three-oh. How much time did I have left? I'd been in the home stretch of this race, still behind but a respectable second, and suddenly I'd whacked right into a fence, lost my jockey and been left in the dust. Behind the scenes there was probably someone loading a shotgun, ready to put me out of my misery.

'Hey,' Emma said, snapping me out of my dire imaginings before I could be packed off to the glue factory. 'It's going to be all right. Trust me. You can do so much better than him.'

I smiled, trying to be brave, but inside I wasn't sure. My parents loved Richard. He was the right combination of dynamic and humble, hands-on and ambitious. He was attractive and generous and… and I'd walked in on him having sex with someone else on my sofa. That was really the only fact that mattered now, wasn't it?

What was I going to tell Mum and Dad? Not the truth, God no. Talk about sex with my parents? I'd rather tell them Richard joined the foreign legion or died in a freak golfing accident.

I decided not to think any more. The vodka was really helpful for that, at least. Emma helped me put new bedding on the guest bed – because like hell was I using the main bedroom. Then we put on *Dinnerladies* and had a floor picnic. We ate a lot of dubious pizza and overpriced ice cream and Emma took out her handbag-sized tarot deck and read my fortune for me. Okay, so she made most of it up, but it made me laugh and that was the point. According to her fortune for Richard, by the end of autumn he'd be awash with regrets and defeated by a dark fairy queen with blood-red nails like crow talons. I'd prefer him to be balding and eaten by bears to be honest. Apparently, there wasn't a card for that. Still, by the time Emma left, I was giggling and tipsy and ready for a good night's sleep.

Only, within minutes, the silence in the flat was weighing heavy on me. I found the jumper I'd finished still in my tote bag and went to throw it into the rubbish sacks with the rest of the stuff. But it was so soft, and I'd worked so hard on it. I ended up carrying it with me to the tiny spare bedroom.

As I got into the guest bed all alone, hugging the cashmere jumper, I couldn't keep from crying. My life as I knew it was over and tomorrow I'd have to start unpicking myself from Richard, one bill and kitchen appliance at a time.

Chapter 7

THE HANGOVER WAS NOT worth it.

My mouth was like flypaper – complete with rancid insects – as I stumbled out of the bedroom and flung the crumpled cashmere jumper at the rubbish bags. I was done being pathetic and done crying. I just wanted to take some paracetamol, drink a pint of orange juice and try to make my head stop banging.

While I was nursing myself through a cup of tea and a slice of dry toast, Emma texted me. *I can handle things today – have a rest and let me know if you need anything xXx.*

I was tempted, sorely tempted, to slink back to bed and emerge six hours from now for a Tesco meal deal and a few episodes of *Bake Off.* But I wasn't an employee any more. I was a business owner. That meant dragging myself out of the flat and off to my place of business to… do business.

I'd get a coffee on the way. I needed it.

God, what if Maeve asked me about Richard? That thought stopped me dead. I shook it off – without actually shaking, because that would have been a mistake in my condition. I couldn't just hide away forever to avoid talking about him. I loved Leaford but that meant sooner or later everyone in town was going to know about the break-up. I just had to live with that.

Wrangling the bulging black sacks of crochet into the lift nearly made me cry. The weight of them only reminded me of how much I'd given to someone who didn't care about me at all. To top it off, my hangover was making everything seem so much harder than it needed to be.

Downstairs I hefted one bag over each shoulder like an old-timey farm worker and wobbled down to the one charity shop in town – Lilac Lawn Hospice Shop. A tiny, warren-like space full of chipped Cadbury Creme Egg mugs and yellowed paperbacks. The stock was in constant rotation but always seemed to be exactly the same – the sort of things you only ever see in charity shops, like 'Live, Laugh, Love' signs and books by Jeremy Clarkson.

The bell jingled as I backed in through the door, catching a waft of vodka from my own pores. I looked up and saw Margaret, the only shop assistant, standing by the till. God, I hoped she wouldn't smell the booze on me. I hadn't woken up with time for a shower and my body spray wasn't doing much to help me out.

'Morning, just a few bits for you,' I felt the need to say as I flopped the bags down by the counter.

Margaret offered me a pursed-lipped smile. A long time ago she'd been the young, mean receptionist at my primary school, before sweet-shop Sally took over. She'd shushed me aggressively when I was babbling away to her, as kids do, and she'd been my nemesis ever since. She probably didn't know she was my nemesis. I'd never been anything but polite to her, but I'd once seen her slip on a dog poo and privately cheered.

'You still running your little shop?' she asked, as she nudged open the top of one bag and frowned at the contents so aggressively that, for a moment, I feared I'd grabbed a bag of recycling by mistake.

'Yup… it's only been a few weeks.'

'Hmm… well, I suppose it takes all sorts. Those don't look very practical for shop work.' She was pointing a frosted pink talon at my shoes. A pair of Irregular Choice cowboy boots inspired by My Little Pony – pastel rainbows and silver glitter all over. I'd needed some of that energy in my life today. Something a little bit fun to make me feel less like smacking my head into a wall.

'They're very comfy actually,' I said – which was a lie, as they were new and I was already regretting not putting pre-emptive blister plasters on my little toes – and turned on my heel to leave.

I walked straight into a tower of *Inbetweeners* DVDs and had to scramble to stop them cascading to the floor. I left the shop red-faced and burning up under my 'Be Happy' yellow jumper. Perhaps I'd gone a bit hard on the whole 'dressing to cheer myself up' thing. I caught sight of myself in the window as I was passing and winced. I looked like a *Blue Peter* presenter having a nervous breakdown. I popped into the bakery and ordered two coffees, thankful that Maeve wasn't working. I didn't have it in me to chat today and the part-time teenager on the till didn't say a word to me.

'Tabitha!' Emma huffed as I walked into the shop. 'I said to take the day off. You look wretched.'

'Cheers,' I sighed and dragged myself to the counter to sit down on a stool, handing her coffee over. 'I feel it. But I can't just sit at home being sad all day in the flat.'

The little surge of vindictive joy at calling the 'apartment' by that name pushed the hangover misery back a little. A tiny placebo but I'd take it.

'I suppose it was sort of the scene of the crime,' Emma said, chewing on her lip. 'Okay, but hand over that muck – the last thing you need is caffeine. Let me make you some mint tea. That'll sort your hangover out.'

I didn't have the energy to fight her as she took my coffee, even though mint tea was like drinking unsweetened toothpaste spit. My stomach flipped over. Ugh, that was not a safe thought.

For the first time I was glad we didn't have any customers in. I leant on the counter and tried to sip the disgusting tea while Emma worked around me. She, I noted somewhat resentfully, had claimed my coffee as well as hers. I didn't have the energy to do anything, and for the first time I didn't even feel like flicking through a pattern book or checking the wholesaler's website for new yarn. I just felt empty, scraped out and numb.

At eleven, normally the time we'd take a little tea break, Emma nudged me out of my seat. 'Why don't you go for a walk and get some fresh air?'

'And something from the bakery?' I said, seeing through her ploy.

'If you like.' Emma patted my shoulder. 'But the walk might do you some good.'

A strong coffee and a muffin would probably help more. I'd just have to finish the coffee before I came back to the shop. Emma could be rather militant about her herbal cures.

Annoyingly, the fresh air was quite nice. Now that I wasn't weighed down with bags of crochet or Margaret's stare, the autumnal breeze was refreshing. My little toes had lost all feeling and it was actually quite a nice walk, all told. The sound of my heels on the cobbles never failed to make me feel whimsical and light.

I went to the bakery and bought some muffins and a coffee from the mercifully silent teenager, then wandered down a side street and peered into the window of Gilly's Gallery. All the pictures were of woodland animals in party hats. She couldn't be selling a lot of those, surely? Though, as I eyed a trio of hedgehogs in Christmas-cracker crowns, I had to admit they were sort of cute. As far as I knew, all the art in there was done by Gilly and the shop hadn't turned a profit, ever. She was keeping it afloat, though, and no one knew how. I wondered which picture she'd put in the harvest-festival display this year.

As I moved on and dallied outside the window of the estate agent's, I wondered what to do about my housing situation. I'd have to move out of the flat and I couldn't afford to rent anywhere around town on my own whilst also paying rent on the shop. I imagined moving back in with Mum and Dad and their regular parties and groaned. I was an in-bed-by-eight sort of person, born into a family that saw sunrise as a challenge. I couldn't see that working.

Maybe I could get into a house share or something. Emma would probably offer to put me up for a while, but she was in a studio and there wasn't space for another person for longer than a few days. If that. Irritation at Richard bubbled up from the chasm of heartbreak in my chest. Yesterday my life was sorted, practically on rails. Now he'd ruined everything and I wasn't even sure where I'd be living next week.

I returned to the shop with a little black cloud floating over my head. The look on Emma's face as I entered didn't perk me up either. I'd expected her to be happy I was back and bringing her baked goods, but her eyes were round with alarm and darting about, avoiding me.

'What is it? What's happened?' I asked, my hands tightening on the bakery bag and my empty coffee cup as Emma just looked at me in mingled panic and awkwardness. 'Is it Richard, has he come in? Is it Mum and Dad, has something happened? Oh God, it's moths, isn't it?' I felt horror run down my spine. 'We're infested with moths eating their way through all our stock. That's it, I'm finished. My boyfriend cheated on me and now I'm being eaten out of business…'

'No, it's not that,' Emma finally managed to get out, holding up her hands to urge me to calm down. 'Sorry I was just… I'm not really sure how to tell you without you freaking out, but you're already freaking out, so that's my bad…'

'Just tell me!' I begged, thinking that if it wasn't moths or something wrong with my parents, I could handle it. It couldn't be that bad. Not 'walking in on a squeaky-bummed vixen on your leather sofa' bad anyway.

'A man came in while you were gone,' Emma said, wincing.

'A… was he weird, or creepy – what happened?' I hurried over to the counter and dumped my stuff on it. 'Are you okay?'

'I'm fine. He wasn't weird or anything. He was just… he was

wearing the jumper. As in *the* jumper. And he had um… two black bags with him.'

'Black… you mean rubbish bags?' I said, a horrible realisation twisting up my insides. 'My rubbish bags? The ones I handed over to Margaret this morning?'

'Yep,' Emma squeaked. 'Look, I don't want you to get upset but…'

'But that awful woman didn't even unpack the bags, did she? She probably just slapped a price tag on them and shoved them on the floor with the sticky Duplo and the VHS tapes of fucking… *Taggart*.'

Emma was tense and looked miserable. She obviously didn't want to be the one telling me all this. I couldn't blame her. I'd already had my heart broken once in twenty-four hours and now it was happening all over again. My gorgeous crochet, treated like someone's old baby clothes, all stained with strained peas and musty from the loft.

'How much?' I asked, dropping onto my stool behind the counter. 'How much did she sell them for?'

'I'm… not quite sure this is healthy,' Emma protested. 'I mean, at least it's all gone, right? That's what you wanted?'

My stomach squirmed, threatening to reject the giant coffee I'd just downed. 'I wanted it gone-gone. Not walking back into my place of business on a stranger. How much, Emma?'

Emma wriggled as if trying to contain the awful secret, but she gave in quickly under the weight of silence. 'Ten pounds.'

'Ten pounds!?' I was going to burn that charity shop down with Margaret inside it.

'Each!' she said quickly, as if that would soften the blow.

'Ten pounds wouldn't cover the cost of the ends I snipped off that lot!' I buried my head in my hands. My one solace had been that the crochet Richard had never appreciated would at least make some money for charity. It was worth over a thousand pounds, even second-hand. Margaret had woefully undervalued it but, then again, so had Richard.

'I know, I'm sorry.' Emma put her arm around me. 'Can I get you a cup of tea, or a hug or… go down there and give Margaret a piece of my mind?'

My head shot up. 'God, no, she'd eat you alive.'

Emma sagged in relief. 'Good because I am so scared of her, have been ever since she practically forced those Lilliput Lane figurines on me. I only went in to ask her to put up a poster about tarot readings.'

I couldn't help but giggle and it broke some of the awful tension. Still, I felt as if I'd had the stuffing pulled out of me by a cruel toddler. All that crochet, all that work, gone for a paltry twenty quid. My talent was worthless. I was worthless.

'He's probably going to sell it all on eBay,' Emma said, as if trying to make me feel better. 'He'll flip the lot and make hundreds more. That'll show her.'

I groaned in annoyance and rested my elbows on the counter, defeated. 'I know I shouldn't care but it just feels really shitty. I did all the hard work and I was okay with the profits going to charity but not to some scummy reseller. What did he even look like?'

'Um… I wouldn't say "scummy",' Emma said, evasively. 'But he was a little… shabby. Around the edges. Sort of like that dog that's sometimes tied up outside the library – cute little sausage dog, one of the hairy ones? Sort of scruffy, three legs, tartan bandana…'

'More about the guy, less about the dog,' I sighed, now face down on the counter.

'Right, um… maybe late thirties. Going grey already, bit beardy and stubbly and… he had a shopping bag with him, from the everything shop down the way. Scissors, bin liners and candles. Which I thought was odd. Maybe he was getting ready for Halloween?'

'Scissors?' I sat bolt upright. Oh my God – was he going to cut the crochet up? Repurpose the yarn, or sell it on as scrap fabric?

'I don't think he was going to use the scissors on the stuff,' Emma soothed, clearly guessing my train of thought. 'He came in to ask me about washing everything. Didn't want to shrink stuff or have it unravel. I gave him a list of temperatures and stuff for the different fibres.' Emma looked quite proud of this display of customer service, and I was pleased she'd been able to give advice. Or would have been if it had been doled out to anyone else but the knitwear bandit.

'He probably just wants to sell it and then, you know, it'll be with people who really appreciate it,' Emma said hopefully. 'And he was wearing the jumper. The cursed one, so… it isn't going to waste.'

'Well… that's that then, I suppose,' I managed to say, trying to sound adequately soothed and not at all like I was having a crisis over some crochet. 'Nothing I can do about it now.'

Emma patted my arm and went to make tea. I sat on my stool and stewed. First Richard, now this. How many more unpleasant surprises did the universe plan to spring on me?

Chapter 8

We were only ten minutes from closing and I was pulling the internal blinds down when I saw it. The jumper. It was walking down the street, fresh from a trip to Londis by the looks of it. I froze and stared as it sidled past without a care in the world. Twice in one day it had been by the shop. If that carried on, I wouldn't be able to stand it. I'd never wanted to see that thing again and now it was practically stalking me.

'Emma!' I called back towards the stock cupboard. 'I've just seen it again!'

She came hurrying over, clutching a bag of polyester toy stuffing – the single item we'd sold that day and needed to restock. 'The jumper?'

'Yeah… it went that way.' I pointed to the left, the way towards the car park and not much else.

'Maybe he's heading home now and you won't see him again?' Emma said, squeezing the bag of stuffing like a stress toy. 'He might have only been visiting for the day. I've never seen him before, have you?'

To be honest, I hadn't really been looking at the man inside the jumper. I'd seen the distinctive pattern, the colours I'd been focused on for weeks, stitch after stitch, and nothing else had mattered beyond the shock of seeing it again. I'd got a general impression of a stocky figure carrying a Londis bag and a plastic-handled mop.

'I hope so,' I sighed. 'God, I wish I'd burned it. Just that one thing, so I'd never have to see it again.'

'It was too pretty to burn.' Emma patted my arm reassuringly. 'You'd have never been able to do it. Not after all that work.'

She was right. Damn it. Set fire to cashmere? I'd sooner burn my own hair – while it was still attached.

We closed up and Emma hovered on the pavement, waiting for me to lock the door. She had her car keys in hand and was jingling them worriedly.

'Do you want to come and stay at mine, for tonight?' she asked, as I shouldered my tote bag. 'Or I could come over? Just so you don't have to be on your own.'

'I'll be all right – thanks, though! And for yesterday,' I said. 'I think I need to decompress and just get my head on straight. I'll be all right by tomorrow and I can start sorting everything out.' This was me lying to both Emma and myself, to be honest. I was trying to be positive because I couldn't avoid these feelings forever. It would be best for everyone if I just dealt with it in private.

'He's not going to pop by today?' Emma asked, chewing her lip. 'Like if he needs clothes or polish for his cloven hoofs?'

I laughed despite the weight in my chest. 'Not if he knows what's good for him. Besides, I'll put the chain on so he can't burst in and surprise me.'

As Emma gave me a quick hug and left for her car, I found myself thinking that, if Richard had bothered with the chain yesterday, I wouldn't be in this mess. Though, obviously, he still would have cheated on me. I winced as I imagined all the other times he'd probably got away with it. All those 'meetings' with investors and weekends spent golfing. He'd probably been laughing behind my back for months. My insides felt like a ball of wool being pulled in all directions at that thought. Oh God, how long had he been at it?

Suddenly the idea of going back to the flat for an early night had lost its appeal. I didn't want to confront all this stuff right now. Not if I could put it off for a little while longer. It wasn't even dark yet, the long evening persisting into a golden sunset. I could go for a walk, get some fresh air, maybe grab some food from the Moonlight Chinese on the way home. Delay the inevitable moment I'd be by myself, surrounded by my life with Richard. A life that I was no longer going to be living.

I set off in the same direction Emma had gone, towards the car park. Halfway down the road a footpath branched off and crossed a field full of lazily droning insects and crisp, fragrant grasses. I followed the footpath of baked earth to the hedgerow at the far side, where some of the best blackberries could be found in August. There, a kissing gate led on to the towpath. There was a long way round – down to the car park and then up the path – but my route had brought me out around the bend from there. I didn't want Emma to see me and decide to come over. Some time alone was what I needed. Time to not be 'okay'.

The air was sweet with the remnants of berries and I had the urge to pick some as I walked up the towpath, watching the ducks drift along. The canal water was a murky olive green, almost black in the shade of the willows. The setting sun was blinding through the trees, setting them ablaze as I walked by. The scents of summer – lavender blooms gone crisp and grass baked to hay, mingled with those of early autumn – the sweetly ripening crab apples and rich damp earth under the hedges. I listened to the cries of moorhens and the raspy bark of a magpie. This, I decided, was what I needed. Peace and tranquillity.

A crash of breaking china snapped me out of my relaxed mood.

'Bollocks!' a voice exploded from upriver, and for the first time I noticed the boat.

It was parked – moored? – up by the viaduct, a red-brick wall shining so brightly in the sun that I'd missed the shadowy little blob under a clump of elder nearby. Not that the boat was particularly eye-catching. Maybe once it had been something special but it was currently peeling paint flakes into the river, the same dull green as the water. The gold writing on its side windows, 'The Lady Di', was almost all rust, and the wooden planters on its roof were fully stocked with weeds gone to seed. It could not have been camouflaged better had someone intentionally tried to hide it.

I was about to turn back and leave this loud interloper to it, when the tiny doors at the nearest end of the boat flew open and a man emerged. He was carrying a box piled with what looked like china dolls. The pile obscured his face, so all I could see was his legs, until he turned and I gaped at his back – the back of my jumper!

Before I could think better of it, I was rushing up the towpath, My Little Pony boots clopping on the uneven tarmac. I was really starting to wish I'd worn more practical shoes, but it felt like acknowledging that would be letting Margaret win, something I refused to allow even in the privacy of my own mind. Even though my formerly numb toes were now throbbing something awful.

'Excuse me!' I called as the man dumped his box on the deck of the boat and turned back to the doors. He was slightly bow-legged, as scruffy as Emma had said he was, squinting at me against the sun with crinkles around his eyes, his shoulders hunched up by his ears. Late thirties, though? Emma had to be joking. Or hiding a serious eye problem. He was maybe thirty, though the premature grey in his curly hair and the stress lines around his eyes and mouth made him look older.

He glared at me. 'I've got permission to be here, so you can bugger off!'

'I'm not…' I started to say, but he'd already gone back inside and slammed the door. Like an aggressive little character on a cuckoo clock. Well, then.

I looked down at the box and frowned. It was china dolls – the same doll but in many different outfits, including a wedding dress. All of them lightly patterned with black mould. Charming. I could only imagine what that kind of damp would do to all the crochet he'd misappropriated from the charity shop.

For a second I considered turning around and heading home. It was unlikely I'd see the jumper again now. The man in the boat hadn't exactly been gadding about town making friends. But, as I dithered on the towpath, I felt a flash of annoyance. Who was he to tell me to 'bugger off'? I had just as much right to be here as he did and, what's more, I wanted my bloody jumper back.

I didn't want to step onto the boat uninvited. That seemed rude, so I leant over from my spot on the grassy bank and knocked on the narrow painted doors.

Footsteps clomped across the floor inside and moments later the doors were wrenched open. The man stuck his head out and I got a proper look at him without the sun interfering. His salt-and-pepper hair was badly in need of a trim and, aside from the jumper, his clothes were ancient – worn jeans and a pair of scuffed-up black Crocs over stripy socks. He leant in the doorway and glared at me.

'Look, if you're from the neighbourhood watch or the council or the bloody WI – save it. I have permission to moor up here.'

'I'm not here about that.' I held up a hand to silence him before he could work himself up again. 'I just… you're wearing my jumper. I made it.'

He blinked and raised an eyebrow, not looking any friendlier than before. 'I bought this today. I didn't steal it, if that's what you're implying.'

'No! I'm not saying that at all.' I felt my face turn red and wished more than anything that I'd never decided to take a walk. Or at least that I had left once I'd spotted him. I knew I was acting irrationally but it had felt so important that I get the jumper back.

I tried again. 'I donated it this morning and…'

His disbelieving look dried the words up in my throat.

'Look,' he sighed. 'I'm trying to get some work done, so either you get to the point or you get off my boat. All right?'

'I'm not even on your ruddy boat!' I looked down, indicated my feet and stamped on the grass to emphasise my point.

At which point I slipped on the wet grass and went careening towards the water.

Chapter 9

I shrieked as I went over, arms windmilling wildly. The man on the boat tried to grab my shoulders but I was already gone. I hit the water and immediately went under, lost in a world of green and dead leaves. I saw the shape of a shopping trolley looming in the weedy dark and had just enough time to think 'there's no Waitrose anywhere near here' before I was surfacing and gasping for air. My mouth tasted like old leaves and what was probably duck shit.

I've never been a good swimmer. In primary school I was the one stuck in the shallow pool with kids four or five years younger than me, while the rest of my class learned to dive off the high board. We had certificates from jellyfish up to shark, and a special book to put them in. My book only ever had the first certificate in it. I was a jellyfish, through and through. In the end I'd used the book to collect patterns from Aunt Lou's magazines.

Treading water as best I could, I looked up and realised to my horror that I was drifting with the current. Already several metres away from the boat. I shared a panicked look with the man on the deck and watched him kick off his Crocs, eyes intent on me as he judged the distance.

'WAIT!' I yelled, nearly swallowing another mouthful of swampy canal water for my troubles.

His intense expression dissolved into surprise and annoyance. His eyebrows knitted together as he gaped at me. 'What?'

I kicked at the water, trying to stay above the surface. 'Take the jumper off first!'

He was definitely more annoyed than surprised now, his eyes flinty and dark. 'Are you serious?'

'It's cashmere!' I yelled defensively, flailing at the water. I could hear a duck laughing at me. I was cancelling my donations to the Wildlife Trust after this.

The man shook his head in disbelief. 'What are you on!?'

'Just do it!' I called, splashing frantically. My teeth were already chattering. Despite the golden sunset, the water was shockingly cold and tasted as green as it looked.

He huffed but pulled the jumper over his head and dropped it on the deck, exposing a flash of pale skin as his shirt rucked up underneath. Within seconds he'd dived into the water and was swimming out to me. I caught sight of his furious face as he executed a precise front crawl and, to be honest, he looked like he was in two minds about just letting me drown.

When he got to me, he hooked an arm around my chest in a business-like fashion and cupped my chin. Something I vaguely remembered from the life-saving session we'd done at the start of every year's swimming lessons. He was stronger than I'd expected him to be, given his height. The baggy jumper had been hiding the amount of muscle on his arms and his chest, which was hard against my back as he towed me along.

He propelled us back to the boat and helped me up onto the deck, where I crawled forward and got to my feet. By the time I had, he'd climbed out and was shaking his head like a dog, flicking droplets of water everywhere. His T-shirt was pasted to his body, chest heaving under it as he tried to get his breath back after the cold plunge.

'Shouldn't you have a… float or something?' I gasped as the air met my soaked clothes.

'It's perished,' he said, through gritted teeth. 'I wasn't expecting some idiot in cheap shoes to turn up and fall overboard.'

'These were not cheap,' I said, appalled. I looked down at my colourful cowboy boots, currently full of water and covered in bits of dead leaf.

'That's worse,' he sighed. 'God, it's freezing.'

'Don't put the jumper on,' I said automatically and saw him roll his eyes.

'Fine… Do you want a towel or something?'

I nodded, because like hell was I dragging myself home soaked to the skin like this. He ducked through the door and I hesitated a second before following after him. While he worked his way through the cluttered interior, I raised my eyebrows and took in the state of the boat.

Every inch of the place was covered in the same two faces. Mostly the one face. Suddenly the dolls made sense, even if their likeness was questionable. Princess Diana beamed down at me from every available surface. A few Prince Charleses – including a life-size cut-out by the window, which had probably been what scared Ian so much – but mostly Diana reigned supreme. The walls held commemorative plates and plaques, shelves of figurines and yet more dolls, both plastic and china. A glass cabinet held mugs and an entire tea service sporting the ill-fated royal couple, and there was Union Jack bunting crisscrossing the ceiling. The two gold chandelier fixtures were hung with Diana Christmas ornaments and the far wall, beyond which my rescuer had gone, was covered in 'art' depicting the people's princess. Cross-stitch, diamond paintings, paint by numbers, collage and even a tapestry.

'… love what you've done with the place,' I said looking away from an eyeless cardboard Diana mask. 'Very… subtle. Understated.'

A tea towel hit me in the chest. I was unsurprised to find that it commemorated the royal wedding.

'Thanks…' I started to dry my hair, watching the man as he lingered in the far doorway. 'Any chance of some dry clothes?'

'I'll see if I can find some that'll fit you,' he muttered, starting to open some cardboard boxes piled behind a rickety shelf stacked with Diana saint candles and bobble heads.

I pulled a face at the implied slight to me and my hips and he must have seen because he huffed a laugh. 'Because you're taller than me,' he clarified. 'Even without those stupid boots,' he added, under his breath, the ghost of a smile teasing at his mouth.

It was the truth, I realised. I was fairly tall at five foot eleven and that had always made me a bit insecure. At school it was an accepted fact that you had to go out with a boy taller than you were and that rule had stuck with me. I'd been pleased to find out Richard was three quarters of an inch taller than I was. He'd measured. The stranger was at least three inches shorter than me, maybe more.

He fished some joggers and a sweatshirt out of a packing box, tossing those over to me. He indicated the doorway behind him. 'Fire's in the kitchen… you can change in the bedroom and then come through. It's the only door that locks, in case that matters.'

'Thank you,' I said, and crossed the museum of Diana into the bedroom on the left. Inside was a neatly-made-up single bed, covered in a familiar bedspread. The one I'd taken off the bed in my flat. A shelf over the bed contained several very worn Anthony Horowitz paperbacks, including the Sherlock ones I'd read with my aunt as a teenager and still loved. So at least he had good taste in books if not décor. A Princess Diana Funko Pop figure looked down at me, with a watercolour of the boat itself propped against it. Even in the picture the boat looked slightly sad and lonesome. Though the art was good, in my uneducated opinion. Better than the Diana craft kit stuff anyway.

I stripped down to my underwear after locking the door. Although my bra and knickers were soaked through, it felt rude to wear a stranger's clothes without underwear, so I kept them on. I expected the clothes to smell musty but, after a tentative sniff, I found that, although they were obviously old, they were freshly washed and still smelled pleasantly of detergent and something woodsy, like pine or cedar. Figured my angry rescuer with the lumberjack arms would use some kind of foresty-smelling man-soap. I picked up my swampy boots and rolled my wet clothes into a ball before leaving the bedroom.

As I went into the kitchen I asked, 'Do you have a…'

The words died in my throat because my rescuer was still getting changed. As in he had yet to find a shirt and had also stripped off his jeans. The lack of underwear in the bundle of borrowed clothes now made sense. Because he didn't appear to wear any.

He had his back to me, an impressively broad back, though pale from lack of sun. My eyes slid over the dip in his spine like it was a ski ramp and landed squarely on his bum. A soft landing at least, I thought, somewhat hysterically. It was a very nice bum, but on a very *not* nice man, I reminded myself. I was still gaping at him as he pulled a fresh pair of ragged jeans up. He turned around while doing up the fly and caught me staring.

'… plastic bag,' I managed to finish, weakly.

For a moment he just looked at me and I wondered what was so interesting about my wet-rat hair and the fact I was wearing his wrinkled clothes. He was probably going to say something sarcastic. I folded my arms around myself for warmth and realised I was, as my mum would put it, 'smuggling peanuts' – aka nipping like crazy. Wonderful. I clasped my arms tighter and cleared my throat.

He ducked his head and quickly found a tatty bag for life to offer me. I stuffed my clothes into it, feeling my face burn with embarrassment. Had he noticed me staring at his bum? Why had I not knocked? Although, to be fair, the kitchen was behind a curtain, rather than a door. Still, I wasn't normally one to gawp and I didn't want him thinking I was. Even if I had definitely been gawping.

He picked up a jumper from a pile of clothes in a plastic laundry bag on the floor. I recognised it as one I'd made for Richard – green cable-knit-effect crochet. Richard had begged me to make it and then worn it maybe twice. The sleeves were a little too long on the man in front of me, and he rolled them up to expose surprisingly delicate wrists and long, nimble fingers.

Oh my God, I was staring again. What was wrong with me? I was acting like I'd been in a nunnery for the past three years, instead of in a committed relationship. Committed on my end at least. The thing was, though, that however snappy this guy had been since we'd met, he was, objectively speaking… kind of hot. In a Gabriel Oak, brawny sheep farmer kind of way.

Damn Aunt Lou for exposing me to *Far from the Madding Crowd* at such a formative age.

I wasn't about to let him know that, though. He already thought I was an uncoordinated idiot in ridiculous boots, unreasonably obsessed with jumpers. I didn't need to give him the added advantage of knowing how nice his bum was. If he'd never been in a double-mirror changing room, there was a chance he didn't know.

'You have um…'

I nearly jumped when I realised he'd come a lot closer while I was thinking of shepherds and their bums. He frowned, hand wandering towards my face, waiting to see if I'd bat him away. When I didn't, he plucked something from my wet hair. Probably a leaf or something. I managed to catch my breath as he backed off, the heat from his fingers practically glowing on my cold cheek.

'Oh good, it's just cellophane,' he muttered, voice rasping a little as he turned away and tossed the scrap into the kitchen bin. 'I was worried it was a condom.'

Lustful atmosphere officially shattered. I couldn't tell if I was relieved or disappointed. To distract myself I looked around at the tiny kitchen-diner.

The collection of memorabilia in the kitchen area was still obvious but slightly less overwhelming. Limited to towels, oven gloves and a tablecloth on the little table by the bench seat. Over the bench was a familiar blanket – my Moroccan tile blanket. My heart clenched to see it there. The blanket that Richard had cheated on me… on.

I tried to be as dignified as possible whilst emptying my boots out into the sink, but I still caught the man smirking at me. Amused.

'Were they actually expensive?' he asked.

I cleared my throat, but I wasn't about to lie – who cared what he thought? 'Two hundred pounds. Or thereabouts.'

He let out a shocked bark of laughter. 'Fuck me.'

I felt myself blush again. 'They were a birthday present, to myself.'

To be fair, Richard had given me a fifty-pound gift voucher, which I'd put towards them. Though he'd been annoyed that I hadn't used it on some 'smart work clothes'. I think it was a gift mostly intended to get me out of my painty T-shirts.

His eyes strayed to the blanket on the bench seat, and he seemed to put two and two together. 'Did you make that too?'

'Yeah, that's one of mine,' I admitted.

He whistled through his teeth. 'Looks complicated. How long did that take you?'

'I don't know,' I said, though I did. 'Maybe… just over a hundred hours.'

It was more like two hundred but I didn't want to go blowing my own horn.

'Jesus,' he said, and crossed over to the kettle on its little gas ring. 'You're shivering, by the way. Hot drink?'

I was. Fuck. I thought of the long walk back to my flat, and the silence that awaited me there.

'Sure. What do you have?'

He knelt and looked below the counter. 'I've got tea, beer…' He looked up at me, eyes crinkled slightly with humour. 'Do you need those options again?'

'Tea, please,' I said, reluctantly cracking a smile. Mostly because I was relieved we weren't talking about the blanket any more.

'So,' he said, straightening. He picked up the copper kettle and started to fill it. 'If it took you that long, why did you donate it?'

Okay, so apparently we weren't done talking about it.

'Personal reasons,' I said, and leant against the wall instead of sitting on the offending blanket. 'Why do you collect Diana memorabilia?'

He huffed a laugh, doling tea bags into a pair of commemorative mugs. 'I don't. This place used to belong to an older couple – they used it as a sort of… shrine. Kept it moored at the bottom of their garden. I'm still working on clearing it out.'

'Mmmhmm… and how did you come to be the recent owner of such a fine vessel?' I asked, as he passed me my cup of tea – handle first. The only acceptable way to do it. I had to get Richard to put cups down before I took them, I'd burned myself too many times. My fingers brushed his as I accepted the mug and I winced at how cold they were. Surprisingly soft too, for a guy living on a boat, just barely starting to roughen at the tips.

His voice was soft too when he said, 'Personal reasons.'

Fair enough. I'd earned that. 'And you bought two giant bags of my crochet because…'

'It gets really cold on here at night. Went in to buy some blankets, a few jumpers, but the woman in there was just sticking prices on the bags and it looked like the best stuff in there. And possibly the only stuff someone's Tory grandfather hadn't died in, on or under.'

That was an understatement. Not to be a bitch but my crochet was leagues above the bobbly old microfleece blankets and knackered M&S jumpers the charity shop usually stocked. He'd be warm as toast in here with all those jumpers and blankets. Not to mention he'd look miles better in them too.

'Maybe you should take that jumper back, though,' he said, cutting off my train of thought. 'Since it's cashmere and all… I'll probably just ruin it.'

'I um…' I felt my face burn hot with embarrassment. 'I don't really want it back. I just sort of freaked out because I wanted it gone and then… you turned up in it at my shop…'

'The wool shop?' he surmised, and I nodded. 'So… bad associations with the jumper?'

'You could say that… I made it for my ex,' I said, deciding there was no sense tiptoeing around the subject. 'I'm surprised it took so many to trigger the sweater curse but it happened eventually.'

'Curse?' He looked amused. 'I thought the woman in the shop was a bit witchy. But she seemed too nice to curse anyone.'

'Emma? Yeah, she's normally the one who believes in curses around here but this one's not so much spooky as an observable phenomenon, apparently.' I realised I hadn't bothered to introduce myself and held out a hand. 'I'm Tabitha, by the way.'

'Well, that's very formal.' He smiled crookedly and took my hand to shake it. 'Cooper. What's the deal with the curse then? Do I need to sprinkle some salt around the place or…?'

I rolled my eyes. 'It's just one of those things. I don't even know where it comes from but, if you make your boyfriend or partner, whatever, a big craft project… thing, they break up with you. Knitters and crocheters mostly. I uh… made him a cashmere jumper and I wanted to surprise him with it, so I went home early…'

'Uh-oh,' Cooper said, deadpan. 'I've seen that film before.'

'Yeah… he was with someone else. In our flat… on my really, really time-consuming blanket.'

I saw him follow my gaze towards the bench seat, nose wrinkling.

'I washed it,' I said.

'Good call,' he said, and looked back at me. 'Your witch friend showed me the label on the yarn you used for that jumper by the way – little handful of that stuff for, like, twenty quid? That must've been expensive.'

I sighed. 'Don't remind me. Probably cost me… well, I know it cost me hundreds in yarn and then… God, if I paid myself minimum wage for the time it took… another, well, I don't have to pay that. It's just my time. And the yarn wasn't all at once, obviously, and I got some discount because of the business, so it's not that bad.'

Cooper leant back against the kitchen counter and blew on

his tea. '… but your time is valuable too, so, with that included – how much?'

I winced. 'Probably around… one thousand seven hundred pounds?'

His dark brows shot upwards. 'Shit! That's nearly more than I paid for the boat – and the engine packed in when I got here. You can't just give that away – you should take it back and sell it. It's like… boutique quality.'

I shrugged. 'I'd be lucky to get a tenth of what it's worth. That's just how it is – you can buy a jumper from some website for twenty pounds. So that's what people think they cost. You should just keep it – I guarantee it'll keep you warm.'

'Hey, even a hundred and seventy pounds is better than a poke in the eye,' Cooper pointed out. 'You could nearly buy some really impractical boots for that.'

The jibe felt more like an inside joke. A soft bat of a teasing cat paw. I smiled and he slowly returned it. I noticed one of his canines was a little crooked, like a book carelessly re-shelved at the library, left at a jaunty angle. It suited him.

'I'd honestly pay that just to not see it again,' I said, and meant it, tearing my eyes away from his smile. 'Please, keep it. You did just save my life.'

Cooper ducked his head, looking uncomfortable for the first time since I'd met him. 'Eh, you'd have probably been fine. Besides, I was ready to jump in there wearing the bloody thing so, like I said, it'll just get ruined. Even if you're not going to sell it, why not, I don't know… burn it? Ceremonially, with your friend, in the woods?'

I laughed. 'In the nude, carrying a sheep skull and reciting the pattern backwards?'

'Hey, it's your Saturday night, not mine,' he said, back to smiling lopsidedly again. Was I imagining it or had his ears gone a little pink at the idea of me in the nude – ritualistically or otherwise? It was probably just the cold. I was drenched in canal water, for God's sake. Hardly prime fantasy fuel.

'Nah… I'm good.' I set my empty cup on the table, obscuring one of tablecloth Diana's eyes. 'I should be getting home but… the jumper's yours now, so… if you want to burn it? Whatever. But you'd be wasting all my hard work if you did. Plus you'd be missing out on, like, the best jumper you'll ever have. Ever. Even if you do eventually get engine oil or something on it, it'll still be warm. And almost illegally soft… and it looked good on you.'

I winced, having let my mouth run away with me. But it had looked nice on him. That was just the truth. He could have that for saving my life.

'No reason not to keep it then, is there?' Cooper huffed a laugh, looking a bit surprised and awkward. As well he might. Me and my big mouth.

I busied myself putting my wet boots back on. Ew, they squished. 'Thanks for saving my life, by the way. Not sure how to pay you back for that.'

Cooper took my mug and set both cups in the sink. 'If it helps, I regretted it immediately.'

I laughed. 'Oh, really? You just talked yourself out of a thank-you card.'

I watched as he rolled his eyes. 'I'll live. Need help getting off the boat, in case you fall in again?'

'I'll manage,' I said, already heading out of the kitchen door. 'Happy cleaning! Hope none of your dolls are haunted.'

Oh, my God, was I flirting? I'd been single for less than twenty-four hours and I was already checking out bums and flirting with… a very confusing man who had 1. Saved my life, 2. Called my shoes cheap and 3. Been basically naked in front of me. All in the space of an hour. I needed to get myself home before I did anything else embarrassing.

As I squelched off up the towpath, though, I couldn't resist a backward glance, and there was Cooper – picking up the jumper and folding it carefully before taking it inside.

Chapter 10

THE NEXT MORNING, I woke up with my hair in a curly nightmare nest and Aunt Lou's copy of *The House of Silk* on my chest. I'd reached for it as a comfort blanket after tucking myself in. I could almost hear her taking a turn reading aloud as we put skeins of yarn through the ball winder, turning it by hand.

Thoughts of Cooper snuck in around the edges of that memory. For a moment he was the one reading the book and I was curled up beside him by the woodstove on the boat. I blinked that image away. Temporary break-up-related insanity, that's what that was.

Glaring at myself in the mirror, Denman brush in hand, I cursed past-Tabitha for showering off the smell of canal and then collapsing into bed for an early night. To be honest, I hadn't wanted to spend much time mooning about the flat. Going to bed right away had at least kept me from wandering into the main bedroom to brood. But there was a price to pay for that reprieve. My head looked, as Mum would say, like an explosion in a mattress factory. Wonderful.

I made my way to the kitchen and found the egg poacher in the cupboard under the sink. I hadn't bothered with dinner last night and I was now completely famished. After dotting butter in the plastic cups, I cracked in two eggs and set a timer. While they cooked, I added wholemeal bread to the toaster and unloaded the washing machine. It seemed it had been running nonstop since I caught Richard in the act. As I draped the borrowed joggers and sweatshirt over the indoor airer, I had to acknowledge that at least it wasn't more sullied crochet. I just hoped Cooper wouldn't mind his woodsy soap being washed away by tea rose and fresh linen.

The timer went and I buttered my toast before topping it with perfectly poached eggs. There was a bit of smoked salmon in the fridge and, after it passed the sniff test, I added that to my plate, because why not? As I sat down to eat, I checked my phone and found several cute animal TikToks and memes from Emma. Clearly an attempt at cheering me up. Which, to be fair, they did.

At least until the front door opened and Richard came in, without so much as a cursory knock. Like this was just a normal morning and he was coming home from a night out with the boys. Stupid, stupid past-Tabitha. She'd left the bloody chain off. I was going to have to have words with her.

Halfway through cutting a bite of toast and egg, I froze, just looking at him. Richard's eyes found mine and the door fell shut behind him with a clunk. I was, abruptly, no longer hungry.

'… Hi,' he said, shifting his keys from one hand to the other. I couldn't help but be surprised at how good he looked. Especially considering how long he'd been separated from his shelf of the bathroom cabinet. After the past two days, I'd thought he'd just be any old guy to me but he was still Richard: perfect hair, cashmere coat, checked scarf. He was clean-shaven and bright-eyed, like nothing had happened. Comparatively, with my tangled-up hair and yesterday's hangover still weighing heavily in the bags under my eyes, I felt like I'd spent a week living under a bush.

'Hi,' I said, and wrapped my dressing gown tighter around myself. 'I'm going to work in a minute but if you wanted to pack some stuff…'

'I actually thought you might be willing to… talk now.' Richard set his keys down on the breakfast bar and eyed my plate of eggs and salmon wistfully. It was the same breakfast

I had made him on anniversaries and at Christmas, I realised belatedly. The smell of it now making me nauseous. 'Maybe have a coffee and just talk things over?'

That actually sounded pleasantly mature. I'd been worrying so much about what was going to happen with the flat and his stuff and everything else. It was honestly a bit of a relief that he'd turned up to discuss it. Even if, ideally, we'd have been doing this over text. Seeing him again was a lot, especially for that time of the morning.

'Right,' I said, nodding. 'Okay, well… I have work but if we're quick. Um… I suppose the biggest thing is going to be who stays here and what to do about the rent over the notice period.'

Richard's eyebrows rose and his mouth lifted slightly into a disbelieving smile. 'You want me to move out?'

'Or I can, but I'd need to check if Mum and Dad have space for me at the moment, because I need to think about rent on the shop,' I said, trying to keep the peace. 'I just thought maybe you'd be moving in with… you know. Her.'

'With… oh!' He pulled a face as if he'd just sipped spoiled milk. 'No, no that's not… she's no one. Just a… what I meant was I thought we could talk about this and get past it. Together.'

She's no one. How could three words make me so angry and feel so devastated at the same time? He hadn't even said her name. For the sake of 'no one', he had torn my world apart. Destroyed three years of togetherness. He couldn't even imagine living with her, apparently, but she was worth spitting on our relationship. I'd had this idea in my head that he was leaving me *for* her. That he'd cheated on me because he just couldn't resist her. He loved her more than me. But no… she could have been anyone. No one. And she was still worth losing me over.

I blinked at him, tears threatening to spill over. Disbelief following hurt and anger until I couldn't breathe enough air. He'd made me feel like this before – slightly unreal, as if our two versions of fact weren't quite meeting in the middle. Such as when I'd special-ordered him a new, criminally expensive golf club he wanted and he assured me four months later that he'd bought it himself. I'd always thought it was just his memory being bad, or me caring too much about silly details. But, sitting there, it felt like I was from an alternative timeline altogether. One where I hadn't walked in on him having appallingly loud sex with another woman on our sofa.

'Together?' I repeated and pushed the plate of eggs away because I was worried I might actually throw it at him. 'Richard... we aren't going to be together any more. You cheated on me.'

He actually looked surprised. Not shocked, but mildly surprised, like he'd walked in to discover I'd rearranged the kitchen slightly. Things weren't as he'd expected to find them. How odd! The tears were still lodged in my throat, but so was a bubble of hysterical laughter.

Richard held out his arms, perplexed. 'Come on, Tabs, it was one time. It didn't mean anything.'

The sight of the congealing eggs and fish turned my stomach. I picked up my plate and went over to the bin, scraping the food into it without looking up. 'Well congratulations on throwing us away for something that didn't mean anything,' I said to the discarded tea bags and eggshells, not trusting myself to look at him.

I put the plate in the dishwasher and quickly went to our room to grab some clothes for the day. I didn't want him to see the cracks in my resolve or how much he'd managed to hurt me. He didn't deserve that kind of access to me any more. From now on, we were strangers. He already felt so far from the Richard I'd loved. *She's no one.* How could he say that? How could he believe that would make it okay? Who even was he right now?

I heard Richard following me and turned to glare at him as I reached the wardrobe. I just wanted him to go away before I fell apart.

'If you want to get some stuff, please do,' I said, as firmly as I could. 'Otherwise, I'm going to get ready and go to work. I don't really want to talk about this any more unless we're going to discuss arrangements for leaving the flat.'

I was proud of myself for getting it out without my voice going all wobbly and weird, but he didn't seem to be listening to me. Or looking at me, as he said, 'This isn't mine.'

I glanced down, wrong-footed by the pained tone in his voice. He was holding a dark piece of clothing, wet and slightly crumpled. The sweatshirt I'd taken out of the washing machine shortly before he arrived.

'Whose is this?' he asked, turning big, wounded eyes on me. 'It's a man's sweatshirt, and I've never seen you with it even when you were doing up your shop… where did it come from?'

'I borrowed it yesterday,' I said and took a step towards him, holding my hand out for it. Richard held it away from me, though.

'From who – Emma? Or a new boyfriend?' I couldn't tell if he wanted that to be the case or if he'd be disappointed if he was right. A small, mean part of me thought he was actually pleased to have something to throw back at me. He never liked to be in the wrong – even over stupid things like who put the wooden chopping board in the dishwasher. But I didn't want to lie to him – that'd just be sinking to his level.

Still, the unvarnished truth felt like something to keep to myself. I didn't want Richard haring off up the towpath to have a go at Cooper. Not when all he'd done was drag me out of the canal and give me some dry clothes. All perfectly innocent. Minus the arm and bum appreciation and the flirting I'd done. If it even was flirting. With the benefit of distance, I was less certain that he had been trying to be anything but friendly, with a side of sarcastic banter. It had just been… refreshing to talk to someone who actually listened to me and responded to what I said instead of brushing me off. I hadn't realised how much I'd missed that.

'I got drenched yesterday and borrowed some things to come home in,' I said, letting annoyance take over from hurt in an attempt to force him out. 'Now, can you leave so I can get changed?'

'Drenched how? It didn't even rain,' Richard said, refusing to let the subject drop.

'I fell in the canal,' I said bluntly, face growing hot in embarrassment.

'Fell… you expect me to believe that? What would you be doing by the canal, for God's sake…'

'I was taking a long walk because *someone*,' I raised my voice sharply, 'someone I thought I was going to spend the rest of my life with – someone I trusted and loved, just broke my heart into tiny little pieces over "no one", Richard!'

That seemed to bring him up short and I ploughed on into the stunned silence. The key was, I thought, just not letting him get away from the truth. If he could edge that out of the conversation, he could talk me round. I had to keep it central, a great big glaring tear through the fabric of our lives. I had to stay strong until he was out of my sight.

'So I went for a walk and slipped and fell in the canal, and had to wear some stranger's clothes to come home in. But even if you were right, and I'd gone out and found someone else in the day and a half since we broke up, that would be none of your business. Because you stopped being my boyfriend when I walked in on you with your dick in someone else.'

I winced. The word 'dick' bounced around the room like a crazy ball from the joke shop. It seemed ludicrously childish for such a momentous betrayal. Perhaps I should have gone with 'cock', or something more stately and serious, like 'member'. Well, it was too late now. At least I hadn't accidentally let a 'willy' slip out mid-argument. That really would have been the worst possible way to say it.

'… fine,' Richard seemed to deflate a little, and dropped the wet sweatshirt onto the bed. 'I suppose I'll pack some of my stuff and… give you a bit of space to think things through.'

I wanted to say I didn't need space or time or any dimension in which to think things through. I needed his absence and a clear plan for a Richard-free future. But saying that now would, I knew, only restart the argument. I just wanted to get to work and hopefully handle the rest of the break-up logistics through text.

While Richard took a holdall from the bottom of the wardrobe, I carried my clothes into the bathroom and locked the door. In there I quickly washed, got dressed and started the process of taming my hair, yanking harder every time I thought about the man outside. My stomach rumbled – fickle creature that it was. I'd just have to get something to eat on my way to work.

'Tabitha, where's all my stuff?' Richard called, confused.

'What stuff?' I opened the door, heated roll brush in hand, and found him frowning over a half-full bag.

'My cardigans and sweaters and… you said you made me a jumper? I saw it when you…' He cut himself off before he could mention me walking in on him. 'It was blue and brown. I can't find it?'

I felt my stomach squirm a little with guilt. All right, so I hadn't wanted to see any of that stuff again, but it was still very much Richard's stuff. I'd made it for him and gifted it to him (though the cashmere jumper was kind of a grey area). I probably didn't have the right to just get rid of it all, but I'd done it now and I wasn't about to ask for forgiveness.

'I donated everything I made you,' I said, 'to the charity shop in town. But I think it's all been sold since yesterday.'

'But you knitted that stuff for me,' Richard said, clearly annoyed. 'It was mine.'

'It was crochet,' I couldn't resist pointing out. 'And between donating the stuff I made you, and you cheating on me, I think I know what's worse.'

He rolled his eyes at me then. 'Maybe if you'd spent less time on your crochet, and your silly little hobby shop, this would never have happened.'

For a second I was speechless. Not just because he was trying to blame this all on me, but because I was afraid – afraid that he was right. I had been obsessing over the shop lately and I had always been very into my crochet. Hadn't I thought, as I cleared out the cupboard, about all the times I'd had a project on the go around him? On a romantic picnic, for God's sake. Was I too obsessed to have seen this coming? Had I basically ignored Richard until he started looking for someone else?

Reality came streaming back in. No, absolutely not. I was not going to take the blame for what Richard had done. I could have ignored him, but the answer to that was to talk to me or to leave. Not to bring any old 'no one' back to our home to have sex on my things. How dare he try to make this my fault? How dare he!?

I felt my patience snap. 'If that's everything you're taking, you can leave.'

I watched as Richard's mouth thinned into a line. His eyes moved over me and I could feel him searching for a comeback, a retort that would give him the win he so obviously wanted.

'Don't give away any more of my stuff,' he said finally, and grabbed the bag, heading for the door. 'And if I find out you've been bringing another man back to our flat, I'll…'

'… remind yourself that you already brought a woman here while we were still together?'

He slammed the front door shut behind him and, for a moment, I was fiercely proud of my victory. Then I sat down on the bed and burst into tears.

Chapter 11

'ARE YOU OKAY?' EMMA asked when I met her outside the shop thirty minutes later.

'Yeah, no… sort of.' I got my keys out, juggling a bag of baps and two takeaway coffees as I unlocked the door. Bless her, but Maeve must have noticed my bloodshot eyes because those rolls were stuffed with a worrying amount of bacon. 'Richard came back to the flat this morning.'

'Shit!' Emma followed me inside, well-kohled eyes round like those of a bushbaby. 'Did he come to get his stuff, or to apologise and get back together? Either way, I hope you told him where to go. Slimy little weasel.'

'Um… well, he didn't actually think we'd broken up and neither was he sorry… but he did pack some stuff,' I said, hearing how brittle my voice sounded and hating it. I'd cried while I finished up my hair and then tried to erase the evidence with probably too much of my precious Erborian concealer. No wonder Emma could tell I was shaken up. I probably looked like a weird reverse panda.

'Ugh, what a dick!' She screwed her face up and pulled out a stool for me. 'I'll open us up. Don't worry about it.'

'Thanks… I'm sorry for being such a mess the past couple of—'

Emma cut me off with a raised hand. 'No apology needed. You were together for three years. It's going to take more than a few days to feel like yourself again.'

I wished she wasn't right. More than anything, I wanted my

body to catch up with where my brain was. Intellectually, I was angry at Richard, so very angry. But my chest was still carved out with sadness and my stomach churned with regrets. How long would that last? How long would I be mourning a man that my higher reasoning told me wasn't worth so much as a proper goodbye?

Emma went around the shop and pulled up the blinds behind the window displays. The lights came up one after the other and she moved the display baskets of half-price yarn out of the corner where they were stored while we hoovered every night. That done, she sat down and we ate breakfast together.

'Do you think he gets it now – that you're broken up?' Emma asked, tearing open a sachet of ketchup and piping it evenly into her roll.

Looking at mine, I tried to muster some appetite. 'I think so. He uh… kind of freaked out because there were men's clothes drying on the airer when he came in.'

Her eyes widened and she paused with the bap halfway to her mouth. 'Fill me in.'

'Nothing happened!' I exclaimed at her salacious tone. 'It was… okay, so I went for a walk by the canal after work—'

'Aww, you should have said, I'd have come with you,' Emma interrupted.

I laughed, because I'd known that was exactly what she'd say. 'I know, I just wanted to be by myself for a bit but I was walking that way and I found that narrowboat everyone's been gossiping about and it turns out that jumper-man lives on it.'

A grin spread across her face. 'You got with boat man?'

I swatted at her arm playfully, amusement and embarrassment at least making a nice change from hurt and doubt. 'No! I was in a weird mood and I confronted him about the jumper… and then I fell into the canal and he had to rescue me.'

The noise Emma made could only be described as a squeal. 'He rescued you from the water? I've seen this film. Did his shirt go see-through? Did he give you the kiss of life?'

'It is really not the Colin Firth moment you're picturing,' I said, stirring two sugars into my coffee. 'More like… grumpy dog begrudgingly fetches tennis ball from filthy canal.'

'… hot,' Emma raised her eyebrows. 'Come on you're telling me it wasn't the least bit sexy? Because I did a rune reading for you and it did say you'd be meeting someone new.'

'… did it really?' I asked, narrowing my eyes.

'Well, meeting someone new or that you'd be given a gift… or give birth. I'm still learning all the configurations but it was very positive.'

I laughed. It hurt all the tummy muscles I'd pulled whilst crying but felt good.

'But he lent you clothes,' Emma pressed, 'and you're telling me there was no spark at all? Not even a little tiny whiff of sexiness?'

The back of my neck went hot as I thought of Cooper's crooked, slightly foxy smirk and his cold, nimble fingers. Heartbroken I might feel inside, but I wasn't immune to… whatever that had been. I cleared my throat.

'More like a whiff of canal. The presence of about five hundred Princess Diana pictures also gave the moment a weird vibe,' I said and then, as Emma's nose scrunched in confusion, I elaborated. 'The boat's full of some older couple's royal family merchandise. He's cleaning it up. And… maybe there was a tiny moment where I thought about… I mean I did see him naked. Ish. Briefly. From behind.'

Emma took a chomp of her roll and nodded sagely. 'From behind is probably for the best.'

'Why?' I felt my face go a bit hot, remembering the moment I'd walked in on him changing. 'Because I'm not ready to see a new dick yet?'

Cock, I corrected myself mentally. Richard had a *dick* but Cooper definitely seemed like the kind of man to have a cock.

I tried to ignore the hot squirmy feeling in my belly at the thought. I'd probably caught a deadly parasite from the canal water. I was absolutely not getting all wriggly thinking about Cooper's…

'Because he'd just taken a dip in the canal… which I expect was freezing,' Emma said pointedly, screwing up her napkin. 'Did he have a nice bum?'

'Oh God, yes,' I said, before I could filter my thoughts.

'Was he… nice?' Emma asked, raising an eyebrow.

'I'm not exactly sure. He was… kind of mean, but funny? And a bit nice, but a lot strange. But it was sort of fun bantering with him. He wasn't exactly Prince Charming but he was… something. It took my mind off things.'

'Well, that's good – that it distracted you a bit. Also… Richard doesn't really do that, does he? The banter thing.' Emma said and pulled a face. 'I saw him parking up at Asda all crooked once and I said "parked or abandoned?" and he literally just ignored me.'

'Yeah, he doesn't really like being the butt of jokes,' I muttered.

'Hmm.' Emma clicked her tongue and looked contemplatively at the lid of her coffee. 'Do you know his star sign? Boat guy, I mean.'

'No.' I couldn't help but laugh as I imagined Cooper's reaction to me asking. 'I am almost completely positive that he doesn't believe in astrology.'

Or underwear, I thought but did not say.

'Are you going to see him again?' Emma asked. 'You could find out his birth date and hour for me.'

'I mean… I do have to return the clothes he lent me, but I probably won't hang around for tea and a chat again. He seemed like he had a lot going on.'

'Again?' Her eyes gleamed. 'You had tea?'

I narrowed my eyes at her in admonishment. 'Like you said, the canal was cold. And we didn't talk long. He just asked me about the crochet and the jumper, which by the way he's keeping – all of it – he just wanted to be warm on the boat, so… and… I told him about Richard.'

That seemed to sober Emma. She reached over and took my hand. 'Tabitha…'

'I know it was… but it sort of helped, a bit. I mean, you've got to take my side because we're friends but he's a stranger and, if he thinks Richard's a piece of shit, then… that helps. It makes me feel like I'm making the right decision.'

'I can see that,' Emma allowed. 'But just be careful, okay? All jokes aside, you don't want to go straight from Richard into a rebound with some… stranger on a boat.'

'I'm not,' I insisted, but felt my cheeks burn all over again. 'It was just one of those moments, you know? The kind you can only have with a stranger and then they never go anywhere and you never really see them again.'

'Except to return their clothes?' Emma said, sceptically.

'I'll probably just drop them off in a bag and not see him,' I said firmly. 'Like I said, he's probably busy de-Diana-ing his boat. Anyway… as we're probably not going to be busy today – again – I think I'll flat-hunt out at the counter on the work laptop.'

'Cool. I think I'll do some affirmations and recharge the crystals before people start coming in.'

Emma bustled off to do just that and I unlocked the drawer under the counter, which held the laptop I'd bought for ordering and bookkeeping. It was second-hand, obviously, a bargain from Teddy who ran the garage and also did computer fixes and refurbished tech on the side. He'd even thrown in a new mouse, two memory sticks and new brake pads. It was time to trawl through the local property listings and try to find somewhere I could afford to rent by myself, whilst also paying rent on the shop in a few months' time.

While it booted up, I drank my coffee and probed my feelings experimentally. Was I thinking about Cooper as a potential rebound? I had been flirting maybe. A bit. I wasn't even really sure. We'd both been sort of bantering back and forth and it had felt natural and easy. The way it felt when I talked to

Emma. Friendly. That was all. Casual. Fun. So what if seeing his collection of well-loved Horowitz books had sent me to the storage cupboard to dig out my own copies? That was just because they comforted me. It wasn't about him or how it had felt to be held tightly and towed to safety.

I thought about his bum again and caught sight of my own panicked expression in the laptop screen. That was enough of that. I was off men for a while, and that included their bums.

I sat and doom-scrolled flats for about half an hour, finding nothing in my price range. Sadly, no wormholes had opened up to the 1980s, where rent wasn't the same price as the ransom for a minor TV star. Leaford property prices were out of control, even for rentals. The quaint streets came at a price, as did our commutable distance to London. The only place I found in my budget was a garage, and even that had a waiting list.

Maybe I could ask Emma about renting a two-bedroom for the pair of us to share? Or was that asking too much of a friend who was also my employee? It was looking increasingly as if I was going to be moving back in with Mum and Dad. I'd have to ring them sooner rather than later. God, the thought of explaining everything to them made me feel so tired. It wasn't that I thought they wouldn't understand, but they'd be so… hurt by what Richard had done. To me and to them. Because they'd had a lot of hopes pinned on him, on 'Richard and Tabitha', the unit. Hopes of weddings and grandchildren. Hopes I was about to crush.

Mum especially wasn't going to take it well. I could already feel the 'but I don't understand, you were so happy together' coming. Somehow this was all going to be my fault, I knew it. If I was permanently in Weightwatchers, or making a roast every Sunday, or making sure Richard never saw me without lippy on, he never would have strayed.

'Um… Tabby?'

I looked up and found Emma standing in front of the counter, holding her phone. She looked nervous, her mouth downturned. Whatever she was looking at, it wasn't good news.

'What is it?'

'I set up an alert on my eBay profile yesterday, just in case that guy tried to flip your stuff? Not that I could stop him doing that, but I thought it might be a bit of a boost if it did end up selling for a lot?'

My stomach dropped. 'He's listed stuff, hasn't he?'

Why was I surprised? More than that, hurt. I'd barely met the man. He was just a stranger, like I'd said. Even if he did hand hot mugs over the right way. I didn't even know his last name. Come to think of it, for all I'd opened up to him about Richard, he hadn't so much as told me why he was on the boat or what he did for a living. For all I knew, he was some sort of fly-by-night crochet dealer, already pootling off to another small town. It was unlikely, but still.

'Do you want to know or…?' Emma asked, biting her lip uncertainly.

But I was already typing and, within seconds, I had eBay up on the laptop and was searching for the most recently listed items under 'handmade crochet'. The screen filled with pictures of the usual hexagon cardigans, water-bottle holders and tote bags. Nice, bright, pretty designs. None of them were mine, though. I scrolled and a familiar pair of mules – dupes I'd made of a Prada pair – popped up.

'I'm sorry,' Emma said, but she sounded far away. 'I know it's awful but… this doesn't mean you can't trust anyone new, okay? Or maybe he meant he was keeping most of the stuff but he didn't have a use for those, or—'

'I didn't make those for Richard,' I said, cutting her off. 'They weren't in the donation bags.'

'Oh,' Emma brightened, but then seemed to think for a second. Her shoulders slumped. 'Oh.'

'I made them for Richard's sister last Christmas. He told me he took them with him on their family get-together and she loved them.' I let out a long breath. 'He never gave them to her, did he?'

I was thinking of all the things I'd made for his family, for Christmases I was never invited to – because the rule was wives only. No girlfriends. The shawl I made his mother, the golf-club covers for his dad, amigurumi toys for his nieces and nephews (whole play sets of fruits and baked goods). I scrolled through eBay and saw it all posted there, some of it already with bids on. Items going for thirty, forty, even sixty pounds, with days left on the auctions. So much stuff.

It looked like Richard was going to get some start-up money out of me after all. That was why he'd been so upset about the jumpers. He hadn't suddenly realised how much he valued me and the symbols of my love for him. He'd been seeing pound signs.

'Are you all right?' Emma asked, breaking my staring contest with the eBay results page.

'Yeah… it's fine,' I said faintly, feeling like there was a fist in my throat wearing some very spiky rings. 'We're broken up now anyway… good riddance, right?'

'Right,' Emma agreed, though she didn't sound that certain. Fair enough, neither was I. This hurt almost as much as the cheating. He'd lied to me for several years now. Not just about Christmas but every time I'd asked him what his family might like for birthdays and christenings. Every time I'd asked if they liked their gifts. He'd lied right to my face about it. Why? Was he embarrassed by my homemade presents? He could have just said they wanted something specific from a shop. I wasn't unreasonable – I didn't want to push my crochet on everyone. I would have understood. God, what if he didn't realise that? Did I really seem like some kind of crazy crafting person who couldn't take a hint?

No matter how angry and upset I was at Richard, I couldn't help but feel a prickle of guilt inside. That maybe, somehow, everything that had gone wrong between us was partly my fault too.

Maybe if you'd spent less time on your crochet and your silly little hobby shop, this would never have happened.

Maybe he had a point.

Chapter 12

I went for a wander at lunchtime, just to take my mind off Richard and the crochet auctions. I'd been refreshing the pages all morning and looking at the bids as they came in, which I knew wasn't healthy or helpful, but that hadn't stopped me.

Richard had set the prices too low but he'd probably still get a good amount for the whole collection. I'd made so many things and he hadn't given any of them to his family. I had no idea where he'd been keeping them. Maybe at work, where he had a large locker for extra suits and his Hunter wellies for more rural property viewings. Hell, maybe he'd just chucked them in a gym bag in the boot of his car.

I wasn't thinking about it. I wasn't. We were finished and it didn't matter any more. To that end, I decided it was time to break the news to my mother. As much as I didn't want to hear what she thought I could have done to prevent Richard from cheating on me, I had to tell her sometime. Even if I kept flashing back to the moment I'd come home crying because everyone at school made fun of my wide-legged trousers and she'd looked me up and down before saying, 'Well, I did warn you.'

I found her number in my contacts and hit 'call' as I took a seat on a bench down the side of the butcher's. Mum answered on the third ring.

'Hi, love. Unusual for you to call – what's up?' I could tell, from the slightly tinny echo, that I was on speakerphone. At a guess, this was because Mum was painting her nails, as I couldn't hear the Hoover and that was the only other time she used hands-free.

'Oh, um… nothing much. I just wanted to call and… check in,' I heard myself say stiffly.

'Ah, well, it's nice to hear from you. I'm looking forward to seeing you at the party, both me and your dad are. It feels like we don't get to spend much time together any more. Still… you've got Richard to be worrying about. I understand.'

'I… do, yes.' I cursed myself inwardly for my cowardice. This exact thing had happened when I was trying to break up with my university boyfriend. Every time we saw each other, he smiled and hugged me or gave me a kiss – how could you dump someone after that? It went on for a month. Mum had been upset to hear about that break-up too, I remembered. She was more excited to hear I had a boyfriend than when I'd told her I got a two:one.

'How is Richard?' Mum asked, and I felt a spasm of shock as if she'd read my mind. 'He's not been around for a while – work must be really busy?'

'It is, yeah, but he's fine. We're both just really, really busy. You know, the shop, his work and trying to set up a business…' I trailed off before I could add 'his affair' to the list.

'Hmm,' Mum hummed, sounding troubled. 'Well, just make sure you're looking after him – cooking something nice and making sure you look your best at the end of the day. You know, the shop is lovely and everything but… Richard is your future. You need to put as much work into your relationship as you do into work, if not more.'

'Mmmhmm,' I got out, through a throat suddenly thick with shame, irritation prickling at my neck. Did she really think so little of me that Richard was all I had going for me in terms of the rest of my life?

'Oh, I have to tell you – your father's decided to repaint the front of the house and we have had a terrible time tracking down the same pink as before. And you'll never guess who we saw at B&Q…'

I let her talk for twenty minutes about paint charts, why Sally from the sweet shop would be buying so much wood glue and what the weather was doing at the weekend. I couldn't tell her. I didn't want to tell her. Even though I knew I had to, that she'd find out sooner or later, I couldn't get the words out. I didn't want to hear that first disappointed 'Tabby...' to come out of her mouth. It would hit me right in my chest, where it was still sore and aching from heartbreak. It was going to hurt and I didn't want to invite that pain in.

Once Mum rang off to do her pedicure, I went for a walk and tried to soak in some positivity. Leaford high street looked lovely in the autumnal sun, the hand-painted signs and red bricks glowing and leaves the colour of dried apricots drifting from the oak trees in the park. Acorns and chestnuts popped under my boots as I crunched down the street and the smell of freshly baked bread and hot coffee wafted from the bakery. Bliss.

Or at least it was until I reached the bakery steps and saw none other than Richard inside. He was probably buying himself some focaccia on his lunch break. Having not had his fix after I caught him cheating and tried to batter him with the bag of baked goods. I backed away in panic and sidestepped. There was no way I wanted to risk talking to him again after the state he'd left me in that morning. I had to hide.

Looking around at my options, I started to panic. I couldn't chance him wanting a paper from the newsagent's or popping into the cheese-and-wine shop for a client gift. There was only one place nearby that Richard wouldn't go, even if it was peeing down with rain in a red-weather warning – the charity shop. The only thing that wrinkled his nose faster than second-hand goods was a shop packed full of them.

I ducked through the door, hoping the bell wouldn't bring Margaret out of the back. Talk about out of the frying pan into the fire. Thankfully, she was on the phone back there. I could hear her droning on about collection dates and parking restrictions.

The hospice shop was a weird L shape. The main body of it went from the front door to the counter, but there was a windowless offshoot that was the perfect place to hide. That was where the books were shelved, along with old magazines, out-of-date maps and sewing patterns. Basically, anything papery that was going a bit yellow and musty. I squeezed between two overflowing racks of old waxed jackets and M&S duffle coats and let out a sigh of relief to be in the dim sanctuary of the book-nook.

I'd just give Richard five or ten minutes to grab his lunch and go, then the coast would be clear to return to the shop. Was it cowardly? Yes. But at least I wouldn't be reduced to tears for the second time in one day. I couldn't bear it.

Margaret shuffled back into the shop front and I heard her huff as she unlatched the jewellery case to add more items to the already overflowing trays inside. The click of beads and scrape of metal on glass were the only sounds in the shop and I held my breath. In front of me a row of deteriorating Catherine Cookson novels sat crumbling and, above those, fifteen copies of the latest 'must read' naughty romance were having a little orgy between James Patterson novels.

The bell over the door jangled and I took the chance to sidestep to the craft books. Maybe I would find some interesting crochet patterns and this embarrassing game of hide-and-seek would be worth it.

'Donations for you,' came a familiar voice. It was Cooper. My stomach flipped over and I glared down at it. Traitor. How could it do that for someone we barely knew?

Margaret made a nasal noise of disapproval and I heard the clink of plates and cups rattling together. I could imagine her sugar-almond claws picking through the Diana memorabilia, her mouth all pursed up as she let Cooper squirm, wondering if she was going to deign to take the bric-a-brac or not.

'I suppose,' she muttered finally.

'I've actually got quite a lot more to bring up, if that's all right?' Cooper asked, sounding almost amused by her reluctance.

'If you must,' Margaret sighed. 'It might shift. If not, there's always the china smash at the fair… you were in yesterday.'

'I was,' Cooper affirmed. 'Thanks again for the blankets and things – though I think you underpriced them. Some gorgeous stuff in those bags. Handmade too. I actually feel like I owe you money.'

My breath caught. He had no way of knowing I was here, right? He wasn't just saying that for my benefit. He actually thought that and he was telling Margaret to her face that he thought she'd marked them up wrongly. He either had a death wish or a deep conviction that had prompted him to tell her.

'Hmf' was Margaret's response. 'No accounting for taste.'

That's it, I was going to jumble her alphabetised DVDs up before I left. The cow.

I heard Cooper click his tongue. 'Anyway, I took another forty out at the cashpoint – you could have got more for it. But pearls before swine and all that.'

Ha! Take that, Margaret! I felt vindicated and sort of as if I wanted to burst out of my hidey hole and give him a high-five. Or a hug. I wondered what he was wearing and if it was one of my jumpers.

Judging by the icy silence that followed Cooper's words, Margaret was giving him 'the look'. I waited for him to turn tail and leave.

As well as avoiding Richard, I had no desire to run into Cooper for another awkward exchange of jabs and jokes. Or rather, I had no desire to have to examine how I felt afterwards. Yesterday had been confusing enough. As soon as the bell went again, I'd count to twenty and then leave. Back to the sanctuary of the wool shop.

But the bell on the door didn't go. Instead I heard the old wooden floor popping and creaking as Cooper browsed the shop and then, finally, stepped into the nook. He was wearing jeans and boots, and the cashmere jumper with the cuffs carefully folded back. My hands twitched with the urge to touch him. It. The jumper. I felt myself blush furiously.

It took him a few seconds to see me in the gloom and, when he did, he went very still. I couldn't help looking stiff and surprised – there was no denying that I hadn't been shopping normally. He'd have heard me moving around otherwise, the floor being so loud and warped. I was caught and we just looked at each other. Then he slowly inched towards me and whispered, 'Hiding from anyone in particular?'

The scent of sharp pine mingled with the mustiness of old books and I took a breath as I tried to come up with something to redeem myself. But I was saved from disaster when he nodded back towards the main shop and pulled a face.

'She's fun.'

I snorted and clapped a hand to my mouth in embarrassment. Cooper's eyes twinkled in the low light and I wanted to both shove him and smile at him. It was a weird, dizzying feeling. Like driving fast over a humpbacked bridge.

'I'm just looking for a good book,' I whispered back, and picked up one of the disintegrating volumes in front of me at random.

'Ah, *The Novice Guide to Rearing Show Rabbits*, that's a thrilling read. I'm waiting for the sequel myself.'

'You never know, I might be going into angora at the shop. We could keep them in the break room,' I said, and felt my insides glow when his jaw ticked with a suppressed smirk. He was enjoying this. I was too. I felt suddenly as if we were a pair of naughty kids hiding away in a cupboard at school, while the mean headmistress stamped about outside, rearranging piles of moth-eaten teddies and balding Barbies. But that was a dangerous feeling – I had only just broken up with Richard. I couldn't afford to get mixed up with someone else.

I returned the book to the shelf and gestured to the narrow exit. 'I'd best be getting back.'

'Tons of angora to harvest, I expect,' Cooper said, stepping aside.

Even though he'd moved, with the shelves boxing us in, I had to inch past him sideways and for a moment we were practically nose to nose. He had to look up at me ever so slightly, but it didn't seem to bother him. He was looking at me as if I was something rare and special he'd spotted on a high shelf. Up close, his generous lips were a little chapped, but they looked soft too. Biteable.

Get hold of yourself, Tabitha! I told myself sternly, as I reached the doorway and glanced back at him. He was watching me, and maybe it was the shadows or good old-fashioned delusion, but he looked just as dazed as I felt. I could still feel his body heat on my clothes and smell the mingled sharpness of pine and mint as I ducked out of the book-nook and into the street.

A blast of autumnal air chased the heat from my skin and I hurried back to the shop. It wasn't until I reached it and stepped inside that I realised I'd completely forgotten to look out for Richard. For the past few minutes, he'd simply ceased to exist.

As the shop door shut behind me, I gave myself a little mental shake. Whatever I thought I was feeling around Cooper, it was just a passing fancy. As temporary as the turning of the leaves. Pretty soon the novelty would wear off and he'd be just another man wandering around town, forgettable as the brown mulch under my boots come November. But just in that moment, my blood was fizzing around my body and I could almost feel the ghost of his lips on mine.

Chapter 13

TWO DAYS LATER, ON a Saturday that was trying valiantly to be more summer than autumn, I drove to my parents' house. If anything could throw cold water over my silly infatuation with Cooper, it would be Mum's garden-party extravaganza. Nothing could kill a crush stone-dead like hanging around with my parents' friends while they talked about colonic irrigation, all-inclusive breakfast buffets and everyone they knew who'd got married or had kids. That last one with a lot of glances my way by Mum. Then the inevitable listing of the ailments and the showing of the bunions, melanoma biopsy scabs and varicose veins.

I had never been able to see the appeal in sitting in your own back garden, yelling over music and drinking paint stripper masquerading as cocktails until two in the morning before passing out fully dressed or throwing up cheese and pineapple hedgehog. It all felt one bowl of keys away from a swinger's party. Or worse, like a nineties kids' party, plus lethal amounts of booze. Give me a nice barbecue, a reasonable amount of wine and a ten o'clock bedtime any day. But Mum was a partier through and through. Even if her clubbing days were mostly behind her, she was bringing the spirit of two-for-one shots and stripper heels to her suburban garden. God help her neighbours.

When I was a teenager, she'd been the one loading up on Bacardi Breezers for my sixteenth birthday, while I trailed after her in the supermarket, whispering about the legal drinking age. She'd wanted skimpy tops, spin the bottle and snogging at midnight. I'd wanted a bonfire, s'mores and scary stories. Sometimes it felt as if I was the frumpy old mother to her teenage party animal. It made me feel like a constant disappointment.

However, her party would at least give me something else to think about. I'd already been using it as a distraction and to that end, I was accompanied by a specially made tropical Eton mess, strapped into the front passenger seat, where Richard should have been.

I reminded myself sternly that he would have been in that passenger seat because he insisted I be the designated driver for my parents' parties, his response every time I asked if we could switch being 'But, Tabs, you know I can't cope with all that sober.' I'd laughed because, yes, the parties were always weird and awkward until you were a little bit sloshed. But thinking back on it, I'm no longer sure he was talking about the parties specifically, and not just my parents in general.

I still hadn't told them we'd broken up. After trying that one time, I hadn't so much as picked up the phone for another go. Let Mum find out from someone else and have her first response far, far away from me – like when I quit drama club because I hated being on stage. It was meant to get me out of my shell. To be honest, I think she'd secretly wanted me to become a child star à la Emma Watson. I didn't want to have to tell her about Richard. Maybe she would just intuit it if I left things long enough, and decide it was too painful for me to talk about, so she'd better not ask.

Fat chance.

'Tabby!' Mum cried, throwing open the front door and nearly knocking the dessert dish from my hands. She wrapped me up in a hug, drowning me in a waft of knock-off 'Hypnotic Poison' that was most assuredly not by Dior, more like Dion from the market. 'Where's Richard?'

So much for intuition.

'He um… he's not coming,' I said and pulled a regretful face. I didn't really mean to lie exactly. I just didn't want to get into it on the doorstep. Or in the hall, or anywhere really. Ideally, Mum would find out while I was, say… camping for two weeks with no phone access. She'd be over it by the time I got back, or at least in the sulking stage rather than the talking one. Maybe Emma could suggest a nice yurt for me to take shelter in on a commune or something.

'Aww, such a shame – well, come on in, you know where everything is.' Mum's sandals slapped back up the hallway and she called through the sliding patio doors to Dad. 'Tabby's here! No Richard!'

A dog barked in the distance and I heard a flurry of PVC windows slam in annoyance.

Now all the neighbours knew. Fantastic.

I put the dessert in the fridge, noting as I did so that it was packed with snack food in various stages of defrosting. From the prawn-cocktail ring to the mini-eclairs and the prefilled vol-au-vents, Mum had gone all out. It brought back all my childhood memories of Bonfire-Night parties with Viennetta and Sara Lee Gateaux on the picnic table by the patio. Birthdays with apple bobbing and caterpillar cake. Mum's Christmas buffet, which must have cleared out at least one Iceland on a good year. I smiled to myself and closed the fridge. Some things never changed, and that was what made them so reassuring. Even if now, as an adult, I was included in the more raucous, exhausting side of the parties instead of being packed off to Lou's after dark.

'All right, Tabby?' Dad asked, ducking in to get a beer from the separate drinks fridge.

Okay, my second chance to just tell the truth was here. Dad was neutral, like Switzerland. If I told him he could break it to Mum later and absorb some of the fallout. I took a breath and stepped forward. I was going to get it over with right now. Then the rest of the party could just go ahead as planned. It didn't have to be a big deal.

'Actually, Dad…'

The doorbell went and Mum skittered past, waving for Dad to go back to the garden and finish setting up. I sighed as he shot me a regretful face and hurried back out. Later, then. It would have to wait.

While Mum welcomed the guests at the door (from all the shrieking, it sounded like her friend Mary from the salon and probably Mary's husband Jim – though he wasn't making a sound, bless him), I went into the garden.

The patio heater was in pride of place and, judging from the greyish sky and the breeze creeping in, we'd be needing it. So much for the last blush of summer. Not that rain was a worry. The huge striped awning had been winched out from its dock on the side of the house and it covered the paved garden and the gravel patches where succulents had once grown. The awning was one of those giant things you see advertised during the day, between reruns of *Midsomer Murders* and *Poirot*. Mum had thrown a party to celebrate its installation.

Dad passed me on his way to the barbecue – a three-grill monstrosity imported from America, which it took him several days to put together. It was gleaming red, like a sports car, and he polished it and tucked it into a weatherproof cover every year.

'Can you give a bit more puff to the flamingos? They're looking a bit limp,' he said, handing over a bicycle pump which he'd been carrying around in his 'sexy bare chest' apron.

'Sure.' Mum's new collection of inflatable flamingos were arrayed around the hot tub (also inflatable) and under a gazebo made of inflated palm trees. One wrong move with a ragged hangnail and that whole end of the garden would be gone. Just blown up into the sky like a leftover birthday balloon. I gave each droopy bird a few pumps to perk them up a bit and then put the pump back in Dad's shed.

Mary and Jim were in the garden now, accompanied by Mary's daughter, Gina, and the few neighbours who were still talking to Mum after successive decades of very loud parties. Graham and Mark from across the way thought she was 'a hoot' and had brought their golden doodle with them. I watched it sniffing at the flamingos and hoped it wouldn't scratch at one.

Mum was busy passing out drinks from a pink tray – they were in glittery martini glasses and sporting skewers of raspberries and pink umbrellas. Clearly her theme for this one was based on the new flamingos. With her distracted, I went into the house to do a quick check on my old room.

As I climbed the stairs, I stopped to look at the family pictures hung all the way up the wall, each frame at precise angles. They'd repainted the downstairs about five times since I'd moved out but the pictures were always the same. Only the frames changed. Currently they were glass with silver glitter stripes. The walls painted a pale green. Combined with the brown stair carpet it gave the impression of mint chocolate ice cream.

On the landing was my favourite picture. Mum and Dad in paper Christmas crowns, raising glasses of bubbly, and sitting on the floor in front of them, was me with Aunt Lou, both of us smiling as she showed me how to crochet a big granny square with my new plastic hook. Even with the distance of time, I could remember the sheer unbridled joy of being good at something. Of not having to struggle or get frustrated as I had on Christmases past. Mum had picked out presents she would have probably loved as a kid, but which only brought me fresh disappointment in her eyes. Days spent failing to master roller blades, a twirling baton, a make-up set and myriad hair-styling tools. The less said of the 'teach yourself Spanish' DVDs the better. To be fair, I think those were because she wanted a translator on holiday.

Crochet made sense to me, right from the start. It was one of the only things in life that always made sense. I smiled at the faded photo and pushed open the door beside it, into my bedroom.

'Jesus Christ…'

I inched around the half-open door – because it wouldn't open further, and found myself looking at a mishmash of gym equipment and what looked like half a Clintons card shop. My room had gone through different life cycles since I moved out. First, it had stayed as a sort of shrine to my pre-university self. Then Mum had turned it into a guest room in shades of sugared lilac. Last time I'd visited, it had been part guest room, part craft space, with a futon and a lot of beading equipment. Now there was hardly room to move.

'Oh, there you are, love.' Mum appeared behind me and stuck her head around the door. 'What are you doing up here?'

'Just... looking around,' I said weakly. 'What's um... with all the stuff?'

She pulled a face. 'Your dad got really into home workouts during the pandemic. Jerry at the health club was retiring and he let him have this lot for cheap. He hasn't really used it much so if you're in the market for a treadmill...'

'No, I mean the other stuff.' I indicated the piles of wrapped presents, studded with bows. The stacks of floristry foam and wire, bushels of faux flowers, multi-packs of candles and sacks of plastic crystals. I was desperately hoping this was all some new hobby of hers, but the look on Mum's face put paid to that. She lit up like one of the forty magic lanterns stacked on top of a crate of disposable cameras.

She slid around the door into the room. 'That's just overflow from the garage. Some wedding stuff I picked up – just in case. You know, it was awful when all the venues closed down before and, if we end up having to do the whole thing ourselves, I didn't want us to be stuck with no supplies. People were panic buying like crazy last time.'

'Yeah, beans and toilet paper, not streamers and personalised champagne.' I tilted my head to read the labels. 'Who are Greg and Silvia?'

'No idea – but they never picked up their order, so it was a steal,' Mum beamed at me. 'We can just make new labels. I've got a machine for that somewhere. Found it on Marketplace.'

My stomach was screwed up into a tight, miserable little ball.

It was like walking in on a shrine to Richard – to our future, our marriage and children. A whole network of events that were now never going to happen. I could hear Mum in my head, handing over carrier bags of candles and wedding favours to some Marketplace buyer, 'These were for my daughter's wedding but she was so obsessed with her little shop that she drove her boyfriend into another woman's arms… yes, yes, I did tell her, but she never listens to me, you see.'

I moistened my lips. 'Mum… I need to tell you something…'

'Have you and Richard finally discussed when he's going to propose?' Mum asked, clasping her hands together. 'Your dad will be so pleased if it's soon – if you have the engagement party before the end of November, we'll be able to free up some space for the barbecue in the garage.'

What in God's name was waiting in the garage? A self-assembly chapel complete with a flat-pack vicar? Or was she raising doves? This was insane. I had to stop it now, before she started filling the deep freeze with DIY wedding cakes.

I took a breath, my heart jumping up and down inside me with panic. She was going to be crushed. At her own party, no less. Why hadn't I done this sooner? Why hadn't I called her as soon as it happened? I suppose for the same reason I was currently struggling – I knew it would hurt her almost as much as it had hurt me. And she would hurt me, all over again, without meaning to. My eyes prickled, but I couldn't let this go on. I braced myself.

'Mum, Richard and I aren't getting engaged,' I said, then ploughed on before her face could register anything other than confusion, my heart in my throat. 'We're not together any more. We broke up.'

Her fingers found mine. The silence was sharper than her nails on my skin as she gripped my hand. As if she was worried I was about to run away. I wanted to, bizarrely. Wanted to escape from this moment, this house, from the lecture I knew was coming. From the look on her face that said I'd ruined everything.

I felt like I was about to be sick all over the dated treadmill.

Somewhere down below, there came a loud bang, followed by barking and yelling.

'Mum?' I said, when she didn't react to what had to have been the death blow to one of her flamingos. The lack of reaction was making my stomach slither into knots. 'Are you…?'

'Why?' she asked, at last. 'You two were perfect together. I thought you were finally going to settle down and move on to the next phase of your life, together. What happened?'

There it was – the blame. Not 'are you okay?', but *what happened?* Her eyes narrowing a little, looking at me as if to say, *what did you do?* It had to be my fault. Richard was perfect. Richard brought Mum flowers every time he came over and helped Dad chop down the crab-apple tree in the front garden. He knew about wine and had advised them on planning permission for Dad's shed. Richard had a good job and great teeth and he was polite, went golfing and laughed at Dad's jokes. Even if I told Mum that Richard complained bitterly every time I 'dragged him' to one of their parties, she wouldn't hear it. Not Richard – he was Mark Darcy, the estate agent. Heathcliff with a protein shake. He was a catch, and I was the terrible fisherman that had let him leap out of the net.

On the heels of her question, I couldn't help but think about all the tiny ways in which Richard hadn't fitted with me properly. The things I'd only allowed myself to start seeing recently. His lack of a sense of humour, how much he didn't like my family, the sterile flat and his distaste for second-hand things, for bright colours and whimsical designs. His lectures on calories and how he never cleaned up after himself. Had Mum really thought we were 'perfect together'? Had she not seen all the ways in which we didn't match? Had she wanted to see? Or, like me, had she trained herself to ignore all of it, because any man was better than nothing? Was she not meant to look out for me when I couldn't see stuff like that for myself?

'He wasn't "perfect"… I caught him cheating on me,' I said, not wanting to give her the full technicolour mental image of what I'd walked in on but also not wanting to let this charade of 'Richard, the ideal man' continue. 'So I ended it. I had to.'

Mum's face did something complicated. Her eyes were sad, the well-sunned crinkles around them smoothed out and soft. But her mouth tightened into a little cerise bud, somehow both defiant and thoughtful.

'Tabby,' she said, softly. 'Are you… sure?'

I just gaped at her. Sure? I'd been hoping for 'all right' or 'okay', even 'going to want your room back for a bit?'. Once the shock and blame laying were over, I'd been hoping for some understanding. Just a shred.

'Sure?' I repeated, trying and failing to keep the hurt from my voice. 'Mum, did you not hear what I said? Richard slept with someone else. What else could I do – ignore it?'

Mum opened her mouth as if to argue, but Dad's voice interrupted, ringing out from the garden below.

'Penny, can you get some string and come down here? The wind's picking up and we've lost a flamingo over the fence!'

I looked at Mum, waiting for an explanation, for her to remove the knife she'd just jabbed into my heart, but she just turned to the door, hurrying to fetch Dad some string. Over her shoulder she threw back a forcefully bright 'We'll talk later, okay, Tabby?'

But I didn't want to talk later. I wanted to go back in time and not have to hear my own mother ask me if I was 'sure' about dumping my cheating boyfriend.

I left the room after her and, as I passed the picture on the landing, I looked at Aunt Lou's smiling face and thought, *you would never have asked me that*. Because it was true. Lou would have made me a hot chocolate and told me I was better off and that Richard never deserved me. That there were plenty of fish in the sea. She'd have intervened before now to tell me she didn't think he made me happy. And she'd have been right. She'd have sat up with me for as long as it took to pick apart his jumpers and re-ball the yarn to make something new out of. Something worthwhile.

I thought all of this as I rushed down the mint-chocolate-chip stairs, and out the front door to my car.

Chapter 14

My phone started to go off as I drove, but I ignored it. By the time I got back to the flat, I had seven texts and one missed call from Mum, plus two texts from Dad. I looked at the notifications in the lift and just felt exhausted. There was guilt too because I was aware that I was being childish. I'd just run away without telling them, never mind confronting Mum about what she'd said. But it was just too much, in the moment. I'd spent days agonising over what her reaction would be, but somehow it was worse than I'd imagined.

In the flat my first instinct was to ring Emma, but I only got as far as opening my contacts before thinking better of it. She'd done so much for me over the past few days. I couldn't just keep dumping all my issues on her. That wasn't fair. Besides which, she wasn't just my friend but an employee. I was taking up enough of her time as it was.

Unfortunately, that didn't really leave me with many options; my other oldest friend was Kate and she lived in Australia now, had done for years. Married, two kids, a nice, safe job. We didn't have much in common any more and rarely spoke beyond sharing memes or birthday wishes. In the three years I'd been with Richard, I'd spent most of my time with him, his friends and their occasional girlfriends. Emma was the exception. She'd come into my life by chance and we'd hit it off. But, other than her, I hadn't really been maintaining or making new friendships. Which was really biting me in the arse now that Richard was gone, leaving a gaping hole in my life.

What's more, I now knew I couldn't really talk to Mum about it. *Are you sure?* What kind of question was that? I kept thinking back and wondering if she'd somehow misinterpreted what I'd said, but I'd been pretty clear. There weren't many ways to interpret 'I caught him cheating on me.' Had she meant 'are you sure that's what you saw?' but surely she knew I wouldn't just throw away three years on an assumption.

I put the kettle on and took a deep breath before opening Mum's texts.

Tabby? Are you coming down?

Do you need anything? – Dad has stop-poos in the medicine cabinet.

I scoffed. So she'd assumed I was trapped in the bathroom or something. No sense at all that it was what she'd said to me that was the issue. I scrolled down.

Just saw your car's gone. Hope you're okay.

Mary said to tell you your dessert is lovely – big hit here!

Her denial was brittle, even in text form. As if as long as she kept talking as if things were fine, they would be. Mum wasn't good at conflict, never had been. She liked to either pretend it wasn't happening or just ignore the upset until it was over. I couldn't count the number of times she'd left me to 'cry it out' in my room as a teenager when all I wanted was a cup of tea and a chat.

I've washed your dish up and I'll keep it till you next pop round

Or I can drop it off to the flat if you need it sooner?

And, finally, a slightly desperate little *how are things going at the shop?*

Dad's texts were more direct: *Sorry you had to go* and *love the Eton mess!*

I put my phone down. No way was I dealing with that right now. I'd just end up getting myself worked up and more upset. Like always, I'd just leave it a few days and pretend it never happened, let things go back to normal.

The kettle clicked off and I raided the cupboard for some

hazelnut hot chocolate. Once I had a foamy mug prepared, with cookies on the side, I retreated to the spare bedroom. On the bed, with the duvet tucked over my legs, I pulled out a few craft books and went through some of the projects I'd dog-eared. I needed a distraction and, if it was one that made me feel closer to Lou, then that was all the better. I wanted her with me so badly that my eyes were prickling.

I was skimming over hats and gloves when I flicked a page over and found some chunky-knit hand warmers staring up at me. It was a simple pattern, similar to some cup cosies I'd made before. Acrylic chunky yarn in any colour you'd like, then front and back post double crochet to create a textured finish. Unbidden, the memory of Cooper's cold fingers against mine made my right hand twitch.

I raided the plastic boxes of yarn under the bed in the other room and returned with a half-ball in bottle green with orange and brown flecks. It sort of reminded me of the leaf-strewn surface of the canal, and a strong chest against my back as I was towed across it. With a hook in my hand and a podcast on my phone, I got stuck in.

It was easy to lose myself in the simple stitches, each one so distinct I didn't have to worry about keeping count. The yarn was soft and comforting between my fingers and the rhythm of the hook as I worked the stitches was automatic and easy. The chunky yarn worked up fast and, before too long, I'd finished the first hand warmer and my hot chocolate. My stomach rumbled, reminding me that I hadn't had any dinner. I'd only had a light lunch, saving myself for the barbecue spread.

In the kitchen I realised I needed to get some shopping in. I'd been sort of drifting since the break-up, forgetting about the normal flow of life – supermarket shop on a Friday night, clean the bathroom Sunday, change the bedding every other Saturday. The flat still looked sterile and clean but, upon closer inspection, I could see the tumbleweeds of fluff in the corners and the fingerprints on the gleaming glass and white countertops.

As much as I didn't owe it to Richard to keep up my routine, neither did I want to live in a dirty flat. I got out the polish and cloth and then found the broom to sweep the floor before mopping. We had one of those robot vacuum cleaners but I didn't like the thought of tripping over it, so it only got turned on when Richard remembered to do it.

While I cleaned, I couldn't help but think about Mum's reaction to the news about the break-up again. Her disappointment had been clear, as was the fact that I was the cause of it. I was twenty-seven, and three years into a serious relationship. At my age, Mum had already had me and I was five. I knew she was worried I was leaving it too late, that she wasn't going to get to be a grandmother while still 'young enough to enjoy her grandkids'. Maybe she was starting to stress that it just wasn't going to happen at all. After all, she'd only been able to have the one kid and she started fairly young – what if I was already past that point and unable to have any?

On the one hand I understood her fears. Some of them were mirrors of my own. I had been concerned that it had been three years and Richard still hadn't even mentioned proposing. Worried I was approaching my thirties and still childless with no clear plan in place for starting a family. I could see where Mum was coming from. But, at the same time, why were her hypothetical grandchildren worth more concern than me, her own daughter? I was the one hurting right now, the one who'd been cheated on. Sometimes it just felt like my kids mattered more than me already, and they weren't even born yet.

I was in a bad mood again by the time I was finished cleaning. I made a quick dinner – tomato soup with cheese on toast to dip – plenty of Worcester sauce on there too. I turned the TV on and put a well-worn sitcom on as background noise. Once I was done with dinner, I washed up and returned to my crochet with another hot chocolate. I was determined to finish the hand warmers before I went to sleep. At least there was one thing I was in control of.

As I finished up the final stitches and sewed in the ends, I couldn't deny it any more. I knew who I'd made the hand warmers for. I wasn't just working away at them because I was too stressed and unhappy to try and sleep. I wanted them finished because Cooper's clothes – clean, dried and folded – were in a bag for life in a corner of the spare room. They'd been there for a few days now and I hadn't had the courage to take them back to him. Part of me was worried that seeing him again might lead to more flirting. Part of me was worried that it wouldn't.

Today I'd had the push I needed to make the trip back up the towpath. There was no point in continuing to wallow or keep myself in stasis, worrying about what would come next. I was going to sort out my housing situation, separate my life from Richard and move on. I had a list of tasks ahead of me, cleaning the flat was just the start. I'd return Cooper's clothes next – along with the thank-you present I'd made – and then 'the jumper incident' would be firmly behind me.

Firm in my convictions, I set the new hand warmers aside and laid down to sleep. Tomorrow was a new start, a new Tabitha. One Sunday that would fix everything by the time it was over. The next time I woke up it would be on a sunny morning, ripe with potential.

I woke, bleary and confused, to hammering on the front door and the persistent chime of the doorbell. My phone told me I'd only been asleep for an hour or so. With a groan, I tripped out of bed and rushed to the door, worried the neighbours were going to be disturbed. I barely glanced through the peephole – I knew already what I'd see. I took the chain off and let him in.

'What are you doing here?' I hissed at Richard as he staggered past me into the flat. He was dressed for his weekend golf session in a polo shirt and navy golf trousers. His shirt was untucked though, which wasn't normal, and his dark hair was falling out of its carefully swept-back gel style. As I flicked on the harsh overhead lights, he recoiled slightly and I saw that there was a stain on the front of his pale pink shirt. He smelled of gin and beer. I wrinkled my nose.

'Tabs,' Richard tried to wrap me up in a beery hug but I took a step back. He wilted slightly. 'I wanted to see you.'

'You're drunk,' I pointed out, redundantly. 'Go home.'

'I am home,' he whined. 'Come oooon, I've been in that bloody Travelodge for ages. I want to come home.'

Travelodge. I'd thought he'd have gone to stay with his 'lady friend' or one of his golf buddies. Apparently not. The nearest Travelodge was outside town, near the train station, on the industrial estate beside a Currys and a Carpet Warehouse. At least a thirty-minute drive. Even in this state he hadn't been stupid enough to try to drive it. He must have walked here from the pub up the canal.

I weighed my options and sighed. I couldn't just push him out on the street. What if he did decide to try to drive and hit someone? Or fell in the canal as he tried to walk back to his hotel?

'Just… go to bed, all right?' I said, relocking the front door and shooing him towards the hallway. He went, stumbling out of his shoes and leaving them in the middle of the room. I rolled my eyes and kicked them to the side, near the coffee table. The last thing I wanted was to trip over them in the morning.

'Taaaaaaabs?'

'Yes?' I sighed.

'… thank you.'

He sounded so pathetic that it killed my anger stone-dead. I sighed and felt my shoulders droop as I turned off the light in the kitchen.

'You're welcome…' I rubbed my face and padded back towards the guest room. 'The sick bowl's under the bed. Good night.'

Chapter 15

THE NEXT MORNING, I woke up and had a brief moment of peace before I remembered Richard had turned up in the small hours. I lay very still under the fluffy, down-filled duvet (one I'd used as a kid staying in Aunt Lou's guest room) and listened hard. No sounds of movement in the flat. Perhaps he'd woken up, hungover and ashamed, and had let himself out?

I heard a clang from the kitchen and sighed. Yeah, that had probably been too much to hope for.

I got up and wrapped myself in my dressing gown before making my way to the kitchen. My new Greens Steel tumbler was on the floor, surrounded by a puddle of protein shake. Richard, in his rumpled golf clothes, was scooping powder into a second insulated tumbler – also mine – and adding water from the filter jug.

'Morning,' I said flatly.

'… morning,' Richard grunted. He dropped a shaker ball into the tumbler and closed the lid, mixing up the protein drink and following my gaze to the mess on the floor. 'Slipped out of my hand. I'll mop it up.'

I didn't say anything. He didn't deserve a little pat on the back for cleaning up his own mess. Instead I sidestepped the puddle and made myself some breakfast – toasted potato scones with pan-scrambled eggs. I made it quickly and took my plate to the lounge to eat, away from the kitchen where Richard was leaning against the counter.

'Any plans for today?' he asked, after drinking his shake in silence for a while.

'Probably going to do some errands,' I said, scrolling my phone as a distraction.

'Yeah, I thought the fridge was looking a bit empty,' he said.

I hummed in agreement but didn't offer anything else. Out of the corner of my eye, I watched Richard carefully refill the filter jug and put it back in the fridge. Something I'd literally never seen him do before. Usually he left the empty jug out, or worse, put it back so I didn't realise it needed filling up again. It was like watching a dog pick its own mess up in a bag and drop it in the bin. Slightly uncanny.

Interesting that he magically knew how to do these things now. This was the man that Mum thought was my 'future'? Maybe I'd created this mess by making out he was perfect for the last three years, to win her approval. God, that was depressing.

I finished my breakfast and left to get washed and dressed while Richard was cleaning up the spilled shake. Something else that wasn't usually his move. Sometimes he'd lay paper towels over a spillage but that was as far as it went.

While choosing what I wanted to wear for the day, I found myself thinking about Cooper and told myself firmly to knock it off. It wasn't that I was trying to dress for attention, but I was wavering over my usual errand-running outfit – jumper, leggings and trainers. What was the harm in looking just a little bit put-together? He was cute, well, hot. And I was single. No crime there.

I wondered what Mum would make of Cooper – older than me but shorter, scruffy and boat-dwelling. She'd be horrified. I highly doubted she'd label him 'my future' anyway, which, to be honest, only made him seem more attractive. Did he have a job, a car? Probably not. I remembered how he'd looked washing and carefully drying the mugs on his boat. At least he'd bloody clean up after himself.

In the end I popped on some blusher and tinted lip balm, a quick dash of mascara. Just my usual make-up. For clothes, I went a little less scruffy than I might otherwise have done – buttery lilac workout leggings, a belted T-shirt dress and a hexi-cardigan I'd made the year before in shades of pale purple and cream. I stuck my hair up in a claw clip with the usual untamed strands escaping within seconds. I wasn't about to do a full wash day today, though.

I grabbed the bag from the spare room and tucked the hand warmers into it, then got my things together to leave. Richard was still in the kitchen, now making himself a cup of tea. It was annoying but I wasn't about to begrudge him a tea bag and some milk.

'You can let yourself out,' I said, on my way to the door.

'Do you want me to transfer some money for the shop?'

I felt a flush of anger pass over me at his assumption. 'You don't live here.'

'Well, I do still—'

I was out of the door and letting it close behind me before he could finish. I didn't want anything from him. By the end of today, I'd be organised and ready to pick apart our lives, like frogging a badly made project back into its component yarns. Separate and ready to start over again as two new things.

The weather was good, despite the grey clouds that had hung over town yesterday. The air was a little crisper and the ground was slightly damp, as if we'd had a light shower but, other than that, the conditions were perfect for a walk. I'd come back for the car later, since I needed it for the shopping.

I didn't meet anyone as I crossed the park, where the community garden was already heaving with pumpkins, swelling between enormous leaves. Soon every one of them would be distributed to a different business or landmark, carved for the annual competition. The winner got to keep the coveted pottery pumpkin trophy for a year and, after the judging, Maeve and the church ladies would serve up industrial quantities of pumpkin pies, sage and pumpkin scones and toasted pumpkin seeds. I was in such a good mood I waved at the scarecrows guarding the vegetable hoard – this year the junior school had made two, Buzz Lightyear and Sally from the sweet shop… though she looked a bit like Taylor Swift if she did her make-up by whacking her face into a paint pallet. I was sure Sally was still pretty chuffed.

I walked through town. Nothing would be open this early on a Sunday. The church bells were ringing out loudly and, aside from the milkman, the roads were empty of vehicles. I felt wonderfully free and unobserved, checking my reflection in the darkened shop windows.

I cut through the meadow, encountering a solitary dog walker – Alistair, the vet who lived across the hall from our flat. I gave him a little wave, enjoying the quiet too much to say anything. I hadn't seen his girlfriend for a while – Cressida, I think her name was. But they didn't live together. I'd meant to ask her how much it'd be for a birthday cake for Richard. Not that I needed one now.

There was a light mist hanging over the surface of the canal and, as I got closer to the viaduct, I could smell wood smoke in the damp air. Cooper had a fire going in his stove. Clearly, he was also an early riser and wasn't one to go get pissed on a Saturday, as if he was still a fresher at uni.

It wasn't until I reached the boat that I got nervous. Maybe he wouldn't appreciate being bothered this early in the morning? I could imagine him inside, reading or at least scowling at a newspaper, as he ate some ruthlessly sensible cereal like Shredded Wheat and drank black coffee.

Having reached the bank near the boat, I stopped and wondered if I ought to just leave the bag with a note. I had my shopping pad in my bag. But that felt a bit rude, cold even. I could knock and then he could decide if he wanted to answer or not, I decided.

I reached over to knock on the door and it opened under my knuckles.

I squealed. It was automatic as the door just opened suddenly and Cooper appeared – tousle-haired and wearing another of 'my' jumpers, this one a grey crewneck with some popcorn stitches around the lower third of the torso.

He jumped, which was slightly validating. One hand flew to his chest, clutching a battered pack of cigarettes and a lighter against himself. The other grabbed the side of the doorframe, as if to keep himself from falling.

'Well… I'm awake now,' he huffed. 'Jesus – just when I thought you weren't coming back. Was the plan to lull me into a false sense of security?'

'Did it work?' I asked, and he laughed drily.

'Just a bit. At least I didn't scream – think of my neighbours.' He gestured to the empty canal and then his eyes fell to the bag I was carrying. 'And here I thought I wasn't even getting a thank-you card.'

My face was warm, a fluttering in my chest. Was I already flirting again or was this just how he talked and it was bringing it out of me? It was hard to tell.

'It's just your clothes. I did wash them, sorry for not bringing them over sooner. I just got a bit busy,' I said, all in a rush.

'Eh, no worries, not like I've got a shortage of joggers to wear. You're up early…' He gave me a considering look, like he was trying to work something out. 'Want to come in for a tea?'

'… um, sure, but I thought you were coming out for a cigarette?'

He shrugged and tucked the packet into the pocket of his washed-out tartan pyjama bottoms, which rucked up over his feet, slightly too long. 'Should give it up really, but I can wait a while.'

He stepped back and I followed him into the boat. He'd clearly been working hard in the past few days. Most of the Diana memorabilia had been sorted into old cardboard boxes and stacked up ready to be dealt with. Without all the dolls and china in the way, the inside of the boat was actually quite spacious, the varnished timber walls slightly sun-faded in the few spots they hadn't been covered in clutter.

'Going well then – the renovation,' I said as I entered the kitchen after him to find him already putting the kettle on.

'Mmm? Oh, yeah. Would be going faster but I have to carry everything down to the charity shop and the woman in there is fucking scary – I mean, you heard – she goes through everything like she's trying to find reasons to turn it down. Miserable old...' He looked round at me and pulled a face. 'Sorry, she's not your mum or something, is she?'

'No!' I laughed. 'God no, Margaret's an absolute nightmare. And she hates me, so feel free not to hold back. I am fully on board with slandering her.'

He deposited tea bags into two mugs and leant back against the counter. 'Hard to imagine anyone hating you. Unless you chased *her* down to demand knitwear?'

'Ha, ha,' I deadpanned. 'How're the blankets and stuff working out for you anyway? All toasty aboard The Lady Di?'

'As cosy as it gets on here, yeah, cheers,' he nodded, and I realised that he looked me in the face when we talked, eyes alert and attentive, not so much as dipping titwards. 'Though I can't stop wondering how much it must've cost to make that.' He gestured at the blanket on the bench seat. The cheating blanket, as it had become in my mind. 'Kind of scared it's priceless.'

'Definitely not any more,' I said, trying to make a joke out of it.

He winced. 'Sorry, I didn't mean to... you said it took like a hundred hours, right?'

'Closer to two,' I confessed.

'Wow...' He poured hot water into the cups and looked at the blanket again, clearly working something out in his head.

'Yeah... well, that was certainly a lot of... wasted time,' I mumbled.

He passed me a cup of tea and the brush of his icy fingers reminded me of the hand warmers in the bag at my feet.

'Not a waste. It's a gorgeous thing – just a shame it's got uh… bad memories attached.'

I sighed my agreement, then picked up the bag and held it out. 'Speaking of bad memories… thank you for fishing me out of the canal – and I, um, made you something.'

'The much-discussed thank-you card?' he asked, mouth quirking into a smile. He was playing with me, not trying to win or score points, just… playing. It was nice. He opened the bag and peered inside, and something soft and fleeting travelled across his expression.

'They're just…' I started.

'They're great.' He set aside the bag and slipped the hand warmers on. I was pleased I'd managed to guess a good length for him, perfect for tucking into the sleeves of his jumper. I watched as he flexed his knuckles and ran his fingers over the soft acrylic yarn.

'I just noticed you have appallingly cold hands last time I was here so, seemed a safe bet.'

'I do,' he chuckled. 'Toes too. I used to get a lot of complaints. My last girlfriend made me wear socks in bed. 'Course that was a few years ago now…' He cut himself off and gave me a slightly subdued smile. 'They're perfect. Thank you. Though I do feel like I'm really taking advantage of your skills.'

'It's not a big deal, I promise. They provided a much-needed distraction,' I half-laughed and busied myself sipping my tea, the word 'girlfriend' buzzing in my brain. I'd given so many crochet presents away since learning to make things, but I'd never felt like this before – sort of squirmy and embarrassed. Watching Cooper continue to admire the hand warmers, I couldn't remember the last time anyone was so pleased with something I'd made. I mean, definitely Lou, before she died. Now it was probably down to Emma. She genuinely seemed to treasure the things I'd gifted her over the years.

Definitely just Emma, I thought sadly. Richard treated my projects as if I'd just popped into Primark to buy them for him, and even Mum and Dad didn't really do more than say 'Thank you' and set aside whatever I'd made for them. None of them would throw on the socks, mittens or hats I'd made as soon as they got them. That was for sure.

'They're acrylic,' I said, trying not to sound apologetic. 'You said about the jumper being too fancy, but acrylic stands up to anything – lots of washes, thorough wear, even if you have to carry a hundred boxes of Diana merchandise, I guarantee they won't get worn out.'

That startled a laugh out of him and whatever that subdued look had been about was gone, his face relaxing. 'Well, thank you. And not that it's at all expected, but the next time you make me something, I promise to pay you what it's worth.'

I waved him off and set my empty mug on the table. 'It's not about the money.'

'I know – but you're not just handing over a blanket, or a pair of socks – it's your time, your skill,' he said. 'That warrants a little reciprocity.'

I smiled at him, pleased, because aside from Emma giving me free tarot readings and charm bags, no one had ever offered me anything back for my work. Even for the stuff they asked me to make. I wasn't sure what to do with the warm feeling building in my chest. It felt like I was about to either hug him or burst into tears.

I decided to leave before I found out which.

'Right, well, best be off. Lots of errands to run,' I said. 'Thank you for the tea.'

'Any time,' Cooper said easily. 'Enjoy your errands. Help yourself to a doll or a mug on your way out… please. Please take one. Or five.'

I was laughing as I left, feeling lighter than I had in days. Near the door I stopped and glanced back to find Cooper watching me. He gestured to the heaps of Diana merch and I rolled my eyes, but took a teacup off the top of a pile. He gave me a thumbs-up and I carried my new acquisition with me all the way back to the car park at the flat, smiling every time I looked at it.

Chapter 16

RICHARD WASN'T IN THE flat when I went up to drop the cup off and pick up my reusable bags. I did notice that the protein-shake spillage had been cleaned up. Sort of. There was some sticky residue there that would need swabbing away. In the bathroom, although he'd obviously taken a shower, he hadn't left his wet towel in a heap on top of the toilet seat. I was starting to suspect he was trying to show he'd 'changed'. God knows why, given our break-up had nothing to do with his lazy habits and everything to do with his infidelity.

I was about to start writing out a shopping list when my phone rang. It was Mum. I sighed when I saw her name on the screen. Maybe it was because I'd just had a nice walk in the fresh air, but I actually felt equipped to answer. That didn't mean I was looking forward to it.

'Hi, Mum. I'm just off out to Asda. Can I call you back?' I said.

'Tabby,' Mum trilled. 'How are you? We missed you yesterday but everyone loved that dessert you made. Mary asked for the recipe.'

Right, still going the denial route. She made it sound like I'd had a stomach upset or something. Instead of leaving the house because I couldn't bring myself to pretend she hadn't hurt me deeply with that one question. *Are you sure?*

'It's Eton mess but with tropical fruit – cream, pre-made meringue and… fruit.'

'Lovely, I'll pass that on to her then.' Mum paused for a moment and I could feel her casting about for something else to say, to keep the conversation going without dipping into anything real. The point of the call was to re-establish contact, smooth things over without having to address what had roughened them up in the first place. The way it had always been – a cup of tea a few hours after an argument. Asking if I wanted anything from the shop so I'd have to talk to her again. 'So… Asda. Getting anything special or just a stock-up?'

I tipped my head back and looked at the ceiling. Jesus. 'Just a weekly shop. I forgot last week. Had a lot on my mind.' The urge to say 'what with my boyfriend cheating on me' was almost overpowering. I managed to resist, just.

'Well, if they still have those multi-packs of Yorkshire Tea, can you grab me one and pop it round? You can pick up your dish at the same time. Or I can come over instead, I haven't been to yours in a while.'

Was she angling to see Richard? Trying to find a way to work things out between us like some kind of unpaid counsellor, or was she just trying to be supportive? I wanted to believe it was the latter. Mum wasn't by nature manipulative, she could just be a bit pig-headed sometimes. Stubborn and relentless when it came to what she thought was the best course of action. Her catchphrase in the face of any and all of my cautions had always been 'no, it won't'.

We should take an umbrella – it's going to rain.

No, it won't!

That vase will leave a water mark on the windowsill.

No, it won't!

If we don't go now, the shop will have run out of school uniform in my size!

No, it won't!

Cut to me, soaking wet, wearing my too-small school jumper and repainting the windowsill. She never listened to me.

'I'll see if they still have them and text you,' I said. 'Gotta go, see you later.'

I rang off and scribbled down a quick list. Only shopping for myself was a change and the scrappy list didn't look long enough once I'd finished. I felt a pang of regret. Was this what it was going to be like now? Buying single onions and half-sized loaves of bread just for one? Why was everything set up for pairs of people and families? Even bloody food shopping.

The drive to Asda was stressful. Sunday drivers were out in force by this time, pootling from A to B and having three to five pints before trundling back. I made it to the supermarket and parked up in the furthest corner from the shop, the only area where there were spaces. With a trolley and my list, I went in and gladly turned my brain off, wandering the shelves on autopilot and grabbing what I needed.

I was in the cleaning aisle, trying to find the cheapest laundry liquid that wouldn't take my skin off, when I stepped back and bumped right into someone's trolley.

'Sorry.' I leapt out of the way and found myself looking right at Cooper. He was still wearing the grey jumper and the hand warmers I'd made, but had exchanged his pyjama bottoms for faded jeans and work boots.

'Hey.' He looked surprised but not unpleasantly so. 'You again. Twice in one morning.'

'Yeah – errands, remember,' I said. I glanced down at his trolley and saw that he'd stacked one end of it with tinned dog food. 'I didn't know you had a dog. Have you been hiding it away?'

'No, just didn't have one until about forty minutes ago.'

'Wow, you move fast,' I joked, and immediately regretted it when his mouth twitched, obviously fighting hard not to rise to my poor choice of words.

'Went out for my much-anticipated first cigarette of the day, once I'd recovered from having the shit scared out of me, and he was just walking down the towpath. Came on board for some head scratches and I kept waiting for the owner to come around the bend but they never did. Must have got out of someone's garden. He has a collar but no tag.'

'Poor thing.' I folded my arms around myself. It was horrible to think of someone calling and calling for their dog, only to get no answer. I had a massive soft spot for animals, but particularly dogs – because I'd never been allowed one growing up. Dad was keen but Mum – the queen of Febreze and Flash wipes – was put off by the potential for smells and muck. Aunt Lou's dog Pete had been my one pet growing up and he hadn't even really been mine in the strictest sense.

'He might have a chip. I sort of had a cat when I was a student and ended up getting his chip checked,' I said. 'It used to come to my window and, once I found out he didn't have an owner, I flea-treated him because he had a bit of a mangy bum. But he stopped coming around once I switched from Whiskers to Lidl cat food.'

'Snob. Though I do prefer Whiskers myself,' Cooper said sagely. 'Keeps my coat nice and silky.'

That startled a laugh out of me and his face lit up when he saw his joke land.

'Did you leave him on the boat?' I asked, once I'd sobered. 'The dog?'

'He's actually tied up outside,' Cooper winced. 'I didn't want to risk him eating a Diana and getting ill. Plus, you know… I have a lot of very valuable blankets that I'm quite partial to.'

'Good call,' I said, trying to ignore the little twinge of pleasure that gave me. 'Can I see him?'

'Sure – though, to be clear, I didn't lure you with a puppy, you very much volunteered,' Cooper said.

I'd fortunately mostly finished my shopping and I could pick up the last few bits later. We went to the checkouts and I let Cooper go in front of me, as he was only buying the dog food and some plastic pots of instant noodles and porridge. He packed everything into a tatty rucksack and then waited while my week's worth of shopping came down the conveyor belt. When I started packing, he picked up an empty bag.

'Need help?'

'Oh!' I was surprised, both that he was offering and that he'd actually asked. 'Yes, please.'

The woman on the till looked at us and sighed. 'You've got a good one there, love.'

'Uh… thanks,' I said, flushing, and then realised I should probably have set her straight. But I didn't and Cooper didn't either.

We packed up my shopping and I paid with a quick tap of my card. I resolutely did not find it insanely attractive that he'd put the eggs on the top of a bag so they wouldn't get crushed. Like a functional adult. As we wheeled our trolleys out, he glanced at my bags.

'You like to cook?'

'Hmm?' I followed his gaze and realised that it was pretty obvious from what I'd bought – lots of vegetables, fresh fish, spices and other essential ingredients. Nothing pre-made in sight. Except the two tubs of Häagen-Dazs and the three bottles of wine. 'I do, yeah. Not that I'm great at it… I take it you don't?' I asked, faintly teasing.

He shrugged. 'Never really had the time before. I think I might try and get into it.'

'You can probably do really nice porridge on that stove – much better than the pots. I'm kind of jealous actually, I've always wanted a woodstove,' I confessed as we left through the automatic doors.

'It is nice, yeah, especially since the wood's basically free round my way, and I am at heart a bit of a cheapskate.' We turned a corner and I saw the dog even before it jumped up on its hind legs and started barking at Cooper. It was a wiry-haired little terrier, white and brown, with enormous bushy eyebrows and a curled over tail like the top of a Mr Whippy cone.

'Oh, he's lovely,' I cooed, watching the dog eagerly welcome Cooper back. He was tied to a bike rack with what I realised was a dressing-gown belt attached to his collar. I knelt down and held out my hand for him to sniff. The dog left off pawing at

Cooper's jeans to turn black button eyes on me and start licking my fingers.

'Wish they'd had a proper lead,' Cooper sighed. 'Would save me from looking like a total prat on the way home.'

Maybe it was the dog's cute little puppy eyes, or the thought of going back to the flat on my own – but I found myself saying, 'I'll give you a lift. If you like?'

'I wasn't fishing for one.' Cooper looked uncomfortable, busying himself with patting the dog and untying him from the bike rack.

'Okay… I'm still offering,' I said, then added, 'if only so you help me pack all this stuff into the boot.' It was fairly obviously an excuse. I didn't have that much shopping and I was used to handling twice as much by myself, but it was enough for Cooper to relax again.

'Sure. Thanks.'

He put the dog in the car and then helped me load the shopping bags while the terrier whirled around in the back seat, exploring every nook and cranny. There was going to be white hair all over the upholstery and I didn't even care. When we got in, I started the car and winced as my *Best of Dolly Parton* CD kicked in. I quickly turned it off before she could fully launch into 'Jolene'.

'Sorry – sort of my go-to for break-ups,' I said.

'Understandable. My guilty pleasure's the occasional blast of her cover of "Harper Valley PTA".'

'You like Dolly Parton?' I raised an eyebrow.

'I think it's impossible not to, isn't it? That's like not liking fun, or cake. Country gets unfairly maligned, I think, but that's just the opinion of a city boy,' he said, putting on an appalling Southern accent.

I giggled. Cooper whistled and the dog shot over the centre console and into his lap.

'You've got him well trained already,' I laughed, manoeuvring us out of the car park.

'Nothing to do with me. He's just a clever boy, aren't you?' He rubbed the dog's head, flapping his ears about.

I had a sudden brainwave. 'I think I have some of my aunt's old dog stuff stored at the flat – a lead and some bowls, stuff like that. If you'd like it, I mean, it's just gathering dust at the moment.'

'That's… really kind of you,' Cooper said, so earnestly that I glanced his way in surprise. I'd been expecting him to make light of it with a joke. 'Thanks. I can come and pick it up later, if that's okay?'

'I could just do a quick drive-by now?' I said and he looked surprised but nodded.

Even though it was my idea, I felt a bit awkward when we pulled up by the block of flats. I hadn't really thought through that I was inviting Cooper over to my home.

Maybe he sensed something because he quickly said, 'I can wait down here if you want?'

'Don't be silly,' I laughed. Though it came out a little strained. Why was this so awkward? 'You're not getting out of carrying stuff that easily. The dog can stay, though – he's probably not going to hotwire the car.'

We left the dog sitting in the front seat and I showed Cooper into the building and to the lift. He stood behind me while I unlocked the door and I felt a tingle running up and down my spine.

'Wow…' he said, as he stepped into the flat and looked around. 'It's very… clean.'

I laughed under my breath. He was trying so hard to hide how appalled he was. 'It's all Richard's idea, not mine.'

Cooper visibly relaxed. 'Thank God, because it's… awful.'

I giggled. 'It is, isn't it? I always think it looks like someone's about to do surgery in here.'

'Yes! Or like the lobby of a really overpriced gym.' Cooper surveyed the kitchen and shook his head. 'On a spaceship.'

'Seriously. I don't know what soft furnishings did to him as a child but it started a lifelong feud,' I said. 'I, um, think I put Pete's things in the spare room.'

'I love a dog with a human name,' Cooper said, following me down the hallway, still looking around in semi-horror at the bland, bright walls. 'Unless Pete was your aunt's boyfriend. I don't want to assume. Or kink-shame.'

I laughed, throwing open a built-in cupboard and hunting around for the right box. 'The first one, but that's very open-minded of you. I think his old toys are in here as well.'

'Ah, this is more like it,' Cooper said, and I turned to find him looking round the room. I'd moved some more things in there to cheer myself up since the break-up and there had been a few of Aunt Lou's ornaments around before then because Richard didn't have to look at them in there. Her Hathaway Rose dressing-table set and the stained-glass wreath of wildflowers hanging in the window. One of her blankets was draped over the bed. Well, we'd made it together but it was her design – three-dimensional sunflowers and sprays of leaves on alternating squares.

'It's a bit of a mess,' I said, gesturing to the wicker chair with all my clothes draped over it and the books on the bedside table, one of which I realised was the Anthony Horowitz one I'd dug out after meeting Cooper the first time.

'It feels like you.'

'Oh, thanks,' I laughed. 'So I'm a mess?'

'Clutter isn't mess, it's… real. Warm,' Cooper said, sounding distracted. He blinked and cleared his throat, suddenly awkward. I guessed he hadn't meant to say that out loud. He thought I was warm and real? Was that a good thing or code for me reminding him of his mother? Why did I care? And why was seeing him only inches from my bed making my belly flutter?

'Found it,' I said, in the ensuing awkward silence. I held out the box, which contained Pete's lead, a few toys, bowls and random useful things like nail clippers. Cooper took it from me and when our eyes met, he was the first to look away. My stomach flipped and felt too light afterwards. I glanced away towards the door. God, what if Richard decided to let himself in? That was a sobering thought. I wasn't really doing anything to feel guilty about – especially given Richard and I weren't together – but, at the same time, this didn't feel entirely innocent either.

Cooper cleared his throat, ears pink. 'Should probably get back before the dog does some mischief in your car.'

'Right, absolutely,' I stuttered out. My heart was beating rapidly and I couldn't keep myself from looking at his mouth. Suddenly the room felt too small, the bed too laden with implications. One of my bras was dangling over the wicker chair. It all felt too personal. Intimate.

We made a hasty retreat to the lift and I felt myself relax once we were back on neutral ground. Cooper seemed more at ease too, and started talking again, about the flats and how they didn't really match the rest of the town. I nodded in agreement, glad of the distraction.

Back down at the car, the dog welcomed him as if we'd been gone for years instead of minutes. It felt like ages to me too actually. My heart was still beating too fast. I made myself breathe normally and tried to focus on anything but the man getting into my car.

Cooper put the box on the floor and wedged it between his feet so he could keep hold of the dog on his lap. I got in and told myself to just act normal for the next few minutes.

'Are you going to put something on Facebook?' I asked, as I drove towards the old-town side of Leaford, where the boat was moored. 'Missing or found pets usually go on the local page – Leaford Community Group?'

He was quiet for a moment too long and I glanced over to see him looking out of the side window. His body was tense and, although he was still petting the dog, he was doing so automatically, not really paying attention.

'I don't really do Facebook,' he said, a beat too late. 'Maybe you could take a picture of him and post it for me?'

'Sure… do you have a phone number at least, so I can let you know if anyone responds? Or do you rely mostly on smoke signals?' I asked, trying to lighten the mood. There was something off about his reaction when I mentioned Facebook. Not the usual 'I'm too intellectual and important to use social media' I'd had a few times from library colleagues. It had felt somehow cagey.

For the first time, it occurred to me that I didn't really know anything about this man. I'd told him about my break-up, he knew about the shop, about Emma and Richard and where I shopped, what car I drove. All I knew about him was that he lived on a boat stuffed with Diana memorabilia. I didn't even know why he lived there or where he'd come from. He said he'd bought it recently but where had he been before? Did he have a job? A last name even?

'… I'll write it down for you,' Cooper said eventually. He picked up the shopping-list pad from the centre console and shifted the dog around so he could reach into his pocket. The phone he pulled out was a cheap little Nokia with a keypad. The kind of phone I hadn't seen in real life since the 2010s. What people in TV dramas would call a 'burner phone' – used exclusively by drug dealers, hitmen and people on the run from the government.

He scribbled the number down from his contact list. I couldn't help glancing at the screen as he did so and saw only three numbers in the directory: 'my number', 'O2' and 'Lloyds Bank'. No family, no partner, not even a Chinese takeaway place or doctor's surgery. I returned my eyes to the road, frowning. What was his deal?

'Cheers,' Cooper said, as I pulled up in the little car park at the end of the towpath. 'You want to get a picture of him for the Facebook post?'

'Sure.' I took my phone out and tried not show my surprise when Cooper got out of the car and left the dog in the passenger seat for me to photograph. He could have just been keen to get his bag out of the boot. It didn't have to mean that he was trying not to be photographed.

I snapped a few pictures of the dog, who grinned adorably at the camera, blinking politely. I ruffled his ears and watched as Cooper opened the door and attached Pete's old lead before leaning in to give me a wave goodbye.

'See you around,' I called, and watched as he took the dog and walked up the path back towards his boat. He threw me a wave over his shoulder and I caught myself smiling slightly, but slowly that smile shrank under the weight of everything I didn't know about him. Accompanied by the knowledge that I shouldn't care what he was hiding.

Chapter 17

Monday morning saw me back in the shop for another week of work, one I was determined to get through without any more upsets or early closings. I just wanted things to go back to normal. To that end, I showed up fifteen minutes early to put the kettle on and get things ready for opening before Emma showed up.

'Morning,' she called from outside, as I unlatched the door. 'You're keen.'

'Ready to get back into a routine,' I said. 'I looked at property listings for three hours yesterday and there's nothing going right now, so that means I might have to pay for the flat on my own for a few months.'

'Is that… doable?' Emma asked, shedding her black spider-web coat.

'It's going to have to be. I can do it, as long as I cut back on some things.'

Like buying coffee, my Audible subscription and eating anything that wasn't from the yellow-sticker section of the supermarket. I'd also need the shop to start making more money and, to be honest, I'd probably also need to put some stuff on eBay just to try and bridge the gap. God knows how I'd manage once the pre-paid rent on the shop ran out. But I could do it. What was the alternative? Ask my one friend and sole employee to also move in with me? That was too much pressure to put on Emma and there was no way I was going to be able to move back in with Mum and Dad after Saturday's disaster.

'Hey, what's that?' Emma went back to the door and pulled a piece of paper out of the letterbox. It was set low in the door, so low down that most of the junk mail distributors didn't even bother to shove takeaway leaflets in there.

'Probably a parish newsletter or something,' I muttered, double-checking the amount in the till so I could note it down before we opened.

'It's an envelope, unsealed… oh, my GOD!'

'What?' I jumped a little in my seat and looked up to find Emma holding a rectangle of paper up at me. Her eyes were wide and for a moment I thought it was an eviction notice or something even more dreadful, like a Reform leaflet. Then she beamed at me.

'It's a cheque! For five grand!?'

I blinked at her. The words made sense individually but not when I put them together. Who the hell would be leaving us a cheque, let alone for that much money?

'Is there an invoice or something in there?' I waved her over and Emma tripped across the shop floor. She handed me the envelope and the cheque. On the inside of the flap of the envelope someone had written (in appalling chicken scratch) 'If you're good at something, never do it for free'. I looked at the cheque. It was indeed for five grand, made out to 'Ewe and Me'. Then I noticed the name of the sender and let out a startled laugh. Although there wasn't a full name, it was easy to tell who was behind it.

'It's a joke,' I said, in answer to Emma's confused expression. 'From J Cooper – the boat guy?' It seemed a safe assumption – I'd never met another Cooper in my life. Odd that he was going by his last name. I wondered what 'J' stood for?

'A… joke?' She looked quite disappointed. I supposed from her perspective the cheque had been the answer to the many crystals and charms placed around the shop. I felt bad for having ruined the mystique.

'I took his clothes back yesterday and we were talking about how much some of my crochet would cost to make – and I think this is just his way of trying to show that he values it, you know?' I ran my thumb over the scrawled signature. What a silly… sweet thing to do!

I looked up from the cheque and found Emma looking at me with her brows nearing her hairline. The last time she'd looked at me like that it was because I'd told a visitor that it was absolutely fine for them to ask me for directions (three times) without buying anything. It was her 'who are you kidding?' look.

'What?' I asked, more defiantly than I meant to.

'"What?" she says, like she didn't just get a cheque for five thousand pounds, from a cute man who "just wants you to know he values you".' Emma folded her arms. 'Who also saved you from a canal.'

'Not a real cheque,' I reminded her, stubbornly. 'And we already talked about the rescue thing and I told you it wasn't romantic or sexy or anything like that. It was just a thing that happened. And now I've given him his clothes and the hand warmers and I'll probably never see him again.' I thought for a second and then corrected myself. 'Unless someone messages me about that dog.'

Emma frowned at me. 'Okay, I have more questions now – what hand warmers and what dog?' Her expression turned incredulous. 'Did you… make him something?'

'Just to say thank-you-slash-sorry for the whole canal incident. I mostly wanted to have a quiet crafting afternoon and he just happened to be the beneficiary of that. Besides I make stuff for everyone.'

'Except Margaret.'

'Because she is evil,' we said, together.

'Yes, exactly,' I said. 'She doesn't need knitwear because she derives warmth from the fires of hell. But I make stuff for everyone else, so it's not a big deal. And the dog was… look, after I dropped his clothes round, I had to do a weekly shop and

I bumped into him at Asda. He was there buying dog food for a stray dog he'd found and I let him have some of Aunt Lou's old dog stuff, then gave them a lift home. He asked me to post in the Facebook group to see if anyone lost him. That's all.'

'You went by the flat?' Emma raised her eyebrows. 'Together?'

'I... yes. Just for a second, to get the lead and bits for the dog. It's not like I haven't been alone with him in his home before,' I said, feeling a bit prickly. Ordinarily would I let a strange man know my address? No, of course not. But Cooper was different. I trusted him. Why that was I couldn't say. Maybe because out of everyone I knew he'd never hurt me, accidentally or on purpose, with a comment or a criticism. He just seemed to accept everything I said and did with interest instead of critique. Even my own mother couldn't manage that.

'Hmm.' Emma drummed her star-and-moon acrylics on the counter. 'So the cute rescuer also saves sweet little puppies. And he just happened to bump into you?'

'At the one supermarket in town,' I pointed out.

'How did he get there? That's quite far to walk, right? And he didn't have a car or a bike with him?'

That brought me up short. I hadn't considered that before. How had Cooper got to Asda by the time I did? It was a long walk, especially with an unfamiliar dog on an improvised lead.

'I don't know, he could have hitch-hiked or... taken the bus,' I said, suddenly realising. 'He probably took the bus. They let dogs on. I saw a man with a duck in a cage on there once.'

That seemed to convince Emma at least. She let the subject drop with a hum and went to make tea in the break room. I finished setting up the shop floor for another day and followed her back there to collect my mug. We returned to the shop front together and, after unlocking the door and turning the sign over, I sat at the counter with her, waiting for customers.

'How was your weekend?' I asked to forestall further Cooper talk. I didn't want to examine that whole mess too closely.

'Pretty good – had to pop to Home Bargains for the new Halloween décor, bought some lovely cushions and a new blanket. Then made myself a little Sunday roast and watched a Catherine Cookson.' Emma blew on her tea. 'How was the party on Saturday, by the way?'

Crap. I immediately tried to think of a lie but I could tell Emma had already picked up on my pause. She frowned.

'Did something happen? Oh God, please tell me that Eton mess on your Instagram made it to the party and didn't fall in the foot well – that happened to me with a trifle. There were sprinkles in my floor mats for months.'

I laughed, but even to me it sounded strained. 'Nothing like that, thankfully. Um… I had a little falling-out with Mum, that was all. So I went home early.' At Emma's surprised expression, I hurriedly corrected myself. 'Not even a falling-out really. It was nothing – she just didn't take the news about the break-up the way I thought she would.'

Understatement of the year. Not even in my most dire imaginings had my mother flatly asked if I was sure I wanted to dump my cheating boyfriend.

'Oh, hon, you could have called me – what did she say?' Emma asked.

'She… asked me if I was sure,' I said, shrugging. 'That was it. I probably overreacted.'

'Sure?' Emma repeated, as if it was an entirely new word to her. 'About breaking up with Richard?'

I nodded.

'Richard, who you walked in on while he was having sex with another woman in your home? On your blanket!?'

I winced at the volume, but nodded again. 'I didn't tell her I'd seen him, just that he cheated…'

'You *told her* and she still said… wow, no wonder you left. I'm so sorry.' Emma put her hand on my arm and gave it a squeeze, her gemstone bracelets tinkling together. 'Have you spoken since?'

'She rang yesterday morning but we didn't really talk about it. You know how she is. But I will talk to her about what she said, I just have other stuff to be worried about right now.'

To be honest, the way Emma was reacting made me feel a bit worse about it. I'd tried to minimise how horrible the whole situation had been. But hearing Emma be so flabbergasted was making it more and more real to me that Mum's reaction to the news of Richard cheating had been far from what normal people would consider appropriate from the mother of the injured party.

I didn't mention Richard showing up drunk because I knew already what Emma would say. She was love and light when it came to saving spiders and putting crystals over the door but she'd be disappointed in me for not telling Richard where to go and throwing him back out into the night. I was sort of disappointed in myself. Even if it had been the responsible thing to do, I could have just called him a taxi or made him book an Uber. I didn't have to let him stay the night, but I had. It was hard. I'd thought I could turn off all my feelings for him and to a certain extent I had. But some of them had deeper roots than I'd anticipated. Illogical, inconvenient roots.

'Well, let me know if you need some moral support,' Emma said. 'Or an alibi.'

'I will do. Thanks,' I said, glad the subject was being dropped. 'And, hey, let's schedule in that "Stitch and Witch", hmm? It can't hurt.' While Emma created a new group chat, I thought privately that, despite her reassurances, I didn't want to keep burdening her with my crap when she had her own life to be concerned with. I could handle Mum and Richard. As for Cooper, he wasn't mine to worry about. He was just a man, on a boat, passing through and soon he'd be off somewhere else doing… whatever it was he did.

Why did that thought make me feel like someone had added weights to my shoes?

In a burst of distracting productivity, I made a free website for the shop and posted links to it in the local Facebook groups. It was nothing fancy, just a few pictures of the shop and stock, the address and our contact information. But at least now anyone googling for craft shops nearby would be able to find us. I'd been naïve to think we'd survive on foot traffic and word of mouth alone. I had to get the shop out there and bring people to us if we were ever going to be more than a brief novelty on the high street. An embarrassment under a 'To Let' sign.

In between customers I checked my phone for responses to the dog post. Quite a lot of 'poor thing' and 'hope you find the owners' replies. A few people had tagged friends and asked 'Is this Poppy?' or 'Looks just like Chalky!' but so far no one had claimed to know who he actually was. But it was still early days. I wondered if he was microchipped and how to go about checking that. I'd have to ask Alistair next time I saw him.

As I was putting my phone away, I got a notification from Mum. I was expecting a reminder about the tea she'd asked me to get for her, but it was a link she'd sent via WhatsApp.

Having a Baby at Thirty: Why You Shouldn't Wait

Terrific.

Chapter 18

I IGNORED THE ARTICLE. Of course I did. The alternative was to open the chat and read it and then Mum would know I'd done so. Better to just ignore it. That was how we dealt with everything as a family. I'd learned from the best.

My vow to have a normal work day was being sorely tested very early on. Fortunately, we had a steady flow of customers for once – apparently, there was a coffee morning at the church hall and it had brought in a lot of foot traffic. People were coming in looking for supplies for their harvest display contributions. We sold quite a lot of the cheaper acrylic yarns, pompom makers, buttons in autumnal shapes and even a fairly expensive set of ergonomic crochet hooks. Things were looking up. I still hadn't had time to get anything done regarding our brainstormed ideas, aside from asking Emma to arrange for her coven to visit. The whole 'Richard and his squeaky-bummed floozy' thing had really ruined my time management.

Even Maeve came by, having supplied cakes and biscuits to the coffee morning. She stopped by with her Sholley packed with leftover shortbread petticoat tails and gossip. Today she was in baby-blue, from her trainers to her bobble hat, one I'd made for her on a whim several months ago.

'I asked around about that dog you posted on the local group – no luck unfortunately,' she said, when I brought her out a cup of tea. She was going through a stack of felt rectangles, hoping to make faux pastries for the display. 'Such a lovely boy though – where is he now?'

'Oh, Cooper's taking care of him,' Emma chirped up as she restocked the baby-weight yarn basket. 'The guy living on the boat up by the viaduct?'

'You know him?' Maeve looked intrigued. 'What does he look like? I've only heard stories from Margaret at the charity shop and you know what she's like. Basically called him a drifter and said he keeps bringing rubbish in for her to get rid of.'

A defence of Cooper was automatically on my lips. 'Not rubbish, he's clearing out a load of royal wedding stuff, Charles and Diana. Some people collect that – it's not exactly worthless. And he donated cash too – forty quid.'

Maeve raised an eyebrow. 'How do you know?'

'She's been on the boat,' Emma said breezily. 'And you'd know him if you saw him. He's sporting some very nice jumpers,' she added, giving me a look that sparkled with a shared joke. My face felt hot – God why did I have to go and form a one-woman fan club for the man?

'Oh! I have seen him.' Maeve's crinkled cheeks pinkened. 'He came in to buy bread and I caught him looking at the iced biscuits – the nice ones I just put out for autumn. I hadn't seen him before so I asked if he had any plans because sometimes, you know, you can upsell people if they've got a party coming up or something. He just said he might have someone pop in for tea and the biscuits would probably be nice.'

I felt my skin tingle. Someone in for tea. Was that… me? Was Cooper expecting to see me again soon? But Maeve hadn't said anything about when he'd come in. It had probably been days ago if he hadn't brought the dog with him.

'Did he buy any?' I asked, resolutely not looking at Emma.

'Eight,' Maeve said proudly, setting her chosen felt aside for purchase. 'Served him right before I left for the coffee morning. He was very polite, and he said he liked my hat.'

Today. 'And he didn't have the dog with him?'

Maeve frowned. 'I'm not sure. Most people tie theirs to the handrail by the front door, but some use the cage round that tree on the little patch of grass. I can't see round there from the counter. So do you know if he's planning on moving on soon? Only I know Margaret and a few others are on to the council about him and he must have permission to be there but you know what it's like when people start their little campaigns. If he has to leave, will he pass the dog on to you?'

'I'm… not sure,' I said, unexpectedly unsettled by the thought that Cooper might just vanish. I'd been reassuring myself with that thought not too long ago but hearing it from someone else made it seem more real. The idea that I might never get to joke back and forth with him again left me feeling a bit sad and grey.

'I can put some posters up in the shop if you get some printed up – I know everything tends to be online these days but not everyone is, you know?' Maeve said. 'I'd hate to think of some poor pensioner missing their best friend and not knowing that he's being taken care of.'

'I can make some on the work laptop – right, Tabitha?' Emma asked. 'Get them printed at the library?'

'Good idea.' I managed a smile, still disturbed by the idea of a Cooper-less future. I had no right to be as bothered as I was. I knew that. It didn't help with the twisting in my chest.

Maeve left for the bakery after buying her felt and a fancy William Morris pincushion (it felt like a pity purchase but I wasn't turning those down these days). Emma went to the back to make a poster and I swept biscuit crumbs off the counter and straightened up the shelves.

'Finished!' Emma called through, and then appeared in the doorway. 'Go have a look, I'll man the till for a bit.'

It wasn't as if she had to, there was no one in at the moment. It seemed our early 'rush' had died off entirely. I went into the break area to look at the laptop. The poster looked very smart, although there wasn't much information on it. Just the picture of the dog, the fact he'd been found on the towpath and was safe, plus my phone number and email at the bottom. It amused me to see that Emma had deployed some 2000s ICT lessons WordArt on it. It was very cute.

I was about to pop back out and tell Emma it looked great and she could raid the petty cash for printing money, when I heard a familiar voice through the bead curtain. Richard's voice.

I didn't even hesitate, just plastered myself to the wall out of view of the door, like a red laser dot had appeared on my chest. I was actually holding my breath, which felt embarrassing in the extreme. But there was no way I wanted to see Richard right now, or ever again if I could help it. Was this going to be my life now? Hiding from Richard like I was playing a lifelong, professional game of hide-and-seek?

'She's not here at the moment,' Emma was saying – bless her, she knew exactly what to do. I was going to make her employee of the month. 'But you can leave them and I'll make sure she gets them when she's back.'

I heard the distinctive plasticky rattle of cellophane against the counter, accompanied by the rustle of tissue paper. Flowers. He'd brought me a bouquet of some sort. Well, not 'some sort' – it would be Richard's go-to arrangement. He always went for a dozen roses (colour dependent on occasion – red for valentine's, pink on anniversaries, yellow on birthdays) with gypsophila and eucalyptus. A combination that I'd thought endearingly classic and vintage. Just then, however, it felt annoyingly predictable. I wondered what colour roses he'd picked for 'sorry I shagged someone else on the sofa'. Hopefully, blue – because they were as improbable as his chances of getting back with me.

'Where is she?' Richard asked, actually sounding kind of sad.

'Just out for a bit.' I was glad Emma hadn't said the café or somewhere he could conceivably chase me down. 'I don't know when she'll be back… sorry.'

'… is she out with him – her new bloke?' Richard asked snippily. My sympathy evaporated. He obviously didn't believe me about Cooper – the hypocrite! But there was also a tiny glimmer of vindictive satisfaction. Ha! Now he was getting a little taste of his own medicine – imagining me moving on with someone else. Of course, then I thought about myself and Cooper… moving on, and had to purse my lips together to contain the squeak of pure shock at my own imaginings.

'I don't think she has one of those.' I could imagine Emma crossing her arms sternly, not giving anything away, and was immensely thankful that she was my friend. She'd make a pretty scary enemy.

'She was washing his clothes the other day. Gave me some cock-and-bull story about falling in the canal and borrowing them to come home in.' Richard was obviously not letting go of his suspicions, and whatever humility his drunken state had left him with was apparently wearing thin. 'She moved on pretty quick.'

Un-be-lievable. The hot, flustered feeling brought on by imagining myself 'moving on' with Cooper (in my head we were now lying in his bed on the narrowboat, cosy and post-coital) was replaced by the urge to burst out through the curtain and slap Richard's idiotic face. How DARE he judge me and the speed at which I may or may not be getting over him? He had cheated on me! Right in front of my eyes!

'I mean… less quickly than you, right?' Emma said sweetly. I punched the air in silent approval. Yes! Get him, girl! 'Besides I'm sure Tabitha's not looking to start washing some other man's clothes for him. She's probably looking for an adult.'

The chilly silence was so intense that I half expected fog to start rolling in through the bead curtain. Emma had never exactly been warm with Richard but now she was treating him like a stranger at the bus stop who'd just flashed her and then offered her a pocket-temperature Dairylea Triangle. It was amazing and awful. I wished I'd recorded it, to be honest. I felt like the time in uni when I'd drunk five Redbulls in a one-hour seminar. I was practically vibrating with energy, and also slightly nauseous.

'Just give her the flowers… please,' Richard muttered. God, he sounded annoyed. Good.

I heard him walk across the shop, shoes rapping on the vinyl floor. The bell jingled and then rattled aggressively as he slammed the door. There was a moment of silence.

'He's gone,' Emma said redundantly. There was a rustle as she picked up the flowers and, a moment later, she came through to the back with them. White roses. Weirdly funereal, but appropriate given he'd killed our relationship completely dead. Though the residual feelings of loss, anger and shame were still churning in my stomach, like an unfortunate late-night kebab.

'You can take those, if you like,' I said. 'Or bin them, I don't really mind.'

'Maybe your mum might like them?' Emma asked. 'It'd be a good excuse to pop round and talk.'

I pulled a face. 'I don't really feel like doing that right now. Thanks for dealing with him, though.'

'No problem. I'll go to the library now, shall I? Get those posters printed?'

Emma took some change from petty cash and left me to it. I stuck the flowers precariously into a mug so they wouldn't die before I could work out what to do with them. They were innocent in all this after all. They hadn't asked to be bought by a knob.

Sitting in the back room, looking at those flowers, I thought of the article Mum had sent me. Okay, so it was poorly timed and borderline offensive that she was only worried about my declining fertility but, at the same time, didn't she have a point?

Starting again with someone else would take a few years. I'd have to find a good guy – and it had taken several years of dates that went nowhere before I even found Richard. The chemistry hadn't been instantaneous but he'd been polite, attractive and not welded to a PlayStation or the sofa. I'd thought he was mature and thoughtful. Maybe I'd been looking for the wrong things. Unbidden, I thought of Cooper half-smiling at my Dolly CD. No, a future was not built on liking the same naff music. Or books.

So there was finding someone suitable, then dating, becoming official, moving in together, discussing marriage, all those little steps to take before the patter of tiny feet. I wanted to do things properly – if anything, Richard cheating had made me firmer in that belief. I imagined having had a baby with him a year or so ago. I'd be stuck right now, not even a chance of spousal support. No, marriage first, baby after. That was the plan.

But I was running out of time to make that plan work.

Are you sure? Mum had asked. Well, that was the thing, wasn't it? I was sure, most of the time. When I was with Emma or at the shop, it felt easy to imagine a Richard-less future. But around Mum or in the flat by myself, struggling to find somewhere to live now that I was starting over, I began to have my doubts.

Richard was many things, but I'd been with him for three years, and I knew him. Right up until he'd cheated on me, I thought he was husband material. Father material. Even now, I was looking at the flowers and wondering if I was being too hasty. He was playing his part in the apology dance, so maybe I was being rash in not doing my bit. Like an adult. The word sat heavy as a toad in my gut. A boring adult, who did things because they were rational and expected and responsible. Even if that meant setting happiness aside to settle for… Richard.

But the memory of what I'd walked in on was still with me. I couldn't forgive cheating. There were probably those out there who could but I wasn't one of them and, if anyone I knew decided to get back with their partner in a similar situation, I didn't know how I'd feel about them. At best I'd maybe pity them, at worst I'd be disgusted.

No, I decided. Even if it was a mistake to start over now. Even if I missed the boat on having kids and getting married, as my mum was clearly afraid I would. It wasn't worth how I'd feel about myself if I took Richard back. That was the end of it.

Chapter 19

I SPENT THE NEXT few days in a flurry of pumpkin-making madness. Leaford had entered into its countdown to the harvest festivities and every shop window was a riot of orange – the gift shop had orange candles, money banks, soft-toy clownfish and pumpkins, and the sweet-shop display jars were all stuffed with orange slices, gobstoppers and lollies. Even Gilly's Gallery had obliged the yearly trend with a series of fox paintings. Emma and I had moved all the yarn in shades from coral to neon orange into the window, flanked by jars of buttons. Even the butcher had exchanged his plastic parsley with faux orange wedges.

The final deadline for the library's harvest window display was looming and I had serious amounts of décor to make. Maeve's salt-dough cornucopia was already sitting pretty in the window, along with most of the other contributions. I was way behind. The felt-leaf garlands were mostly just cutting and a tiny amount of sewing but the crochet pumpkins were another matter entirely. I'd committed to at least ten in multiple sizes and, although the pattern was fairly simple, the larger ones took some time to work up.

Sitting in front of old *Charmed* episodes, surrounded by tumbleweeds of hollow fibre filling, I worked for hours on my pumpkins. My fingernails were permanently speckled with fabric glue from doing the stems and velvet fibres from the chenille yarn. I was seeing pumpkins in my dreams – laughing at me. But I managed to get them all finished in time, though one was slightly wonky where I'd run out of stuffing. That was fine, he could go at the back. If anyone asked, I'd say he was a butternut squash.

Thursday afternoon we had early closing, so I went to drop everything off. It was a bright day with just a hint of autumnal chill. A light breeze caught the bat bunting and the orange lights strung down the high street. Battery-powered candles huddled in the hedgerows, their timers set to dusk.

As I walked through the market square, being careful of the cobbles in my Mary Janes and admiring the straw bales and seating being set up for the pumpkin competition, I wondered if Cooper was warm enough on the boat. I then stumbled after accidentally picturing him in bed, bare-chested with one of my blankets slung low over his hips. It would be just my luck to get my libido back and then break my ankle.

I still hadn't heard anything about the dog. I guessed Cooper was going to have to keep him for a while. Though I could always offer to drive him to the vet to get his chip checked, presuming he had one.

I'd worked at the library for years before leaving to start my own business. It was my favourite building in the town centre and I'd loved having a claim to it. The red-brick building with its brass clock and steepled roof had once been the town hall, before the modern one was built over the river, and was subsequently closed due to asbestos. Inside it was gloomy, with high ceilings and narrow leaded-glass windows. The dusty shadows added to the ambience, as did the creaking wooden stairs, which popped and cracked underfoot as they were climbed. The air still smelled of instant coffee, dusty radiators and yellowing paper. Even the front desk, trimmed in brass rails and with a leather blotter, was a work of art.

Dan was manning the desk that afternoon. Or, at least, he was sitting at it whilst reading a Sherlock Holmes puzzle book and making notes on a jotter. I gave him a wave as I walked past, and he nodded at me. We'd never really been close as colleagues and, to be honest, I hadn't really made that many work friends. It was the building and the job that I loved more than the people I worked with.

I walked through to the back, where the children's library was. Vintage teddy bears and work from the local school competed with World Book Day posters and beanbags for space. The tiny Wendy house was neatly put to rights and I checked my watch, smiling slightly when I thought of the chaos that would be wreaked in here when the school emptied for the day. On week days the library was usually quite quiet – we had a few old boys in reading the newspapers, ladies exchanging one pile of Mills and Boons for another, mums attending toddler story-time and the occasional student on a free period, checking out comics or just using our free Wi-Fi. But, come the afternoon, at least twenty kids would come in straight after school, dragging PE kits and lunch boxes, all of them competing for the best beanbag and reading-challenge bragging rights. Mostly because the bus back to Fenlowe didn't come until four, and the stop was right behind us. That was my favourite part of the day, to be honest. I'd accepted more than my share of underbaked Food Technology cookies and handed out many a reading badge.

The window display was in the big bay window off the children's area, protruding onto the pavement outside. The main thoroughfare to the bus stop. Everyone would be able to see it as they walked to the school or the shops and classes came on little trips to put their items into the window and take pictures with them. It was already quite full. The butchers had donated a vase of pheasant tail-feathers and several antlers. Maeve's cornucopia sat beside it, the florists had made garlands of faux leaves, acorns and squashes. There was Gilly's chosen painting – the hedgehogs celebrating with pumpkin punch. Sally had filled a pumpkin-shaped jar with Irn-Bru jelly babies and set it in a nest of lollies. My crochet offerings and bunting would fit right in. Space had been taped off for the children's remaining town models and clay animals in pride of place. The boat-turned-clock-tower had already been delivered. You had to look really closely to see that it used to have a stern.

The stillness in the library was as restorative as I remembered it being. The ancient radiators were rattling away to chase the chill from the air and I could hear the book cart with the wonky wheel moving about upstairs. The turning of a page was loud in the silence and yet it took me a while to realise I wasn't alone back there. Someone else was in the stacks.

Between the front desk and the children's library was the non-fiction section. The adults' fiction area took up the entire first floor, so everything else had to be squeezed in downstairs. I heard pages turning and at first thought it was Dan doing his puzzle book, but I realised after a moment that it was closer than that. Then I heard the scuff of a boot on the polished parquet floor. I absorbed all this at the back of my mind, until I heard someone muttering under their breath.

'Come on, I cannot be the only person that needs to know this…' followed by the thump of a book being set back on the shelf.

I knew that voice. It sent a thrill through me and drew me closer. Before I knew it, I was setting my last pumpkins down at random. I ducked through the stacks and found Cooper there, glaring at the spines of the books. He was in front of a shelf with three subjects, ordered by code instead of alphabetically, so 'organised religion', 'reptiles' and 'vehicle maintenance' were packed in together. I had tried to change this 'system' but Laurel, our head librarian, had put her foot down. She'd worked at the library since it opened, and we were all a little scared of her.

'Starting a church or adopting a python?' I asked, as he scanned the titles.

He jumped and I realised it was the second time I'd made him do so. He was a little twitchy for a devil-may-care drifter. He recovered quickly but still looked a bit uncomfortable.

'Sorry, didn't mean to startle you,' I said, and then, feeling that I should try to make up for accidentally jump-scaring him,

I added, 'I used to work here. I can probably help you find what you're looking for.'

'Oh, right…' He gave the books a bewildered look and raised a hand to push his unruly hair out of his eyes. 'I was trying to find literally anything about engine maintenance for boats. The uh, Lady Di conked out as soon as I got her here. Haven't been able to get her started since.'

'Really?' I felt an unpleasant little jolt. 'Is that why you're still here then? You just can't get away?'

'Something like that.' He shrugged. 'To be honest I don't really have anywhere I need to be, but if the local council of busybodies get their way, I might have to shove off. I'm having visions of trying to row downstream while a bunch of pensioners and school-gate mums chase me with rotten vegetables.' There, his twinkle was back, and he graced me with a sighting of the cutely crooked tooth as he smiled.

I laughed. 'Can't have that. I'm not sure there's much on boats unfortunately…' I scanned the titles on offer and nibbled my lip. 'If you look something up in the online catalogue, you can request it.'

Cooper scratched the back of his neck. 'I actually don't have a card – I was just going to read it here and take notes.'

'No problem. You can sign up for free – government didn't get that one yet.'

That startled a little huff of laughter out of him. 'Good to know, but I don't really have an address, so it's just really complicated…'

'Just use the shop.'

What? What did I just say? I had to catch up with myself. It had just come out automatically. Maybe something about being back in the library had put me in 'customer service' mode, where I just had to try to sign everyone up, no matter what. Cooper looked just as shocked as I felt, his eyes losing their cute crinkles as they widened and his brows shot up.

'That's really kind of you. I really don't want to cause any problems for you and I can just order a book or something and have it go to one of those Amazon lockers at the supermarket. It'll just take a while to arrive, that's all.'

'That's… AHA!' I grabbed a thin book off the shelf.

Cooper jumped again and I pulled an apologetic face. 'Sorry! I just saw this. *Essential Boat Maintenance* – not very long but it'll do the job.'

He snorted, and I rolled my eyes. 'Funny.'

'Sorry, that's just usually my line.' He was chuckling now. I glanced down and then back up, sure he'd caught me looking, but he just continued. 'But yeah, no, that sounds like it might be helpful. I'll just have to copy down what I need.'

I flicked through the book doubtfully to cover my sudden embarrassment. 'Looks like a lot of diagrams. How good are you at drawing?'

'Not too bad actually,' he said wryly, as if making a private joke, then he peered down at the book. 'But not that good, what even are those symbols?'

'I'd say "Take a picture on your phone" but I've seen it and I doubt you'd be able to read anything if you used that thing.' I was hoping this offhand comment might prompt him to share the story behind that shady phone. Maybe he'd dropped his iPhone in the canal and it was just a stopgap until he got a new one. But he didn't offer any kind of explanation. Not that he owed me one at all, I was just sort of hoping he'd be able to put my doubts to rest.

'Too right,' he sighed. 'I suppose it'd be bad form to admit that the other option is to steal it – seeing as you used to work here. Though,' he leant in conspiratorially, warm breath tickling my cheek in a minty rush, 'that would mean you know all the security measures, you could help me out – make it an inside job and I'll cut you in for half the appendices?'

I could tell he was joking, but there was an air of slight desperation about him. He obviously needed the book and, for whatever reason, he seemed reluctant to get a library card sorted out. Which was a shame because it was useful to have, especially for someone in his position – the boat probably didn't even have internet. Free internet was the most popular service aside from the printers and the photocopier. The actual books weren't really on the top of anyone's list these days.

'The photocopier,' I realised, and snapped my fingers. 'We can copy the pages for you and you can take them.'

'Genius – see, knew it would pay to have insider knowledge,' Cooper said, seeming to relax now that we'd found a solution that didn't involve his lack of address or personal information. Interesting that. But it wasn't on me to pry.

I led him over to the photocopier – ancient and temperamental as always – directed him on which change it would accept and which it would simply swallow (anything round was a no-go – fifties and twenties only). The copier churned out warm pages with the incomprehensible diagrams on them. Cooper rolled them up and tucked them under his arm like a swagger stick, then offered me a salute.

'Cheers. Now I just need to work out what they say and if it's useful, and then how to implement it – easy.'

I laughed. 'Well, if you need any other books or a lift to Halfords, let me know. I know a bit about engines too – though that's mostly cars.'

'That's… unexpected,' Cooper said, then looked embarrassed. 'Jesus, that was awful – I sounded like my dad.'

'It's fine.'

He shook his head. 'It's really not. I'm sorry – I've spent the better part of thirty years trying to be just like him, but not any more. And that was a shitty thing to say. Sorry.'

The seriousness with which he was taking it was intense. I reached out and put my hand on his arm. He looked so angry with himself and the muscles under my hand were miserably tense.

'Thanks for apologising – I know I don't look like a car nut,' I said, trying to lighten the mood. 'I'm not, to be honest. I'd much rather let the mechanics do their thing. My dad is just a big believer in life skills. I can plaster too. Not well or anything, but passable.'

'Starting to think there's nothing you can't do,' Cooper said, relaxing under my touch. He didn't say it in the way Richard would have. In that 'all right, we get it' kind of way. He was dead serious and earnest. He was looking at me like I was this competent, put-together person. It felt good, having him look at me like that. Being allowed to be proud of myself without worrying he'd take it as some kind of slight.

I realised I still had my hand on his arm and let it fall. He glanced at my retreating fingers as if he wished they were still on him. My throat was suddenly dry.

'You know what they say – Jack of all trades, master of none. Except crochet,' I said, flustered.

'I'll remember that. Thanks.' He smiled at me and watched me for a beat too long, making me blush slightly. I hadn't realised how close we'd drifted together. His voice was low and we were in our own private world. 'I was actually heading back to the boat now, if you wanted to come back for a tea and a poke around the engine block – or just to check on the dog, you know. In case you were worried about him.'

'I'm sure you're taking good care of him – which is good because no one's claimed him yet. But yeah, tea and a dog cuddle sounds good,' I said softly.

I was thinking about Maeve and what she'd said about the biscuits. Had he planned to invite me back to his and it was just chance that he'd managed it so quickly? Or had they been intended for someone else?

Why did it matter? Just because he made me feel as if I was a person first and a woman second. Just because I was standing inches from him in the library and wishing he would kiss me. I was astounded at how badly I wanted him to. Had I ever wanted Richard this much? Ever felt this way before? The full – butterflies in my stomach, skin overheating, breath catching in my throat, practically giddy with it – need?

Outwardly I tried to seem normal, though inside I was alternating between the urge to kiss him and guilt over how quickly this was all happening after Richard. We kept chatting about the dog as we left the library. The sky had turned a menacing gunmetal grey and the air smelled of coming rain. Wonderful, maybe it would cool me off. I'd left my umbrella at the shop as well. My boucle coat wasn't exactly waterproof either.

'Poor bastard,' Cooper sighed, as we walked down the chilly street. 'I hope someone comes forward soon – he deserves to find his way home. He's a good dog, even if he is eating me out of house and home. Boat and home, whatever.'

'He at least deserves a name,' I said, easily keeping pace with him. Occasionally our arms swung in such a way that our fingers brushed – it was electrifying. What was wrong with me?

'Mmm, weird no one put it on his collar,' Cooper muttered. 'I've been…' He cut himself off, apparently embarrassed.

'What?' I couldn't help but ask, already half-smiling. 'You've been…?'

'It's nothing,' he waved me off, pulling his oversized waxed jacket tighter around himself. At the collar I could see the edge of the cashmere jumper poking out. I wondered if the jacket was something he'd bought at the charity shop or found on the boat. He didn't seem to have much stuff of his own that I'd seen and it was adorably big on him. I found myself thinking that I could easily fit inside it with him if I wrapped my arms around his waist. He'd probably offer too, if we were waiting in the cold.

'Come on, what?' I nudged him and he sighed, but he was smiling now too.

'I've been calling him Charlie. As in…'

'As in Charles and Lady Di,' I giggled. 'Does that make him the boat's official mascot?'

'Hey, I'm the official mascot – he's the captain.' A few raindrops fell and Cooper tucked the photocopied pages under his coat for protection. 'I think he knows more about that boat than I do. He's definitely been in all the nooks and crannies since he moved in. You should see some of the stuff he's dragged out of the little cubby holes. So many old doilies and dusty Dianas.' He shuddered theatrically. 'Haunting.'

'Or haunted.'

We were outside the shop now and the rain was pattering down. Not heavily as such, but leaving two-pence-sized dark splotches on the pavement. I ducked into the doorway and fumbled for my keys.

'Let me just get my umbrella a second.'

'All right, but you'll have to hold it – tall person's burden.'

I laughed. 'Okay, deal.'

I was trying to get the stiff old lock on the door to cooperate and was very glad that we were under cover. The scent of petrichor rose up, reminding me of school playgrounds at the end of summer, the first heavy autumnal showers driving us inside to play board games instead of skipping. I was so absorbed in the nostalgic scent that it took me a moment to realise that Cooper had stiffened beside me.

I glanced around and saw an unfamiliar car moving slowly past us. Obviously not a local – they were crawling along like they were looking for an address and were going the wrong way in the one-way system. Besides, I'd have remembered if anyone in Leaford had a shiny red BMW with a 2025 plate. I wasn't really a car person, but that really would have stood out amongst the school-run Land Rovers and banjaxed two-door runabouts of the local population. Myself included.

'Fancy,' I said, offhandedly, but Cooper didn't respond. Instead he turned towards the shop, hunching his shoulders inside his too-big jacket and dipping his head down. He was hiding, I realised. From the car and whoever was driving it.

A prickle went up the back of my neck. All the odd little things I'd noticed about him were suddenly not just quirks and slightly weird niggles, but a solid red flag waving in front of me. Burner phone, lack of personal details, jumpiness and now hiding from a strange, posh car. Cooper wasn't just an eccentric, he was actively trying to avoid something. Or someone.

The question was why?

And what was he so scared of?

Chapter 20

I FINALLY GOT THE door open and Cooper followed me inside, quickly closing the door behind us. Outside the rain was falling steadily now and I was fairly certain that between the rain on the windscreen and Cooper disappearing into his jacket, the person in the car couldn't have recognised him. I guessed he was thinking the same, because he visibly relaxed once we were inside.

'Bloody weather, eh?' he said, jerking a thumb towards the windows. It was too performatively casual, the way he said it. It was all wrong and my insides twisted uncomfortably. A moment ago I'd been desperate to kiss him, now I was doused in the cold realisation that I still barely knew him.

'Yeah,' I muttered, twisting one of my hands into my scarf anxiously. Was I really going to say something? But, in the end, it just sort of slipped out. 'So… what was that about?'

'What?' His expression was open and innocent, those brown puppy eyes big and confused. But underneath it there was a sliver of tension in his jaw. He knew I'd noticed something going on. I think we were both surprised I'd actually called him on it.

'You sort of freaked out a bit when that car came past. Like you were worried someone was going to jump out and grab you,' I said, trying to keep my voice light.

Rain rattled off the windows in the silence and Cooper was the first to look away, glancing down at the floor and shifting his boots around. I waited, and inside I could feel my good mood fading away. The temperature was dropping rapidly and it wasn't just the rain behind it. So it wasn't just Richard who'd lied to me. Were there any honest men at all?

What hurt the most was that I didn't even really have any right to feel upset or angry. Who was Cooper to me, really? I'd met him a handful of times and chatted a bit and yes, I'd felt a pull towards him. A spark there that I'd tried to ignore but maybe that had all been delusion. A weird aftershock of my break-up. Literally the day after I caught Richard cheating, I'd happened upon Cooper, and it was hard to ignore the implications of that. First the break-up, then the mysterious stranger – it was like a film. I'd let myself get carried away.

'Look, you don't have to tell me,' I said, as neutrally as possible. 'I know I don't have any right to know about your life, and it's none of my business, but… it's sort of obvious that you're worried about something, or someone. That you're running away or hiding… and if you want to talk about it, I'd like to help. If I can. You don't have to deal with it all by yourself.'

Cooper's jaw worked for a second and I watched the way his lip moved as he ran his tongue over his teeth, chasing words as he looked for something to say. I stood there, watching him and listening to the rain lashing down outside, and told myself that whatever he said next, I would try to be supportive and not let shock get the better of me. Even if he said he was on the run from a drug dealer, or that he'd stolen money from his last employer, or he had a wife and child somewhere. I could be a good friend. He clearly needed one.

Then he cleared his throat. 'You know what, you're right…'

I took a steadying breath.

'… it is none of your business.'

The words stung like a slap, not just because they were unexpected and mean, but because he was right. I didn't have any right to probe into Cooper's secrets. We were basically strangers. In fact, I felt it more so in that moment than I had when we'd first met. He was so cold and sharp, looking at me as if he'd caught me going through his things. I shivered and wrapped my arms around myself. Before I could think of anything to say to that, he'd turned and let himself out into the pouring rain.

'Cooper!' It burst out of me in shock. I ran to the door and threw it open, ignoring the jingling of the bell, which was quickly swallowed up by the downpour outside. 'Don't be ridiculous, it's pouring!'

But he was already running down the street, a blur in the rain, his hair plastered to his scalp. The shadows of the oncoming evening gobbled him up and I was left with just the rain and the hissing of a passing car. Damn it.

I shut the door and leant against it. It wasn't just the weather that had me trembling. I hadn't been afraid of Cooper at all – not when he'd shouted at me when we met, or when I was getting changed on his boat, not even when he randomly showed up while I was shopping. I wasn't afraid of him even now I knew he had a secret. But, at the same time, I did feel really, really stupid. Who was he really? He was just a random man that chance had thrown in my path. I didn't even know his first name. Yet I'd just trusted him immediately – borrowed his clothes and let him into my car, my home, into my shop after hours. I'd offered him the use of my business address only a half-hour ago.

Just me being a naïve, trusting little fool all over again. Exactly as I'd been with Richard. I sat down behind the counter, ashamed and angry with myself. Given all the risks I'd taken, I was lucky all I'd got was a scathing remark. He could easily have gone through my handbag while I was changing on the boat, or used my address to commit fraud. Whatever Cooper's secrets were, they were nothing I wanted to get involved with. Really, he'd done me a favour by throwing my concern in my face.

With my umbrella in hand, I left the shop and was careful to lock up properly. The time to be open and trusting was over. I'd let myself be taken advantage of twice now, by Richard and then by Cooper. Mum had always told me I was too idealistic, that I expected too much of people. Maybe she was right.

I knew where I needed to go.

Back at the flat I got into my car and drove over to my parents' house. It was still raining buckets and the stick-on butterflies on the front of the house were flapping wildly in the onslaught. I rushed to the front door and rang the bell. The distinctive sound of Mum's marabou-trimmed indoor wedges came slapping down the hallway. She was wearing a bright pink sweatshirt and offensively floral leggings, as if she was still clinging to summer. She took one look at me and her face fell.

'Oh… sweetie.'

I didn't quite throw myself into her arms, but it was close. Because she was so much shorter and slighter than me, she rocked backwards on her heels. Within a minute she'd hustled me into the living room and we were curled up on the blindingly cyan leather sofa she'd had specially made when I was a teenager. She picked up a white furry pillow and threw it at my dad in his armchair.

'Make us some tea, love.'

Dad fled to the kitchen and I heard him rattling spoons and mugs with purpose. I knew from experience that he would bring the tea and then vanish again, either to the pub or to the shed, his two safe zones whenever emotional upsets were detected. As long as there was someone else there to offer support, he was eager to duck out.

'What's up, sweetie? Is it work?' Mum asked, slowly stroking my back. I shook my head against her shoulder. Even though the shop was struggling and I had no idea how to fix it, or how I was going to even afford the rent on it in a few months. The awful feeling in my chest was not about pending financial ruin.

'… Richard?' Mum seemed reluctant to bring him up and I wondered if she was thinking of my hasty departure from her garden party. Maybe she did feel bad about that after all.

Dad returned with two cups of tea and moments later I heard his keys jingling as he left the house. It was probably too wet out for him to go down the garden to the shed. He'd have driven to the pub. Mum would text him the all-clear later once things were resolved.

I sat back and wiped at my face with my sleeve. Mum tutted and whisked a tissue from the bedazzled box on the table. I dabbed at my eyes and blew my nose.

'It's so stupid,' I muttered. 'I just… I feel like I've been a complete idiot, trusting all the wrong people and getting let down…'

'Oh, honey, it's not your fault for trusting him. He just made a mistake, that's all. It's nothing to do with you.' Mum rubbed my arm and looked at me ruefully. 'You mustn't blame yourself.'

I nearly let out a wet little laugh at that. Of course, now it wasn't my fault – now that I was literally sobbing on her sofa. Why did it take me breaking down to earn a bit of genuine concern? It was as if she couldn't tell I was upset without me bawling right in front of her. My own mother, who'd known me from birth, who'd raised me, couldn't tell when I was hurting.

I sucked in a stuttering breath. 'But there must have been red flags and I didn't see them. Didn't want to see them. Like an idiot,' I sighed. 'And then you asked me if I was sure I wanted to break up with him and now I'm… maybe I'm not sure and I'm just rethinking a lot of my choices lately and wondering if I should even be allowed to make my own decisions, because I keep making things worse.'

'Like what?' Mum asked, confused. 'Other than Richard…'

'Oh just…' I didn't want to talk about Cooper, it would take too much explaining. I'd feel like even more of an idiot telling Mum I'd been crushing on a stranger. 'With the shop. Like maybe starting a business wasn't the best idea. Like you said, I'm too idealistic. I went into it with a dream and now the reality is so much different. Just like with Richard.'

'Is the shop really not doing so well?' Mum asked softly. 'Do you need some money?'

'No! No, I don't want… I don't know, maybe I should stick it out. See it through, you know?' I sniffed. 'Giving up just because it's hard… I'd only be making it one hundred per cent my fault that it folded. At least if I try, I'll know it wasn't down to me not making an effort.'

'So…' Mum said carefully. 'Are you thinking about… giving him another chance? Putting the work in to forgive him?'

Just like that, the shop – my business – was waved aside. Mum had tunnel vision on my love life. The thing was, I hadn't been thinking about forgiving Richard. But sitting with her, talking about it, I was starting to wonder if that was exactly what I needed to do. Everything was falling apart and it had all started when I broke up with Richard. Had I binned off three years of my life and potentially left myself homeless and the owner of a failing business because I was too rigid to see that he was sorry?

He'd brought me flowers after all and hadn't snapped at Emma when she was (rightfully) mean to him. He'd been trying to win me back – talking to me, cleaning up after himself at the flat, trying to still give me money for shopping – and I'd been throwing it back at him out of anger. But was I really perfect? All right, so I hadn't cheated but I also hadn't really listened to any of his opinions about the inheritance money. Instead of setting up a joint business, I'd put it all into the shop and then basically ignored him for months while I worked on that.

I took a deep breath. 'I keep thinking about how you always used to tell me I expect too much of people – like, remember when I stopped being friends with Chelsea Walker in middle school?'

'Because she stole your pink gel pen,' Mum nodded, looking amused. 'I remember.'

'It wasn't that she stole it. It's that she just refused to admit she had. I mean, it was clearly mine, it was the same brand as all my pens and she only had the one of that kind. It was the same level of gel…' I cut myself off because this was well-worn ground. I'd been annoyed about it since I was ten. 'It wasn't that she took it. It's that she was so obviously lying and she just expected me to let it go.'

'I remember the fallout from that one. You two didn't speak for three weeks,' Mum sighed. 'But you made up in the end, didn't you? At the summer hog roast? I think because you realised it was just a silly little thing. It wasn't worth your entire friendship.'

I sighed. 'Yeah, we did make up. And then two years later she found out Jamie liked me, and she wanted to go out with him instead, so she told everyone I was a lesbian.'

'Well, there's nothing wrong with being a lesbian,' Mum said. 'So that says more about her than about you.'

'I know there's nothing wrong with…' I sighed, frustrated. Especially given that my mother had never acknowledged the fact that her own sister was gay. 'The point is, I forgave her for the first lie and then she told an even bigger one to get what she wanted. And then I got bullied by idiots over something that wasn't even true, and she went out with Jamie and ghosted me.' I screwed the tissue up into a ball and crushed it in one hand. 'What if I forgive Richard for a "one-time mistake" and next time he lets me down even worse? What if we get married and have kids…' I felt Mum twitch slightly like she was suppressing an excited fist-pump. '… and then he just walks out on me with someone else, leaving me looking like an even bigger fool than I do right now?'

I looked up and saw Mum nibbling her lip, gazing sideways at Dad's empty armchair (also hideously bright cyan with a Mongolian sheepskin cushion on it). She looked, for the first time since I'd arrived, kind of perturbed.

'Mum?' I asked, sensing something was off with her. Normally she was full of soothing platitudes, so long as she wasn't the cause of the upset. But right now, she was worryingly silent. 'What is it? What's wrong?'

Mum's eyes flew back to me and she looked a little wide-eyed and helpless. A fluffy bunny caught in the headlights. I'd never known her to be lost for words before.

'Sweetie…' she said eventually, 'I want to tell you something, and you have to promise me, that you won't let it... that you will try and understand. Okay?'

'... Okay?' I said, warily. Was she about to admit that she knew the sofa was blindingly awful and had done this entire time? Was she colour-blind? Because that would explain some things.

Mum took a deep breath. 'When we were first going out, your dad and I, long, long, before we were married and had you... your father cheated on me.'

My heart felt like it was being clenched in a fist. 'Dad cheated on you? With who? When? How long have you known about it?'

Mum held up her hands, cutting off my questions. 'Like I said, it was a very long time ago, and I don't want you to hold it against him, because we were very young, he was very sorry and I forgave him. It doesn't matter any more.'

'It does to me! I can't believe he'd do that,' I said, skin crawling in horror. 'He's... Dad.'

Mum laughed. 'He wasn't always "Dad", honey. Anyway, it was a few weeks after we started going out together and he went drinking with his friends. One thing led to another and they ended up at a house party... and he slept with someone else. I was furious and your dad was mortified... but after a while I forgave him.'

'Why?' I asked, trying to make this information match up with what I knew of my dad. My tool-hoarding, parking-charge-protesting dad. 'I mean, how could you forgive him? That's... unforgivable,' I finished lamely.

'I know it probably seems that way. But, in the end, I decided that I believed he was sorry and that when he said it would never happen again, he was telling the truth.' Mum shrugged, like it was just that easy. 'After the anger fizzled out... I realised I missed him. That I was just making myself miserable for the sake of being "right" and that maybe someday, years down the line, we'd be married and have a wonderful daughter... and that one night wouldn't mean anything compared with that.'

There was a lump in my throat as she looked at me. I could see she meant it. It wasn't just a story for my benefit, to convince me to give Richard another shot. Mum genuinely believed – knew – that she had made the right decision. That her marriage and her life with Dad was worth swallowing her pride over his one mistake and giving him a second chance.

'And you've never… regretted it?' I asked.

'He's never given me a reason to,' Mum said firmly. 'In all the years we've been married, he's never so much as looked at anyone else. I think he was so scared of losing me that, when I took him back, he couldn't believe his luck. I think he realised once he'd lost me, for those few days, the value of what he had.' She smiled slightly. 'Not to toot my own horn, of course.'

I laughed, but sobered quickly. 'I'm just… what if he's another Chelsea, instead of another Dad? What if he makes me look stupid?'

Mum covered my hand with her own, her engagement ring and wedding band warm against my skin. 'You weren't stupid to trust Chelsea again. She was an idiot for betraying your trust and losing you as a friend. So if you do decide to give Richard a second chance and he wastes his last shot with you, he's the idiot – not you. Don't let the fear of disappointment keep you from believing in people, sweetie. No one's perfect.'

'I know,' I said, and I thought of Cooper – who'd rescued me from the canal and charmed me, only to turn so cold and distant the second I asked a question he didn't like. 'I suppose you never really know what someone'll do if you give them a chance.'

'Exactly.' Mum smiled softly. 'All you can do is wait and see what they'll do with it.'

Chapter 21

I HAD A LOT to think about on the short drive home. Thankfully, the rain had petered out and I was left with the soft hushing of tyres on wet tarmac, accompanying my reeling thoughts.

Dad had cheated on Mum and she'd forgiven him. It was hard not to feel a bit weird about my dad being with someone other than Mum. Point of fact, it was weird to think of Dad at a party which she hadn't organised. But I was relieved that, when I probed my feelings over it, I didn't feel any resentment or anger towards him. I wasn't appalled at him on her behalf, because Mum had seemed so accepting of it as just a part of their story. This other woman, whoever she was in her nameless, faceless existence, was just a complication in my parents' rom-com. The halfway point before they got together and lived happily ever after with me and a flock of inflatable flamingos.

No, the real headline of the afternoon was that Mum had told me about it. I could count on one hand the number of times in my life that we'd had open, honest talks about stuff that actually mattered. Hell, I could count it on three fingers – Dad's cheating, when she gave me 'the talk' when I was eleven and when she told me where meat came from. That was it. This was actually the first time Mum had ever shared something really personal with me. I was kind of stunned. Maybe things were changing and we'd had a kind of breakthrough over the whole Richard situation. Maybe this was the start of us understanding each other and being close. I smiled at that. God, it would be great to finally be the kind of daughter who ran to her mum with things, instead of avoiding her.

As I manoeuvred through the drenched roads of Leaford, I found myself imagining a future where I forgave Richard. We'd talk it out and he'd promise to never betray me again. Sure, things would be cold and awkward for a while but we'd get past it and back to normal eventually. Parties at Mum and Dad's, weekly shops together, curling up in bed at the end of the day – our lives would be as they were. Then Richard would propose, with red roses and dinner, a classic move. We'd announce it and my family would be thrilled, his too. I'd go dress shopping with his mother and my mum, sample cakes and pick floral arrangements. Mum would tell me all about what married life was really like over wine. She'd tell me all the little secrets and tips to make it work and cry on my wedding day. We'd marry and honeymoon and soon I'd find out I was pregnant and we would focus on creating a perfect home for our first child. Mum would be there at the birth, coaching me through it.

One day in the future I might sit that child or those children down and explain to him, her or them that once, a long time ago, their father made a stupid mistake. But that all this – the house full of family pictures and shared memories, every picnic and beach day and even their very existence, had come about because I forgave him. That together we had worked through it and that what we had now was worth the temporary awkwardness.

I pulled up outside the block of flats and imagined a second scenario. Me, alone, in a house share in my forties. My business having failed and the library having not taken me back on. I'd be working somewhere boring and soul-destroying and coming home to no one but the twenty-somethings who avoided me like the plague. Going over to my parents' house at the weekend while they tiptoed around the subject of dating and children. That fledgling closeness with Mum having died a death as I spurned her advice and ignored the fact that she'd opened her inner life to me. Getting dressed up and going on a few dates before I lost interest or the will to make conversation. Or before the man I'd met revealed some secret or snapped at me and I walked away. But at least I'd know that I was the better person. The better, lonely, sad little person.

I got out of the car with a sigh and went inside, taking the lift up to the flat. Maybe Mum was right – I couldn't be sure Richard wouldn't make another mistake but, at least if he did, I'd have tried to make things work instead of giving up and wondering what might have been. I'd have a child, a marriage, instead of nothing.

'Tabitha?'

I looked up in shock at the sound his voice. The last I'd expected to hear.

'Richard?'

He was standing by the front door, his pea coat black with rain. He looked small and apologetic, like a wet puppy. For a moment I wondered if he was drunk and looking for a place to sleep it off again but, as I moved closer, I could tell he was sober. There wasn't a whiff of alcohol about him and he looked miserably present.

'I came to… well, I need to get my things, but more than that…' he sighed helplessly. 'I wanted to say I'm sorry. I really am and… I'm even sorrier for not respecting that you needed space. So… I'm going to leave you alone, once I've grabbed the last of my stuff.'

My first instinct was still to deliver a sarcastic retort. To make him feel even worse, but with Mum's words still swimming around my brain, I resisted.

'Thanks… come in.' I let him into the flat and watched him start looking through the kitchen cabinets and depositing protein-shake tubs and sports bottles into a bag for life.

'Do you want a tea?' I asked.

'Mmm? Oh, sure,' he smiled at me shyly. 'Got a bit caught in the rain when I popped to the shop for some bags.'

I held out a hand. 'Let me put your coat on the heated airer.'

He looked pleasantly surprised by the offer and handed it over to me. Once I'd plugged the airer in and draped the coat over it, I made two mugs of tea and slid one across the counter to him. By that time, Richard was packing his car-cleaning stuff from under the sink.

'I uh… went to see Mum today,' I said, breaking the silence. 'Had a bit of a weird day all round, to be honest.'

'Is it the shop?' Richard frowned.

'No… not really. But I went over there just to have a chat, you know what it's like when you just need to go home for a bit.'

'Yeah.' Richard took a seat on one of the breakfast-bar stools and gave me a slight smile. 'I've been going to see Dad more than usual since… mostly he just tells me I'm an idiot and that you deserved better – which is true.'

I huffed a laugh. Richard's dad had always liked me. He thought I was a 'good match' for his son, probably because I was different from Richard's exes, most of whom would have been at home competing on *The Apprentice*. His mother had never really treated me badly but she'd been a bit cool to me ever since I'd brought homemade tiramisu to her New Year's Eve party. This was apparently interpreted as me 'showboating' my baking skills. Which was laughable, because I couldn't bake, the sum total of my skills with dessert could be described as 'assembling'. No matter how many times I complimented her pre-packaged petits fours, the insult had already been dealt. Still, we got along fine outside of that.

'Well, mine told me I should give you another chance,' I said. It just sort of came out. I was still too busy processing to engage my filter.

Richard looked at me, hope evident in his dark eyes. He looked so soft and hesitant that for a moment he wasn't my ex who cheated on me; he was the man I'd fallen for when we'd met by chance at the library.

Thinking of the library brought Cooper to mind and I felt a stab of shame and annoyance at myself. I'd really misjudged things with him and made an idiot out of myself. What else had I been wrong about – the shop? Leaving Richard?

I took a deep breath. 'It turns out Mum knows a little bit about second chances and forgiveness and if she didn't, then I wouldn't be here, so… there's that.'

Richard swallowed hard. 'So… does that mean you're… that you want to give us a second chance?' He lowered his voice. 'Give *me* a second chance?'

There it was, the pivotal moment in all my imagined futures. Forgive or walk away. I looked at Richard, really looked at him. The man I'd been with for three years, through birthdays and summer holidays, broken appliances and heatwaves, lazy Sunday mornings and getting stuck on the M25. We had a life together and a history. Ballast, to keep us grounded. He wasn't some mysterious stranger with a pack of secrets and no first name in a house that could literally float away. He was a good bet, a solid guy. For the future.

'… I think so,' I said quietly. 'If you can promise it won't happen again, then…'

'It won't.' He reached out and took my hand, earnest and intense. 'Tabs, I love you. I want to spend the rest of my life with you. She meant nothing to me. Less than nothing. And I know that doesn't make it better – shit, it makes it worse – but I would give anything to go back and never make such a stupid mistake again. I know now that… you're everything. You mean everything to me.'

My eyes welled up, an ache in my chest making me sniffle. Richard set his mug down and rounded the counter. He put his arms around me and held me to his chest. It felt so familiar and safe. He smelled the way he always did, like Paco Rabanne 1 Million and flat whites. He pressed his cheek against the top of my head.

'I'm so, so sorry, Tabs,' he said softly. 'Not just for what you walked in on but… I shouldn't have sold the stuff you made for my family. I shouldn't have blown up about it but I think I was just angry because the only other option was feeling guilty and I couldn't take it.'

I sniffled into his chest, half laughing, half crying. It was so Richard – the way he'd said it. But he meant it. Hearing him finally admit to what he'd done, instead of brushing it off, had brought me to the edge of tears. The anger drained out of me. He knew he was in the wrong. He knew and he was admitting it to me. For the first time ever, really, in our relationship. Just like things with Mum, this felt like a watershed. We were growing, together.

'Why didn't you give them their presents when I made them?' I asked, sniffling. 'Why lie to me about it?'

Richard was silent for a long moment and then he sighed. 'You remember the tiramisu fiasco – they would have seen it as showing off or something. But you liked making the stuff so much and I couldn't bring myself to tell you the truth… so I just bought gift sets and said they were from you.'

I pulled away a little bit and looked him in the eye. Despite the quaver in his tone, his eyes were dry, but he looked deeply apologetic. 'You have to promise that we're going to be honest with each other from now on.'

'I will,' he said immediately. 'Completely and totally honest… Tabs… were you seeing someone else? The guy from the boat that's been hanging around town? I don't care if you were, but I just want to know.'

I shook my head. 'No. It was just… I don't know what I thought was going to happen but it was just a few chance meetings. Nothing happened.' My heart felt heavy, sore as if it was bruised. Nothing had happened. So why did I feel so sad, so lost?

Richard seemed to relax a little.

'And… her,' I said, hating myself. 'The woman you were with… is she…?'

'She's gone,' Richard said quickly. 'I haven't spoken to her since that day, just told her it was all a mistake and it was never going to happen again. I meant it, Tabs. I only want you.' He cupped my face. 'I want a future with you.'

I sniffed, offering him a watery smile. 'I want that too.'

We hugged tightly and he kissed my cheek. It all felt so familiar and so safe. Looking at him, I saw all the little parts of him that I'd come to know and love – the tiny mole on his cheek, the one hair that grew against the grain in his left eyebrow. The way the tip of his nose brushed my cheek when he kissed it. He was the Richard I'd known for years now – my Richard. Of Richard and Tabitha. No more secrets, no more uncertainty.

We went to bed that night in our room, the first time I'd slept in there since we'd broken up. When I woke up in the morning beside him, it felt like a return to normalcy, to routine. Like the first morning in your own bed after the long journey home from a stressful trip.

It was over. The whole messy episode. Richard had apologised and we'd recommitted to each other. I looked at his sleeping face, his nose adorably scrunched as he dreamed. This was the man I wanted to marry and have kids with. And just as it had with my parents, it would all work out eventually.

After so many days and weeks of uncertainty and worry, everything was back to normal. And yet, as I got up and checked my phone, finding a text from Emma, I felt slightly ashamed. What was she going to say about me getting back with Richard after she'd spent so long supporting and reassuring me? What if she was disappointed in me?

I brushed my teeth, searching my own face in the mirror. Did it matter if Emma disapproved or didn't understand? What mattered was that I was happy. And I was.

At least I would be.

Eventually.

Chapter 22

'YOU'RE... BACK TOGETHER?'

I took a sip of my tea, looking away from Emma as she gaped at me. The shop was empty, as per usual for that soon after opening. We were sitting by the counter and having our morning tea as we exchanged plans for the weekend. Emma had just finished telling me about an axe-throwing date she'd decided to go on with a woman she'd met online and so I'd passed on my own nugget of news.

She looked upset but also worried, like I'd just told her I planned to quit the shop and become a nun. She looked at me like I wasn't making any sense at all.

'Yeah... he apologised again. He seems to really mean it, so...' I shrugged, hoping she'd drop the subject if I could just telegraph how nonchalant I was about it. 'So have you seen this axe-throwing babe before or...?'

But she wasn't taking the bait. 'Tabitha, I'm happy if you're happy, you know that but... I'm just a bit worried because you were so heartbroken and so sure you were done with him. This feels like a massive one-eighty and I just want to make sure it wasn't... caused by something major.'

'Like?' I asked.

Emma looked really uncomfortable now. 'I don't know, the housing situation maybe? Or you're worried about starting to date again? It just feels like maybe you're sort of rebounding on Richard... with Richard.'

I felt my face start to grow hot. 'I'm not "rebounding", I'm just… being realistic, for a change.'

That only seemed to deepen Emma's confusion. 'What do you mean "for a change"? When have you not been realistic? I thought you were handling things really well since he moved out.'

'Well, look at this place for starters,' I said, my flush deepening. 'I had this big dream about a yarn shop and I didn't really think it through. I just acted on a whim. I haven't managed to do anything to bring sales in. I just started this without any sense of what was realistic. I mean, a shop like this in a town this small? It makes no sense and we're probably going to have to close down eventually.'

'… Oh,' Emma said, crestfallen. Her eyes were huge with worry. 'You're closing the shop? What about the Stitch and Witch? When were you going to tell me I'd be looking for a new job?'

'No! We're not closing, like, right now.' I was getting flustered now. Why wouldn't she just leave it alone? 'I'm not planning to at the moment but, come on, it's hardly buzzing in here, is it? It feels like we're on borrowed time and have been since we opened. I'm sorry… I thought that was obvious.'

'But what does that have to do with Richard?' Emma persisted, her expressive eyes narrowing. She tilted her head like a particularly savvy crow, her long gemstone earrings swaying. 'Is this whole "reunion" about money worries, because, if it is, you know I'll help any way I can, you're not alone…'

'It's just about me planning for the future,' I said, standing up and taking my mug to the back in an attempt to forestall further comment. My hands were shaking. 'I'm nearly thirty and everyone I went to school with is getting married and has kids. Kids plural! I can't just keep wishing and hoping that I'll get the life I want. I have to do something about it.'

'And that something is settling for Richard?' Emma asked, coming to stand in the doorway. 'Is he really who you see yourself spending the rest of your life with? Thirty isn't dead – you've got decades of life left after that.'

'I know, and I'm not settling, I'm being realistic. He's a successful, intelligent, stable guy.' It had all been so clear last night – why was she doing this to me now? I could feel a headache coming on.

'And he cheated on you. What's to stop him doing it again?' Emma pointed out, unnecessarily in my opinion. I'd been there after all, I'd seen it. It happened to me, not her. Embarrassment was turning to annoyance as this conversation continued.

'And he said he was sorry, so I forgave him. That's what adults do. They talk through their problems and fix them,' I said, my voice sharper than I'd intended it to be. 'They don't throw salt at it and wish it away. It's time to grow up!'

As soon as the words were out, I wanted to snatch them back. I hadn't meant to throw in an insult to Emma's witchy beliefs, but it was too late. I saw it land. I saw it hurt her and watched as she quickly covered that hurt up, as if she didn't trust me with it. That was almost worse than seeing it to begin with.

'Emma…' I began, stomach churning with guilt. 'I'm sorry—'

'It's fine,' she cut me off, but her lip was quivering. 'Look, I need to restock the embroidery floss, so I'll get on that.'

She vanished to the other side of the shop and I wrapped my arms around myself, feeling awful. She was obviously desperate to get away from me so she wouldn't have to pretend not to be upset. Nothing needed restocking. The loaded shelves were hung with discount signs as it was. We'd barely opened for the day and had refilled the shelves yesterday to get ready for an influx of sale customers who were probably never coming. She was avoiding me. No wonder, really, after I'd snapped at her for just being worried about me. Snapped and personally insulted her in the same breath.

Ever since we'd met, I'd known how important her spirituality was to her. Although I didn't really believe in all that stuff, I'd always respected the fact that she did. We could make fun of each other about a lot of things, but I left that alone. Until today, when I'd felt backed into a corner and under pressure. The worst time to suddenly go right for her biggest insecurity.

To my shame, I hid away in the back for a while, afraid to come out and face her. I was thinking about how much time she'd given me since I broke up with Richard. How she'd come to the flat with booze and snacks, covered for me at the shop, sent him away just because I asked. I'd just thrown all that back in her face. I'd taken Richard back and now she had to be wondering where she stood after basically talking shit about him with me for weeks now. Obviously, she had a right to be worried. She'd been involved in the whole mess from the start.

The thing was I didn't really know what to say to her. I'd never taken someone back after a break-up before, let alone one as fraught as the one I'd had with Richard. I'd never even imagined I would, not until Mum told me all about what happened with Dad. That had really shifted my perspective.

The rest of the day was tense and stressful. I kept wanting to apologise but the words just wouldn't come. I'd manage to say her name and then end up offering her a cup of tea or something so banal it made me want to curl up and die. The only respites from the awkwardness came when a customer wandered in or when we took our lunch breaks. Aside from that, we worked in a tense silence punctuated by overly polite offers of tea or comments on the work that needed doing.

The arrival of some bills did not improve things. Our first electricity bill had come in and was much higher than I'd been expecting. The cost of keeping all the yarn free of damp by having the heating on in the badly insulated shop was astronomical. I could have cried when I saw the amount. I needed to do something.

To escape the tension for a while, I dived into everything I'd been too preoccupied by the break-up to do, namely, actually trying to save my business. Looking at the optimistically misnamed 'profit' spreadsheet, I could see in black and red that we were spiralling towards closure. If I didn't do something drastic, we'd be closing down before the rent was due, because we wouldn't be able to afford insurance or to keep the lights on.

So I put a post on the local Facebook group, offering 'to-go crochet kits' with instructions and materials. Then I widened that to the local pages for the next five villages and two towns. I typed up instructions and tried my best to make them look cutesy, then dug the supply of brown paper carrier bags out of the storage cupboard and lined them up as if I was making packed lunches for fifty people in the break room. A ball of yarn, a basic five-millimetre hook, snippers, and a blanket needle taped to a business card. I only hoped people came to buy one.

Towards the end of the day, I got an email from Emma asking for annual leave for the next three days, finishing out the week. I felt blindsided and upset but what else could I do but approve it? I wasn't going to force Emma to be around me. God, what were we going to do about her coven coming in for a craft session? That was going to be fraught, if it was even still happening now.

By closing time, I was miserable and still desperately wanted to apologise for my comment. But as soon as I started closing up, Emma squeaked out an excuse about trying to get home early for a delivery and left. I closed up by myself, unable to blame her for making her escape so quickly. Maybe tomorrow I could message her to say sorry and then, when she returned to work after her time off, I could bring her in some breakfast and apologise properly.

With the shop closed, I stood on the pavement and contemplated going home. Richard would be in soon and he'd said he was going to cook for me, which was nice of him. Probably his go-to of lasagne with red wine and garlic bread. He was obviously really trying to make an effort and I appreciated that. Even so, I didn't want to go straight from the atmosphere at the shop to the flat, taking all this tension with me. It was the last thing we needed on our first day back together.

I wandered vaguely instead, trying to dispel the lump in my throat and the twist in my belly. I was thinking about what would go into arranging crochet and knitting classes at the shop and if the outlay on nibbles and drinks would be worth it, plus the extra electricity used being open for an added two hours.

The weather had turned sticky since the rain, humid and clammy. It wasn't really great weather for a walk, much less in a long cardigan and UGGs, but I refused to give up. A bit of clean air would improve my mood, even though that air felt as if it had been recently microwaved.

It was hard to say whether I noticed I was walking towards the towpath or not. Maybe it was intentional and I was just deluding myself, or maybe it was coincidence. But I found myself walking that way anyway. The canal was its usual languid self, green and still, aside from the dimples of water bugs and the occasional commotion of ducks somewhere under the willows. A few decorations had escaped containment from the town centre and solar-powered light-up ghosts gathered under the trees. There were mini-pumpkins and gourds along the back of the benches by the path.

The further I went up the towpath, the slower I was walking. What if I met Cooper? What if I didn't? What was it exactly that I was hoping for? I could imagine bumping into him and getting a gruff apology for his snappiness yesterday. Or he might just ignore the issue like my parents usually did. What if he was still angry at me for prying?

If I did see him, I could tell him I was back with Richard. But why would I? It wasn't even his business – and what reaction was I even hoping for? He wouldn't care. I was literally a stranger to him.

I just missed him. Which was crazy. We'd barely known each other a month. I didn't even know him at all. But still I wanted to see him, to talk to him. So badly that it made my chest hurt.

All of this was on my mind as I rounded the bend in the path and looked towards the viaduct. My heart dropped and I felt for one horrible moment as if I might cry. The strength of my reaction surprised me. If I hadn't spent the day walking on eggshells around Emma, perhaps it wouldn't have hit me so sharply. But, as it was, when I looked upstream and saw that the peeling green boat was gone, it felt like coming home to find my front door kicked in. Like something safe and certain had been ripped away from me.

Even though it was pointless, I walked the rest of the way to the viaduct itself. The boat was gone, with nothing but a flattened patch of yellowish grass to show where the boarding plank had been. Not so much as a cigarette end to indicate that Cooper had been there at all. The thoughtful, civic-minded bastard.

What had I been expecting? A note addressed to me and weighted down with a stone? Some sort of folksy sign of goodbye, like a whittled rose or half a Charles and Diana plate, split down the middle and left for me. Matching the cup that was sitting on my bedside table, full of hair grips, making me smile whenever I saw it. No, there was nothing. Not even a note about Charles the dog or what I should do if someone did message me about him.

Standing there like a lemon was just making me feel worse. I walked back the way I'd come and sat down on the first scarred and well-scrawled bench I came across, my back to the cutesy pumpkins. I didn't want to leave the canal entirely. That felt like giving up. Even though I knew logically that Cooper wasn't about to come steaming upriver, having just popped to Asda in his home.

Was it my fault that he was gone? I felt my insides twisting about unpleasantly. I'd asked questions about his past and tried to get him to be vulnerable with me. Now he was gone. It was hard not to draw a line between those things and call them cause and effect. He was obviously troubled by something, trying to leave something or someone behind. I'd got in the way of that.

But then, as my panic started to recede a little, I gave myself a little shake. It was very self-involved to think that I was the sole reason Cooper might have left the area overnight. He'd seen that car after all, that was why we'd had our falling-out. That car that had been crawling down the street as if looking for something. The car that didn't belong in Leaford, as far as I could remember.

A cold little ball of worry settled in my chest. Had whatever Cooper was trying to get away from finally caught up with him? The person in the car might have recognised him after all. It had driven in the direction of the towpath and the car park. The same way Cooper had bolted after I'd questioned him. They could have parked up and seen him rush past, then followed him to the boat.

Who was it? I'd worried he was involved in something shady – something criminal. Perhaps he'd stolen money or fled debts and that was all catching up with him here. Maybe I ought to be going to the police and letting them know that he might have been kidnapped or forced to leave?

Then again, maybe his issues were more personal than that. I had no idea if he had a wife or a child he'd run out on. What if he was just a deadbeat trying to stay off-grid to avoid spousal or child support? Someone had probably thought he was a good, safe bet, and he'd let them down. Just went to show, you couldn't predict the future. You just had to take a chance.

I stood up and dusted my skirt off. At the end of the day, was it any of my business? Without any indication that Cooper was in real, imminent trouble, I couldn't exactly alert the authorities. It was probably just the local busybodies that had finally moved him on and he'd left because, well… why would he stay? There was nothing to keep him in Leaford.

Nothing at all.

Chapter 23

'Hey, you're back late,' Richard called from the hob as he whisked cheese into a béchamel sauce. The air was full of the scents of garlic and tomatoes. I'd been right about the lasagne. Normally, it was one of my favourites, and the one indulgent thing he made, but just then the thought of eating anything made me want to cry.

'Yeah… sorry. Things at work got a bit… complicated,' I said, dumping my bag and cardigan on the sofa and going to sit on one of the bar stools. I propped my elbows on the counter and watched as Richard started layering up the lasagne.

'Sounds tough, at least you're here now,' Richard offered, glancing up and giving me a quick smile. I tried to offer one back, but inside I was urging him to ask me what was wrong. I needed to talk about Emma and the argument. It was eating me up.

After a few minutes of silently watching him assemble the pasta dish and put it in the oven, I cleared my throat. 'Emma and I had an argument. A sort of… falling-out. Earlier.'

'Mmm?' Richard poured two glasses of wine and slid one over to me. 'What about?'

I winced. 'She was a bit surprised we were back together, that's all. I ended up being quite short with her. I insulted her beliefs and I don't really know how to make things right.'

Richard stopped swirling his wine and scoffed. 'Her "beliefs" are cuckoo, though, aren't they? I mean, you don't believe in all that witchy-woo stuff so why should you pretend to for her sake?'

I felt my back stiffen. 'I might not believe in it but she does. I don't have to pretend to believe in anything to make her happy but, at the same time, it was out of order to throw it in her face and insult something that's important to her because I was upset.'

He raised his eyebrows. 'Upset about what? If she upset you, it's hardly your fault an argument started.'

'She wasn't *trying* to upset me…' I started and then, as I looked at him, I realised I didn't have the energy to explain it all if he wasn't going to listen properly. 'It doesn't matter. I'll deal with it on Monday when she's back from annual leave. She booked the rest of the week off today.'

'Today?' Richard gave me a look. 'Are you sure you want to set the precedent that she can book leave with basically no notice? I mean, I know she's your friend and everything but she's also your employee. She needs to remember that and so do you – especially if she's causing issues for you at work.'

'She isn't "causing issues",' I sighed. 'Besides, it's not like there's any reason she can't have leave. We're not rushed off our feet. Honestly, there's barely any work for two people there at the best of times.'

'Hmm,' Richard hummed contemplatively. 'So… why not let her go?'

'Fire her?' I said, aghast. 'I can't do that.'

'Well, you just said you don't need her working there, so that'd save you quite a bit of money, right?' Richard pointed out, tapping his fingers on the counter. His gold signet ring rapped on the marble. 'I get that she was useful during the renovations but is keeping her on a wise business move?'

I picked up my glass of wine and took a hasty gulp. It unfortunately didn't do anything to calm the swarm of ants scuttling and biting in my stomach at the thought of letting Emma go. She wasn't just 'useful' during the renovations. She did half the work, alongside me. She was there at all hours helping me to paint and strip wood and lay rat traps. She was the one who'd driven said traps out into the distant countryside to release the confused rats into the wild. Even if there wasn't a huge amount of work at the shop now, she was still making stock for me. Her stitch markers were moving well now that I had managed to list them for sale on the website and she was keeping me company and bolstering my resolve to keep the shop going. Hell, she was coming up with ideas to try to bring more business in.

'Well, she's still contributing a lot – like the Stitch and Witch.'

'The… what?' Richard looked at me like I'd just said I was going to teach dogs to make mittens.

'It's like a "stitch and bitch", where you chat about stuff and do crafts? But it's her coven, so a bunch of witches talking about stuff while I teach them to make tarot bags and things.'

Richard's eyebrows were in his hairline, but he didn't say anything. He didn't need to. It was beyond obvious that he thought it was a stupid idea.

I wanted to defend Emma and her ideas to Richard but I was just so tired already from the long day. He'd have an argument for every point I could raise and he wouldn't drop it until he felt as if I'd come around to his way of thinking. For the sake of some peace, I just shrugged noncommittally and turned away on my stool, hoping he'd let it go.

'How was your day at work?' I asked as a distraction, and Richard launched into a story about a house he'd been showing for a few months now with no real interest. Mostly due to all the underlying issues the property developer hadn't banked on when they built the place.

'I had a new couple viewing it today – first-time buyers, very eager – they couldn't believe the price on it. I mean it's three bedrooms for a hundred and forty thousand, where else are you going to find that round here? 2002? New build as well, they were over the moon, practically offered to name their first-born after me.' Richard's mouth curled scornfully. 'Then the bloke ruined it all – walked right out the back door while she was talking my ear off about schools in the area. I never let buyers out back, always say I've not got the key for the doors, but the bloody gardener had left them unlocked.'

'What happened?' I asked, because Richard had previously told me that the entire bit of decking outside the back door was unstable, due to the mining history of the area. It had kind of troubled me that they were even trying to sell the place. But Richard had pointed out that if not his firm, some other estate agent would do it. I pushed aside the thought that I remembered all that, yet Richard still couldn't remember the difference between knitting and crochet. That was the old, immature Tabitha talking.

'He went straight through the deck is what happened,' Richard rolled his eyes. 'Screamed like a girl too. I had to help him out and then, of course, it was sort of obvious that the concrete under it was all broken up and they started asking questions about the rest of the house. Once he said "subsidence", I knew it was game over. Bloody *Homes Under the Hammer*'s got everyone too clued up for their own good.' He took a swig of wine and shrugged. 'Still, better luck next time. The developer's going to slap a bit of cement over the cracks. It'll be fine.'

'Jesus!' I pulled a face. 'Sounds like he should be reported.'

Richard chuckled. 'Eh, "buyer beware" and all that, you know? They should have seen that price and known it was way too good to be true. Some things are just too perfect to believe.'

I thought of Cooper and how easy it had been to talk to him and warm to him. How he'd remembered how much I'd said the blanket cost and followed all the crochet washing directions religiously. I held my tongue because Richard was right. Some things were too good to be true. At least you knew where you were with an obvious fixer-upper.

While the lasagne cooked, I opened WhatsApp and tried a couple of times to get an apology to Emma written out. I struggled to get across how sorry I was for snapping at her but, after a few attempts, I had something that sounded right.

Hi Emma, I'm really sorry about today. I was completely out of line with what I said and I didn't want to give the impression that I don't respect what you believe. I know you were just concerned for me and I'm sorry for blowing up at you. Just wanted to say this now, and I will apologise when you're back in at work. Enjoy your time off and don't stress about anything – it's all on me. Sorry again.

I sent it off and crossed my fingers for luck. Hopefully Emma would see it and then not worry about our argument on her days off. I was still going to apologise when I saw her again, but the idea of leaving this hurt to fester for days didn't sit right with me. With that message sent, I felt a tiny bit better and hoped that it would ease any worries Emma had.

A notification popped up for Facebook. Maeve had sent me something from the local group. I opened it to find a picture of the canal. It must have been taken after Cooper left, because the caption said 'FINALLY!!!!' Before I could think better of it, I clicked into the comments.

I was quickly reminded why I tended to avoid Facebook these days – at least for non-work-related stuff. Almost every comment was a nasty remark about 'cleaning up the area' and 'bringing down the tone'. Most people were calling 'the bloke on the boat' a dosser or a shifty character. I wondered how many of them had actually met Cooper or even seen him. As far as I knew, he'd kept himself to himself. He'd certainly left no traces by the canal, not even an empty crisp packet.

One or two people – Maeve amongst them – were scolding people for being so closed-minded and aggressive when he'd literally done nothing to anyone. Some others were speculating about where he might have gone. They were tagging friends and family in the surrounding area to ask if the boat had come through. I found myself reading every comment, looking for a hint as to where Cooper had moored The Lady Di now. As soon as I realised what I was doing, I exited the app and put my phone down.

I made a green salad to go with the lasagne and Richard and I sat down to eat. He told me some more about work and I mostly just nodded and let him talk. I didn't have any stories of my own that I wanted to share. Aside from the fact he wouldn't get half of them without me explaining stuff, they just reminded me of Emma and Cooper – and that made my stomach clench up with guilt.

After I'd put everything in the dishwasher and washed up the lasagne pan, we watched some TV and then went to bed. As soon as we were both under the duvet, Richard moved in for a cuddle. I snuggled up with him and tried to relax, but my brain was awash with guilt and muddled anxiety about the shop. After a while, Richard started stroking my back and that turned into skimming his hands progressively further under my pyjama bottoms.

'Rich…' I muttered, and shifted away a little. He took this as a cue to get into the crook of my neck, kissing and nibbling. 'I'm really tired.'

He stopped and sighed, then rolled onto his back. 'Okay… night then.'

Before too long he was snoring and I was left wide awake and staring at the ceiling. In the dark I lay there thinking about crochet kits, Aunt Lou, electricity bills, Emma, taxes and Mum. My mind was a horrible alphabet soup of HMRC jargon and personal drama. Sleep wasn't in my budget. Sleep was for business owners who had the slightest clue if they'd have a business in three months.

I thought my way through the forest of work worries and found myself thinking about how Lou hadn't had anyone in her life after her 'friend' Gail passed away. Maybe she'd been too heartbroken or maybe no one else had met her standards. Gail, she used to tell me, was one of a kind – a true and honest friend. The other half of her soul, who just knew her. They clicked from the moment they met in a dog-walking group. As far as I knew, Lou hadn't been close to many other people and she'd obviously had no children, no one to leave her worldly things to but me. She'd ended up alone.

Then my brain, unwilling to let me just get some ruddy sleep, turned to Mum. She'd been married to my dad for over thirty years. They spent every day together, pretty much. They'd had me, bought a house, and built a lifetime of memories. All because Mum had forgiven Dad for his one mistake.

That was the choice I was making, I thought to myself, awake in the dark. I could end up alone with my high standards and my romantic ideals. Or I could have something real and solid.

I only had to let myself be happy with what I had, instead of thinking about anything, or anyone, else. I just wished I could convince myself of that long enough to get some sleep.

Chapter 24

The 'Emma-less' days at the shop were awful.

It wasn't as if it was hard work. I'd been honest with Richard that there wasn't really enough to do to justify two full-time workers. But the fact that I could handle the workload alone easily didn't change the fact that I missed having Emma around. Missed our chats and our jokes, the companionable tea breaks and watching her rearrange her crystals and charms around the place. I missed my friend.

The shop had literally never been cleaner or more organised. I tried to distract myself with all the little tasks that would normally take me a week or so to get round to. But by the middle of day two, I really had nothing left to do except sit and wait for customers to come in. The crochet kits were moving, but slowly. All in all, not a great time.

It was only made worse when Margaret popped in. I came out of the back room and she was just… there. It had been so long since I'd seen her anywhere else that I'd sort of started to believe she couldn't leave the charity shop, as if it was a crypt warded with holy symbols that kept her locked up. When I came out and saw her, I actually shrieked.

Peering over her varifocals, Margaret favoured me with a stare of disapproval.

'Not wise to leave the till unattended,' she said.

'No… I suppose not,' I said, not wanting to risk starting a conversation by pointing out that I'd been two feet away, behind a bead curtain. It wasn't as if I'd left the shop or been sat back there, drinking shots with my headphones in.

She wandered around, poking at various items before selecting a single needle-threader from a basket of them on the counter (fifteen pence), which she paid for in small change. She left without another word and I was genuinely torn between finding the entire exchange amusing or irritating.

Things at home weren't much better than they were at the shop. Richard and I were back together and that was… fine. Things were back to normal and our routine was as easy as ever to get lost in. But I couldn't quite seem to convince my body to let go of all the stress and annoyance that had built up towards Richard in our time apart.

For example, on Saturday, the last day that I would be running the shop without Emma, I was making breakfast when Richard woke up. Just a quick feta omelette with a handful of spinach wilted on top. He went straight for the Nutribullet and made himself his morning shake but, as it was blending, he wrapped his arms around me from behind.

And I flinched.

He gave me a quick kiss on the cheek and let me go, but I could tell it bothered him. A lot. We hadn't had sex since getting back together and I'd been reluctant to cuddle in bed because he kept trying to initiate. I just wasn't ready. Worse, I kept thinking about Cooper and how I'd brushed against him in the book-nook. That thrill of excitement it had sent through me. I couldn't feel that for Richard right now. I didn't know if I ever would again and that was really depressing.

Once I'd eaten, he made me a coffee in my travel mug and our hands brushed as he handed it over. They were warm and soft as always, but the goosebumps that rose up on my skin weren't from excitement. They were a side effect of my skin crawling as I tried to smile gratefully and take the cup from him.

It was a relief to get out of the flat and walk to work. It had only been a few days. Things would get easier eventually, I was sure of it. Maybe it would be a good idea to ask Mum how long it had taken her to let go of the past and be present with Dad again after he'd cheated on her. Just to get a ballpark idea of when this awkwardness would end.

On my way in, I quickly checked Facebook and found that no one had messaged me about Charlie. So either his owners weren't on Facebook or they weren't looking for him. A quick check of my chat with Emma showed that she had still not responded to my message but she had read it. That was all I could hope for.

'Morning.'

I nearly dropped my cup and my phone when I heard her voice. I stopped short and looked up at Emma, who was waiting outside 'Ewe and Me', looking a bit sheepish. She was wearing an ombré jumper I'd crocheted for her in purple and grey. Her hair was piled up and glittering with crystal clips and she had two cups of coffee in her hands.

'Hi,' I said, then had to clear my throat and try again. 'Hi – I thought you were off until Monday?'

'I was going to because, honestly, I was really angry with you. To start with. But… I've sort of run out of things to clean at home and I… missed you a bit. A lot. We haven't really gone more than a day without talking since we met.' She shrugged as if trying to pass that observation off as casual, when in fact it meant everything to me. She was right, we were almost constantly in contact. Emma flicked a loose strand of hair over her shoulder. 'I got your message… thanks. It meant a lot that you didn't want me to spend my time off obsessing over what would happen when I came back.'

'I'm really sorry,' I said, unsure if it was okay to move in for a one-armed hug or not. 'I wanted to bring you in breakfast on Monday and apologise properly but… I am really, really sorry. I shouldn't have snapped at you when you were trying to be there for me and I shouldn't have said what I said. I didn't mean it.'

'You sort of did,' Emma shrugged a little. 'I know all the woo-woo stuff isn't your thing and that I've been bringing it to work and that probably made you uncomfortable…'

I felt awful all over again. 'No! No, it really, really didn't. I love your "woo" – and okay, so, even if I don't believe in it – it's still appreciated. That you're putting so much effort into the shop when you don't have to.'

'Just because it's not my shop doesn't mean I don't want it to succeed,' Emma said. 'But thank you for apologising and, for what it's worth, I'm sorry for prying. It's not my business if you decide to get back together with Richard. You're a grown-up and you don't need to explain yourself to me.'

'You definitely practised that,' I said, before I could think better of it. Fortunately, this made Emma laugh.

'Just a few times on the drive over,' she admitted, then her expression turned serious again. 'Tabitha… look, I don't want to create more problems, so this is the last time I'll ask but… getting back together with Richard… Are you absolutely, one thousand per cent sure that's what you want? You were just so hurt before and I hate that he did that to you.'

I felt my shoulders slump. A few days ago, when the decision was freshly made, and I was so convinced it was the right one, I'd been more than ready to fight for it. What a difference a few days could make!

'I don't know that I'm one thousand per cent sure but… I'm at a reasonable eighty-five per cent and… I think I just need a bit of time to work on things. We both do. After three years, I think I owe that to us, you know?' I sounded pleading, even to my own ears.

Emma looked at me for a long moment and my stomach seemed to chew on itself in anxiety. Then she nodded.

'All right, if you're committed to forgiving him, then I am here to support you.' She moved in for a quick hug. 'But I am equally here for whatever you decide to do next, okay? You don't have to explain it or justify it. I'm in.'

'Really?' I asked, hardly daring to hope that at least one person in my life would support me no matter how many times I changed my mind about the future.

'Absolutely. Look, you might not believe in my woo-woo but you respect that it's a part of my life. And I can give that same respect to Richard if he's going to be part of yours.'

To be honest, I wasn't sure I fully believed her. There was a tiny part of my mind that was whispering that having a few crystals around was less taxing on me than tolerating Richard was on her. I knew she didn't like him, even before the cheating. But at least she was offering to try. That was something.

'And,' Emma continued, 'I know that if tomorrow I were to become a Buddhist or a reiki healer or a… vicar, you'd only need to know that it was what I wanted to do to be supportive of me.'

That was true. I would. A few years ago, Emma had got really into ghost hunting around Leaford's historic buildings – from the old forge to the crumbling church ruins. I'd kept her company on several drizzly nights while she set up her Ouija board and EMF detectors, sitting in a darkened room with a flask of hot chocolate, crocheting.

'Well… I appreciate it. Thank you. I really missed my best friend the past few days.'

'Missed you too.' Emma gave my arm a squeeze, then nodded at the shop. 'Shall we?'

'We shall.' I unlocked the door and let her in, glad that we were somewhat back to normal after the biggest argument we'd ever had since she lost her car keys on a visit to Tintagel and we had to climb the whole bloody cliff again to find them. And that one had been settled with a pub lunch and a knickerbocker glory.

'Wow, it's looking pristine in here,' Emma said, looking over the militantly arranged shelves. 'I should take days off more often.'

'Please, no,' I pleaded jokingly. But also meaning it. 'It was very dull without you. And besides, you're my favourite employee.'

She set the drinks down on the counter and raised an eyebrow. 'I'm your only employee.'

'That too.'

She clocked the remaining brown bags lined up on the shelf under the counter. I'd finally got rid of enough of them that we had the break room back.

'Those are doing well! Great idea by the way,' Emma said. 'I didn't really know if you were still game for it but I haven't called off the Stitch and Witch… is that okay?'

'More than okay,' I said firmly. 'I've got some Fleetwood Mac LPs on standby. It would be my pleasure to host.'

Emma beamed. 'Great! I'll tell Patricia and Artemis that you're still keen. And don't worry about laying out nibbles or anything. We'll bring cakes and things – everyone's already baking up a storm for Halloween. What are you going to have us make?'

'I actually did some googling and I think we can do a nice tarot pouch as a beginner project. But we can work up to a conical hat if they're keen to come back.'

Emma looked ecstatic at this news. I'd done some very quick maths and between the ten pounds per person to cover hot drinks and my tutelage, plus materials costs, this could make a big difference to the shop's bottom line for the month.

We went through the usual opening routine and took our seats behind the counter. I had high hopes of a good sales day seeing as it was the weekend, I'd been posting a LOT about the shop and the Leaford market was on. This close to harvest festival, it had been relocated to the school playground and side streets instead of the square. Leaford overflowed with the usual bevy of food stands – jams, chutneys and wine, artisanal cheese from the new owners of Hollyhock Farm, Cressida's Cakes and a charcuterie stall. Then there were crafts – macramé plant holders, felted animals, hand-thrown earthenware mugs and leather goods. The air smelled like hot sugar near the crepe stall and incense near the tarot reader. It was always a busy day in town. The sounds of people meeting up and haggling, competing with buskers, the school brass band and the shrieks from the bouncy castle. People invited their friends and families to stay and the whole of Leaford turned out for it.

Emma being back had really lifted my mood. I asked her about her upcoming date and what she was planning to wear and we talked a little about what restaurants might be good for after axe throwing. Then Emma started peeling the cardboard sleeve off her takeaway cup, a sure sign she was anxious about what she was about to say.

'I, um… noticed the boat was gone, when I left early the other day. I went for a walk to clear my head and didn't see it.'

My insides squirmed and I remembered the confrontation I'd had with Cooper in the shop. I hadn't told Emma about it. There hadn't been a chance to. The headline last time we'd spoken had been me getting back together with Richard. I hadn't wanted to muddy the waters by bringing Cooper into it. Even though I wanted to tell her now, it felt like opening the door to more questions. Ones I didn't want to answer. Ones I couldn't answer, even in the privacy of my own head.

'Oh?' I said instead. 'Yeah, I think I noticed later that day, actually. He must have moved on somewhere else. I bet the Facebook crusaders are pleased.'

'Yeah, the whole community group was going nuts over the news. More comments than when they announced the new wind farm,' Emma said meaningfully. 'Bet they're foaming at the keyboard to see he's back.'

'He's… back?' I repeated, a tingle of surprise and relief running through me. 'When?'

Emma pulled a thoughtful face. 'Not sure. He wasn't there yesterday afternoon, because Margaret and some of the other busybodies went up there to post pictures of some flattened grass like it was the latest North Sea oil spill. But, when I parked up this morning, I was a bit… nervous… about coming in, and I went for a walk and the boat was there, puffing smoke. I saw the dog on deck, tied up to the railing. He's cuter in person – or… in dog – than he is in that picture you took. Such a sweet, smooshable lil face.'

'Yeah, that's Charlie,' I said, still processing. Cooper was back? Why? Or, to be more accurate, if he'd left for a reason, what had made him change his mind?

Emma was looking at me strangely and I could see the questions forming behind her eyes. She was putting things together and I couldn't escape before she took a breath and asked, faux-casually, 'So, you knew he was gone… did you find that out the same day I did or…'

It was so obvious she thought that Cooper leaving had been the thing that spurred me to get back together with Richard. It was both annoying and uncomfortably close to the truth. If I hadn't been so wrong-footed by Cooper's outburst in the shop, I never would have gone to see Mum and found out about her and Dad's relationship. But I wasn't back with Richard purely because Cooper had pushed me away. I hadn't even been certain I was interested in Cooper. Just he made me feel… happy, when I was around him. At least he had until he turned into a completely different person, all cold and shuttered.

'Yeah, I found out the same day you did,' I said, truthfully enough. 'We must have just missed each other on the towpath, to be honest. I'm not sure why he'd leave and come back again.'

Emma's look of consideration lingered for a moment longer. 'Maybe he needed to stretch his legs, so to speak? Or he realised he wasn't quite ready to move on.'

'Hmm,' I hummed noncommittally and distracted myself by tidying a basket of ribbon bows that didn't need tidying.

'… Tabby?'

I looked up to find Emma watching me, nibbling her lip. 'I don't want to start prying again but… maybe this could be a good thing for you. You could go and see him. I thought you two were really hitting it off.'

'I don't really think I have any reason to go up there,' I shrugged. 'I gave him his clothes back and no one's messaged me about the dog, so we're pretty much done. Cup of tea?'

We'd only just finished our coffees but I escaped to hang out by the kettle and avoid further questions. When I returned with fresh brews, Emma didn't broach the subject again. Whatever she thought she knew about me and Cooper, she was mistaken. There was nothing to know. Nothing to speculate over. He was just a random guy, outside the unit that was me and Richard. What did I care where he drove his boat?

Though later, as I busied myself with a budget spreadsheet, I kept finding myself looking up at the shop windows, waiting for a familiar jumper to pass by.

Chapter 25

By the time lunchtime rolled around, I was toying with the idea of going for a walk by the canal. Just to see if Emma was right and Cooper really was back. Not because there was a magnetic pull that had me wanting to be in the same space as Cooper. Nothing like that whatsoever. The more sensible side of my brain was telling me to get a sandwich from the bakery and ignore the boat entirely, but I was curious and the boat was nagging at me like a half-finished project in my crochet bag. I needed to see him. It. I had to see *it*...

At five to twelve, though, the door jangled open and Richard came in. He was dressed for work in a dark blue suit and pink shirt, brown loafers tapping on the floor. He must have come straight from a viewing. He still had his zipped-up folio under his arm.

'Hey,' I smiled at him, feeling a little awkward because Emma was just in the back room behind me, making a Pot Noodle. I wasn't sure how she'd react to seeing him. 'Didn't expect to see you until tonight.'

'Eh, I binned off a few rental viewings – thought I'd take you out to The Black Swan for lunch.'

'Really?' I couldn't help bursting out. The Black Swan was a swanky gastro-pub up past the viaduct, nestled into a bend in the canal. It was the sort of place you went for special wedding anniversaries, not a quick workday lunch. Mum and Dad had been for one of their friends' retirement parties and said the food was 'finicky'. I'd looked their menu up and seen the prices jumping out at me, prices starting with twos and threes, for *sandwiches*.

Guillotines had been built for less.

'Yeah, really,' Richard laughed at my expression. 'You deserve a treat – you've been working really hard.'

'I'll be back in the hour, though, right?' I asked Richard, uncertainly.

He pulled a face. 'Come on, Tabs, live a little. Close up for the afternoon. You can invite Emma if you want. I can afford it.'

While I dithered, Emma appeared through the beaded curtain, noodle pot in hand. 'I'll mind the shop,' she told me, without really engaging with Richard. 'Don't worry about it. I can make some posters to advertise the Stitch and Witch on the laptop, get a few more people in.'

'If you're sure,' I said, not wanting to put her out after we'd only just made up.

'You've been here on your own for a few days, I can handle one afternoon,' she said, still not looking at Richard, which I could tell was bothering him from the way he moved around a little further into her eyeline. 'Have fun and I'll hold down the fort.'

'Great!' Richard said, without waiting for me to make up my mind. He took my hand and tugged me out from behind the counter. 'Let's go – car's outside.'

Richard's car was fancier than my little run-around. He needed to be able to run clients to and from the office for multiple showings where necessary and the car was a reflection of the company. I relaxed into the leather seat and enjoyed the air-conditioning as he drove us out of Leaford and through the lanes to The Black Swan.

'This is a nice surprise,' I said, as we went over a stone bridge and I looked down at the canal flowing under it, smiling at the sight of moorhens zipping about after each other.

'Like I said, you deserve it.' Richard reached over and squeezed my knee. I managed to suppress the urge to pull back. Just.

We drove up to The Black Swan, the car crunching over pristine white quartz gravel. The pub itself was a Tudor building that had always been some form of alehouse or other, as was proudly noted on the sign outside. Now painted charcoal grey with black beams and a sign picked out in gold, it looked the perfect mix of modern and traditional. Outside, the slate planters were full of late summer flowers, all of them so dark purple that they appeared velvety black. I felt a pang for the garden that I'd probably never get to have, not in a flat anyway. Richard wasn't keen on a house and loathed the thought of mowing grass every weekend. Apartment living was the future, according to him.

Richard practically dragged me across the car park in his excitement and, once we reached the door and were greeted by a smiling hostess, I hoped he'd relax a bit. He was making me nervous and it was only lunch, for God's sake.

'Table for Hollings?' he asked.

I watched as the petite brunette hostess ran a scarlet manicured finger down her reservation book. She looked up and smiled. 'Party of four? Right this way.'

Four? I looked askance at Richard but he avoided my gaze and followed the hostess. She led us through the main restaurant area, where the wooden floors and tastefully rustic décor felt warm and inviting. Our table was in the attached conservatory, surrounded by beds of more black flowers and within view of a mini-orchard of ripening apples. Beyond the trees the canal was surrounded by reed beds, almost hidden.

We were seated at a table for four, covered in a black tablecloth. The tableware was white with gold trim and I didn't really want to touch any of the delicate glassware in case I broke something. In terms of celebrating our reconciliation, this felt like a little much.

'Who's joining us?' I asked, unable to keep a faint note of suspicion from my voice. I wondered if this was some sort of investors' lunch for his business and he was trying to kill two birds with one expensive meal by inviting me along.

Richard took a breath and reached for my hand on the table.

'Tabby!'

I jumped a little and the table full of expensive glass and china rattled alarmingly. Richard shot me an admonishing look. But my flicker of irritation over that was quickly swamped by the surprise at seeing both my parents entering the conservatory. The hostess ushered them in and I took in Dad's suit (the classic black one he only got out for funerals or weddings) and Mum's eye-wateringly bright fuchsia and coral floral wrap dress. What were they doing here, dressed up?

I glanced at Richard and saw him smiling at them, polite and without teeth. Oh God. Was he… was this how he was going to propose? Right now, after only days of us being back together? That felt too soon. Much, much too soon. Panic made sweat prickle all over me and I tried to discreetly wipe my palms on my skirt before getting up to hug Mum and Dad.

'Mum, Dad, this is a surprise,' I said, trying to smile as if I wasn't suddenly a nervous wreck inside.

'I know!' Mum's voice ricocheted around the glass walls and I saw Richard wince. She was clearly pleased with how this reveal had been carried out. As she and Dad took their seats, she kept looking at me and beaming. I wanted to mouth 'what's happening?' but sensed it would just spur her on.

The hostess brought menus in black leather covers and a carafe of lemon water. I poured myself a glass and tried not to neck it.

Richard was in no hurry to get to the point of this lunch, it seemed. He and Mum chattered about the menu and Dad scoffed at the prices. I was in private agreement. I could appreciate good food as much as the next person but eighteen pounds for grilled asparagus on sourdough? Twenty-two for a bowl of soup and some bread? Had the world gone mad?

I dithered over the menu so long that in the end, when a waitress came to take our order, Richard just said I'd have what he was having. Mum 'awwwwed', like this was adorable. In fact, I was slightly embarrassed but didn't want to make a scene. I could pick the anchovies out of the starter, and it wouldn't kill me to eat salad for both the first and second course. At least it wasn't as expensive as the eight-ounce steak and truffle frites. I'd had water bills for less.

'This is so nice,' Mum sighed, smiling at the pair of us, while the waitress brought out the wine Richard had ordered and poured for us. Dad was still looking slightly poleaxed by the menu prices, goggling at the vase of flowers in front of him with a slight eye twitch. I could only sympathise.

'It is,' Richard agreed. 'Always so good to see you two, and it seems especially important now… when Tabs and I are moving into a new phase of our relationship.'

Oh, God! He *was* going to propose. The sheer panic the idea filled me with made me feel physically sick. I was immediately overcome with guilt that this was my response to Richard planning for our future. What was wrong with me? I was in a very nice restaurant with my parents and my boyfriend of three years and he was apparently about to ask me to marry him. And my instinct was to push over the table and sprint for the nearest toilet?

'I've recently been doing a lot of soul-searching, a lot of thinking and preparation for the future,' Richard said, picking up his glass and clearly getting ready to give a toast. 'In the past few days, it's become clear that big changes are on the horizon.'

Mum made a high-pitched noise I'd previously only heard One Direction fans produce. She was fixated on Richard, as if he was about to pop the question to her rather than me.

Richard reached over and took my hand. To my embarrassment, I twitched away slightly and had to stop myself from whipping my fingers away from his entirely.

He ignored this and cleared his throat. 'Tabs, you are… everything to me. You're the fuel in my engine, the scaffolding on my skyscraper… the sparkle on my diamond.'

Mum grabbed Dad's hand with such force that he jumped, jolting everything on the table. Richard glanced peevishly at him for a fraction of a second, before returning his attention to me.

'Tabitha – I'm all ready to take us to a new level. All you have to do… is say yes.'

A trickle of cold sweat had formed between my shoulder blades. I felt like I had the one and only time I'd got food poisoning. I found I couldn't meet Richard's eyes and my gaze skittered away to the window and the reeds bordering the canal. The conservatory felt stifling all of a sudden, as if the air was being sucked out of it.

'Will you be my business partner?'

The oxygen came rushing back in as if a switch had been flipped. My lungs filled and I took a great big gasp at the same time as Mum did. Though for different reasons, I'd bet. I met her eyes and saw she was trying to hide her disappointment. Dad just looked mildly perplexed.

'You want Tabby to go into business with you?' Dad said, hesitantly.

'Yes.' Richard squeezed my hand, smiling at me. 'I just heard from my last investor yesterday and Hollings Property Development is officially fully funded and ready to move into the next phase. And, as a future Hollings, I want you to be a part of it with me.'

Mum made the 'OMG, is that Harry Styles???' noise again, though slightly less aggressively this time. More of an 'I think I've just seen Zayn Malik' whistle instead of a full-on squeal.

'But… I already have a business,' I pointed out, hating how hesitant I sounded. It was obvious, so why did I feel bad about pointing it out? Like I was the one ruining everyone else's good time.

At that moment the first course came out and there was a general stiltedness as we waited for the two waitresses to set down the plates and leave. I eyed Dad's quartet of mushroom ravioli jealously over my own salad of pea shoots and samphire.

It looked like something you'd shake out of a lawnmower, complete with anchovy slugs.

'I know you've got the shop to think about for now,' Richard said, once the waitresses left. 'But given our conversation the other day, it sounded like you were aware that you weren't going to be able to keep running it forever. This business is going to be ours – our family business. And after the amazing job we did renovating the shop, I think you can agree property development makes a lot of sense for us.'

We? The amazing job *we* did? I looked at him, speechless. But there wasn't even an ironic twist to his mouth or a hint of embarrassment around his eyes as they looked beseechingly into mine. He'd put my wonky sign right and that was pretty much it, as far as I was aware. Well, that and spent weeks complaining about the smell of white spirit on my clothes or the bits of sawdust I managed to track into the flat.

Mum leapt into the silent void of my disbelief. 'That is a great idea, isn't it, love? Just imagine the pair of you working together. You'd get to spend so much time with one another – so many couples don't get that these days.'

'And Tabby does have a lot of construction knowledge,' Dad put in proudly. 'You'll be able to let Richard know what needs doing.'

I tried to suppress a little laugh at the frown this put on Richard's face. Even as I did so, I was mildly hurt that Dad didn't think I could, or should, do any of the things he'd taught me to do. I was knowledgeable but he'd much rather it was Richard getting his hands dirty. He still thought Richard had done most of the work on the shop too. Because that's what I'd allowed him to believe. I was so embarrassed by Richard's lack of interest in helping that I'd replaced Emma with him in the renovation stories I told my parents. They thought he'd been mucking in with me every day, that it was him who'd taken the captured rats away to release them in the wild. I'd even made extra effort to get the paint off my hands and the smell of bleach off myself, so they wouldn't guess how much of the work I was doing.

I'd done it all for the same reason I'd lied to them about Richard being busy at work when he didn't want to go to their parties or Sunday dinners. The same reason I never told Mum that he hated her cooking, or Dad that he regularly insulted contractors as 'not having a single GCSE or a tooth between them' – because I wanted them to like my boyfriend. More than that, I wanted them to see at least one aspect of my life as being successful. Mum was happiest and most approving of me when I was in a relationship and it was going well. So I convinced her and myself that it was.

I felt suddenly very hemmed in by my own mistakes and lies. Sure, Mum and Dad were happy that Richard wanted to go into business with me, that he wanted to marry me someday soon. But how much of that was due to the things I'd allowed them to believe about him? That he was hands-on and chivalrous and loyal? Would Mum have urged me to give him a second chance if she really knew him?

Well, yes, probably. She was so dotty over the idea of grandchildren, she'd probably encourage me to get hitched to the Devil himself as long as he was fertile and owned his own car. But Dad would have his doubts. I was sure of that.

'So, thank you for coming to our celebratory lunch,' Richard said, and I realised that my 'yes' to this whole plan had been taken for granted. That we were celebrating that acceptance and not the offer itself. I wanted to speak up but I couldn't get my thoughts straight, couldn't think of a way to put things that wouldn't cause a scene.

So I just nodded and smiled, and ate my pea shoots, valiantly trying to make my stomach stop churning.

Chapter 26

Somewhere between the dressing-less green salad and grilled chicken, and the berry compote and clotted cream (hold the cream), I decided I needed some air. Dad had gone outside to vape and Richard was having his ear talked off by Mum, so I muttered something about the 'ladies' and left the conservatory.

In the pub itself I ignored the signs for the toilets and found a rear door propped open into the gardens. It was just a bit of grassy bank out of view of the conservatory, with a falling-down drystone wall to stop people going into the canal. I stumbled over the lush, wet grass and leant my hands on the crumbling stone. If I hadn't left my bag at the table, I'd have called Emma. As it was, I only had the willows and nettles for company. After a few deep breaths of cidery autumn air, I opened my eyes and looked down at the slow, green water. Suddenly, all I wanted to do was talk to Cooper.

'It's okay… it's all going to be okay…' I told myself softly.

'You sound like me on my wedding day.'

'Jesus! Dad!' I whirled around and gaped at him, where he was leaning against the wall of the pub. 'What are you doing back here?'

'Same thing as you, I think. Trying to get my head around what my other half's thinking.' He shook his head and tucked his vape back into the too-tight jacket of his suit. 'God love her, but your mum is a mystery to me sometimes. Like when she ordered that bloody sofa… and today.'

'I don't know what you…' I trailed off at his look. Dad wasn't the most emotionally articulate person but he knew when he was being blatantly lied to.

Dad tramped over the grass and came to stand by me. Together we looked out over the canal and the woodland beyond. A rabbit hopped through the undergrowth and I thought about how wonderfully simple its life must be – munching grass and sleeping in a nice warm burrow. Sure, there was the ever-present danger of being hit by a car or eaten by a fox but that had to be better than relationship drama, doing laundry and paying taxes for the rest of my life.

'She wants you to be happy,' Dad sighed, and I tore my eyes away from the rabbit to look his way.

'I know. I just don't think she really knows what that would look like. I'm not that sure any more either.'

We stood in silence for a moment. I knew Dad wasn't about to go delving any deeper. He wasn't one to invite emotional upset into his life. But he was giving me a moment away from the table, from Mum and Richard and all their expectations. I appreciated that. He knew something was up, he just didn't really know how to ask or talk to me about it.

That didn't mean, however, that I wasn't going to ask him about stuff.

'Dad?' I asked, with the drawn-out cadence that still felt second nature, after years of begging for lifts, twenty quid to go shopping, or the last Celebration in the box.

'Hmm?'

'When you and Mum were first going out…'

'There you are!'

We turned as one and I tried not to look as annoyed and disappointed as I felt to see Richard striding over the lawn towards us. He was smiling, but he looked a little stressed. Probably from being left alone with Mum for several minutes without a buffer.

'They've brought out the desserts and I've got champagne to

open,' Richard said, threading his arm through mine. There went my chance of speaking to Dad. Out of the corner of my eye, I saw him scurry gratefully back towards the pub. He'd clearly sensed the weight of my unasked question and was glad to have escaped it. For now.

I smiled at Richard and let him steer me back inside. I kept that smile up through my fruit compote and champagne, the drive home and all that evening. All while Richard talked over 'our' plans for the future, the properties he wanted to bid on at an upcoming auction and all the ways we could save money on renovations.

When he finally ran out of steam – it was early evening and I was making us falafel wraps for a light dinner – I set down my spatula and took a deep breath. We were alone and there was no chance of him ganging up on me with Mum to steamroll my objections. It was time to talk it out.

'Rich… I'm really glad you're excited about the business and I think you're going to be great at it,' I began.

'We will be.' Richard wrapped his arms around my waist and kissed the back of my neck.

I winced. 'Right… the thing is I'm just not sure it will be a "we" thing, at least not for a while.' I felt Richard tense up against me and knew he was taken aback. So I hurriedly continued. 'The shop hasn't been doing great, but it's also not on the verge of closure. Things are actually turning around – we're selling out of the crochet starter kits and we have an event planned. The online store's gaining some traction… we're still not there yet but there's no timeline on when or if we might close and, before we did, I'd want to be sure I'd tried everything possible to keep it going. For Emma, and for Lou. She knew this was my dream and she'd want me to give it my all. Not have one foot out the door.'

Richard peeled himself away from me and circled the island. When we came face to face his expression was incredulous.

'Why am I just hearing about this now?' he asked, eyes wide.

'I didn't really have a chance before…' I began, but he interrupted, eyebrows shooting up in exaggerated surprise.

'But you said yes?' He let out a breathy laugh of disbelief. 'I took you and your parents out for hundreds of pounds' worth of lunch to celebrate the fact that we were going into business together – now you want to tell everyone that it was a mistake?'

'I think maybe we should have talked about it before the lunch—'

He groaned like I was being annoying on purpose and I was surprised at how angry that made me and how quickly. He was the one who'd created this situation, not me. 'Then it wouldn't have been a surprise, would it? I was trying to do something nice, Tabs – now you're telling me I shouldn't have bothered?'

'It was nice, and it was great to see Mum and Dad… but this is kind of a big decision and I think we should discuss it before one of us just unilaterally makes a decision—'

'Isn't that what you're doing by saying "no"?' Richard said, waspishly.

He'd cut me off again and I gritted my teeth in frustration. Had it always been like this and I'd just not noticed before? Richard talking over and across me, not listening, bulldozing me. If he was hoping I'd back down or just go along with his plans, those days were over. I was done being pushed down someone else's path.

'I'm not saying "no",' I sighed, frustrated and clinging to my last shreds of patience. 'I'm saying… maybe, but not right now.'

'What's the difference? Sounds like a no to me.' Richard shook his head and then reached for his keys and wallet on the counter.

'Where are you going?' I asked, stunned. 'I'm about to dish up.' The first time I'd even halfway stood up for myself and he was just going to storm out and not talk to me. I thought we were meant to be doing this differently. That he was meant to be the 'new Richard' and adult. But he was acting like the same old selfish, childish man who'd cheated on me.

'Stick it in the fridge, I'll have it later.' Richard was already up and on his way to the door, slipping his feet into his gym trainers. 'Maybe I need some time to think too.'

He didn't quite slam the door but I winced anyway at the abruptness of his exit. That had gone terribly, but I wasn't willing to take the blame – he was the one who'd sprung this on me.

Irritated and monumentally fed up, I ate my falafel wrap in front of the TV and contemplated messaging Emma. In the end I sent a text just to say thanks for watching the shop and wishing her a good date for that evening. She messaged back fairly quickly.

How was lunch? Fancy a post-mortem at mine tomorrow? I'm in if you bring brekkie! :)

Honestly, that was the best thing I'd heard for a while. I messaged back in the affirmative and we set a time. With nothing much else to do except sit and be anxious about where Richard had gone and why, I got out some leftover yarn and started working on a much-used pattern for a winter hat. The sort of thing I could make in my sleep. It was the perfect distraction and I let the rhythm of the stitches and the burble of the TV slowly unwind the knots of tension in my shoulders. I might be shit at relationships and possibly also at business but at least I could crochet a hat without even trying.

I had half a hat done before my eyes started to feel heavy. After making some waffle batter and sticking it in the fridge for tomorrow morning I did my night-time skincare routine and settled into bed to listen to a podcast.

It was weird sleeping in the main bedroom without Richard there. It took me a while to fall asleep and, when I did, I had nightmares about stripping woodchip wallpaper while Richard lectured me about our 'business values' and a screaming baby swung off my leggings, while another sat on my shoulders, slapping the top of my head with its chubby fists.

I jerked awake in a cold sweat to hear someone moving around in the flat. I tensed up but then realised it was Richard coming home. I checked my phone and saw that it was two in the morning. He'd been gone for hours and the local pubs closed at eleven. Where had he spent the intervening three hours? My stomach clenched. The first thought that entered my head was that he'd been with someone else. With her. The other woman.

Was that what I was always going to be afraid of, forever?

Richard staggered in through the bedroom door and snapped the overhead light on. I screwed up my face and could almost feel my pupils shrinking to pinpricks under the sixty-watt assault. Richard, discarding his clothes over the floor, didn't seem to notice that I was awake.

'Where've you been?' I asked, scrambling to turn on my bedside lamp and then heading for the main light to switch it off. The blessed gloom was a relief for my eyeballs.

'At the pub with the boys.' Richard was struggling to remove his shoes and I saw that he'd tracked leaf mulch into the bedroom. Ugh!

'They close at eleven, though.'

'Yeah…' he said slowly. 'We had a few beers at Rob's after.'

'Right,' I said, wishing I believed him. 'Have you had water too?'

'Hmm? Ah, no… can you get me some, babe?' he whined, pulling off his shoe and handing it to me as if he was tipping me with it.

I got up and collected his other shoe, dumping them on my way to the kitchen. I came back with a pint glass of water and set it on the bedside table. Richard was already in bed, wrapped up in the bulk of our duvet.

'There you go,' I muttered.

'Thanks…' He didn't open his eyes, already sounding half asleep. 'Turn that bloody light off, will you?'

I got into bed and switched my lamp off. Lying beside Richard as he started to snore, sweating yeasty beer into the sheets, I wondered how Mum had managed to trust Dad again. If there was a point where she'd just had to make the conscious decision to take what he said at face value. If that was the case, why couldn't I do it? Why was I wide awake and thinking about all the things Richard might have been out doing?

It was a sleepless hour and a half later when I remembered him telling me that Rob was away in Tenerife for two weeks. My heart thumped painfully and I knew then for sure that Richard was lying to me. Again.

Chapter 27

Emma's neat little studio was nearer Fenlowe than Leaford, in a housing estate built back when I was still in primary school. A sweet little purpose-built village intended for families buying their first home, which had been carved up by landlords before the grass had seeded.

It was still a reasonably nice place to live but suffering a bit from decades of neglect and overoccupancy. Emma said she paid a management fee to 'maintain the grounds' but she had no idea where it went. As I got out of the car I nearly slipped on a crisp packet left on top of a dog turd like a festive hat. The gutter practically rattled with discarded Monster cans and the surrounding front gardens were ragged and piled with bin after bin, the only sign of the overcrowding within the houses.

Emma's was a ground-floor place and her garden was startlingly green and lovely, compared with those surrounding it. The bordering hedge was clipped, and inside, a herb garden provided a riot of greenery, even now the weather was turning. Between the plants, Emma had peopled her garden with gnomes and fairies, mosaics of broken plates and glass, and a concrete birdbath caked in moss. It was the perfect cottage garden at the centre of an otherwise weary world.

I let myself in through the gate and up the brick path, tapping on the door. Emma opened it in a tie-dye fleece, purple leggings and Crocs studded with little crystal charms she had probably made herself. She raised her perfectly pencilled eyebrows at the sight of the pile of boxes in my arms.

'Goodness, hon – I said bring brekkie, not start a humanitarian relief effort.'

Okay, so I might have gone a teensy bit overboard on breakfast. I'd decided on waffles with crispy sausage patties, maple syrup and a jug of banana and vanilla smoothie. That had sort of spiralled into a yoghurt parfait, freshly baked almond croissants (from frozen, I wasn't that much of a psychopath), some bacon and egg bites and a fruit salad.

'Well… at least you'll be well-fed through the week,' I said. 'Gotta keep my best employee fuelled up and ready to go.'

She smiled, but there was a wary twist to her mouth that made me feel terrible. We still weren't past the damage I'd done to our friendship. I planned to keep trying until I had made up for it.

Emma let me slip past her into the studio flat. I was always pleasantly surprised at how cosy it felt. I was probably just too used to the sterile chill of my own flat. Hers was hung all over the place with tapestries and her big squashy sofa was piled with huge comfy cushions and blankets. Her kitchen was spotless and warm and full of handmade pottery mugs and jars of herbal tea blends. It felt more like home than anywhere I'd ever been, except Aunt Lou's house. And Cooper's boat. A boat I was never going to see the inside of again, I told myself firmly.

Emma flipped the kettle switch and turned her oven on to reheat the food. We hugged and sat down at her kitchen table. There were a few late roses in a glass of water on it, pearls of dew still on them. Emma must have picked them right before I arrived.

'How was lunch yesterday?' Emma asked, at the same time that I said, 'How was your date?'

'You first,' I said, with a smile.

'It was fine – good. Axe throwing is fun, as it turns out. I'm not sure we really have a lot in common but sometimes that can be interesting, you know? You don't want to be dating your twin, just someone that gets you.' She shrugged. 'She complimented my cardigan and I told her you made it for me – turns out she knows the shop but hasn't ever been in. I think I might have convinced her to give us a try.'

'That's great,' I said, as Emma got up to pour hot water into a pot of tea. 'If she does, you'll have to point her out so I can be nosy.'

Emma chuckled, bringing the pot and two heavy handmade mugs over. 'I will do… now, tell me about lunch. Because you seem stressed about it.'

'Is it that obvious?' I sighed.

'To me? Yes.'

'Okay… it was kind of a big production. Richard had arranged for Mum and Dad to be there—'

'Oh, my God – did he propose?' Emma looked as horrified as I'd felt in the moment, which was somewhat vindicating. Her eyes searched my ring finger like she was looking for a landmine.

'No, and believe me, I was worried he might, which… doesn't seem ideal. He wanted us to celebrate going into business together – as property developers.' I watched her face crinkle as she tried to understand this. 'He got the funding sorted out for his business and he basically said that since the shop was going to fail anyway, I should come and steam wallpaper and strip paint for him.'

Emma opened her mouth as if to speak, then closed it again, pressing her lips into a line. I watched her as she clearly tried to sort through what she wanted to say, like a deck of tarot cards, trying to find the most diplomatic ones. In the end she gave up and slammed 'The Devil' down between us.

'Is he out of his tiny little mind?'

I laughed and, honestly, it felt so good to just laugh at how stupid this whole situation had become. All the fretting and worrying and overthinking and I just laughed it away for a moment. Emma joined in after a shocked little pause and we were both giggling, making each other crack up again every time our eyes met.

'I know,' I wheezed, once I managed to calm down. 'It was such a bold move I was almost impressed, you know? He was acting like I'd already agreed – more than that,' I added, warming to my theme. 'He was acting like I didn't just take him back after he cheated on me. Like it could be taken as read that I'd be over the moon to go straight into business with him and get married and have kids…' I stopped, appalled at the way my skin was crawling, just thinking of it. What had I done? More importantly, what was I going to do about it now?

'Are you… ready to tell me about why you did forgive him?' Emma asked, carefully. 'I feel like I missed something important somewhere – because none of this sounds like you.'

I looked down at the surface of the table and nodded. It didn't really sound like me at all – was it only a few days ago that I'd convinced myself that Richard was my future? I felt like I was waking up from a trance.

'I went to see Mum – I was already upset but then she told me that… my dad cheated on her when they first started going out.'

The timer went off for the reheated breakfast food and we both got up, scrambling to plate everything. As Emma slid crispy sausage patties onto two plates, she was still obviously reeling from this news.

'I can't believe she told you that – out of the blue,' she said, as we retook our seats with heaped plates. 'I mean, obviously it was meant to get you two back together, right?'

'I suppose so… and it worked,' I said unhappily, cutting into a warm waffle and dipping it into maple syrup. 'She wasn't happy about the break-up from the start, to be honest, and I suppose I just started to think, if they could get past it and have a whole life together, then maybe I could forgive Richard and we could get back to normal. Move on.'

Emma chewed a cube of melon meditatively. 'I can see where she was coming from,' she said slowly. 'But… a lot of that isn't about forgiveness, it's about what happened afterwards. About how your dad proved himself and what they committed to together. Have you spoken to him since you found out? Asked about it?'

'I tried to get into it at lunch but Richard interrupted.' I took a sip of my tea and let it warm me through. 'I should get his side of things. I know that. I didn't mean to rush into anything but it all happened so quickly. I saw Mum and she talked to me about it and I started spiralling. Then, when I got back to the flat, Richard was already there and he was apologising. If I hadn't messed things up with Cooper, it never would have happened.'

'Cooper?' Emma raised her eyebrows and a piece of sausage fell off her fork, landing in a puddle of syrup. 'He was why you were upset?'

I winced and wished I'd kept that part to myself. It just made me feel so stupid. That I'd made such a big decision based on an awkward set-to with a virtual stranger. I set my cutlery down and poured myself a glass of smoothie as a distraction.

'I bumped into him at the library and we were walking back to his place when it started raining. Everything was fine, he was fine. But then this car went past and… I don't know, he acted scared almost. Hiding his face from it. So I asked if he wanted to talk about it and he told me it was none of my business and ran off into the rain.'

'…and then his boat disappeared,' Emma said, filling in the blank like it was the final clue in a weekend crossword. 'I did wonder if that was connected to what was going on. Jesus! What do you think it was about that car? Is he in some kind of trouble? Legally?'

'No idea. But whatever it is, it must be serious. He was really freaked out. I um… wondered if he was running away from his family. He mentioned not getting on with his dad that well. Or that maybe that's his wife's car or something and she's looking for him.'

I couldn't look at her while I said it but, when I glanced

up, Emma was watching me with an odd expression. Sort of troubled but sympathetic. She reached over the table and covered my hand with hers.

"What?' I asked softly.

'I know I was teasing you, but I didn't realise how much you liked him.'

My face burned. 'I…'

But it was useless to deny it, because I did. I liked talking to him, I'd felt my heart lift every time we bumped into each other. And the thought of not seeing him again had been like a stone in my chest. I liked him. I cared about him. I just wasn't sure if he cared about me.

Emma tilted her head to the side. 'Tabitha, even if you're not ready to think about anyone else romantically… it's kind of obvious you care about him. Since he's back, you should go and talk to him. Get a straight answer out of him.'

'He didn't want to give me one last time,' I pointed out.

Emma patted my hand, her silver rings catching the light and sending up sparkles from the moonstones and amethysts there. In her warm little kitchen, it was so much easier to believe that Cooper might want to talk to me. I felt as if, in there, I was safe from the pressures of Richard and my mum. Emma gave me the confidence to believe in my own thoughts and wants. Whereas Richard made me doubt myself at every turn.

'Last time he'd just been jump-scared by a car,' Emma pointed out. 'Maybe he overreacted and, if you talk to him again, he'll handle it better. He came back after all. There must be a reason.'

'And if he doesn't react better?' I asked.

'Then he's missing out. And just because he doesn't want your friendship, that doesn't mean you have to be with Richard. Because it's obvious he's making you miserable – and he was even before you broke up. You were always making excuses for him and pretending it didn't bother you that he was never there when you needed him. I mean, he ditched you on the opening day of your business and now he wants you to work for him?'

Emma scoffed and gestured at me with a chunk of melon on a fork – like a magic wand. 'That's… pants.'

I laughed, and she let go of my hand with a smile. It was good, sitting there and eating brunch with my best friend. As if the cracks that our argument had left were closing. I should have just been honest with her from the beginning – about Richard, about Cooper, all of it. But that would have been almost the same as being honest with myself. Emma and I were so close, it would have been impossible to manage my catastrophic levels of denial if I admitted how I felt to her.

She must have seen my expression shift. 'I should have said something sooner, about Richard. I didn't ever really think he was good enough for you.'

'I should have been willing to see it,' I said.

'I promise to never let something like that slide again.' Emma held up her tea as if in a toast. I clinked my smoothie against it.

'And I promise to listen to your excellent advice, even when I've got my head firmly shoved up my bum.'

We dissolved into giggles. This was what I wanted my life to be like. Warm and filled with laughter, understanding and love. It wasn't about hitting milestones and making other people happy and it certainly didn't have to come from a man. I just had to hang on to that when it became harder to believe.

Still, as we finished eating and Emma made another round of tea, I thought of Cooper and wondered if he'd be happy to see me. If he'd missed me like I'd missed him. Only there was somewhere else I needed to go first.

'I think you're right,' I said to Emma, hands cupped around my mug. 'I need to talk to Dad.'

Chapter 28

It was Sunday afternoon and that meant one thing – Mum was in the kitchen making a roast and Dad was in the shed 'pottering'. That's a word that usually conjures up images of compost and gardening gloves, fixing things or hand-carving toy soldiers. In reality, Dad's 'shed' was quite a large construction with its own electricity, a TV and a wall-mounted bottle opener over a table topped with hundreds of resin-covered bottle caps. A man cave in all but name.

Mum let me in and took me through to the kitchen. Sunday-dinner preparations were in full swing; the Paxo was rehydrating, Aunt Bessie's frozen roasties were cooking in the oven along with a slightly alien-autopsy-looking roasting bag full of chicken, bulging onions and carrots. Mum picked up the jar of Bisto and started measuring it into a Pyrex jug.

'Dad in the shed?' I asked, despite already knowing the answer. It was mostly a precursor to me escaping out there to talk to him. But first I had to appease the gatekeeper – would I be allowed to pass or would I have to sacrifice half an hour, or make an offering of laying the table?

'As per,' she sighed. 'You can take him out a cup of tea, if you like.'

Permission granted.

It was weirdly nostalgic, nudging the frozen jam roly-poly out of the way to get at the kettle, making Dad a tea in his favourite mug. All at once I could have been fourteen again with maths homework to do before tomorrow, and a heap of 'heatless curler' technology crammed on top of my head, an acne face mask smeared over my skin.

'That was nice of Richard taking us out for lunch yesterday,' Mum said, while I stirred sugar into Dad's tea. 'How are things going with you two now?'

'Oh, you know… the same as they were before,' I said truthfully, hoping she'd hear what she wanted to without me having to lie. The thing was, even before the cheating, things hadn't been perfect, or even good. I just hadn't let myself see it and, by extension, hadn't let my family see it either. But now my eyes were wide open.

I still had no idea what to do about Richard. By taking him back, I'd really muddied the waters and made things even more complicated. But I still couldn't find it in myself to fully let go of the years we'd spent together and the future I'd imagined with him. I just wasn't sure if I wanted him in that future, which was all kinds of messed up. I needed some extra perspective and, hopefully, Dad would deliver. As long as I could keep him in the shed and not allow him to nip out to the pub to escape. I contemplated hiding his car keys.

'Tell him there's no pigs in blankets,' Mum called after me as I let myself out of the back door. 'They didn't defrost in time and I don't want him to get his hopes up and sulk!'

Outside I picked my way down the garden, past the extravagant barbecue and the bar, both now covered over for autumn with matching hedge-pattern tarpaulins. Dad's shed was right at the bottom, screened from the rest of the barren garden by a fake-ivy-covered trellis, which stood out against the grey stone and gravel. I went up to the metal door and knocked on it.

'Enter!'

Inside, Dad was sitting in his recliner, space heater plugged in beside him and the TV showing a live football match. He looked surprised to see me, then clocked the tea and perked up.

'All right, Tabby? You staying for lunch?'

'No, I'm very full of brunch actually,' I said, and settled into the second recliner, usually reserved for Dad's friend Terry. 'I just popped by for a chat.'

At the word 'chat' Dad started to look uneasy. I watched his eyes dart to the door and decided to press on before he could come up with an excuse to leave.

'I talked to Mum the other day and she told me something about when the two of you first got together… that you were also sort of seeing somebody else?'

I wasn't going to come out and say 'sleeping with' not to my dad. It was hard enough knowing that he'd done it even once, to get me. That he'd had not one but two women was unthinkable. Especially just then, sitting in his man shed and seeing him in his West Ham slippers and 'Number One Dad' T-shirt. A shirt, by the way, that I hadn't bought him, he must have found it on sale and not bothered to read it. As with the 'World's Best Sister-in-Law' mug he'd inexplicably bought himself.

'Ah… right,' he said, still looking longingly at the door. 'Well… that is true.'

I'd assumed as much. Mum was keen on Richard and me staying together, but not so keen that she'd just make a story like that up. But it was good to have confirmation.

'But she forgave you,' I prompted.

'She did, yeah.' Dad squirmed in his chair and glanced at the TV as if Gary Lineker could phase through the screen and come to his aid. 'What's this about, love?'

'Richard cheated on me,' I said quietly, and that at last got Dad to look at me.

'I'll wring his neck,' he said, sitting up straight. 'That little scrote.'

'Dad!' I couldn't help the giggle that escaped me at the outraged look on his face. 'You cheated too.'

'But that's different. You're my daughter,' he huffed. 'No one bloody cheats on my Tabby – I always had a bad feeling about that tosser. Right – when are you moving out? I'll borrow Terry's van. He won't mind. He's actually not legally allowed to drive since his last eye test. Bloody Asda opticians snitched on him.'

'I'm actually not sure we're breaking up,' I said, holding up my hands to calm down his tirade. 'I mean, I did break up with him but what Mum told me… it sort of convinced me to give him another chance.'

'… oh,' Dad subsided slightly. 'Well… that's… your choice. Though I'm surprised your mum told you about all that – it's ancient history now.'

'She said it didn't seem important any more,' I confirmed. 'But… I don't know how to feel about Richard right now. I wanted to ask you how you managed to get Mum back. How you stayed loyal all this time. Basically, see if it would help me understand how to deal with this.'

I had the sudden, horrible thought that he might be about to admit to me that he hadn't been faithful at all and had in fact been carrying on a years-long affair. I didn't want to know that and, frankly, if Mum found out, she'd probably cremate Dad on his own massive American barbecue and mix his ashes in with the gravel.

'Well…' Dad started, then stopped, apparently hunting for the right words. He looked at me quizzically as if I'd asked him to explain the offside rule. 'We sort of just… moved on.'

Very helpful.

'But what changed afterwards? What did you do?' I asked, trying to herd him towards some specifics.

'I can't really say that much did change,' Dad shrugged.

The TV emitted a roar of crowd noise and his head snapped round, having missed a goal entirely. He huffed.

'Nothing changed?' I asked, surprised. 'At all?'

Dad turned back to me and sighed. 'Tabby… it was all very different back then. We didn't do all this talking stuff. I was drunk, I made a mistake and I regretted it. Your mum accepted my apology – and a few weeks of grovelling with flowers and chocolates – and we moved on. She knew that I wished it had never happened and that if Margaret and I hadn't been drunk, it wouldn't have.'

'Margaret?' I didn't so much say the name as dry-heave it. That's the trouble with living in a small town, you know everyone. And I only knew one Margaret. 'You slept with Margaret… from the hospice shop?'

Dad turned the same shade of maroon as his slippers. 'It was a long time ago! She used to be quite a looker.'

My bellyful of brunch churned around inside me. Ugh! That was so not a mental image I ever wanted to have. Dad and Margaret. Even back when I'd been in primary and she was the school receptionist, she'd had a tiny little cat-bum mouth all pursed up and mean, and wicked red talons which she filed endlessly. I couldn't imagine her attracting a wasp, let alone my dad.

'As I said,' Dad continued, still flushed with embarrassment. 'It was a house party, I'd just been paid and I was very, very drunk. I couldn't remember my own name, let alone that I was head over heels for your mother. Margaret was hitting the advocaat pretty hard and, the minute we sobered up, I realised what I'd done and… honestly, I could have slapped myself into next week. I was that mortified, that scared I'd lose your mother… I had to tell her right away.'

'You… told her?' I was shocked. Mum hadn't mentioned that. Come to think of it, I'd just sort of assumed that she'd found out from one of her legion of girlfriends.

'Of course!' Dad looked as surprised as I was that this detail hadn't made it into the retelling. 'I went straight round from dossing in the back room of that house. Stinking of beer, crying, I was a mess.' He was flustered. Clearly, he hadn't wanted to admit as much. 'As soon as she answered the door, it all came out.'

'You just blurted out that you'd cheated?'

'No, I threw up in her Mum's peonies,' Dad said, with a rueful half-smile. 'But the second thing I did was tell her what happened. She slammed the door in my face, then opened it again to tell me… well, let's just say the air was pretty blue.'

'And then what?' I leant on the arm of my recliner, enthralled.

'Well, then she went to tell her parents what happened and her dad, bloody hell, he was terrifying.'

'Grandpa Steve?' I laughed.

'Your Grandpa Steve was my Mr Groats,' Dad said darkly. 'That man never forgave me for that – or for the time I leant against his Morris Minor.'

I chuckled, and Dad laughed guiltily. 'Bless 'im… grumpy old arse. Anyway, by the time Mr and Mrs Groats came outside to shout at me, I was hosing out the peonies – which I think got me a little leeway. But they chased me off and I ended up sending a letter instead. Which I think went over well… she agreed to see me anyway, and then, I apologised again and told her that I didn't deserve her, that I regretted that night more than anything else in my life and that, if I got a second chance with her, I wouldn't need a third, because I'd never risk hurting her again.'

'Awww, Dad.' I reached over and patted his arm. He looked quite bleary-eyed and I wondered if he was going to cry – something I'd only seen him do twice. Once when Granny Grey died and once when he put a full tank of petrol in our diesel car while we were on holiday in Wales.

'Ah, pssshht!' Dad waved me off, still very pink about the cheeks. 'I was a soppy idiot about your mum. Still am. But she took me back and I didn't drink again until the night we got engaged. Just to prove to her I was serious.'

I thought of Richard and his apologies. He'd told me that the other woman, the one I'd caught him with, meant nothing. Less than nothing. I'd even said back to him that he'd thrown me away for nothing. He hadn't been drunk on a night out. He'd been sober, in the middle of the day, in our home. Dad had done everything he could to make it up to Mum but, most importantly, he'd given her space. He'd sent a letter and waited for her to reach out. Richard had kept hanging around, waiting like a vulture for me to be defenceless.

Worst of all, Dad had promised to never risk losing Mum again, and had stayed sober for a year and a half. Richard was lying to me again less than a week after I took him back.

'Tabby?'

I looked up and found Dad looking at me seriously. 'It's up to you if you want to take Richard back. Not me and not your mum. I know she's… very keen to see you married and everything, but it's up to you. She only wants it so much because she thinks that'll make you happy. That's all we want really – for you to be happy.'

'And you'll be okay with him if I do take him back?' I asked.

'If Richard makes you happy, that's all I need to know,' Dad said.

The TV resounded with cheers and cries of 'GOAL! but Dad didn't glance its way. He squeezed my hand.

'Do what makes you happy – and we'll both be happy for you.'

I leant over for an awkward armchair hug, and Dad patted my back firmly, like he was trying to make me cough up a Starburst that had gone down the wrong pipe.

'Now, are you sure you won't stay for lunch?' Dad asked.

That reminded me. 'No, I really can't fit a whole roast right now. By the way, Mum said to tell you there are no pigs in blankets.'

Dad inhaled sharply. 'Bollocks!'

Chapter 29

I LEFT THE SHED chuckling but, by the time I reached the back door to the kitchen, I was anxious again. I'd realised while talking to Dad that most of the pressure on me to stay with Richard was pressure I'd put on myself. My parents loved me and would support me no matter what I decided to do. In theory. In practice, all I could think of as I approached the house was that Mum was going to be so disappointed.

I opened the door and stepped into the steamy, chicken-scented kitchen. Mum was at a chopping board, peeling the film off a frozen apple crumble. Double dessert, she was really trying to make up for those missing tiny sausages.

Should I tell her now that I was thinking about breaking up with Richard again? I decided that would be a bad idea. She could easily make me doubt myself again. I needed to make my mind up first. It wasn't like she'd do it on purpose but, just because she was so sure, that made me feel uncertain. It had always been that way. When I was eight and had no clue how to roller-skate, she'd talked me into going to a roller-disco birthday party. I'd been going back and forth on the invite for weeks, but Mum was so sure I'd enjoy it that I ended up going. Less than an hour in and I'd fallen over and cut my head open. The worst part was I hadn't even been having fun before then. It was like Mum thought, if she could just push me enough, reality would warp and her assurances would become truth. If she just kept saying 'You'll have a great time!' or 'He's so charming!', that would make it so.

I never felt sure about anything really – my GCSE choices, boyfriends, hair styles, whether I was a dolphin girl or a horse girl. I was always struggling with decisions and working out who I was, except when it came to the shop and crochet. I'd been very clear on that goal and had kept it as a dream for years before going for it as soon as I had the money. I wanted to follow that feeling more. Even if things were difficult at the shop right now.

'Are you off, love?' Mum asked, fluffing the boulders of crumble with a fork. 'There's plenty if you want to stay for dinner.'

'Sorry, can't. Maybe next week?' I said.

'Okay. Anyway, I expect Richard's taking you out somewhere nice to celebrate all the good news – you two getting back together and starting a business. Seems like he's really turned over a new leaf.'

'Mmm,' I hummed, thinking that really Richard had dropped his 'new man' act fairly quickly. The last time he'd cooked had been that lasagne several days ago, when I'd had my fight with Emma. Since then, he hadn't so much as made me a cup of tea. I wondered what Mum would say if I told her that, if maybe she'd agree with Dad then that I should do what made me happy instead of clinging to what wasn't working. I wanted to believe it but, as much as I knew she wanted what was best for me, I wasn't sure if she was ready to let go of Richard and what he represented yet. I knew what that was like.

Feeling distinctly guilty about all my half-truths, I gave Mum a hug, refused her parting gift of two 'mostly good' courgettes and a cauliflower, and made it out to my car. It was only a temporary deception, I told myself. Next time I saw her, I'd be certain in my choice and able to defend it.

I checked my phone. When I saw the text notification from Richard, my heart sank. Internally, I immediately felt a powerful urge to scream 'go away!' at my poor innocent phone. That was probably a sign that I should break up with him. A big one.

I tapped the notification anyway.

Hey Tabs, sorry for late notice but going to a bit of a thing at the golf club. Back late. Save me some dinner, yeah?

'Well, isn't that just perfect?' I muttered to myself, gripping my phone so hard that the plastic case creaked.

I decided not to respond to the message, mostly because, if I started to, I might accidentally type something like 'Hope you drown in a water hazard'. Which felt unnecessarily mean, even if he had cheated on me.

Instead I checked the time and wondered if around four in the afternoon on a Sunday was an acceptable time to drop by someone's boat to check in. I decided, on reflection, that I couldn't wait until my lunch break tomorrow to see if Cooper really was back and if he was still angry with me. Besides, I had the Stitch and Witch to prepare for then.

It felt rude to arrive empty-handed so, as I drove through town, I stopped at the petrol station to get a gift. It was the only place still open at that time on a Sunday – that's small towns for you. I paid an extortionate price for a carrot cake and a tin of fancy dog food, then went and parked up by the towpath. Sitting in my car, I took a deep breath and told myself the worst thing that could happen was that Cooper would tell me to get lost.

As I was walking up the towpath, a thin rain started to fall. I pulled my cut-off denim jacket around me and wished I'd worn something waterproof. Or that had a hood. I had a blanket-style scarf around my neck and, after a few minutes, when the rain worsened, I took it off and wrapped it over my head to keep the worst of it off.

A haze rose off the canal as the rain hit it and the ducks were diving and splashing in the unexpected shower. A few frogs, disguised as mottled autumn leaves, hopped across the path and I skirted the squashy yellow slugs that were crawling out over the slick tarmac path.

The boat was back, now moored a little further from the viaduct, under some dripping willows. It looked reassuringly the same as it had last time I'd seen it – peeling paint, rust-spotted gilt lettering and the same planters, though these were now empty of dead weeds. Smoke was drifting from the chimney, adding the aroma of wood smoke to that of rain-soaked greenery and damp leaves.

And I felt sure. So I followed that feeling.

I hurried the last few metres, glad I was wearing more sensible biker boots today. Reaching the boat, I stepped over onto it and rapped on the door. From inside I heard the skittering of nails on wood and a low woof as Charlie came to the door. He started to whine and paw at the door itself and I drummed my fingers on the wood.

'It's okay, Charlie, it's only me.'

He woofed again – happily this time – and rushed off. I waited for Cooper to come to the door. Waited and waited, with rain trickling down my back and my feet growing cold in my boots. I knocked again but this time Charlie didn't come running. Almost as if he'd been shut somewhere, like the kitchen.

Cooper was on board – he wasn't stupid or thoughtless, he wouldn't leave the fire going with the dog inside while he went out. He'd taken the dog with him to Asda on a dressing-gown cord, for God's sake. No, he was in there and he was avoiding me. Well, there was my answer then. He didn't want to see me. My feelings had led me astray again, just as they had with the struggling shop. Obviously, I couldn't trust my own judgement.

Feeling stupid and naïve all over again, I left the cake and dog food by the door, then stepped off the boat and back onto the footpath. I stood there a moment, looking at The Lady Di, at the smoke from the chimney and the sliver of light coming through the curtains in the living area. At the far end I thought I saw the kitchen blinds twitch, but I could have been imagining it.

The rain began to peter out as I walked back to the car, dejected. I got back into the driver's seat in my damp clothes and took the scarf from my head. Well, that was that then. I knew where I stood now with Cooper. Which was nowhere near him.

But where did that leave me with Richard? It wasn't that I didn't want to end one relationship without another in the offing. But I was questioning my judgement now. My certainty was leading me astray, so how could I trust myself to make a good decision about Richard? What if I ended up alone and miserable and cursing myself for dumping him?

Knowing he wasn't going to be at home anyway, I was reluctant to head back to the flat to sit in silence and worry about what I was going to say to him. I couldn't go back to Emma's or to Mum and Dad. Cooper didn't want to see me and it was Sunday, so even the café in town was closed. I sighed and looked up at the tiny crochet plant dangling from my mirror.

I knew where I wanted to go.

Aunt Lou's cottage was on the outskirts of Leaford, near a piece of woodland where we'd once picked blackberries and nettles to make dyes and blackberry tarts. It was down a winding lane and, as I drove down it, I didn't meet anyone coming the other way. It was very quiet down there, and the driveway outside the cottage was empty. So much the better. I didn't want to run into the new tenants and have to explain myself.

The cottage was rendered white and had a gabled roof of red clay tiles. The front still had Aunt Lou's roses climbing up it, the sweetest pink and yellow marbled flowers I'd ever smelled. Of course, right now there were no flowers, but I could almost smell them in the damp air anyway. The memories were so strong I felt tears prickling in my eyes.

Beside the hedgerow on the left-hand side of the property, there was a narrow public footpath. I followed it around to the rear of the cottage and looked back at the house from this new angle. The new people had put out patio furniture, and through the French doors, I could see that they were in the process of repainting the living room a deep forest green. Aunt Lou had kept it the same shade of toast brown as long as I could remember.

It didn't make me sad to see the house change. Wherever Lou was now, she wasn't in that house. Neither was she hanging around the little Leaford graveyard where her headstone was. I didn't sense her in either of those places, but sometimes I thought I could feel her with me. I'd only told Emma about it, and she'd nodded sagely and said that was to be expected. Lou wasn't tied to a stone or a house – but she would always be a part of me.

So why was I out here in the wet, poking around behind the cottage? I suppose I just wanted to go back to a time when I knew for certain that someone had my back, whatever I decided. Something I'd lost since losing her. Emma was the closest thing I had to that, but it was different with a friend. Lou was like my second mother. Older and wiser and so kind and patient with me. I wanted her back so badly. She'd have known exactly what to do.

I followed the footpath off into the woods, picking my way around the worst puddles of mud. The woods out there were the site of so many of my favourite memories with Lou, from teddy-bear picnics and fairy hunts to building camps, animal watching and foraging. We'd even camped out there a few times, though the land didn't belong to Lou. Just laid our sleeping bags out and watched the stars – sprinting back to the house in fits of giggles at two in the morning when it started to rain that one time. I could see Lou in my head, the bells on her long skirt tinkling as she ran over the springy moss barefoot.

I found one of our camps in the far corner of the woods. The area wasn't very accessible and I had to climb a steep bank and slide down the other side to reach it. That was probably why it hadn't been disturbed much. Though other people had definitely used it in the years since we'd built it. There were a few rusty cans of beer and chunks of charred wood amongst the weeds from a long-extinguished fire. But the camp was still standing. We'd built it like a wigwam, triangular and made of logs and branches leaning against each other. The gaps were plugged with moss which had grown since we'd packed it in, making the whole structure green and velvety on the outside. A bird had built a nest on top of it and white feathers were scattered over the surrounding clumps of dead bluebells. Emma would have called them angel feathers. I was just relieved to find part of my history with Lou still standing.

As I gathered the cans together to take away with me, as she would have done, it started to rain again. Droplets rattled through the autumn leaves, striking the dirt heavily. The air was thick with an approaching storm and the temperature was plummeting. I ducked into the den itself and found that someone had left a log round in there as a seat. Perched on it, I looked out at the rain as it lashed down through the trees. Leaves fell with it and the undergrowth rustled with the ferocity of the rain.

It was surprisingly cosy, sitting there in the little hideout Lou and I had built together. Mostly Lou, to be honest, as I must have only been thirteen or so when we built it. The age was showing, some of the logs were rotting away to powder, breaking away under my nails, but those on the inside were holding up well.

I took my phone out and used the torch in the gloom. Many, many people had decorated the inside of the camp with their initials, swear words and various graffiti marks, all carved into the logs or Sharpied on. I had to really look for it, but I managed to find the first piece of graffiti that had graced its walls. Lou had written our names and the year of construction in silver marker pen, her swirly handwriting standing out under a layer of other messages. I touched the faded silver of her name and wished she was there for me to talk to. But, even as I wished it, I realised something. Possibly the thing that had drawn me all the way out here on a wet Sunday.

I'd been doing Lou a disservice over the past few weeks. My aunt, who I loved so much, whose cottage had felt like home. The woman who'd supported my dreams and shown me what it was to be good at something. She'd given me my entire identity and yet, ever since Richard cheated on me, I'd been telling myself that ending up like Lou was the worst fate I could imagine.

Tears started to flow then. I was horrified at how I'd acted, the things I'd thought about that life in the privacy of my own head. I hadn't really connected them to Lou until I found myself sitting in the camp she'd built with me. Who the hell was I to say that her life had been empty and sad without a husband or children of her own? If anyone else had said it of her, I'd have stamped on their toes.

Aunt Lou had lived in a house so warm and full of love that it had become my escape. She'd had so many hobbies and skills and had shared them with me, because they'd brought her so much joy. She was never left sitting alone and sad, because she had so many friends, so many clubs and societies. Like the one where she'd met Gail.

All the memories I had of her, like building this camp, those were part of a life that hadn't featured marriage or children of her own. The kind of life I'd been going around thinking about as if it was the worst thing that could happen to me. I was ashamed of myself then, looking at her curlicue writing. Her life wasn't the lesser of two options. It wasn't the absence of a man like Richard that had made it. She had built it for herself, like this place. Intentionally and proudly. Because it was what she wanted.

'I'm sorry,' I said aloud, to the dripping rain and creaking timbers. 'I've been acting like a total melon, haven't I?'

I could practically hear her laugh, and I already knew what she'd say.

Just a little. What are you doing out here in the rain? Come inside and get warmed up – tell me all about it and we'll see what we can do.

'What if there's nothing to be done right this minute?' I asked the air.

Well, then we'll have a hot chocolate and not worry too much until tomorrow. And then we'll see about getting things all straightened out, mmm? You're a smart girl, you already know deep down what you need to do.

She was there with me. Not because I was in the camp or because I was near her house, but because I'd shut out all the clutter and buzz that made it hard to hear her soothing voice. Aunt Lou was right, there was nothing I could do today. Richard wouldn't be back until so late that I'd already be asleep, and I wouldn't be back at work until tomorrow. I could take my business and my relationship by the horns tomorrow.

I knew what I wanted and it wasn't Richard. If the options were Richard or being alone – I'd gladly take the latter. Of that I was completely certain.

Chapter 30

It was a good plan in theory but, as it turned out, it lacked a little in the execution. For starters, it was quite hard to break up with your boyfriend when he was never bloody around.

Not only was Richard not in the flat when I went to sleep, he was not there when I woke up. He'd been there – the blender was full of protein-shake sludge and the shoes he'd worn yesterday were in the middle of the floor, a wet towel left in the bathroom. But Richard had come and gone, presumably to work, though I wasn't prepared to bet on it any more.

So the break-up would have to wait. I didn't want to do it over the phone. It had to be in person or he'd only want to meet up and talk it over. Try to 'manage' me as if I was a potential buyer that had just discovered a rat in the master bedroom of one of his properties. I sent him a text saying we should have dinner together tonight and then got ready for work.

While I tried to repair the damage the rain had done to my hair yesterday, I thought about Cooper. I didn't want to think about him, but there he was. Clearly, he didn't want to talk to me and whatever had brought him back to Leaford after his short absence wasn't related to me at all. He'd probably been laying a false trail for whatever creditors or scary characters were trying to find him. It wasn't my problem. He'd made that very clear.

I left the flat and walked to the shop, blushing furiously when I saw Margaret putting a bin full of DVDs out on the pavement. She was wearing her usual scowl and a rollneck jumper over stirrup trousers that she had to have bought in the nineties. No one sold them any more, surely? As she turned, she spotted me and I tried to arrange my face into an expression that said, 'I have no idea of your history with my father and no wish to find out.' I hurried past her and she shunted the DVDs into place with an irritable shove, before disappearing into the mothball-scented embrace of the charity shop.

Emma was never going to believe me when I told her about Margaret. I barely believed it and I'd heard it from my dad's own mouth. Much as I wished I hadn't.

When I arrived at the shop, Emma was already waiting outside, playing a game on her phone. She had an umbrella with her today and had brought in the tubs of leftover brunch for us to polish off before work. She brightened when she saw me and put away her phone.

'Sooo, how did things go yesterday with your dad?' she asked as soon as I was within talking distance.

'Unbelievably,' I said, unlocking the door. 'As in, if I hadn't heard it myself, I would not believe it.'

Inside, while the microwave whirred away to make our breakfast, I filled Emma in on the sordid details. The advocaat, the peonies and Margaret.

'Ugh, you could have waited until after I'd eaten – my GOD!' Emma pulled a face. 'I can't believe it – your dad and… I don't know what to do with this information.'

'Repress it?' I suggested, piling a paper plate with food and handing it over to her. Despite her protestations, Emma dug in immediately. 'That's what I'm planning to do.'

'Aside from the trauma of that mental image… did you get anything out of talking it through with him?' she asked.

'A bit,' I hedged. 'I mean, he said he gave Mum space and then, when she was ready to give him a chance, he promised her he'd do better. He didn't drink again at all until they got engaged. That was over a year later.'

'Wow, sounds like he was really serious about making things

right with her… and not repeating the same mistakes,' Emma said.

I heard the pointedness in her tone, as much as she tried to hide it. She was right, more than she knew. Richard was already backsliding into his old habits – lying and going off to the golf club without any hint as to when he was coming back.

'I mean,' Emma continued, 'it makes it clear that he made a mistake – being so drunk that he'd sleep with Margaret of all people. Instead of just… choosing to cheat.'

'Yes, I get it, thank you,' I said without much heat.

Emma winced. 'Sorry. I know it's your decision…'

'And I've decided to break up with Richard… again,' I said.

Emma threw her hands up, sending a piece of waffle flying through the bead curtain. 'YES! Thank God, I am so proud of you!' She hugged me and I couldn't help laughing.

'Obviously you're on the fence about it,' I giggled.

When Emma pulled back, her cheeks were pink. 'I was really, really trying to be impartial.'

'You're awful at it.'

'I know!' She cracked up. 'But honestly, he's a waste of your time – I'm glad you're breaking up… again. I meant it when I said I was here for you no matter what, but I was basically just trusting that you'd make the right decision for yourself eventually… What was it that finally convinced you?'

I felt a small smile twitch at my mouth. 'Aunt Lou.'

'A wise woman,' Emma nodded.

'Wiser than me. But… I just sat with it for a moment and thought about what she'd say and how unfair it was to think of her life as being worse than life with Richard. She was happy with her hobbies and her friends… and I have a really great friend who's actually there for me and cares about my interests. And who I've been taking for granted while I focus all my time on a man who couldn't tell the difference between knitting and crochet at gunpoint. I'm sorry, and I promise not to do that again.'

She 'cheersed' her plastic fork to mine. 'Welcome back, bestie! And hey, you don't need to be sorry. We all lose our heads from time to time. Especially when it comes to love.'

We got back to our plates but, a few moments later, Emma swallowed a bite of sausage and tapped her fork on the edge of my plate.

'Speaking of love… have you been up to the boat yet?'

'Emma!' I chased her fork away with my own and she looked abashed. 'Just because I'm breaking up with Richard doesn't mean I'm about to go chasing after Cooper.'

'I know! But… did you go up there?' Emma asked, eyes twinkling.

'I… yes, okay? I did,' I admitted. 'But only because I wanted to see where we stood, you know? If he was maybe more open to being friendly now that the shock of seeing that car was over.'

'And was he?' Emma asked.

'He didn't answer the door,' I muttered, sinking into myself a little. 'I could hear the dog moving around and there was a fire burning but he wasn't answering.'

'Oh… are you sure he knew it was you?'

That was a fair point. I wasn't exactly hallooing him with my full name while standing on the deck. But if he was hiding from someone specific, why not peek to see who it was? Either he didn't want to see anyone, including me, or he didn't want to see me specifically. I wasn't sure one was better than the other.

'I don't really want to talk about it,' I said eventually.

'Okay, sure thing. Let me clear up from breakfast and we can start getting the Stitch and Witch supplies together and planning those crafting classes we were talking about – I think we can even get a temporary licence to do wine and cheese one evening.'

I was grateful to her for knowing when to push and when not to. I wasn't really ready to talk about Cooper and how him ignoring me had made me feel. Step one was breaking it off with Richard again. Step two would be finding somewhere to live. I was right back where I'd started before the bust-up with Cooper. Fantastic.

Between us we planned out some ideas for the crafting classes, from specific projects like market totes and Croc liners to more general skills like granny squares and crochet in the round. By the end of the hour, we had a full syllabus, which Emma could type up, and I was going to print them out at the library and post them in as many windows as possible. With the exception of the charity shop, because I could never go in there again now. I'd also pop the details online and hopefully draw in enough people to turn a nice profit.

The supplies for the Stitch and Witch – black, purple and orange sparkly yarns, hooks, pattern sheets and stitch markers – were all set aside for later. Emma had even brought in a black lace tablecloth and I had my record player in the boot, along with some of Aunt Lou's crystal dishes for snacks.

I updated my spreadsheet and was surprised to see how good the numbers were looking. If sales held firm and the classes and Stitch and Witch had even half attendance, we'd be comfortably in the black by the next rent period. The shop might actually not be a colossal mistake. It might just turn into a real business. I'd spent so long thinking of it as a failure that the prospect of mild success sort of blindsided me.

By the time Emma went on her lunch break, I was feeling quite positive about the classes. I'd already found some more cheap brown boxes that we could rubber-stamp with the shop logo and post kits in, for anyone who wasn't local but wanted to join in virtually via our website. I had a webcam somewhere that would work for that.

I was hunting around in a box of cables for it when the bell over the door went. I stuck my head over the counter and saw a woman with dark curly hair all around her shoulders wandering towards me up the centre aisle. She was wearing jeans and a grey leather jacket over a Breton stripe top. She smiled at me, and I took a second to marvel at how precise her red lipstick was. I always ended up looking like the Joker.

'Hi – I'm Addy,' she said, 'I was hoping you could help me.'

'I'll certainly try. I'm Tabitha, by the way,' I said, filled with newfound enthusiasm for customer service now that I wasn't an abject failure at business. What a difference one spreadsheet could make.

'Nice to meet you,' she said, digging around in the black tote hanging on her shoulder. It was Kate Spade and I was expecting her to pull out a pattern she wanted help with, or a magazine picture she intended to dupe from *Vogue*. Instead she produced an A4 piece of paper and handed it over to me.

I found myself looking down at a colour photo of Cooper, printed along with a phone number and an email address. Above the picture was typed 'any information gratefully received'. Holy crap, was I holding a missing poster?

'I've been asking around, seeing if anyone's seen him,' Addy was saying. 'Not that I'm having much luck. The bakery's closed for deep cleaning and I got chased out of the charity shop before I could even hand out a leaflet. What is that woman's problem?'

'Probably something psychological,' I said automatically, still looking at the leaflet. 'Who is he? No one dangerous, I hope?' I said, fishing for info.

'Oh no, nothing like that. I just really, really need to get hold of him. And he's avoiding me. Avoiding everyone, actually,' she said, with an eye roll of annoyance. But there was tension around her mouth. She was making out that it wasn't serious but I could tell she was desperate for any information. But without knowing who she was, I couldn't bring myself to offer Cooper's location up. I glanced down and noted the wedding ring on her hand with a tinge of anxiety. I wasn't sure if she'd seen me looking but she quickly whipped her hand off the counter as her phone started to ring.

She answered, but put her hand over the receiver. 'Sorry, have to get this. My number's on the poster – please do ring if you see him. And don't tell him about me – he might get the wrong idea and scarper again. Hello, Adelaide speaking,' she trilled, already turning away. She was out of the shop before I could scrape some words together to call her back. I wasn't even sure I wanted her to come back.

I looked down at the picture of Cooper again. He looked younger, maybe as much as five years younger. Or perhaps he'd just gone through a lot recently. It was hard to tell. There was a little salt in his hair in that picture, and he was smiling, which made it harder to tell if he had those permanent crinkles around his eyes yet. He was dressed differently, smarter, in a white shirt and dark blue tie with navy suit trousers. What really hit me was the confetti on the grass behind him. The half of a rose arch intruding in the background.

The picture looked as if it had been taken at a wedding.

Addy had looked around his age, maybe a little younger. She had the same sort of dry, intelligent voice and I could easily see them sitting in bed together doing a crossword and sipping coffee of a weekend. If they had been a couple, though, if she still was his wife, why was he hiding out in Leaford? And why was he acting the part of a penniless drifter in his charity-shop knitwear, when his wife was carrying a Kate Spade bag around and wearing a massive diamond on her finger?

The bell went again and I looked up, but it was just Emma coming back from her break. She was carrying a can of Monster and had a library copy of *Spirit and Destiny* tucked under her arm.

'FYI, the bakery's shut. I saw Maeve in the newsagent's and she said they had a pan of caramel boil over and the floor's under about an inch of… what's wrong?'

I slid the piece of paper across the counter towards her and watched Emma's eyes widen when she saw the picture. I looked past her and out of the front windows but there was no sign of Addy, and no way to tell which way she'd gone. Damn it!

'There's a woman going round asking if anyone's seen Cooper,'

I said. 'Long dark hair, stripy top – did you see her as you came in?'

'No, I was looking at my phone,' Emma said, nibbling her lip. 'Why's she looking for him, did she say?'

'She took a call before I could really get much out of her. But she said if I did see him, to call her without telling him she'd been around. Which seems like a massive red flag. She was worried he might run off if he knew about her.'

Emma's eyebrows were in her hairline. 'Jesus… well, you should warn him that she's sniffing around, right?'

'What if she has a good reason to be looking for him?' I said, glancing down at the poster again. 'Like… they might be married or something?'

Emma made a noise of indecision, then tapped the picture meaningfully. 'You know him better than you know her so… I say give him the benefit of the doubt. If you even suspect that she's trying to blindside him, you should tell him.'

Caught in indecision, I gnawed at my thumb and glanced at the window again. Despite my indecision, deep down I was sure Cooper wasn't dangerous or shifty. He deserved my help.

I grabbed my bag from under the counter. 'Hold the fort?'

'Consider the fort held,' Emma said, giving me a salute. 'Ring me if there's trouble and I'll come running, with the entire coven if need be.'

'Thanks,' I said, struggling into my teddy fleece and rushing for the door. 'If Richard comes by, tell him I'm out to lunch!'

Chapter 31

WAS IT FATE, OR just my need for a footwear-based pick-me-up that had inspired me to put the bloody My Little Pony boots on that morning? They'd been dried out and I'd polished them over with clear wax, and now I was risking them again in a mad dash up the towpath. Well, maybe 'dash' was putting it too strongly. I was fast-walking, adding in the odd sort of scuttle every now and again. I hadn't properly run anywhere since I went up to an F cup in sixth form.

I took the shortcut to the towpath and hurried upstream towards where Cooper was moored. It wasn't until I saw the boat still exactly where it had been the day before that I realised I'd been expecting him to be gone again. I was relieved to see it still there. Still more relieved to see no sign of Adelaide on the towpath, though, if she'd rushed up here, she could already be inside. I couldn't rule out the possibility that someone else had seen Cooper and knew that he was the man living in the much-discussed narrowboat.

As I got closer, the curtain in the living area was nudged aside and I saw Charlie's furry face through the gloomy glass. He barked sharply, and a moment later he was swept away and the curtains tugged closed again.

I glared at the curtains. That wasn't going to fly today. It was time for Cooper to put his big-boy pants on and deal with me like an adult. Of course, if I said that to him, he'd probably only point out that I wasn't exactly wearing my 'grown-up' boots. Instead of annoying me, the idea made me smile.

Emma was right, I did like him. Damn it!

Taking extra care to avoid falling in, I stepped over onto the boat and rapped hard on the door. Predictably, no response came from inside.

'I know you're in there!' I called through the door. 'And I know you know it's me!'

Charlie was barking inside and I thought I could hear someone moving around, probably trying to herd him into the bedroom to muffle the sound. I knocked again. Okay, so it was less of a knock and more of a pound.

'Cooper! Even if you don't want to talk to me, I need to tell you something – someone came to the shop looking for you and—'

The door was wrenched open and Cooper stood there looking at me in mingled shock and horror. The sight of him made my heart do a tiny flip in my chest, like a gymnast on the high bar. My first instinct was to hug him, and I quelled it. He was wearing grey joggers tucked into thick woollen socks. I noted little dabs of green and brown paint on the grey fabric and wondered if he'd been decorating. He was also wearing the jumper – my jumper, with the sleeves rolled well up away from any painty mishaps. The jumper that had led me to him in the first place. I saw him glance down, clocking my boots, and I wondered if he appreciated the strange twist of fate that had brought us together again, just like that first day.

'Hi,' I said, more pointedly than I'd intended to. 'Thanks for opening the door this time. I see my cake was welcome inside, even if I wasn't. You're welcome.'

He had the good grace to look slightly embarrassed, stubbled cheeks turning slightly red. He took a step backwards and waved me in, glancing around as if checking to see if I'd been followed. Jesus, he really was worried. What was going on?

Inside, Charlie leapt at me, pawing at my favourite lilac tights and trying frantically to lick my hands. I knelt to give him a good pet and then looked up at Cooper, who was still hovering anxiously by the door.

'Who was it that came looking for me?' he asked, sounding very tired all of a sudden.

'A woman called Adelaide, very pretty, fancy handbag. She's passing out pictures of you and asking for any information.'

Cooper shut his eyes for a second and swore under his breath. 'Did you tell her where I was?'

'Oh yeah, obviously. I drew her a little map, then I just decided to rush up here to tip you off because I love drama,' I said, giving him a look. 'I didn't tell her anything.'

He seemed to sag slightly in relief. 'Okay… thank you. That's… good. Ugh, I should have known this would happen eventually. She's so bloody stubborn.'

'You have something in common then, don't you?' I said. 'I mean, you could have just told me you never wanted to speak to me again, not left under the cover of darkness and then skulked back to hide from me.'

I know I'm being somewhat – okay, a lot – bitchy but he hurt me quite a bit. And I'd only been trying to help. It still smarts, actually, that he couldn't just tell me he'd handle it.

'Skulk… oh, God!' Cooper looked annoyed but also rather embarrassed. 'I didn't flee the area, for God's sake – I went for a test drive and my engine conked out again. Took me a while to get it running. Turns out I could have used your know-how after all. That book was not idiot-proof.'

'Oh,' I muttered, feeling myself turning red, my anger losing all its momentum in the face of relief. He hadn't run away from me on purpose. My heart skipped a little when I realised that. He'd also come back as soon as he could. 'Well, I didn't know that… but you have been avoiding me and you did run off when I was just trying to help and…'

He ran his hands over his hair. 'I know, I um… I'm sorry for that. I shouldn't have snapped at you.' He sighed and leant against the wall. For the first time I noticed that the remainder of the Diana clutter had been cleared away. The boat was dark, with all the curtains drawn, but even in the dim light I could see that it was roomier and that a lot of the display cabinets had also been turfed out. He'd been working hard, not sulking.

'I probably shouldn't have been prying so, you know… takes two to tango,' I said – rather magnanimously, in my opinion. Diana would have been proud. 'If you're in some kind of trouble, I want to help, but you don't have to let me.'

Cooper seemed to waver for a moment, then gestured. 'Shall we talk in the kitchen? I think I'm going to need some tea.'

I went through and noticed on my way that there was a weird shape at the far end of the living area. For a moment I thought it was some kind of horribly misassembled modern piece of furniture, then I got closer and saw that it was a table easel on top of an old ironing board.

Cooper saw me looking and laughed awkwardly. 'Cheapest standing desk around. Found it in a skip.'

'Do you paint then?' I asked, peering at the easel. There was a pad of paper on it and I could see a palette of watercolours and a paint-stained Charles and Diana mug cluttered with brushes and pencils.

'… I do, yeah,' Cooper said, sounding tense.

'Oh!' I turned to him. 'Did you do that watercolour in the bedroom? The one of this boat? I saw it when I was getting changed before. It's really good.'

'Yeah, I did that one.' His voice was soft and I realised that he was shy, looking down at the floor. 'I'm not a professional or anything.'

'You could be – honestly that's a really great picture.' I left the easel alone and moved into the kitchen, where the blinds were open and Charlie had retreated to the bench seat to watch us. Cooper was blushing when he came in behind me and quickly went to a kitchen cabinet, peeling at the edges of some masking tape that held an A3 painting up.

'That's incredible,' I said, before I could stop myself, because it was clear he was a bit self-conscious about his art. But it really was amazing: a large watercolour filled with details hatched in with black ink. A whole flotilla of narrowboats with a pub in the background and a field beside it, with a pair of donkeys watching the world go by. It was somehow both lifelike and pleasantly whimsical. I could easily see it being used to illustrate one of the old-fashioned children's books Aunt Lou had read to me.

'Thanks… did it while I was stuck waiting for a new engine part. Had to have it delivered to that pub.' He indicated the one in the picture. 'They were really good about it actually.'

'You're really, really talented,' I said, still taking in all the details. There were people outside the pub and on the boats, almost painted like flowers – shapes and colours springing up everywhere. The first time we'd met I'd thought he had nimble fingers – artist's fingers, I now realised. I heard a scuffle of papers behind me and saw Cooper rounding up more artwork from the kitchen table, where he'd apparently been sketching in pencil when I came knocking.

I caught my breath, recognising the shape of an as-yet-unlettered sign. It was the wool shop. I reached out to still his hands and he let me take them. He was saying something about them not really being ready yet but I was transfixed. He'd sketched most of the key buildings in town, the ones with historic features anyway – the old church and the Victorian schoolhouse, the library and the chocolate-box cottages near the duck pond and even the ruined blacksmith shack further down the canal, with its rusted anvil still outside and the carved granite water trough. But he'd also drawn my shop, which was nowhere near as interesting. And though all the other pictures had abstract little people in them, there was a fully realised figure at the shop window, caught in the act of turning the sign over, a wistful smile smudged on her little graphite face. Me.

Cooper's fingers joined mine on the page, ready to take it from me.

'Sorry,' he said softly, so close to me. 'I know I should have asked but it was after I'd left and… sketching was the only thing keeping me sane. Well, that and Charlie.'

Hearing his name, the dog perked up, then seemed to realise he wasn't about to get a treat. He settled back down, watching us with expressive chocolate-button eyes. I took a step away from Cooper, trying to still the trembling in my chest.

'It's fine, honestly – I mean it's not like you drew me topless on a Harley,' I joked, lamely. 'I was just a bit surprised – it seemed like you were more of a landscapes guy.'

'I am these days, yeah. Haven't done a portrait since…' He broke off and carefully added my picture to the pile, then made a frustrated noise before saying, overly brightly, 'How about that tea then?'

'Shouldn't you be getting ready to leave?' I asked, reluctantly. 'Now that someone's about to find you?'

'Couldn't even if I wanted to – boat broke down again as soon as I got back here. Like fucking fate,' he muttered, then his shoulders slumped. 'I suppose I should have known this wasn't going to last forever.'

I didn't push for more information. Cooper made the tea and we settled down. He took the slightly rickety stool and I sat on the bench beside Charlie, scratching at his ears. Cooper cupped his hands around his mug and cleared his throat.

'I didn't mean to snap at you that evening. I was just… I panicked, quite frankly. I've felt awful about it ever since and I was too embarrassed to see you again. Didn't think you'd want to see me, to be honest. That car was exactly like Adelaide's and I'm still not really sure if it was her or not. But it freaked me out. I'm not ready to see her, or anyone else from my family. But, Jesus… Addy's going to kill me, she doesn't deserve this.'

Oh, my God, she was his wife. Or girlfriend. Something. Either way he wasn't single.

'I've been a shit brother,' he sighed.

It should not have been as big a relief as it was. But thank God. She was his sister. I couldn't help but let out a sigh as the tension in my chest eased. Even if, as it did so, I had to face just how much I'd wanted him to be single and not a cheating tosser… because I really, really liked him. More than that, I wanted him.

'Stepsister, technically. Her mum's been in my life since I was two, I've never known anyone else. But Addy's always been a good sister, just so pushy, which is part of the reason I…' He cut himself off and huffed. 'Jesus Christ, why is this so hard to talk about?'

I felt bad all over again and wanted to hug him. 'You don't have to—'

'I want to,' he said, cutting me off gently. 'I want… you were honest with me that day about your ex and that jumper and I wanted to be as open with you. It probably would have helped but it's just difficult to talk about. I was never really encouraged to talk about this kind of thing. It's not something men do, is it? All this emotional… stuff.'

I could hear someone else's voice in those words. Cooper wasn't saying something he believed, it was something he'd been told. He was trying to get past it and struggling.

'That's okay, take your time,' I said. 'I'm not going anywhere.' I really wasn't. Nothing in the world could have moved me from that spot across from him.

The corner of his mouth lifted into a shy smile. 'Okay… right, well, have you ever felt like… your family has your whole life planned out for you and, any time you make a decision for yourself, you're just…'

'Messing up their schedule?' I said, and he nodded, face relaxing. 'Yeah, I know the feeling. Intimately.'

'It's shit, isn't it?' Cooper huffed. 'I'm over thirty and I'm still sick at the thought of letting my dad down. Which is what it feels like every time I do something other than what he wants. He's sort of a strong personality.'

I thought of my parents. 'I'm also familiar with that. Parents are… complicated.'

'Aren't they just?' He laughed under his breath, then sobered. 'The thing is… before the past few months I was someone else.

Someone… who had a life I didn't like very much. If I had it my way, I'd have gone to art school, but the painting was always something I had to hide because… well, it wasn't what I was meant to be doing. Not something that added any value to my future.'

There it was again, that other voice. That had to be his father. He'd said at the library that he'd been trying to break out of living in his image. It seemed like it was deeply ingrained in him. The same way Mum's desire for grandkids was imprinted on my brain.

Cooper sighed. 'Recently I got back into art, to do a portrait for our parents' wedding anniversary. I've never painted professionally – I wanted to because, honestly, it's the only thing I've ever been good at – but I never did – I just kept it up as a hobby really. A sort of release, but Dad was very scathing.' He gritted his teeth for a second and then forced himself to relax. 'He started laying into me at the party, that if I had time to be "messing around" with that stuff still, then I clearly wasn't working hard enough and no wonder I wasn't where he was at my age.'

I frowned at him, trying to piece together the components of what he was saying. His dad sounded like a dick, but that didn't seem like it would send most people running off in a dodgy old narrowboat. Cooper had obviously not finished, though.

'I'm… I *was* a solicitor, like my dad. Like my grandfather. It was what I was always meant to do, right from when I was little and Dad used to take me to work and show me round. He had me doing Latin at GCSE, work experience at his office, multiple languages at A level, every advanced tutor and course he could get for me. I worked my arse off to get my degree and become a fully-fledged solicitor… and I hated it.' He took a swallow of tea and hunched over further on the stool, hands rubbing over the soft arms of the jumper. 'I wasn't good at it, nothing about that life came easy to me. It was like I was this animal forced into an unnatural environment. Like a fucking fish in an aviary.'

I laughed, then clapped a hand to my mouth. 'I'm so sorry,' I mumbled.

Cooper snorted. 'It was a stupid analogy – I like making you laugh, though.'

'So… you hated being a solicitor?' I prompted, my insides fluttering pleasantly despite the seriousness of the conversation.

'Oh, yeah, completely. The hours, the stress, the other people. I mean, the money was good but all I was spending it on was cleaners and ready meals. The rest was just piling up in my account because I had no life to spend it on. I couldn't balance the job with having a life and the only other people I met were so into the work that we had nothing in common. Um… the last time I actually dated someone was three years ago. We met at work and she was so into it, you know? But I felt like I was lying every time we planned for the future. In the end I had to let her go. We weren't right for each other, because I was pretending and she wasn't.'

I thought of Richard and swallowed a hard ball of guilt. On some level, I'd been pretending too, as I ignored all the ways in which we weren't compatible.

Cooper took a breath. 'I think the painting incident was the final straw, but it had been building for a while. I just… couldn't cope. I wanted out. I needed it. Which in itself was humiliating. I was thirty-one and having a midlife crisis.'

He looked so ashamed that I went to reach out, then thought better of it and brought my hand to wrap around my mug. 'That's not your fault. You obviously gave it everything you had.'

He gave me a small smile. 'It wasn't enough. I uh…' he scoffed at himself, 'I had a bit of a… mental thing. I don't really know what to call it – "breakdown" sounds too dramatic for what it was. I just stopped going to work, didn't answer their calls. It felt like, if I got fired, then at least I hadn't quit, you know? Like it was a loophole into getting out of that mess without making a decision. I stayed home and just lay in bed, couldn't make my mind up what I wanted to do so I just did nothing. Then a week or so into that, I had to get out of there and I went for a drive, parked up in a random village and walked around for a bit. I saw the advert for the boat on a bus shelter. It was like being in a trance. I took the poster down and rang up about it and, a few hours later, I owned a boat. I didn't pack anything or even sell my car, I just went. I didn't tell anyone where I was going – not work, not my family… I didn't even leave a note. And then, by the time I was moored up for the night and sat here with about a million Dianas looking at me and thinking "what the hell have I done?" I couldn't bring myself to tell anyone that I'd lost it. Dad doesn't really "do" mental health… it just seemed like it would be easier to never look back.'

'… and now Adelaide's found out you're staying here,' I finished. 'Oh, Cooper, she must be frantic. She obviously cares a lot about you.'

I immediately felt bad for adding to his misery. But it was too late to take it back now. Cooper nodded, like he was already thinking it anyway.

'It's my own stupid fault – I used my card when I was stranded at that pub and had to order that part online. I hoped he wouldn't but the landlord might have told her I came from here. Or she's found me from people online complaining about the boat. I just don't know what to say to her. To any of them,' he muttered. 'I felt like such a failure and then you…' He stopped himself, clearly embarrassed.

'Me? Me what?' I said stupidly. 'I nearly drowned and that reminded you that regrets are a waste of time?'

He laughed. 'No, but… you did remind me what it's like to be… passionate about something.'

He was looking at me with such a soft-eyed openness that it almost hurt to look at. But, at the same time, I didn't want to look away, even as it made my heart ache in my chest. I didn't want to be anywhere else but right there, on that boat, with that man. I reached over the table and he took my hand.

'To be fair, at first I did think you were slightly mad,' Cooper said, mouth twitching cheekily. 'But as soon as you started talking about the jumper and the crochet… how much it obviously hurt you to give it away, it reminded me of how I felt when I was painting. How special a thing it was to make that portrait for my parents and give it to them, to share something I was so proud of…' He squeezed my hand, looking down at our interlaced fingers. 'You sort of made me see the point in trying again. In valuing my own skills.'

'You'd already painted the boat, though,' I pointed out. 'You don't need to give me credit…'

'Yeah, well… that was me freaking out on the first day I spent on here. Painting that made me feel more in control, and it…' He laughed at himself drily. 'It sounds stupid but it took me right back to when I learned watercolours at school. To when it all just clicked for me and I was happy and it felt like I had my whole future ahead of me.'

Warmth flooded my chest. 'That's not stupid… that's how crochet makes me feel. When I'm sad, it's like having my aunt there with me. And it helps.'

Our eyes met and the warm weight of understanding travelled between us. Even though his eyes were reddened and he was unshaven and tired-looking, I'd never been more attracted to anyone than the way I was to him at that moment. I wanted to put my arms around him and be close to him. It just felt easy, like reaching the end of a row with a perfect stitch count, the right tension, everything aligned to make the pattern turn out exactly right.

I watched his throat bob as he swallowed, a tiny frown creasing his forehead. 'Why didn't you pay in the cheque?'

'The… oh, that… was that not a joke?' I asked, my heart skipping over itself.

Cooper's frown became more playful. 'I don't tend to write many "joke cheques" because that's a really stupid way to lose a lot of money. I wanted you to have it because your work was worth it – it's really good, I have no idea how you do it and, from what you said, it seemed like what's-his-face didn't really appreciate it any more than my dad did my painting so… hence the cheque.'

I giggled. 'Hence?'

'Verily,' Copper snorted. 'Christ, I don't know. It made sense at the time. As you can probably tell, I'm not exactly doing great in the decision-making department.'

I groaned. 'Same… I, um, I got back together with "what's-his-face" after… when we stopped speaking.'

Cooper's eyes were as dark and curious as Charlie's. 'When we stopped speaking,' he echoed.

My cheeks burned. 'It wasn't like you drove me back into his arms or anything. I just, it was a low point and I went to my mum for what turned out to be some well-intentioned, but ultimately not that applicable, advice.'

'Ah,' Cooper nodded, though I could see he still had a lot of questions. 'So you've broken up with him again?'

'Um… sort of but not really?' I said, feeling awkward. 'I decided I wanted to break up with him, but then he stayed out late and left early, so it's sort of a "when I see him next" thing. I thought doing it over text or the phone would be a bit insensitive.'

Cooper nodded. 'And, obviously, you want to be sensitive towards the guy who brought another woman into your home,' he said, pulling a face.

I squeezed my eyes shut and let out a long sigh. 'I know… but, for my sake at least, I want to keep it civil.'

'That's because you're a good person – much better than me,' Cooper pointed out. 'If I'd walked in on someone cheating on me, I'd… probably buy a boat and run away.'

'Sounds like a better strategy, if I'm being honest,' I sighed.

'It has its moments but, I wouldn't recommend it.' Cooper looked around the kitchen and then down at our joined hands. 'Since coming here, I've been struck with the realisation that most of what was making me miserable wasn't the job or my family, it was the stuff I carry around in my head. All the regrets and wasted time. I can't outrun those.'

'But that doesn't mean they're going to be there forever,' I said, thinking of my own epiphany in the woods. 'There's always time to change and try again, now you've had some room to think. You can go back and talk to your family and start over the right way this time.'

Cooper's thumb traced over mine, the whisper of a new callus against my skin. My breath stuttered. 'I'm not sure I want to go back, not physically anyway. There's… I think I'd regret going before I found out what could happen here.'

'Here?' I echoed, and leant in a little at the same time as he did, over the pile of Leaford sketches.

'Mmm,' Cooper hummed in agreement, and his mouth brushed mine, autumn-chapped lips and stubble taking my breath away.

Both of us jumped as someone started pounding on the outer door.

Chapter 32

We pulled back from each other and Cooper's frown neatly mirrored my own. The interruption, cutting off our first kiss, was most unwelcome, to say the least.

'Who the hell is that?' Cooper muttered, then looked pained, probably thinking about Adelaide. Cooper got up and I followed him back into the gloomy living area. Charlie shot past us both, barking manically at the sudden intrusion.

To my shame, I was about to say 'Who cares? Ignore it!' when the banging came again, even louder. Accompanied by an irritatingly familiar voice.

'Oh, my God!' I groaned. 'It's Richard.'

'The soon-to-be-ex-boyfriend?' Cooper looked torn between annoyance and amusement. 'How does he even know you're here?'

'God knows, but I really don't want to deal with him right now.' No, right now I wanted to thread my fingers through Cooper's grey-dusted hair and kiss the crinkles at the corners of his eyes, run my hands under his jumper and just be here with him. Richard had taken enough of my time already, three whole years of it. Couldn't I have just an hour or two before he had to make his presence known again?

'What do we do?' I asked softly. 'He might not know for sure that I'm in here – he's probably bluffing.'

'I have you on the "find my phone" app,' Richard called through the door. 'There's no point pretending you're not here!'

How was he doing that? This was probably the first and only time in our relationship where I suspected him of being able to read my mind. He'd really picked his bloody moment on that one. I made a mental note to delete that app and possibly make an entirely new account, just to be safe.

'I don't think we can hide in here forever,' Cooper said, clearly slightly amused by the tantrum Richard was throwing outside, sputtering and harrumphing at his door like he was a middle-class wolf and we were the two little pigs.

'We could try?' I whined.

'We could… but I haven't done a food shop in a while and the boat's engine's knackered, so we'd be stuck in here starving to death. Probably better to face it head-on.'

I gave him a look.

'I realise that's incredibly hypocritical,' he said, raising both hands in surrender. 'But even so.'

The knocking and bellyaching were suddenly replaced by a general scuffling and muted conversation. For a second I thought I heard Emma out there, and prayed she was seeing Richard off so I wouldn't have to deal with him right now, in front of Cooper. Then the female voice outside rose imperiously and I realised it wasn't Emma. It was Adelaide.

'… will you move? My brother's in there, I don't care what you…' Someone slapped the boat's door with the flat of their hand. 'Jarvis! Jarvis Cooper, I know this is your boat – come out and face me like a man, or I'll wriggle through a porthole!'

I looked at Cooper. He looked at me.

'Jarvis?' I sputtered, struggling not to full-on giggle.

'Tabitha,' he said pointedly, though his ears were turning pink.

'Still think I should face it head-on and open the door?' I asked, folding my arms.

'I… yes. I think we both should.' Cooper looked at the door, then winced. 'Or we could switch things round on them? I take yours, you take mine?'

'If it were a physical fight, I'd say you're on, but I think we should probably talk to them,' I sighed. Then I held out my hand for his. 'But we can do it together? Moral support?'

'Is that not going to upset him, a lot?' Cooper looked more amused at the prospect than reluctant.

'I think it probably will but it's no worse than what I walked in on,' I pointed out.

Cooper took my hand and we moved towards the door. Opening it was like coming out of a cinema screening at midday. For a moment there was so much bright autumnal light that the two figures on the deck were blurry dark shapes. Then they resolved into a red-cheeked Richard, and Adelaide, who looked markedly more put-together. She was carrying a bottle of apple juice and I realised she must have gone into the newsagent's to buy it, and any of the busybodies currently gossiping in there would have told her about the boat. Even if they'd only told her when it had shown up, that had to be enough of a clue for her to look into it.

She looked surprised to see me. I felt a small flush of pride, maybe I was actually good at subterfuge. Conversely, Richard looked grimly satisfied to have his suspicions confirmed and he even shook his head at me as I stood with Cooper in the little doorway. Richard ignored Adelaide entirely, though I caught her giving him a look of distaste out of the corner of her eye. Clearly, she wasn't impressed with his performance.

'Jarvis.' Adelaide's shoulders slumped a little and she raised a half-smile for him. 'Do you have any idea the places I've been trying to find you?'

'I know, Addy… I'm sorry,' Cooper said. 'I wanted to—'

'I knew it,' Richard interrupted, lip curled. 'I knew you were lying about him the moment I saw those clothes. How long has this been going on then, hmm?'

Trapped behind our legs, Charlie barked at Richard. Something I wished it was socially acceptable for me to do, honestly.

'Oh, for God's sake – I haven't been seeing Cooper behind your back,' I snapped, even though technically I had sort of nearly kissed him before Richard started banging on the door. But that was slightly different – I had been about to break up with Richard. Bloody well would have if he'd bothered coming home or been there when I woke up. He was on borrowed time as it was.

'Sure, I believe that,' Richard scoffed. 'You must think I'm an idiot.'

'And what do you think I am, if you really thought I'd buy that you were out with Rob, after you told me he was spending a fortnight in Tenerife!' I couldn't keep my voice from rising, ringing out over the canal and sending a moorhen thrashing across the water as if terrified of being included in our drama. That or it was off to spread the gossip to its little moorhen friends.

Richard's mouth clamped shut and his eyes flicked from me to Cooper and back again. I could see him looking for an excuse or a way to turn this around and get angry with me all over again – for 'spying' or 'checking up' on him and I didn't want to wait for that.

'Richard, I made a mistake taking you back,' I said, as firmly as possible. Cooper's hand in mine made it easier to look Richard in the eye and make him hear me. 'I think I was right the first time.'

'Are you breaking up with me?' Richard sputtered.

'I think that's fairly obvious,' Adelaide surprised me by interjecting. 'Now can you piss off so I can talk to my brother?'

Richard glared at her, then back at me. 'We're not over until I agree we are!' Richard stamped on the deck and I caught Cooper's wince out of the corner of my eye as the heel of Richard's shoe left a dent in the old wood. 'And I think you need to take responsibility for your part in…'

'You screwing someone else on her handmade blanket?' Cooper said, reaching up and leaning against the doorframe in what I realised was an attempt to look taller than Richard. Bless him. 'What happened, she left an impractical boot on the floor and you tripped and fell into someone else?'

A laugh squeaked out of me and Richard shot me a poisonous look. Behind him I saw Adelaide's eyebrows fly up. Clearly, she hadn't expected so much extra drama when she confronted her brother. But she didn't seem displeased. If anything, there was a smile struggling to escape through her huffy demeanour.

'Maybe if she spent more time on me and less on her fucking knitting, I wouldn't have gone elsewhere,' Richard sniffed.

'Crochet,' Cooper and I said at the same time. I squeezed his fingers and he nudged against me. Richard looked at the pair of us in disgust.

'Whatever!' Richard clenched his fists. 'That's still no excuse to go off and screw the first… homeless river dweller you come across. God, have some self-respect, Tabs. He's *ancient*.'

Adelaide's startled laugh was like a blackbird's call, and she covered her mouth immediately. Cooper glared at her and I couldn't believe I'd ever thought they might be married. That was pure sibling communication. The universal language of 'oh sure, you can find it funny, but just you wait'.

'I'm only thirty-one,' Cooper muttered.

I slowly removed my hand from Cooper's so I could wrap my arm around his waist. Cooper, after a slight pause, slipped his around me too. I glanced up at him and it all felt so right. So easy. I couldn't believe I'd spent so long agonising over Richard and whether leaving him was the right thing to do or not. If it was that hard, and we hadn't even reached the marriage and kids discussions, didn't that tell me what I needed to know? It hadn't felt right and I wasted so much time trying to work out why, when really the answer was simple. It felt wrong because it was. We were all wrong for each other.

And everything that had happened with Cooper since he'd arrived had been telling me he was right for me. From his tatty books and easy smile, the banter and his penchant for Dolly. We weren't the same but, as Emma said, that wasn't important. He just got me and I got him.

Richard looked like he was about to bite through his own tongue. 'This is a new low, even for you. You have no idea what you're… is that my fucking jumper?'

'Well… mine now,' Cooper pointed out. 'Cheers for that, by the way – it's great.'

'It's actually really nice,' Adelaide put in. 'Which is surprising, because you usually just order in bulk from the M&S sale page, like someone's grandad.'

'Thanks – it's cashmere,' Cooper said, with a smile like a cat looking at the sun. 'Tabitha made it.'

'For me!' Richard snapped.

'For my boyfriend,' I retorted. 'And you stopped being that when you cheated on me.'

'So, what, you took me back for a few days, now you want to bin me off and make this… drifter your boyfriend?' Richard said scathingly.

'I…' I stammered, face flaming. 'I mean… we hadn't really discussed if… but if he was open to it…'

'He is,' Cooper said quickly, like he was telling me a secret, giving my waist a squeeze. 'He's very open to the idea. Super bloody open.'

I turned towards him, my pulse singing in my veins. 'Really?'

'Yeah,' Cooper's eyes flicked to my mouth and my heart skipped like a stone over the water.

A loud splash made both of us jump. I turned to see Richard floundering in the water, spitting and cursing as he tried to thrash his way to the bank.

'Honestly, Jarvis – you can't steal a man's girlfriend and then take your eye off him – obviously he's going to try and push you overboard – it's not like he'd stand a chance in a fair fight,' Adelaide chided, brushing water droplets from her leather jacket and stepping away from the side of the boat. I couldn't believe she'd pushed him, but I wasn't exactly annoyed about it. If he'd managed to shove Cooper, I'd have gone over with him.

'I wouldn't call it stolen – I was basically donated,' I said, looking down as Richard dug his fingers into the wet bank and struggled to climb out of the water. 'He gave me away really.'

'Oh… shut up,' Richard growled, as he got to his feet, which squelched in their expensive loafers. 'Just wait until I tell your parents about this. They'll probably have you sectioned.'

I ignored him. If he wanted to go crying to my mum and dad about how I'd broken up with him, that was just one more reason to be glad I'd done it. Mum might try to talk me round but I didn't fancy Richard's chances with Dad. Especially not once I told him that Richard had tried to shove Cooper and, by extension, me, overboard.

Richard stormed off down the towpath, dripping water and shedding wet leaves as he went. The pitiless laughter of ducks following him out of sight. Then it was just me and Cooper and Adelaide, standing on the deck of The Lady Di.

'So then,' she said, 'are you going to invite me in?'

Chapter 33

'THIS IS LOVELY,' ADELAIDE said, peering around the kitchen, as Charlie wormed his way closer to her under the table. 'Though I have to say I never pegged you for a royalist.'

There was, indeed, still a heavy Diana presence in the kitchen. Though the majority of the decorations and displays were gone, Cooper had kept most of the practical items – mugs, tea towels, chopping boards, etc, which bore the faces of Charles and, more prominently, Diana.

Cooper shrugged, putting a fresh cup of tea in front of her. 'She was the people's princess… so… how is everyone?'

Adelaide rolled her eyes. 'You mean, since you disappeared without telling a soul where you were going, how are we all doing? It's a mess, Jarvis. Mum's been involving the police but, apparently, you're "low-priority".'

He snorted. 'Sounds about right.'

'Oh, boo-hoo!' Adelaide said, sharp as her scarlet nails. 'I mean that you're not a child or someone's doddery old gran – you're allegedly a functioning adult, who can take care of himself.'

Cooper scoffed and sat back on his stool beside me, arms crossed over his chest. He looked like such a sulky little boy that I wanted to elbow him. Only the knowledge of what he'd been going through made me relent. He apparently still didn't know how to tell his family, even his sister, what it had been like for him. I understood what that was like.

'I can wait outside if you two need some space,' I said gently, but Cooper shook his head.

'Stay… please?'

"It's okay with me,' Adelaide said, shrugging. 'Even if you did lie to me.'

'I thought you might be coming to break his legs or something,' I said. 'Or… you know, that you might be his… wife.'

Adelaide retched and Cooper screwed up his face like he'd just eaten half a cockroach buried in a sandwich.

'All right! Give me a break, I called it wrong,' I huffed. 'Like you're so perfect.'

'Fair,' Cooper said, looking pensive again as he looked back at his sister. 'I'm sorry about upsetting you and Mum.'

'Dad's been out looking for you too,' Adelaide said, softening. 'He says he's going to the pub "because of the stress" and then he drives around to different places – hospitals, shelters, bus stations… anywhere someone might have seen you.'

Cooper slumped lower in his seat. 'I didn't mean to worry everyone. I wasn't thinking.'

'That much was obvious.' Adelaide sighed and looked at him beseechingly. 'What happened? We got a call from your work saying you hadn't been in. I went to your flat and you'd not been there in days, but you hadn't packed anything. Then when I checked your bank activity…'

'Oi!' Cooper bristled.

'Well then, don't disappear and leave your logins written under your keyboard,' Adelaide huffed. 'Anyway, when I saw you'd taken out a load of cash and vanished, I was thinking… I don't really know, that you'd got into something through work and had to lie low for a while. Go off-grid. Can't say I imagined you'd gone full *Rosie and Jim* into the bargain.'

I snickered, and even Cooper laughed under his breath. But Adelaide sobered first.

'Are you in trouble?'

'…no,' Cooper sighed. 'No, I'm not "in trouble". I'm just… I couldn't do it any more, Addy. The job, that life… Dad. It all got on top of me and I realised I didn't like anything about my life. I didn't know why I was bothering to live it. Just that doing anything else felt too hard with him set against it.'

Adelaide's eyes went shiny and she reached out and laid her hand on his arm gently, as if worried he might run away again. Cooper sniffed and patted her hand with his own.

'I wanted to get away for a bit and breathe. That's all. Just find some space to breathe. To think, but then, the longer I was away, the harder it seemed to go back and I kept imagining what Dad would say, until just picking up the phone was impossible. He's going to be furious when he finds out I left my job.'

'He'll be happy you're okay,' Adelaide murmured.

'For about fifty seconds, before he gets angry,' Cooper said. 'You know what he's like about me and my painting, and that's what I've decided I want to do. I've got money, he did that much for me by pushing me into this career. I'm not struggling for a living and, for the first time, I'm not going to let him tell me what is and isn't a waste of my life… you never had to deal with that.'

'Yes, because I'm a lowly girl-child and nothing was expected of me on the professional front – which was obviously peachy for me,' Adelaide said acidly.

Cooper's ears burned pink. 'Sorry.'

She deflated and waved him off. 'Eh, my issues with Dad are old news – even my therapist is probably bored of them,' Adelaide said, tapping her fingers on her mug. 'Suffice to say… I get it. Okay? He's not easy to get on with and he's very set in his ways. But I'm not and you could have spoken to me before running off. I would have told him for you if you didn't feel like you could. I wouldn't even have given up the goods on where you were. He could never make me do anything, you know that.'

Cooper looked genuinely surprised by this, though that was quickly swallowed by anxiety. 'Are you going to tell him where I am now?'

Adelaide looked between us and idly petted Charlie with her free hand. '… No, I won't. I'll tell him and Mum that you're okay and that you're taking a break for a bit. But you have to promise you'll phone me twice a week so I know you're okay and that you'll at least email them and your boss by the end of the month to start straightening things out. You'll feel better once you've properly cut ties with work and let Mum and Dad know how you feel. I promise. I certainly did when I told them Eric and I weren't having babies. It's never as bad as you imagine.'

Cooper made a doubtful noise and Adelaide kicked him under the table. Charlie took an interest in this new game and sat up, wagging his tail.

'He still has that painting, you know,' she said, avoiding Cooper's eye. 'I know he was less than complimentary at the party, but it's in the dining room. Pride of place.'

'I didn't know that,' Cooper muttered.

'The things you miss when you don't come to Sunday dinner,' Adelaide said with a half-smile. 'I mean it, Jarvis. Call me twice a week or I'll be back down here making your life difficult… I might do that anyway, actually. This place is actually quite charming.' She turned to me. 'I imagine we'll be seeing a lot of each other, "Tabitha from the wool shop".'

'Hopefully. Though I'll make sure he calls you anyway,' I said, and she cracked a smile.

'I like you.' She waved a red nail at me. 'She's sensible – you need some of that. Adore the shoes, by the way.'

I gave Cooper a triumphant look, my maligned boots having been approved by his stylish sister. He snorted.

'Anyway, I have a room booked at a lovely B&B with a spa, so, now I know you're not lying in a ditch somewhere' – she gave Cooper a reproachful look – 'I'll leave you two to do… whatever it was you were up to before that idiot and I turned up.'

'Thanks,' Cooper said. 'For coming after me, I mean.'

'What else are little sisters for, if not for finding you when you don't want to be found?' Adelaide said, standing and brushing Charlie's shed hair from her jeans.

'I'll show you out,' Cooper said, and we rose too.

'It's a narrowboat, Jarvis, not the Tower of London. I can let myself out.' She gave him a hug and swung her bag onto her shoulder. 'Take care of yourself, okay? Oh, and check at the Post Office occasionally. Now I know where you are, I can send you some things – starting with your hairbrush, a razor and some normal mugs. It was lovely to meet you, Tabitha, by the way. Thank you for protecting my brother – even if you didn't know from what exactly.'

We said our goodbyes standing in the living area and Adelaide let herself out, letting the narrow door swing shut behind her. A moment later, I heard her jaunty step on the towpath and turned to find Cooper watching me.

We were alone again. No more Richard, no more running. I knew his name, his history, his secret. He knew mine. There was nothing hidden between us any more. This was really, finally happening.

Cooper – he'd always be Cooper to me – met my eye. 'Sure you still want a mess like me?'

'You're not a mess, you know,' I said softly. 'You just got a bit lost. I know what that's like, believe me.'

'You don't look lost to me.'

'I'm not. Not any more.'

My skin tingled as I thought of our interrupted kiss, and I could tell Cooper was thinking about it too. He took a step towards me and I reached for him. Our lips met in a kiss that started light but deepened by the second. Cooper's hand cupped the back of my head, fingers threading into my hair. My own hands wandered over the soft cashmere of the jumper, pulling it up and caressing the warm skin beneath.

Cooper pulled back, with a parting nip to my bottom lip. 'We should lock the door.'

I pressed closer to him. 'Presumptuous.'

We kissed again and I turned us, stumbling back against a wall and weaving my arms around his shoulders. He really was the perfect height for me, my neck wasn't twingeing at all. Cooper leant against the wall, scooping me against himself.

'Bedroom?' I broke away to ask.

'Very presumptuous,' he murmured.

'I am… Lock the door?'

Cooper rushed to bolt the outer door, skidding on a stray scrap of sketchbook paper as he went. I tried not to giggle, watching him trip over his own socked feet. He reached me and swept me towards the bedroom, kissing the join between my neck and my shoulder. I grabbed my handbag on the way, knowing I had condoms in there from my last weekend break with Richard. I couldn't remember the last time I'd felt so alight with need – the last time I'd actually craved someone else's touch like this.

God, I really had been deluding myself into staying with Richard. Never again.

Cooper turned me and I went to sprawl on the bed, then he stiffened and held me back.

'What is it?' I asked.

He grabbed the crochet blanket from the bed and folded it up, depositing it onto a battered little IKEA footstool that he'd acquired since I'd last been in there. I raised an eyebrow.

'What?' He said defensively. 'It's new, I don't want it to get ruined.'

'You—' I laughed, then squealed as he dived at me, and we both fell onto the bed in a tangle of limbs. My handbag hit the floor and a ball of black yarn bounced out, an aluminium crochet hook rattling across the floorboards.

Outside, Charlie whined and scratched at the door, then pattered back to his bed. I wrestled the jumper over Cooper's head and he unbuttoned my blouse. Our eyes kept meeting, gleeful and sharing the delight that we could do this, we were doing this. Finally.

Still, when Cooper pressed me against the mattress and I wrapped my legs around his waist, he paused, hands on his fly.

'Are you sure?' he asked, softly.

My answer was immediate and brought a smile to my lips.

'Oh God, yes.'

Chapter 34

'I CAN'T BELIEVE YOU brought that with you,' Cooper said, waking from a doze and stretching under the duvet. We were both curled up in the warmth of his bed, sated and boneless. As lovely as watching him sleep had been for the first forty minutes, a girl could have too much of a good thing, and I'd never been one to sit with idle hands.

'I never leave home without a project, or the means to start one,' I said, carefully completing my stitch before laying down my hook and the beginnings of a sock on the duvet. 'And, you know, since we're taking a break...'

'Romantic,' Cooper chuckled, rolling over to lie on his front, chin propped on one hand while the other stroked my thigh.

'I'm making this for you and your ridiculously cold feet anyway – that's romantic as hell.' I leant over and kissed him. 'Speaking of, get those hand warmers on, you. I don't want to be jumping out of my skin when we get going again.' I picked up my hook again. 'Not because of the cold anyway.'

He rubbed his stubble over the inside of my knee and I shivered pleasantly.

'Yes, miss,' he muttered. 'Cup of tea?'

'Oooh... yes, please.'

Cooper rolled out of bed, pulled the jumper over his head and padded to the kitchen. Looking at the slightly too-big jumper, and his lovely bare legs, I thought it was worth every hour I'd spent on it after all.

My handbag, still on the floor amongst my cast-off clothes,

started to hum. I grimaced but hunted for my phone anyway. I'd been too occupied to notice but there were several missed calls and texts waiting for me. Two from Emma letting me know that Richard had come by the shop looking for me, and another to say she hoped I was okay. I shot her back a quick message that I was in fact great (so great), and remembered with a wince of guilt that the Stitch and Witch was happening tonight and I would need to get back for it. I messaged to assure her I'd be there.

Then there were also several messages from Mum and one from Dad. He wasn't a big texter and it just said 'glad u r shot of him'. Mum on the other hand was going off in my messages. Not exactly scolding me or getting arsey, but she seemed confused and hurt.

Richard's here, he said you're seeing someone else and just broke up with him? What happened?? You were going into business together! Now he's crying in the front room – I had to put him on a towel, he's all wet! He said some man pushed him in the canal?

Of course he'd said Cooper did it. Richard would never admit that a woman had topped him over. I rolled my eyes and quickly read her other messages.

He said it's the boat man everyone's talking about on Facebook. Are you all right, Tabby? Is it the stress from the shop? I'm sure Dad and I can help out if you're stressed, there's no need to throw everything away.

Dad just threw Richard out – he won't tell me what R said to him but he's very angry with him. I rang the shop and your friend told me about this river person – she said he gave you a cheque for 5k as a joke?? That's not something people do, Tabby!

Okay, so she was right about that one. I wondered what Richard had said to make Dad snap and throw him out. I could only imagine. I was glad he wasn't at their house any more, though.

Richard didn't belong there any more than I belonged on his beloved golf course. If he'd ever even played golf there. For all I knew, he'd been with that other woman the entire time. He was probably with her now, mourning the fact that he wouldn't have me stripping wallpaper for him for free.

My first idea was to message Mum so I could avoid a direct confrontation. But I'd been doing enough of that. It was time to face her head-on and treat her with the respect I was asking for. It was only fair.

I tapped her number and she picked up almost at once. 'Tabby? What is going on?'

'Hi, Mum. Everything's fine. I um… I broke up with Richard again and he didn't take it too well.'

'For this… boat man?' Mum asked.

'No, for cheating on me and for being a terrible boyfriend. He wasn't right for me, Mum. I'm… sorry, because I hid that from you and it wasn't fair of me to make you think he was perfect and then kick him to the kerb without explaining. I should have just been honest from the start.'

'But he was perfect for you—' Mum started.

'He really wasn't,' I interrupted, gently but firmly. 'He didn't care about my business, he thought my best friend was a flake, he was ungrateful, messy and obnoxious… and I had to practically force him to come and visit my family.'

That stunned her. 'But… he always seemed to like coming over for our get-togethers.'

I took a breath. Time to tell the truth. All of it. 'He called your garden a "lower-middle-class eyesore" the first time I brought him over. And I don't think he kept a single present you guys ever got him for a birthday or Christmas. He once told me he saw you guys in Asda and ran away so he wouldn't get "trapped talking to you". And I was too desperate to keep a boyfriend that you liked to realise that I didn't like him, and if you knew him, you wouldn't either.'

There was a long pause as Mum digested this. Or rather,

choked it down like a fish bone. I knew it was hard to swallow the truth after so long feeding myself a diet of lies.

'… what a… tosser,' Mum said slowly. 'Tabby, I had no idea! I'd never have suggested you take him back if I knew he was such a…'

'Grubby little classist worm?' I supplied.

'Exactly. You're better off without him. And… I'm sorry too, for not listening to you that day, in your old room. I've been talking to Dad and he made me realise that maybe it's not always obvious that I just want you to be happy. I don't mind if that's on your own, or with a man, or a woman! Like your Aunt Lou.'

My jaw dropped in shock. 'Aunt Lou?' I repeated.

Mum laughed. 'Well, yes. Tabby, don't tell me you never knew she and Gail were together.'

'I did know but you never talk about it,' I sputtered.

'She was so hurt when she lost Gail, I suppose I just got used to not talking about her,' Mum sighed sadly. 'That and this town hasn't always been as accepting, old habits are hard to break.'

You're telling me, I thought.

'Anyway…' Mum said, 'you're welcome to move back in. I'll see about shifting a few things to Dad's shed—'

'Oooh, actually,' I interrupted, having a brainwave. 'Do you think Dad would mind if I moved into the shed for a while? Then I could have a bit of… space?'

'I don't see why not. He can always pop round to Terry's to watch the football,' Mum said. 'Leave it with me. I'll sweet-talk him.' She paused and I could almost hear her mind working. 'So… about this river man… are you seeing him? Is he…'

Homeless?

Jobless?

A good future father for my grandbabies?

'… coming to Sunday dinner next week?' Mum finished. 'Only if he is, I'll get a family-size pud out and get a bigger bit of beef.'

'That… would be great actually, Mum,' I said, surprised at her welcoming attitude. Maybe I needed to stop pre-emptively upsetting myself over comments she may or may not make. 'That's really nice of you.'

Mum made a 'pssshht' noise. 'If you like him, that's all I need to know. Anyway… it'll be one in the eye for Margaret, he's public enemy number one in her book,' she trilled gleefully.

I giggled as Cooper returned with two mugs of tea, a packet of custard creams dangling from his teeth.

'All right, calm down, Satan… We'll see you on Sunday.'

Cooper raised an eyebrow as I hung up. 'Are we going somewhere?'

'Mum's invited you over for Sunday lunch,' I said, suddenly realising that I really ought to have asked him first. 'You don't have to…'

'A hot meal and a chance to see your embarrassing teenage pictures? You try and stop me.' He set my mug down and carefully turned the handle towards me. 'Besides, I've got a great new jumper to show off.'

'That you do.' I grinned as he set the custard creams down. 'Tea *and* biscuits? I'm very spoiled.' I pulled the duvet aside so Cooper could get underneath and warm up again. The boat really was quite chilly.

'Full service aboard The Lady Di,' Cooper said. 'Though I've been thinking of changing the name.'

Charlie, who'd followed Cooper in, leapt up on the bed, interested in the biscuits and my bare feet. I wondered where his owners were and if they'd ever contact me. If I was being honest, I'd been thinking of him as Cooper's dog for a while now. From the way Cooper looked at him, I wasn't the only one.

'Got to get the engine working first,' I pointed out. 'Maybe after this, I can take a look? You still have those photocopies?'

'I do, though they're a bit covered in oil and my tears,' Cooper huffed. 'Gorgeous and knows her way around an engine – you're not leaving this boat.'

I kissed him, buzzing with warmth. 'I will have to, unfortunately. I've got Emma's coven coming in for a crochet night tonight and I really need to get back for it. Then there's the cleaning up after…'

'Your luck's in – I am really good at cleaning,' Cooper gestured around us. 'Exhibit A.'

I swatted his leg through the duvet. 'You don't want to clean the shop with me.'

Cooper took my hand and kissed it. 'I'd snake the drains if you were there.'

'Charmer.'

'I try. Besides, a gaggle of crocheting witches? This could be the most interesting evening of my life.'

I loved the way he said it. Not as if he was poking fun, but as if he was genuinely excited to see what was going on. To be part of my life, of my world. I didn't have the slightest qualm about him meeting Mum, I realised. He really was perfect – for me anyway. Which was all that mattered really, when you got right down to it.

Tea and the start of a new sock forgotten, we fell back into bed. Scandalised, Charlie skittered back to his bed with a snaffled custard cream. Outside a goose honked and water lapped at the sides of the boat. I smiled against Cooper's mouth. I couldn't help but think that Aunt Lou would have approved.

Epilogue

One Year Later

Autumn was turning the meadow into waves of gold, umber and sienna. I knew that because those were the colours Cooper was using to capture it. He'd left the little tubes on the draining board, promising he was going to cut them open and get the last of the paint out later.

He'd set his easel up on the roof of the boat, out of the way, and was working on the third in a set of paintings with Charlie at his side. The subject was our house – currently covered in scaffolding and workmen. In spring the old farmhouse had barely stood out from the green grass and dark waves of ivy. By the time he did the summer painting, it was free of the tangled undergrowth and the old granite was golden with sunlight. Now the dark paint and rust of the scaffolding and building equipment looked almost picturesque in the autumnal image. By winter, he said, there would be lights in the windows and smoke from the chimney. The two of us all moved in and off the boat for good.

We'd both been working hard on the house. My DIY skills and Cooper's willingness to get his hands dirty and learn on the job paired well together. Emma had also thrown her shoulder to the wheel, coming over at the weekends to help hack at brambles. Even Mum and Dad had done their bit, lending tools and bringing over food shopping to keep us going.

Charlie had done his part, killing three rats and patrolling eagerly for more. We'd finally located his owners via the out-of-date info in his microchip. As it turned out, he'd belonged to their great-aunt, who'd passed away and left them taking care of him. They didn't want him and hadn't been too fussed when he'd run off, escaping from their garden one morning. His old name was 'Cuthbert' and Cooper firmly believed that this was why he'd run away. So he was ours now, and had the tag to prove it.

The meadow with its ruined farmhouse was ideal for us. I had plans for the meadow once the house was finished. I'd have sheep moved onto the land and a shed built to allow for processing wool and dyeing it on site. Cooper had lots of space and subjects to paint and we were both happiest when surrounded by nature and old-fashioned buildings, instead of being hemmed in by traffic and soulless flats.

'Tea?' I called out through the window.

'Love a cup,' Cooper called back. 'Are you sure I can't come in?'

'It's bad luck!' I laughed. 'I'll bring you another blanket, though. We shouldn't be too much longer.'

'We hope,' Emma muttered, holding up a crochet hook and a tangle of fine yarn in consternation. 'Is this right?'

'Yes,' I said, after some consideration, as it was upside down.

'But you're going to look like Madonna.' Emma pointed her index fingers out from her chest meaningfully.

I giggled. 'It's going to get turned inside out, it'll be less pointy – you'll see.'

'Hey, it's your dress, not mine,' Emma shrugged, going back to work while I rattled mugs and hunted around for tea bags. 'When're you two tying the knot anyway?'

'Hopefully, before Christmas – once the house is finished and we have time to plan. Thankfully, Mum's already got literally every supply we could ever need on hand so it shouldn't be too hard to book a slot at the registry office and get things sorted. Then we're doing an outdoor ceremony in the woods behind my aunt's old cottage.' It had just seemed right, as that was the place where I'd finally decided what it was I wanted. I'd told Cooper the whole story and he'd surprised me with a painting of the little hut Aunt Lou and I had built. That place meant so much to me, and Cooper said it felt special when he went there – reminding him of one of the few good memories he had of growing up with his dad and making bows and arrows out of sticks on holiday.

Mum thought I was mad for not having a big wedding, but Cooper's savings were already ploughed into the house and land. I'd contributed what I could from the shop's profits, now that the classes and kits were in full swing. I also wasn't paying half the rent on a fancy 'apartment' or spending money on cashmere yarn to try and 'earn' my boyfriend's approval. Cooper loved me for me and, no matter what they were made out of, he wore anything I made him with pride. Even the silly things that weren't for public consumption.

'Do you think they'll come? You know, his family?' Emma asked, lowering her voice.

'Addy will, with her husband Eric – and their dogs – I think his parents will too but, it's going to be a little bit tense.'

I'd only met Cooper's parents once, when we went up to Wiltshire so he could see them in person for the first time since disappearing. They'd exchanged letters, emails and a few calls but it was clear that things were frosty between him and his dad. That didn't look as if it was going to change, but they'd reached a sort of truce, where they tiptoed around the subject of Cooper's career. Though he did send them a link to his art show at the town hall, where he'd exhibited twenty paintings of Leaford. The one of me in the wool shop was wrapped up, ready to hang in our new house.

I knew I wasn't the person Cooper's dad wanted him to marry. A country girl with a little shop, my parents in their former council house. But I didn't let it get to me. I wasn't ashamed of who I was or where I came from. The good thing was that Cooper's mum liked to make lace, so we had plenty to talk about and were in regular email contact. Cooper also loved my mum and dad. He actually had a monthly meet-up with Dad to watch football, now that he had his shed back.

Mum was another story. It had taken a few visits for her to warm up to Cooper. It helped that Margaret hated him, and that Cooper was polite and charming. The pair of them had also met accidentally at a beginners' cooking class after Mum's microwave exploded, and now had weird little inside jokes about it. It was adorable.

'You'll have gorgeous babies,' she told me last time I met her for coffee on my lunch break.

'Probably, yeah,' I'd responded, refusing to be drawn into that conversation. It was funny really. I'd stressed myself out so much about marriage and babies with Richard, had this invisible deadline in my head. Now it was just gone. It was weird how little I worried about the future now that I was content in the present. Cooper and I had talked about kids but, even if it never happened for us, I'd still be happy as we were. Well, once we were living in the house anyway.

I took his coffee out to him in a thermal cup and he leant down to take it from me. I handed him an extra blanket to put over his knees as well, in the misty morning chill, then climbed up to see what he was working on. We had plans to keep the boat as a floating studio-cum-shop for his artwork, which was doing well online and in a few local bookshops. It was repainted now, in classic red and green, with its new name in gold on the side – Cooper's Rest.

'Gorgeous, thanks!' Cooper set the tea to the side, pink cheeked and fresh-faced in the cool air. 'Speaking of, I was thinking of adding us into this one – about there?' He gestured to the painting.

'Hmm… a little to the left,' I said, wrapping an arm around him and stooping to kiss the top of his head. 'Perfect.'

Acknowledgements

This book would not exist were it not for the help, input and hard work from the people listed below. All of whom inspired or helped bring this novel to publication. I could not have done it without you all.

Thanks belong to the real life Emma, who shares almost no similarities with her fictional counterpart, but nevertheless championed this project from its humble beginnings to its publication. I believe she is still working hard on manifesting a film deal and to that I say – God speed, I'm rooting for you.

I'm also incredibly grateful to Dandy Smith – fellow author and one-time fellow creative writing student – who read my first rom-com back in 2011 (sorry for dating us both) and has been ordering me to write more ever since. This book would not exist had you not prodded me to take the idea to my agent.

Speaking of my agent – thank you to the talented and hardworking Laura Williams at Greene and Heaton. Together we've had a very busy few years and I'd have been a gibbering wreck long ago if it weren't for your quiet confidence and invaluable insights. Both you and Kate Rizzo continue to be a delight to work with.

I'm exceedingly grateful to Bedford Square and particularly my editor, Rebecca Weigler for taking a chance on Tabitha and not only helping to polish the manuscript but for seeing two books where I'd only imagined one. Returning to the world of Leaford to pen the upcoming sequel was such a joyful experience and it was lovely to share it with you. Thank you to Polly Halsey, Production Editor, for her tireless efforts.

This book is partly based on several locations that were dear to me growing up in Hertfordshire. I'd like to thank everyone from my former village who has bought my books and who continue to support me even though I've moved away. I wonder if you can work out where is where?

Honourable mention to the staff member in the Cornwall Air Ambulance where I purchased a few bits of Charles and Diana memorabilia for future Instagram posts. You were so nice when I accidently broke a plate and your comment that 'It's what she would have wanted' really tickled me and is exactly the reason I chose Diana merch to feature in this book.

Lastly, thank you to everyone who took a chance on my first traditionally published rom-com, I hope you had a few laughs and enjoyed visiting Leaford with me.

About the Author

Photo credit © Clifton Photo

Amelia Wildwood is a lifelong dreamer and hopeless romantic who longs to trade her tiny office in for a boat on the waterways, a cabin up a mountain, or a camper van. Until that dream comes true she'll have to make do with writing about it instead. Born to crochet but forced to work, Amelia lives in Cornwall with a permanently sandy dog.

Bedford Square Publishers is an independent publisher of fiction and non-fiction, founded in 2022 in the historic streets of Bedford Square London and the sea mist shrouded green of Bedford Square Brighton.

Our goal is to discover irresistible stories and voices that illuminate our world.

We are passionate about connecting our authors to readers across the globe and our independence allows us to do this in original and nimble ways.

The team at Bedford Square Publishers has years of experience and we aim to use that knowledge and creative insight, alongside evolving technology, to reach the right readers for our books. From the ones who read a lot, to the ones who don't consider themselves readers, we aim to find those who will love our books and talk about them as much as we do.

We are hunting for vital new voices from all backgrounds – with books that take the reader to new places and transform perceptions of the world we live in.

Follow us on social media for the latest Bedford Square Publishers news.

@bedsqpublishers

facebook.com/bedfordsq.publishers

@bedfordsq.publishers

bedfordsquarepublishers.co.uk